UGLIER

KELLY VINCENT

KV BOOKS LLC

For everyone who needs a little luck finding their people

PART I

SOMETHING
TOTALLY NEW

"What's your name, young man?" asked the white-haired old man at the reception desk in my new dorm at the Oklahoma Academy of Mathematics and Sciences. I instantly deflated. Not this again. My little sister Isabella took my hand in support.

"She's a young woman," Mom said to him. "Her name is Nic—Nicole—Summers."

"Oh, I'm sorry," he said, smiling in a friendly way. "Welcome to OAMS, and welcome to Burnside."

He started typing in the computer.

His apology for misgendering me caught me off guard. Usually, people weren't sorry, and they looked annoyed at me for tricking them or something. But we were in a suburb of Oklahoma City, so maybe things were different here compared to my small home town.

The man reached into a box on his desk and pulled out a keycard. He scanned it on a machine and handed it to me.

"Room 201. Second floor, last room on the left, that way."

He pointed to the nearest stairwell. "Welcome again, Nic. You can head on up, but I need your mom to stay and fill out paperwork."

"Okay," I said. Mom smiled at me, and Isabella and I headed for the stairs. We started up, with me dragging my giant blue suitcase up along with me.

When we reached the second floor, the door into the hall was closed. Hand on the doorknob, I held my breath. I could be somebody totally new here. Maybe not everyone would be like the old guy downstairs. And I needed to be somebody new. I couldn't carry on being the loser everyone thought I was back in Emerson. I was done with the constant harassment.

I pulled open the heavy stairwell door to my floor in my new home for the last two years of high school.

There it was, my first glimpse: ordinary off-white textured walls and industrial blue carpet.

Oh, man. This was a bummer. I'd expected something different, more welcoming. This looked so sterile.

"Let me see," Isabella, who had just turned eleven, said from behind me. She pulled the door all the way open and squeezed past me and my suitcase.

A sign indicated we should go right for room 201. We headed down the hall, Isabella, in her pink shirt and white skirt, skipping all the way and singing a new Beyoncé song.

A sense of regret mixed with fear flashed across my heart. I wouldn't see my little sister every day anymore. I'd miss her so much, even if we were polar opposites in almost every way. I was going to be away from everyone and every-thing. It was scary.

But it was also good. A perfect opportunity to reinvent myself. If I could pull it off.

"Here it is!" Isabella said as she hopped to a stop in front of the last door on the left.

I dragged the suitcase the rest of the way and pulled the keycard out to unlock the door. The thin carpet in the room was an orangey beige, and there were bunk beds against the wall to the right, a desk in the corner behind them, and another desk on the left wall. There was also a small table against the wall across from the beds. I wondered what on earth that was for. The room felt abandoned, a box with no personality at all. Even the air smelled stale.

My roommate—a girl named Sophia who was from some small town in southeast Oklahoma that nobody'd heard of—obviously hadn't arrived yet. At least she was a junior, too. She wouldn't know anyone else, either.

Isabella raced in and sat on the bottom bunk, bouncing. "Which bed are you going to take?"

Here we go. Actual anxiety. "Oh, man, I don't know. It's impossible to know what Sophia will be like from a few texts. She seems so *normal* on social media. But also she's so busy on social media, making videos all the time."

"What's wrong with normal?" Isabella asked with narrowed eyes.

"Nothing. I just can't relate to it. You know that." This was strictly the truth—normal annoyed me on most people, but I accepted it on Isabella because she was the best little sister ever. I dropped my backpack on the floor near the end of the bed. It was a brand new one in this really nice teal color.

"Let's do a selfie!" She hopped up and we had to take a picture of both of us with the beds in the background.

Seeing the result, I wondered how Isabella still liked me. She was always cute and happy, and I was a grumpy potato.

"Your hair looks good today, and I'm always jealous of your freckles," Isabella said, which was random.

I looked again at the photo and my hair just looked like normal—long, straight, and light brown. "Freckles aren't considered attractive, Isabella."

"Whatever. You should take the top bunk," she said. "Fun! Which closet are you going to take?"

Another choice. The closets were to the right, on the same wall as the door. They were floor to ceiling doors on either side of a mirror over a chest of drawers. I had no experience with roommates at all, and my substandard social skills weren't going to help me. This was going to be rough going.

Isabella got up and opened the closet on the left. "Cool!" There were a couple drawers on the bottom, and a rack for hanging clothes and also some storage at the top. "You can take this one. I'm sure Sophia won't mind."

"Okay, you're right." At least somebody around here could make a decision. Well, it's not that I couldn't make decisions, but it was hard unless I felt like I had all the information, and if it required social knowledge, I never felt like I had all the information.

Isabella sat back on the bed and I looked at the two desks. There was one on the right tucked between the window and the bunk beds, and the one across from it, with nothing around it. I honed in on the less exposed one, and dropped my backpack in the chair.

That done, I opened my suitcase and started loading things into the closet. That was when I realized there were no hangers and I hadn't brought any. Crap.

"Oh, hi," a voice said from the door. "You aren't Nic."

"No, I'm Isabella."

I backed up and turned to see a girl of average height,

with long, curly dark brown hair, looking at me with a stiff smile and suspicious eyes, a familiar judgy look. She had a full face of makeup, like almost every girl I knew, and was holding a tripod. Sophia.

"*You* must be Nic," she said.

"Yeah."

"Little sister?" Sophia asked, cocking her head toward Isabella.

"Yeah."

Isabella smiled and waved. "Which bed do you want? Nic can't decide."

"Oh, I don't care," Sophia said as she opened the closet on the right. She moved her light pink suitcase, which was covered in stickers of animals and trees, to an open spot on the floor.

I still didn't know what to do, and the anxiety was roiling in my stomach. I didn't really believe her, but that didn't help me decide. "I guess I'll take the top?"

Sophia looked up. "Oh. I was hoping you'd pick the bottom."

Oh, man. This was as bad as I'd worried it would be. "You can have the top. I really don't care."

Sophia smiled more genuinely this time and grabbed a bunch of clothes out of her suitcase. "Perfect." She started loading up the closet. She'd been smart enough to bring hangers.

I finished stacking everything on the bottom of the closet and put the suitcase in there, too. It was weird to see all my clothes in this new place. All I had was jeans, some shorts, three pairs of shoes—all Vans, in purple, red, and black-and-white checkered—a bunch of graphic and plain t-shirts in various colors. The underwear and socks were packed away in the drawers at the bottom of the closet. This pretty much summed up my fashion sense.

The art supplies I'd brought went on my desk, along with all the fantasy figurines I'd painted. Those would line the shelves in front of the textbooks I'd have and the novels I'd brought from home. I tossed the sheets I'd brought onto the bed—I'd make it later—and closed my closet doors, a magnetic click sounding when they were shut.

My stomach did not feel good about my future in this room with Sophia.

Isabella bounced on the bed some more. "This doesn't feel like a normal mattress. It's hard. I don't know how you're going to sleep on this."

"I'm sure it's fine. Let's go find Mom and Dad. I need some hangers."

Isabella raced to the door. I looked toward Sophia, who was still filling her closet, and said, "See you later."

"Bye." She sounded disinterested.

Yeah, this was going to be rough.

I was kind of zoning out while the senior resident advisor—she said to call her the dorm mom—was going on about the rules for kids who had cars. They weren't allowed to use them except to go home over the weekend. Whatever, didn't apply to me. I was originally supposed to be getting a cheap car on my sixteenth birthday, but my parents got in financial trouble and that never happened.

Mom, Isabella, and I were all gathered for the Parent Info Session in the downstairs lounge area of the dorm, off to the left of the front desk. There were some refrigerators lining a wall, a TV in front of the back windows, and some boxy mustard-colored couches. Dad was going to Walmart to get hangers. At first I was worried that maybe kids shouldn't be here since it was for parents, but it was standing room only and there were whole families. Some early arrivers had snagged the couch spots. I looked at the family clusters in the room. There were a lot of younger siblings here, so it wasn't just us.

I was glad Isabella was here, but also glad my brother Caleb hadn't come. He was such a jerk now, only a year younger than me and convinced I was ruining his life by being so uncool.

I was staring absentmindedly at the front door when a slim black-haired boy came in with a blue backpack and two duffel bags. He was wearing gray cargo shorts with a wallet chain running into his pocket. He also had on a t-shirt with something printed on the front, though it was way too far away for me to see it. His hair was short and spiky and his skin was darker than mine, like probably more than a tan. I couldn't put my finger on why, but he looked cool. Maybe the chain thing. He went to the front desk for his keycard, but he had to wait for a bit. That was when he turned and caught me staring. Oh, my God. I quickly turned back toward the dorm mom, but not before I saw a smile on his face.

I was a total idiot. But that had been a nice smile.

Isabella caught my eye and mouthed, "I'm bored."

"Me, too," I replied, glad to be distracted from my embarrassment.

The mystery boy was going to have to walk through the lounge area in order to get to the boys' wing, so I needed to not stare at him again. Even if he did have a nice smile.

But after a bit, he still hadn't come by, and I stole another look toward the desk. No sign of him. Where had he gone?

The front door was the only way to get into the building, although there were some other exits he could've used to leave.

Weird.

Isabella was right. This session really was boring. Mom wrote down all the info about Thanksgiving, Christmas, and Spring Break, and how we'd have to leave the dorm for all of them. She had this little notepad she'd put in her purse at the last minute.

Isabella tapped my arm. "I'm glad you are coming home for breaks," she whispered.

"Me too." I side-hugged her.

I looked around. Sophia was on the other side of the room, next to a tall guy in cowboy boots and a cowboy hat. There were four other such dads in hats in the room, though everyone else was holding theirs rather than wearing them.

I was nervous thinking about how these cowboy kids would react to me. In my experience, cowboy people were even more offended by my unfeminine appearance than others. Apparently the only kinds of t-shirts girls were supposed to wear had those weirdly short sleeves and were close-fitting. Good old toxic masculinity.

I hoped Sophia wasn't going to make my life too difficult this year. I really needed to try to be friendly. I could start OSIN back up again. Operation Social Interaction for Nic was something my best and only friend Sam and I had started to help me make more friends before she moved to Scotland last year.

Thinking of OSIN and Sam being gone made me sad. I still couldn't believe she'd been gone so long. Over eight months. I'd visited her in Scotland in March, but it still felt unreal to me that someone so important to me could be so far away.

Making friends was something I sucked at. I did end up becoming friends with a girl from my art class last spring, but we didn't have much in common besides art, and it wasn't like we were going to stay in touch now that I'd left Emerson. Being friends with her wasn't like being friends with Sam.

I needed to really try this year. I didn't have a reputation here for being the shy, meek wimp everyone back home thought I was. I should try to be braver, not so shy.

This meant I had to talk to people. I had to convince myself that not everyone judged me instantaneously, even if some people, like Sophia, still did. I needed to give people the benefit of the doubt.

This made me queasy. I thought of the boy with the smile. Maybe he'd be my friend. I smiled, imagining it. I should run my own OSIN here. I might have to work on that. For once I felt hopeful. I could really change who I was here.

The meeting finally broke up and people began scattering.

Mom smiled at me. She'd had her blonde hair recently cut, I think for this occasion. "So much to remember! But this is exciting, Nic. You impress me so much, being brave enough to do this at only sixteen."

Me, brave? I shrugged. At least *some* people in the world believed in me. So maybe there was some truth to it, and I could draw on that bravery in my social life, too.

"Let's take a picture," Mom said.

I flinched. "Do we have to?"

"Yes!" Isabella said.

We all got in the frame of Isabella's camera and she snapped it. When we looked at it, it was so obvious that Mom and Isabella belonged in the same picture, and I didn't. I still didn't have everything figured out, but I'd decided last year I was gender nonconforming. But I hadn't decided what to do about that. Changing my pronouns would have been horrible in Emerson. It could be different here. I didn't know.

"Let's go see your room," Mom said. She gave me a side hug.

"Mom, I need to pee," Isabella said.

We walked toward the girls' stairwell and Mom asked at the desk if there was a restroom nearby.

While I was waiting, the dark-haired boy from earlier emerged from the hallway behind the girls' stairwell. He was only a few feet in front of me, and my heart jolted. We made eye contact that felt weirdly intense and he stared for a second before continuing out the front door. Where was he coming from? The only thing back in that direction was the girls' lounge.

Even though he didn't smile this time, he had really friendly eyes. I couldn't help but think about that.

It turned out there was a bathroom around the corner, so I left Mom and Isabella and headed on up to the room. When I got there, I noticed Sophia had made her bed up. She had a fluffy pink-and-white plaid comforter and a white satin pillow case.

I should have made my bed earlier, too. Pulse still racing from the near-collision with that weirdly cool boy, I unfolded the sheets and started putting them on the mattress. Isabella wasn't wrong—it was stiff foam. This would take some getting used to.

I'd left the door open, and I could hear Mom and Isabella talking in the hall, so I sat on the bed and watched them come in.

"This is nice," Mom said, looking around the room.

I laughed. "Really, Mom?"

She smiled. "Okay, it's a little bland. You can put some of your art up."

Isabella pointed to a stained part of the wall. "Put something here. You can cover this smudge."

"We'll see," I said. I doubted Sophia would appreciate my work. I could hang something on the wall next to my bed, though.

"Hello?" Dad called from the hall.

"In here, Dad," I said.

"I come bearing hangers." He handed me a stack and I set them on the bed.

"This is nice," Dad said, which made the rest of us laugh.

"What?" he said.

"Is it, really?" Mom asked.

"Okay, I see your point." He looked around bit more. "Should we go get dinner?"

"Sure," I said, sort of wanting my family out of the room. It felt weird with all of us in there. We headed out and I locked the door before starting down the hall.

Would I see that boy again soon? And would I be brave enough to talk to him? Time would tell.

Later that evening, after my parents were gone, I was sitting at my desk, staring at my art supplies, while Sophia sat at her desk doing who knows what. Mom had given me a journal with art paper and a really nice teal leather cover.

I was flipping through the blank pages when there was a knock at the door. Sophia said, "Yeah?"

"Can I come in? I'm your RA."

"Okay," Sophia said.

I turned around. The door opened and this small, skinny woman came in.

"Hi, I'm your RA!" she announced. "My name is Marisa."

Her light brown hair was in a high ponytail and she had on booty shorts, which threw me.

I stared at her.

"I see we have Nicole and Sophia in this room," Marisa said.

"I'm Sophia." She didn't sound very impressed.

"So that means you're Nicole," she said, eyeing me unapprovingly.

"I go by Nic."

"Of course you'd have a boy's name." She laughed like she was being funny.

Rude. "It's not a boy's name. It's not spelled with a 'k.'"

"Oh, okay." She looked a little chastened and pointedly looked at Sophia and smiled. "I just wanted to remind you of the orientation downstairs at eight. It's mandatory."

Sophia nodded and said okay, and then Marisa said, "Okay, then! See you later!"

After she was gone, we both turned back to our desks. It was seven forty so I had some time to kill. I got my fantasy figurines out and put them on the shelf above my desk along with the novels I'd brought.

I was glad I'd chosen this desk because it was kind of nestled in a cozy corner. My bed backed right up to it, so I could throw crap on there while I worked.

By the time I'd finished, it was about ten minutes before the student orientation was supposed to start.

I wasn't sure if Sophia was going to say something about going downstairs. I didn't know the protocol here.

But it was getting late, so I decided to be proactive and stood up.

"Are you, uh, ready?" I asked the air.

"I guess." She stood up and grabbed a small purse off her desk, but she didn't look at me. We headed toward the door and she said, "We don't have to do everything together."

Well. Okay, then. Since we had literally not done a single thing together, "everything" was a bit of a stretch. I locked the door after we were both out.

"You don't have to lock the door," she announced, halfway to the stairs.

Um, WTF? "My computer is in there. Obviously we're locking the door."

"I don't have my keycard."

"Well, either we're going to have to do one more thing together, or I can let you back in now and you can get it." Where had that come from? I never had good comebacks. I had a rush of unfamiliar confidence and good feeling. Maybe I could make things different here.

She made an annoyed grunt sound. "Let me back in."

"Okay, sure." I went back and unlocked it and then passed her as I headed toward the stairs.

I was still reveling in some small pride at standing up for myself. Why would anyone leave their door unlocked? She'd better lock it on her way out.

The stairwell fire door was super heavy and covered in so many layers of glossy white paint that the frame scraped some of it off. Before I even reached the bottom of the stairs, I could hear the big crowd that must be filling the lounge. Apparently all students had to go to this, not just juniors.

Two RA's were chatting and laughing at the desk when I passed it heading into the lounge. It was even more crowded than I'd expected. Lot of noisy chattering. The sun was low, coming in through the windows.

This time it was only students, no families, so I could get a real look at the people I'd be dealing with every day. Kids were on the couches and the floor and there were people standing at the far wall and in front of the fridges. Were they going to leave me alone, or harass me like so many back in Emerson? Many of the kids looked totally geeky, although others could pass as popular in my old school. Definitely a higher proportion of nerds here, however.

An adult I didn't recognize smiled and greeted me and pointed to a table with white paper bags on it. "Take one."

I did and then went to stand a ways back from the edge of the people standing near the last fridge. This had to be almost everybody. I looked in the bag and saw a chocolate chip cookie, a blue whistle on a chain, some Jolly Ranchers, a pen and pencil, an eraser, and some correction fluid. Kind of random. I never used correction fluid, and it was a junk eraser.

I looked around and didn't see the mystery boy. It looked like everybody else had already made friends, as almost everyone was talking.

Actually, that wasn't true. There were a few kids looking awkward and like outsiders. Maybe I could be friends with some of them. Not that I had the skills to approach people. I sensed movement to my left and turned to find the boy I'd been obsessing over for no good reason.

He smiled at me and I noticed that his t-shirt had a picture an owl reading from an open book. Very cool.

I was frozen at first, as per usual, but then the new brave Nic broke the silence. "Hi." Look at me, talking first. Where was all this boldness coming from? I liked it.

"Hey. I saw you earlier." His voice surprised me, higher

than I would have expected. He was exactly my height. I had a passing thought that I was glad I wasn't taller than he was.

"Yeah. I saw you too." Okay, that was mortifying.

But he gave a warm laugh, and I relaxed. And laughed.

"Did you get your cookie and whistle?" He held up his bag.

"Yeah. Seems weird."

"The whistle?" he asked. When I nodded, he continued, "Colleges do that because they think it helps keep women safe from rape—since they can't be bothered to actually put any money toward teaching men not to rape."

"Oh." I was sort of shocked. I'd forgotten about that problem. I guessed it happened at boarding schools, too. It was kind of like going to college. Especially since our buildings were on a college campus.

"Don't worry about it. You won't be going to any wild college parties. We're tucked in safe in the dorm by ten thirty on weekends."

You don't have to go to wild college parties to get sexually assaulted, I knew. I'd been molested in my own home when I was little. But I wasn't going to bring that up.

"Well, that's good to hear. Parties intimidate the crap out of me." Why had I volunteered that, right off the bat?

He laughed. "Introvert?"

Might as well run with it. "The understatement of the year."

"Same. What's your name?"

"Nic."

"Oh, cool," he said, sounding little surprised. "A fellow single-syllable name bearer. And finishing up with a hard *k* sound. Even better. I'm Mack. Nice to meet you."

"Nice to meet you, too." Nic and Mack. Sounded like they went together.

"Okay, everyone," a loud, commanding voice said from the front of the room. "Let's get started. I'm Mr. Townsend, principal of OAMS. I'm going to start with an introduction and officially welcome you to the 2022-23 school year, and then hand things over to Ms. Patton, your dorm mom." He offered a short, cheesy welcome, and then Ms. Patton got up there and started going over the rules and how everything worked.

Mandatory study time Sunday through Thursday, eight thirty to ten thirty. So, eight thirty curfew except Friday and Saturday, which was ten thirty like Mack had said.

He looked over at me when she said that and mouthed, "Safe in the dorm."

I nodded, loving that he was still talking to me.

Lights out at eleven during the week. We could go anywhere on the college campus, but had to get permission to go off campus.

Mack cocked his head and mouthed, "Better get permission. Don't be naughty."

No car usage except to go home for the weekend. No boys in the girls' lounge, no girls in the boys' lounge, except when an adult was in there.

I glanced over at Mack, expecting a comment on this rule, but he was staring straight ahead.

There were weekend shopping trips to the mall and Walmart, but we had to sign up in advance. Would Mack and I ever go shopping together? That could be fun.

Blah blah. On and on.

Bored and restless, I twirled my hair around my finger. I wanted to talk to Mack, not listen to this lady rattle off information that was probably available in the student manual they gave us when we moved in.

Now she was going on about PDA, something that had

zero impact on me. This time Mack did look over and waggle his eyebrows, but then he mouthed "boring" to me.

Ms. Patton eventually stopped. People started to disperse and Mack said, "Great meeting you, Nic."

"Yeah. Nice to meet you, too."

It was. I was excited that it seemed I had already made a friend. I couldn't wait to see where it went.

I still flying on cloud nine when I passed the front desk on the way to the stairs.

"Stop," came a voice from the desk.

I turned around to see a lady with cat eye glasses staring me down.

"No boys on the girls' side."

Idiot. "I'm not a boy." I didn't give her any time to figure it out and just turned and went up the stairs, half expecting her to chase after me.

I made it to my room and sat on my bed, to fume for a minute. Really? This again?

But then I remembered Mack. Okay, maybe not everything would be different, but some things were. I should focus on that, and see where things went.

At 7:15 on Monday morning my alarm went off and I hit snooze, so nine minutes later it went off again, and Sophia said, "Are you going to get up?" She made no effort to hide her annoyance. I was about to say something about her early morning noisemaking—she'd gotten up and turned the light on and was opening and closing drawers and doors —being far more annoying, but I bit my tongue. New me was apparently wanting to stand up for herself.

I turned the alarm off, anyway, then got out of bed.

Sophia was doing her makeup and I had to squeeze past her and the bed to get to my closet. This was going to be something I'd have to deal with every day, which put me in a grumpy mood. Sophia didn't mind taking up all the space. I grabbed clothes, a towel, and my new shower caddy and headed off to the shower.

And of course, I hadn't considered that there might be a bunch of other girls with the same idea when I calculated how much time I'd need to be there for an 8:15 class. There was a line of three girls in the hall. Everybody looked tired, with the first two resting their heads against the wall.

It crept along. There were three shower stalls, but most people weren't doing those environmentally friendly two-minute showers. The first two girls in front of me were talking about their upcoming class. They were probably seniors because they knew the instructor. The class was nuclear chemistry. It was pretty neat that you could take a class that specialized in high school. Even if it wasn't something I was interested in.

They eventually managed to get through the door, and I had a weird urge to ask the remaining girl something. I didn't know what, but I apparently wanted to talk.

Who was I? This was crazy. I couldn't possibly turn into a social butterfly, could I?

In the end, I didn't say anything, and eventually I got my turn at a shower. I was fast because I had no idea what time it was by then. The hall was empty by the time I left the bathroom. I must have been the floor's late-riser.

I did a quick check on what I'd chosen to wear. I had on knee-length gray shorts and one of my favorite t-shirts, a white one with a sharp-edged red dragon on the front, with the words, "There's a reason they write so many books about me."

To my shock, Sophia was still doing her makeup when I got back to my room. She was doing something around her eyes, but I didn't know what. How long do people spend on that crap? I had no idea.

It was 8:01 now. I squeezed past Sophia to grab socks and my red Vans to match the dragon. Then I almost knocked my blue knight figurine off the shelf when I pulled down notebooks to put in my backpack. Ready, I headed to the door, butterflies filling my stomach at the thought of all the new stuff I'd be dealing with today. I left for the classroom building, mentally prepping myself for a new year of school. It would be totally different this time because it was a different place, and I was going to be a different person. I was sure of it.

I got to my first class about ten minutes before it started. The room was empty, which stressed me out because I couldn't gauge who was sitting where and where would be the best place for me, to minimize harassment. There were four rows of tables the width of the room, split down the middle, with dinky black rolling chairs. I stood frozen for a minute before I noticed someone standing behind me.

"Oh, sorry," I said as I moved out of the way.

"'s okay," muttered this short girl. She stepped in and stopped, staring at the empty room.

She was as intimidated as me.

"Where are the jocks going to sit, right?" I asked.

"I'm hoping there won't be any," she said quietly.

"Do we even have PE here?" I didn't remember anybody mentioning it. But maybe I wasn't paying attention.

"I heard it's only in the second semester."

She was so quiet, I could barely hear her.

Four much more confident people abruptly burst into the room and snagged the front row.

My fellow shy girl headed to the seat next to the window on the second row and I picked a seat in the back. Gradually, more kids came in and filled the first three rows, but no one sat near me. Next came the teacher, who looked frazzled, with several three-ring binders and a large book in her arms, a stack of papers clutched in one hand.

She dropped the papers on her desk in front of the whiteboard, and then set the rest down.

She was wearing a long, simple brown dress, and her hair was all gray and short, with these big curls. I didn't think she was someone who spent a lot of time on her appearance, which made me like her.

"Everyone, go ahead and grab your textbook for this year while I get organized. Our morning meeting ran over. Take one of the syllabi, too."

I didn't know what she meant by syllabi. But the table in the front corner of the room held a stack of giant textbooks.

Everyone shuffled to the front and this Black kid with a short afro and I tried to get into the aisle at the same time, and we both muttered sorry and stopped, and then we each tried to go again at the same time and said sorry again. God, it was like a comedy skit. He finally motioned with his hand for me to go, so I did, but it didn't clear the flush from my face.

Maybe I'd be braver here than I had been in Emerson, but not enough to classify it as actually brave.

While I was waiting at the front to get to the table, I glanced over at the teacher—Dr. Jones according to the whiteboard—and she was eyeing me. She didn't look friendly and I couldn't help but notice the large silver cross necklace she had on. My anxiety level instantly shot up. Before I turned back, someone bumped my shoulder. The girl who did it returned to her seat in the front row without saying a word. We finally all had our books—and the syllabus—and I sat back down without further incident.

Class got started. Dr. Jones explained that junior physics had two distinct sections that corresponded with the semesters. She told us about each of the semesters and said the second was harder than the first, but she insisted that if we did well this semester and applied ourselves, we'd do fine in the second one. Then she went through the syllabus, which was basically a plan for the semester, with all readings, assignments, and tests listed in detail. She said it was also in our LMS, but I liked the idea of having it on paper. I could cross stuff off.

After she finished talking about the syllabus, Dr. Jones starting talking about vectors, and I tried to take the best notes I could, drawing long skinny arrows all over the page.

The rest of the morning went by, with the physics seating challenge repeated in every class—chemistry, world history, and Spanish. But I didn't dither and instead went straight to the back row every time. I was apparently going to be a back-of-the-classroom kid now. It was nicer being able to see everyone else and not having people behind me who might talk about me.

I was sort of dreading the end of Spanish, because it meant I'd have to go to lunch, and I had no idea how I was going to navigate that. But eventually class ended, and I entered the crush of kids heading to the lunchroom. These two guys stepped right in front of me to high-five each other and I had to stop suddenly, and then the girl behind me ran into me.

"Watch where you're going," she said. When I turned around to say sorry, she glared at me.

What a mess. It was stupid because she would have fully seen the idiots blocking my way.

I decided to stop in the bathroom. I found the girls' bathroom and as I pushed on the handle, someone called, "Hey, that's the girls' bathroom."

This girl wearing two tank tops stood right next to me.

"I'm aware," I said.

She didn't look convinced, but I wasn't going to give her a long explanation of how I wasn't a boy.

I pushed the door open and went about my business.

When I got to the lunchroom a few minutes later, I scoped it out. There was a huge line along the left wall, stretching into the hall. I couldn't help but look to see if Mack was in the line. I didn't see him. At the back of the room were tables with these blue containers that obviously held some kind of hot food. The rest of the room was full of the same light gray tables they had in the classrooms, and the same rolling chairs.

Kids were working their way through the line, and only a few were already sitting down. I didn't know how I was going to find a place to sit after all these people got their food and picked a spot. My stomach twisted, but I made myself get in line. My stomach wasn't only telling me I was nervous—it also demanded food.

As I moved through the line, I watched the tables fill up and my anxiety only grew. There were very few empty tables left, and there wouldn't be any by the time I had my food.

People were talking all around me. A guy carrying a tray walked past and abruptly stopped when he saw me.

"Whoa," he said in a strong southern accent. "I heard about freaks in the big city. My first girl freak."

I flinched. Why did this crap always surprise me? He'd moved on but I was still trying to recover. How was I such a freak, anyway? I had on generic shorts that ended right above the knee and a graphic t-shirt, plus my red Vans. What was the problem? He'd been dressed about the same, basically nondescript.

I remembered how I always felt so alone back at Emerson, even in crowds like this. It was better when Sam could eat with me. We would meet in the stairwell to eat and talk so we could avoid the crazy cafeteria, with all the politics and posturing. But she often ate with the band kids, so I was sometimes on my own.

I missed Sam. And it was weird to be somewhere she had never been. After she'd moved last year, I had to go back to the school where we'd spent so much time together, and do all the same stuff without her. But here, I didn't have memories of her. It should have been a good thing, but it made me kind of sad. Would we grow apart?

I couldn't keep myself from frowning, but I wouldn't keep thinking about downer stuff. I'd already noticed that the meal today was chicken with some kind of tomato sauce and scalloped potatoes, so I was trying to focus on the fact that I was going to be eating potatoes and cheese, a combo that can never go wrong.

I again scanned the room for Mack, in case he'd snuck in without getting in line. I didn't spot him.

Finally, I'd moved far enough up to get a plate and soon enough I was through the line and looking for a place to sit. I was so queasy that I was going to have to just sit for a minute before I could eat, once I found a stupid seat.

In the middle, on the side of the room with windows,

there was a table with four empty spots. I headed over and managed to snag one on the end. The other kids at the table didn't say anything. It was several girls, who all looked like they were supposed to, with the right amount of makeup and cute clothes, and one guy with the nerdiest square glasses, but who seemed totally boisterous. He was telling some story about this road trip he'd been on over the summer.

I was still sitting there, staring at my food while my stomach calmed.

"Are you praying?" the guy asked, out of the blue. That question had been directed at me.

"What? No!" I answered.

"What's wrong with praying?" one of the girls asked, either offended or pretending to be. She looked between the two of us.

I blushed and muttered, "Nothing."

Fortunately everyone went back to their conversation. I started eating and on the third bite a clump of tomato sauce landed right on my shirt, right between my boobs over the dragon's head so there was no way to miss it.

Oh, my God. It was a white shirt. And then to make things worse—the theme for today apparently—I realized I hadn't even picked up any napkins.

I would have to run back to the dorm and get a new shirt. So annoyed with myself, I powered through my lunch, then quickly cleared my tray and added it to a rack in the corner near the exit. I raced over to the dorm, with only ten minutes to get changed and back.

But the good news was that my next class was art, so at least I didn't have to worry about trying to focus on something hard while being flustered. It would be nice.

After computer science, my last class, was over I headed over to my room. I'd thrown the dragon shirt onto my bed after I'd put the stain treatment stuff on it. I moved it and lay down on the bed to relax, closing my eyes and taking stock of my day.

Art had been a big disappointment. Apparently the teacher was out with a family emergency, so we wouldn't start the class until Wednesday. I hung out in the library during that class period.

The boy who I'd almost run into in physics was also in art, and he also ended up in the library. I think everyone else went back to the lunchroom.

After I went through the three sections which appeared to be all science and math stuff, I found an English section with some classic novels. I wasn't in the mood for that, so I sat in a mustard yellow chair in front of a glass half wall that let me look down on the front of the building, where the staff were.

I regretted not bringing my own book to read, which was unlike me.

I finally remembered that I did have a few Kindle books, so I managed to open up one of those on my phone app and read for a while. It wasn't something I'd really been interested in. Kindle books were my emergency backup. It was the worst way to read. I wanted the feel of paper between my fingers, and a visual sense of how far along I was, not just some percentage.

When I looked around after a while, I saw the boy from class in another chair, reading a paper book. Smarter than me.

At least my chair was comfy.

I got back to the book, a retelling of Robin Hood that wasn't bad.

A few minutes before my next class, pre-calculus, I headed to the classroom and found my seat on the back row.

Math class here was like math class in Emerson, just without the jocks being annoying. There really didn't seem to be any jocks here. The school didn't have any sports teams. They'd mentioned some intramural stuff, but I didn't know how many people participated.

Then I went to English and computer science. Both were fine. We were reading *Pride and Prejudice* for English, which was fine with me. I'd already read it freshman year.

The door to my room opened, bringing me out of my reverie, and Sophia came in. She didn't look at me, just dropped her backpack on the floor before sitting down at her desk.

Yeah, it was clear she and I weren't going to be friends. I didn't know why she didn't like me, but she obviously didn't.

Oh, well. Not a problem I needed to worry about. I had my part of the room and she had hers.

I'd just focus on my homework and hope I'd run into Mack again. I had a good feeling about him.

Tuesday evening, I came back from dinner—my second one alone, but it was less stressful than lunch because there were more places to sit and I'd been able to find my own table both nights—and when I got to my room, I heard talking on the other side of the door. I opened it.

"Shit!" Sophia said. "I was filming!"

"Oh, sorry. I didn't know." Also, why should I have to hesitate to open my own dorm door?

"It's fine. I can edit it out."

I headed over to my desk, skirting the tripod she had set up. She was standing in front of the window. I sat down and started going through my backpack.

"I'm going to finish filming," Sophia said. "Do you mind being quiet for a minute?"

What the hell? I turned and looked at her.

She was grimacing. "Sorry, I didn't mean to sound snippy. Do you mind if I finish, though? You're usually so quiet it won't be a problem."

She actually looked embarrassed after being so rude, avoiding eye contact.

"Let me figure out what I'm going to study, and I can read."

"Okay, yeah, that sounds good. Thanks."

I pulled my physics book out and got situated with it on my desk. "Okay, have at it."

"Thanks." She started back up. She was talking about the Galápagos Islands and the giant tortoises there, and about how they—I didn't know who—ate them instead of studying them. But then she wrapped it up, saying, "So basically, even someone who became as great a thinker and scientist as Charles Darwin made huge mistakes early in his career. So let that stick with you. We're rarely perfect."

She must really be into science if she was making a podcast about Darwin. I was sort of impressed.

But she was done and I got back to reading physics. I had to start over because I'd been eavesdropping.

Even though we didn't like each other, Sophia was way more interesting than I'd first thought. I got up to head to the bathroom and saw she was doing something on her phone with earbuds in. Presumably editing her video. I was really curious what her user name was, even though I didn't spend too much time on TikTok.

My focus was going to be on school. The second day hadn't been particularly eventful, but I already had plenty of homework.

Right before I reached the bathroom, Marisa's door opened and she emerged.

"Ack!" she said. "What are you..." She narrowed her eyes. "You know this would be much easier if you would just wear makeup."

This caught me off guard and I didn't know what to say. But what the hell? What was it with people being rude today? One of the teachers had tried to keep me from going into the girls' bathroom at school, too. And later, this guy bumped my shoulder in the hall and didn't say anything. I couldn't tell if it was on purpose or not. I was trying to not let it bother me, but Jesus.

I kept going and did my bathroom business before returning to my room, hoping I wouldn't do something else to annoy Sophia.

My mere existence seemed to be a problem for some people.

After Spanish the next day, I followed the herd to the lunchroom. I waited in a long line and eventually got my lasagna and some kind of pre-made salad. I nervously looked around. It was almost full, but I spotted Mack sitting by himself, with some empty seats around him, and I stopped. My heart was already racing. He had on a white t-shirt and his black hair looked tousled, like he'd just run his hand through it.

Should I go over there? I was going back and forth in my head. I shouldn't crowd him, but I wanted to talk to him some more, and maybe he wouldn't mind. I stared so stupidly long, wavering, that he finally looked up and we locked gazes. I panicked, but then he smiled and I knew I would look like a total idiot if I didn't go over there now.

So I did.

He watched me walk over. I knew I should still ask, but I couldn't decide between "Is this seat taken?" and "Is it okay if I sit here?" so what came out of my mouth was, "Is it okay if I seat taken?" And here came the blush.

"Sure." He motioned toward the empty spot across from him.

I set my tray down and took a seat without additional blunders. There was a Brandon Sanderson novel next to Mack's tray.

Before I could say anything about the book, Mack smiled and asked, "So how's your first week going? Are you getting your bearings?"

"Yeah, it's good. I do think it's going to be a lot of work."

Mack nodded while chewing on his own bite of lasagna. He looked like he wanted to say something, so I waited for him, stirring my salad to get everything coated with dressing. I was antsy, but also happy that he wanted to talk to me.

I stabbed some lettuce with my fork.

Mack continued, "It is a crazy amount of work here. Like, they tell you that before you start, but you don't really understand what that means until you are actually here. But you get used to it. What are your main interests?"

He must mean subjects. "Uh, well, I didn't really come

here for the classes, specifically. I came because it was somewhere different from where I was."

And I was already so glad I had. I might have already
made a friend.

Mack laughed. "You aren't alone in that. Same here." He
extended his hands out like a balance scale. "Tiny town—
Kingfisher, if you were wondering—or a suburb of Oklahoma City?" He moved the sides of the scale up and down
until the Oklahoma City side ended much lower.

"Okay, good. I was worried. I'm actually more into art.
But now I'm not sure I'll be able to do all the math and
science classes. I mean, I was always fine at them, but I
didn't study that hard or anything."

"You'll do fine. It's just a matter of putting the time in, if
you don't take the hardest classes. Stick with the basics."

"Okay." That seemed like sound advice. I wondered
what he was focusing on, but he spoke before I could ask.

"What kind of art do you make?"

"Actually," I said, pointing to his fantasy novel, "stuff like
that." I was excited that he liked fantasy, too. It was another
thing we had in common.

"Fantasy?"

I nodded. "I love dragons mostly."

"Very cool. Anything you can show me?"

"Yeah, sure. Give me a second." I pulled my phone out of
my pocket and opened up the folder I kept all my art in. I
went to the infamous dragon fight drawing I'd finished
earlier this year.

"Oh, wow, that's great." He squinted. "Why's it brown? Is
that some fancy technique? It's interesting."

"Yeah, that. The brown. So I worked on this thing for
months. It was huge." I motioned with my hands to show
how big. "And on crisp white paper. And then I finished it

one afternoon and went upstairs for a break. When I came back down, one of my brother's friend's poured coffee on it." I closed my eyes for a second, reliving that feeling of horror as he'd tilted that cup enough so the coffee poured out.

"Oh, my God. What an *asshole*." He said it loud enough that people at the next table looked over. Mack's upper lip was curled in mild disgust.

"Yes, he is that. So I immediately went into action and ended up dyeing the whole thing with more coffee, hoping to give it an antiqued look. Didn't totally work, but you can still see the dragons well enough." I still felt that tug of disappointment that it was ruined, even though I'd done what I could to salvage it.

"Yeah." He zoomed in on the phone and looked around at different parts of the drawing. "This really is good."

"I've got other stuff in that folder. You can look through it if you're curious."

The noise in the cafeteria would normally be stressing me out, like it had at Emerson, but here it didn't feel intimidating. I ate some more salad.

He began flipping through the pictures. "These are really good. Did you know they're adding the A from STEAM to the school next year?"

"What do you mean?"

"They haven't settled on the name yet—OAMSA, OAMAS, who knows—but they're adding art, music, theater, and dance."

"Really?" That could be awesome. Would there be more opportunities for me because of this? Or would I be stuck in the science track?

"Yeah. Some alumnus donated a ton of money and there's a new building going up nearby that will house all that stuff."

"Will the arts students be doing all the math and science stuff, or just arts?"

"I'm not sure, but I doubt they would be expected to follow the same stream as we do now. Maybe you can switch to that track next year."

"That sounds awesome."

I took another bite of the lasagna, which had gone cold because we'd been talking. But this was great. I was pretty sure I was making a real friend. Probably not quite like Sam, but Mack and I had more in common than the girl in my art class who I'd gotten to be friends with last year. Plus, he was cute. I'd never paid a lot of attention to people's eyes before, but his were a nice dark brown that made him look kind of intense.

We ate quietly until Mack wadded his napkin up and tossed it on his plate, half the lasagna left.

"So what are your favorite books?" He asked, leaning back in his chair.

I swallowed and said, "I read mostly fantasy and sci-fi, a mix of YA and adult stuff. I like Marissa Meyer and Neal Shusterman. Leigh Bardugo."

"Did you read the Poppy War series?"

"R. F. Kuang? Yes!" Oh, my God—he liked that series too? "I loved it so much, even though half the time I didn't know what was going on. But it's one of my favorites."

Mack laughed. "Yeah, I can relate to that. It's complex. But I love that series."

"Have you read her other book?"

"Not yet. I'm sort of saving it for when I need something intense that I know I'll like."

"Yeah, I haven't either. I need to." How could we have this much in common? This was so awesome.

The electronic bell on the wall chirped.

"Ten-minute warning," Mack said. "What do you have next?"

"Art, which I'm totally looking forward to, obviously." At least we had a few more minutes to talk.

"Yeah." He put his book in his backpack and zipped it up before standing. "I've got to go do something before class. See you around?"

He was leaving already? My disappointment was an overreaction, but I didn't know how to stop it.

"Definitely," I said.

"Just as an FYI, I usually do something else at lunch, so I'm not always in here." He grabbed his tray and dumped the trash before putting it in the rack.

So what was it that he did at lunch? He seemed a little mysterious.

But then I realized he had told me this because he wanted me to know that he might not be here, and it wasn't because he was avoiding me. This made me smile.

I figured I'd go on to class, so I gathered my stuff and followed him. He was far enough ahead of me that he didn't see me. I was heading down the hall to my class when I saw him turn right, toward the administration offices. Where was he going? There were only offices that way.

All the way to the studio, my heart was beating faster with the intoxicating feelings of a growing friendship. It had been so long since I'd been through this process. It was with Sam in middle school. And that had been awkward and rocky at first, when she aligned herself with a group of mean girls whose main form of entertainment was making fun of me, but eventually she got away from them and we became genuine friends.

Maybe this would work out, too.

PART II

REMINISCING ON A BETTER PLACE

As soon as I walked into the art room, I wished I'd come earlier. There were six tables, and most of the front four tables were full, but there was a spot next to one kid—the skinny boy from physics. I wanted to sit at one of the empty tables in the back, but it might be rude not to sit next to him. I was trying to be bolder, anyway, so I sat next to him. I was only a tad bit nervous.

He didn't look up from his doodling on the cover of a red spiral notebook, the coil spine wire sticking way out. His doodle was of a character punching his fist, cartoon-style.

An Indian woman sitting behind the desk at the front of the room looked up and smiled at me. "Welcome," she chimed. "What's your name?"

"Nic."

She looked at something on her laptop. "Summers?"

"Yeah."

"Great. Welcome to the class." She picked up a multi-colored mug and took a sip from it before standing up and walking around the table. She wore a long textured olive dress with a big, knotty necklace. Her hair was loose and long, and she had on several thin gold bracelets. She didn't look like most of the other women I'd seen around here. I didn't think she had much makeup on, if any. I'd never had a teacher who looked like an actual free spirit before, and that's what I thought of when I looked at her.

She clapped her hands before saying, "We're all here now, so let's go ahead and get started. I already know most of you, but we're going to do some introductions for the new people."

A shiver of panic coursed down my spine. What would we have to say? I hated stuff like this. We hadn't done it in any other classes.

"I'm going to write some questions on the board, and if you could answer them, that would be great." She started writing on the whiteboard, saying out loud what she was writing. "Your name, if you're a junior or senior, and pronouns."

Pronouns? Mind blown. I'd never heard that question in real life before. On TV, sure. Maybe I could change my pronouns here. I didn't know. There was a rumbling of excitement in my stomach. That little bit of questioning inside reignited. I'd settled on the label "gender nonconforming" last year, but maybe it wasn't that simple. It was so hard to know.

The teacher was still talking. "Where you're from. Why you came to OAMS. What your career plans are. Your favorite type of art to make. And your favorite way to spend your free time on something other than art."

She turned back around and smiled again. She was quite the smiler. I already liked her.

"I'll start us off. You can call me Ms. Mangal, and I use

she/her pronouns. I'm from Chicago but people often ask where I'm really from. Don't ever ask that of anyone, but I'll tell you in case you are quietly curious: my parents immigrated here from India. I went to art school in San Francisco. I moved back to Chicago and taught for a while before coming here for this job. I am mostly a painter, working in both watercolor and acrylic, but I also like pen and ink sometimes. I'm a big knitter in my spare time."

She looked at the front right table. "Rachel, why don't we start with you?"

A tall girl with wavy brown hair said, "Sure. I'm Rachel and I'm a senior. I'm also president of the art club. We're having our first meeting today after school, at 4:30."

An art club? That was nice. I wondered what they did, and if it was like the one I'd been in at Emerson. I should join it.

Rachel continued, "I really consider myself from Houston, but we moved to Bartlesville for my dad's job a couple years ago. I came here because I want to get into MIT to major in economics. I'm not super-serious about art, but I do like to draw, mostly in pencil. I find it soothing. For free time—not that any of us here know what that is ..." She paused for a ripple of laughter to run across the front tables. But then she finished, "I love reality TV."

"Great," Ms. Mangal said. "Your pronouns?"

"She, obviously," Rachel said, waving her hand dismissively. "And also, for the new people, I just want to quickly mention that we have several people involved in Young Life here, if you are interested in that."

"Okay, Rachel," Ms. Mangal said.

Rachel's views on pronouns obviously did not involve empathy for anyone who didn't look or act like she thought they should. And I didn't know what Young Life was, but my guess was that it wasn't something that would interest me, since it was her thing. I doubted we had much in common.

The other conventionally pretty girls went one after another. A bunch of names I'd never remember. They were all from small towns and most liked to paint and draw. It ranged from nature scenes to animals to people. I did catch one of their names—Lily—because she did marker art and that stuck out to me. It seemed almost rebellious among her group. Markers usually made me think of sequential art— comics and graphic novels—which nice girls didn't really make. But she looked like a run-of-the-mill pretty, popular girl type. She was slim and had long, straight blonde hair.

Then Ms. Mangal got to my table and started with the boy.

"Uh, I'm Jacob." His voice was pretty low for a skinny kid. He stared at the board for the questions, presumably. "I'm a junior. I use he/him. I'm from Tishomingo. I came here to get out of a small town, I guess. I don't know what my career will be, but I like math a lot. I make comics. In my free time I read."

"Thanks, Jacob." She looked right at me and said, "And last but not least ..."

I stared at the board like Jacob had. "Um. I'm Nic. I'm a junior and I'm from Emerson. I use she/her pronouns." For now, maybe? Who knew what would happen. "Uh, I also came here so I could leave Emerson. I really want to be an artist for my career. And I love to draw fantasy characters, especially dragons. I mostly read in my spare time, if I'm not drawing."

"Okay, great, thank you, Nic. Thanks everyone. Art is often personal, and we make things based on our life experiences and interests, so I love to hear a little bit of what makes everyone tick, and it can help us understand each other's work better, too."

She clapped her hands and leaned back on her desk. "The seniors know the score, but for you juniors, this art class will likely be different from what you're used to. We're more serious in here because I've found that students who take this class truly want to be here, so we will be learning to critique each other's work. Now, you don't absolutely have to join in the critiques if you aren't serious about your art, but if you really want to grow, I strongly recommend it."

What? My pulse instantly quickened. We were going to judge each other's stuff? Oh, my God.

"Now, don't worry." Her gaze landed on me. "Nic, you look concerned."

Everyone turned to look at me.

My cheeks flamed. That was embarrassing. I didn't know what to say. Why couldn't I keep my feelings off my face?

"Critique does not mean criticism," Ms. Mangal said to the class. "We focus on the positives and talk about opportunities to make changes that will help you achieve your goals with your pieces. There is no room for cruelty in this classroom. We focus on growth. When it comes time to do our first critique, I will share the rules with you. We will all be gentle."

She clapped her hands again. She was apparently a big hand-clapper. "Okay. Another thing we do in this class that's different is that I will be creating a development plan with each of you. These are as intense as you want them to be. If you're in here for mental health like Rachel"—this made Rachel smile—"then we'll make a plan that focuses on those goals. But if you might be art school-bound, we will work on preparing your portfolio. And we'll deal with your needs anywhere between those two." She looked at me when she said that last part.

She finished with, "I want you to get what you need out of this class."

That was cool, but also intimidating. But mostly cool. She could actually help me get into art school. I could have a real chance at a competitive school. My stomach was all fluttery at the thought. I mean, that would be amazing. It could change everything.

Ms. Mangal turned around and picked up a clipboard and handed it to Rachel. "I'm going to pass this around. Please sign up for a meeting and give me a short summary of what you think your top one or two goals are for this semester."

She said she was going to talk about all the different media we could work with. We all watched her while she proceeded to point out the wheel and other ceramics supplies. Rachel passed the clipboard to the next girl. I was stressing, trying to figure out what I was going to write for goals. I had no idea.

Ms. Mangal finished up with the ceramics stuff and started talking about the dry media supplies a large cabinet held. I might be interested in doing more with colored pencils. The clipboard went to the next table. My stomach overreacted by twisting with dread.

Next was the wet media cabinet, a much smaller one, with ink mostly. The idea of ink was starting to intrigue me. Black-and-white line drawings could be so dramatic. Even more so than pencil. There were some comics artists that were so expressive in black and white that they didn't bother to color their work. I should look into that. Of course, it was much less forgiving than pencil—I was a big eraser when I worked in pencil. That was something that stressed me out about colored pencils—you couldn't really erase them. I guessed you'd just have to be more cautious with ink, work slower.

The clipboard went to Jacob. I was going to have to figure out what to write pretty quick.

Ms. Mangal was going over the paint cabinet. There were all sorts of paints to choose from, even oils.

Jacob passed the clipboard to me. I noticed that his fingernails were bitten short. The next available time slot was during the Friday class, so I picked that. Then I wrote, "I'm not sure. Maybe ink? Maybe painting?" That was the best I could do. Hopefully she'd be able to help me figure things out. I was the last person to get the clipboard so I put it on the edge of the table in front of me.

Soon, Ms. Mangal finished her talk and locked up all the cabinets. There also were large cubbies for everyone—we were supposed to label them with painter's tape—and we could keep our art in them.

Ms. Mangal picked up the clipboard when she came back over to the tables. "The first assignment you all have is to do a depiction of something fun you did over the summer, or a recent trip you took."

I thought of Scotland. I would do something from there. The statue in Glasgow with the traffic cone on its head?

The instructor leaned against her desk again. "This will be the only assignment you all will be doing, as your subsequent work will all be part of your custom plan we come up with. I want to loosen you up and get you back into art in case you've taken a break. It will keep you busy while we get through all the planning sessions."

I was really looking forward to talking to her. This might be a life-changing situation.

"We're almost done for today, but I also wanted to let

everyone know about an exciting opportunity for those of you who are more serious. A well-known Oklahoma City artist, Clee Greenwood, takes on three local students as mentees each semester for free. She will be taking applications for next spring soon."

My ears perked up. A mentorship? That sounded really awesome.

She continued. "It's competitive, but getting to work with her would be great if you're serious."

Would I really have a chance if I applied?

I absolutely had to try for this. It would be a huge disappointment if I didn't get it, though. But I needed to grow up a little and risk rejection, because I would miss out on things anyway, if I didn't try at all.

Ms. Mangal concluded, "I am happy to talk to any of you about this when we have our individual meetings, so make sure to ask me. The application isn't due for a while."

I would definitely be asking.

But then the bell chirped and class was over. I was bummed because it seemed so short, and now I had to go to pre-calculus. I packed up my bag.

Math was an official killjoy.

Just as I got my sketchbook packed away, Rachel appeared at my table. She put on a big smile and asked, "Are you interested in Young Life? I'd be happy to mentor you."

Her intensity made me nervous. Why was she singling me out? "I don't know what that is."

"It's a Christian youth ministry group. We do lots of fun stuff. You should join."

Oh, my God, was she barking up the wrong tree. "Oh, I don't think that's my scene. Uh, thanks for asking."

"Okay, let me know if you change your mind," she said, turning on her heel, her brown hair swinging out.

"Sure." No chance in hell. I really didn't like religion. People could do their own thing, but it was never going to be my deal.

Art club, though. That was another thing.

～

After my last class that day—computer science—I got to the art room about five minutes before the art club meeting was supposed to begin. There were five girls in there, including Rachel, the club president, and Lily, the marker artist from class.

They all looked so normal, all with perfectly made-up faces. I didn't think any of them would become my friends. Normal and me were like oil and water.

I started doodling in my new journal.

Last night had been pretty productive. I would have to be a lot more organized here, because these classes were going to be harder that my old school. I'd never been a perfect, straight-A student, and I wasn't planning on that here, but I didn't want to be making a bunch of C's, either.

Ms. Mangal appeared from a back room carrying a laptop, a stack of paper, and her colorful mug as three more girls came in and sat at the tables behind me. One of them was from my art class, but I couldn't remember her name. They all looked pretty normal, and I was disappointed. Where were the weirdos when you wanted them?

Not that even the freaks back in Emerson had wanted to be friends with me. But this was a new place. It was disappointing that the differences between here and Emerson weren't going to show up in art club.

I also realized I was being pretty judgmental. That girl from my art class in Emerson had also looked normal to me, and we ended up being friends. She'd even stood up for me once, when a guy made fun of me in class and I froze, as usual. Maybe being like everyone else in some things wasn't automatically bad. I mean, if any of these girls were serious about art, that was a pretty significant thing to have in common with me.

Ms. Mangal set the computer on her desk before leaning back against it. She clapped—the clapping was pretty funny —and said, "Let's get started." She looked around the room. "Where's Sarah G.?"

"She decided she couldn't be in the club this year," Rachel announced.

"Really?" Ms. Mangal said, a slight frown on her face. "That means we'll need another secretary. Anyone interested?" She looked expectantly around the room and everyone looked down except for Rachel and her friends. "We can talk about it later. I'll first explain how the club works for the new people."

"Okay." She clapped, which was still cracking me up. "So, we are a chapter of the National Student Artist Society. Normally, there is a membership fee for students, but OAMS covers that for you. You'll have to fill out a form so I can register you." She partially turned around and picked up the papers, before handing them to Rachel to pass out.

Rachel gave everyone a form while Ms. Mangal continued explaining what was expected of members and what the club offered in return. It was a lot either way. They did do fundraisers, which I hated, but only one each year, and it usually involved selling chocolate, although it was up to the board to decide.

I hated selling stuff. At Emerson, the only sales I ever made were to my parents and their coworkers. I wasn't a door-to-door kind of person. Besides, it was dangerous to go door-to-door now. A lot of people didn't want to see someone like me on their porch. Maybe if I'd been a cutesy cheerleader-type. My sister always did well. When I was in Key Club, we did some in-person things like staffing a table for a food drive at grocery stores, which I was also bad at, but it wasn't as horrible as going door-to-door.

Ms. Mangal was still talking about the club. They had scholarships you could get for your first year of college, and then there was the annual contest.

My ears perked up at that last point, obviously.

"It runs at the end of the year, so I'll talk about it more next semester."

This was exciting. The art contest at Emerson last year wasn't bad, but this was national and would mean more.

Of course, I immediately doubted myself, because that's what I did. But also, I wasn't even the best at anything at my tiny school in Emerson last year—how could I think it would be different on the national scale? That wasn't rational.

Ms. Mangal clapped again. "Okay, now for our chapter's specific business. We are down one board member and will need to fill that position. But first let's talk about the current board and everyone's responsibilities." She started going over the board, starting with Rachel, the president, and then went over the others and what their positions involved. The secretary position was open, and I started to get nervous because Ms. Mangal looked at me a couple times while going over the responsibilities of that position.

She finished by saying, "Volunteering is a great thing to have on your resume, too. Anybody interested?"

Should I do it? I didn't know. Could I even be a secretary here? I'd been elected secretary at the Emerson art club for this year, but obviously I wasn't there anymore.

When no one answered, Ms. Mangal asked Rachel to pick up the forms. Then she said, "I'll ask Lise to enter the membership details from the forms, and I'll pass things off to Rachel. But before we all leave today, we'll need a secretary if we want to stay an active chapter. And the board needs to stay afterward for about ten minutes to talk shop."

Rachel started her spiel. "So this year I want to do a mural this semester. I'll be scoping out a few possibilities, but I think the children's hospital is a good possible site for this semester. This will be a big deal for us and we'll have to work on some Saturdays. Plus we have to design the mural itself. Who would be interested in the painting?"

This sounded fun. I'd never been involved in a mural before. I know the art club at Emerson had done one when I was in middle school, but I wasn't old enough to get involved then.

"And the design?"

About half of us raised our hands. I did, too, even though I had no idea how to design a mural. Hopefully there would be somebody who had enough of a vision, and I could help. I doubted they'd want a dragon scene. A fight scene popped into my head, making me smile to myself. I was sure. Ms. Mangal would have to be involved in the design to some degree, so she could help us if we were struggling.

"Great. That should be plenty. The other major thing we'll need to plan for is the fundraiser in the spring. We can do what we did last year, which was selling the chocolate bars, or if somebody has any other ideas, let me know. We have to sign up by mid-November for the chocolate. We'll vote on it well before that, so get your ideas to me as soon as possible."

Behind her, Lise was typing away while Ms. Mangal

leaned against the wall, watching everyone. Her gaze fell on me again. I looked at the table.

Rachel talked about the club t-shirt design for a minute, swished her brown hair, and then Ms. Mangal moved to the front of the room and clapped her hands, of course, but then she said, "Last item. Who's going to be our secretary?"

There was silence, though all the board members looked around, and then I noticed Ms. Mangal was looking at me and so were a couple other people.

What, did I have SUCKER tattooed on my forehead? God.

"How about it, Nic?" the teacher asked. "You think you might be able to help?"

My stomach dropped. For some reason, it sounded terrifying. I didn't know these people, and they were all seniors and already knew each other and were apparently friends. How could I possibly fit in?

But then again, I was braver here, and technically, this might be a karmic event. I was already supposed to be secretary at Emerson, but since I wasn't there, they would have to rope someone else in, too. It felt inevitable. "Okay," I said slowly. "I guess I can do it."

She smiled and clapped her hands. "Great! That's it for this meeting, then, but I need the board to stay on for a little bit. Thank you for stepping up, Nic."

Great. Everyone else filed out and Rachel beckoned me to her table, so I moved over there. Rachel smiled at me and I felt bad for judging her. "You need to sign some stuff," she said.

I forced a smile back and we all signed some forms and Ms. Mangal printed off the responsibilities that I had, which would start next meeting. Basically, we had a club page, like a wiki, where I had to record notes from our board meetings. They all helped me do a quick one for tonight's meeting. It wasn't a big deal. The board met on Tuesdays every other week, so the first was in couple weeks. It didn't seem like it would be that much work. And maybe I'd make some friends. These girls seemed nice enough, even if Rachel might be a tad over the top. I was guessing she was bossy, and that always annoyed me.

However, I needed to not dislike people just because they were like everyone else. That was not the way to make it in the world, and I was determined to give myself the best chance in this new environment. It really was a fresh start.

Thursday afternoon I was waiting for a campus tour with Ms. Patton, the dorm mom. We obviously knew our way around the OAMS campus already, but it was situated inside a big college campus, and there was a lot more to see.

There were about fifteen other juniors waiting in front of the dorm with me. It was four o'clock, pretty much the hottest time of the day—this walk was going to wear me down. I pinched the front of my t-shirt and aired myself. Not that it really helped, but you have to try.

I was standing kind of off to the side when I sensed someone rushing up from behind. They stopped beside me and turned and said, "Made it."

I felt a millisecond of shock that another student was casually speaking to me, but recovered and said, "Yeah, I think we're about to go."

My new walk neighbor was a girl with a hoop nose ring and short, spiky brown hair. She was maybe an inch taller than me, but slim, and although it looked like she was wearing makeup, she was dressed pretty casually in a nondescript yellow polo shirt and blue shorts. But the nose ring that made her stand out. I hadn't seen her before.

"I'm Nic." Look at me, introducing myself first.

"Jenna," she said. "Where are you from?"

Ms. Patton raised her arms. "Okay, everyone, we're going to get going. Follow me."

"Emerson," I answered quietly.

"Near Tulsa, right?"

"Yeah."

"I'm from OKC." She had virtually no accent, unlike almost everyone else I'd met here. At least among the students.

"Cool." I was trying to think of something to say. Even with my new bravery, I hadn't suddenly sprouted social skills.

"What's on your shirt?" she asked.

I turned to face her as we walked and pulled on the bottom of the shirt to straighten it out so she could see. It had the words "So say we all" above an insignia.

She grinned. "*Battlestar Galactica*! Nice."

I was completely taken aback.

"My dad made us watch that a few years back, every time we were at his apartment for the weekend," she explained. "I pretended to not like it, but I actually did."

Wow. A surge of excitement coursed through me. What were the chances of finding someone into the same stuff as me so fast? "My dad was also the one who got me to watch it, once I got into sci-fi. It was kind of our thing because nobody else liked it."

"That's awesome. Dads are okay sometimes." She laughed, which made me laugh, if a little less enthusiastically, out of nerves.

The sun bore down on us, bringing sweat beads out on my forehead.

As we reached the sidewalk near the building that was across the dorm's lawn, Ms. Patton started speaking again. "This is McCarthy Hall." She pointed at the building as we passed it, another white-painted brick building just like ours. Almost all buildings on campus were short, brick, and painted with the same bright white.

"You may already know that we're at the northwest corner of campus, and now we're heading south. We're going to pass another dorm and then we'll see the gym. I'll be able to take you in for a quick look around. Your student ID will get you into the gym."

"I don't think I'll be utilizing that perk," Jenna said, which made me laugh.

"Me neither."

"You don't spend hours a day on your core?" She said it in a mocking voice that was really funny.

"Somehow you guessed right." I was finding it easy to talk to her. Easier than usual. This might really be a new world for me.

"Okay, everyone, that building up ahead is the gym. But there are several nice workout areas and classes available to everyone else through this door."

As we followed Ms. Patton toward the door, Jenna quietly sang, "One of these is not like the others," and motioned at the gym and then the white buildings on either side of it. The gym was a big, two-story modern building of steel, totally out of place here.

"Yeah. It's really weird."

The chilly air was a relief once we were inside. Ms. Patton showed us around quickly, and then we were back outside again. The heat enveloped me. I fanned myself as we continued south. To the right was a short cement wall that enclosed a narrow, raised grassy area with some trees in the middle. This was a common sight here.

Soon we reached the student union. Ms. Patton took us around the food court and then through a room with very tall, dark wood booths, and walls painted pale green, that she said everyone called Booth Forest. I could see myself sitting in here with my new, hypothetical friends, laughing it up.

Jenna leaned in and said, "That pale green is hideous. They should have gone with dark green. Like pizza-shop-booth green."

I laughed lightly. I knew exactly what color she meant.

Then we were back outside, with sidewalks snaking off in three directions. Ms. Patton pointed to and talked about various buildings on either side, but then we went along the middle path and she pointed out the art gallery, which had studios and music rooms. I couldn't see into the windows that were instead reflected back a sweaty, chubby girl with long hair parted in the middle. I looked away quickly before I could notice anything more about myself.

"This is Joy Harjo Library," Ms. Patton announced, pointing to a five-story modern building.

"I think it's so great it's named after her," Jenna said to me.

I wasn't entirely sure who she was, but I had a fuzzy memory. "She's a poet, right?"

"U.S. Poet Laureate for three years in a row, and she's from Oklahoma, and she's also Muscogee/Creek. First Native American to be Poet Laureate. *So* cool." The admiration in her voice was infectious.

We rounded the corner, still following the dorm mom. Jenna must be an English nerd, maybe even a poet herself. I wondered if she came to OAMS for the same reason as me, to escape a bad social situation. But she wasn't from a small town, so it wasn't the same. I should ask, but I was feeling nervous again.

"That is pretty neat," I said. "Though I'm surprised a poet donated enough money for a building at a technical college."

"Yeah, her second job is robber baron." Jenna laughed. "Actually, it was a donor who asked that it be named after her. It is a library, after all."

I nodded. "Makes sense." How did she know all this?

Ms. Patton started again. "And now we have the library. This isn't a public library—you're not going to find any Nora Roberts or Stephen King in this one—but there are many places to study quietly in here, and obviously there are many books. Your student ID will allow you to check out ten books at a time, for four weeks each. That's paper books or ebooks. Follow me."

We all trailed inside after her, stopping in the giant foyer. The circulation desks were off to the right, with a room full of computers to the left. Continuing straight ahead were metal shelves full of books.

"Most of you will have no idea what I'm talking about, but this spot right here is where the library's huge card catalog used to stand. Before everything was computerized."

Jenna looked at me and whispered, "Old people love history."

It made me smile. She was not wrong. She was also hilarious. Talking with her was fun, even if all I knew about her was that she wasn't into exercise and knew about poets. But the conversation was practically flowing, like I'd always imagined it did for extroverts.

Ms. Patton led us through some of the library, showing

us study rooms we could book, some solo and some for groups. It could be cool to study here. Though I'd never really studied in public before, and I wasn't sure if I'd be able to concentrate. Maybe for a group project or whatever.

We went back outside, the heat pouring over my skin, and waited for everyone else to emerge. Straight ahead there was this giant metal sculpture on a large, round cement platform, surrounded by pink and white flowers. I looked at the sculpture more closely. "Is that a sundial?" I asked.

Jenna narrowed her eyes and studied it. "I think it is. That's one big honking sundial."

"I guess that's how old people tell time," I joked.

She punched me on the shoulder and laughed.

Ms. Patton came out and called for everyone to start following her again. I started to get bored hearing about more buildings and was staring off into the distance when I noticed a guy walking toward one of the buildings. Something about his gait was familiar. And then something glinted in the sun—a chain running into his pocket.

I squinted and studied him. He was wearing a white shirt and tan shorts, with fluorescent shoes.

Was that Mack?

"What are you looking at?" Jenna asked.

"I think that's Mack. He's a senior at OAMS."

"Ah. I don't know him." She laughed. "But then I hardly know anybody."

"Yeah, we talked at orientation and at lunch. He's cool."

"Do you *like* him?" she teased.

For once I was glad for the heat, as my face was probably already red so she wouldn't see the blush. "He's nice," I offered.

"Nice. Code word for 'I like him.'" She elbowed my arm.

Mack was disappearing behind another building.

"I don't know. He just seems different from so many other guys. You know, the toxic-masculine type."

"Ugh. Yeah. I know what you mean. Good ol' boys. Let's get noodlin'."

I nodded at first. "What is noodling?"

"People go into rivers and stuff and stick their arm inside a catfish's mouth to pull them out of deep parts. Sometimes they drown because they dive too far down and can't get out of the water fast enough."

"Um, what?" I was confused, but also distracted. Mack was heading vaguely in the direction of the dorm, but I had no real idea where he was going. The fact that he was so not a toxic-masculine guy made me wonder if he ever felt gender nonconforming, like me.

"Just a different way to catch fish," Jenna said. "But good luck with Mack."

"I think we're just friends," I hedged. "Which is fine. I think we're going to be really busy here."

"That's the truth. What's he like?"

Before I could answer, Ms. Patton pointed out another building, where the nuclear engineering department was based. We turned left and continued on.

"Nuclear engineering," Jenna repeated to me. "It's always weirded me out how that name uses a reference to such a small thing to mean something that can get so big it can destroy the world. Science is weird."

I nodded, my mind still curious about where Mack was going. Was he meeting someone?

"Anyway, what's Mack like?" Jenna asked.

"You know, it's kind of weird. I know almost nothing about him. He gets me to talk about myself, which usually I don't do because I'm sort of pathologically shy."

"You?" Jenna looked genuinely surprised.

"Well, you're easy to talk to, too. Normally I'm awkward and quiet." It was true that it felt odd talking this much. "But I think I'm a different person here. It's weird. Apparently everything is weird to me now, since I keep saying it."

"Well, you're in the big city now. Sort of. Near one. Though what is it they say—you can take the girl out of the country, but you can't take the country out of the girl."

I laughed. "Emerson isn't really *country*. It's just a small town. It's almost a suburb of Tulsa." I thought for a second. "No, who am I kidding. It totally is country. But I'm not. Besides, I am leaving Oklahoma as soon as I can, and I'm not going to always live in a small town." I wondered how I would handle comments like Jenna's if I did come out as nonbinary, since she obviously assumed I was a girl. I didn't know.

"Good for you. Me too. I don't fit here either. After graduation, I'm also outta here like a fart from a baby."

I barked a laugh at that and had to cough to cover it up as everybody turned to look. Jenna was smirking, obviously amused with herself.

"I just made that up, right here," she whispered.

I shook my head and avoided looking at her as Ms. Patton gestured to some more buildings that didn't really relate to us. More white brick.

"You do realize you compared yourself to a fart," I whispered.

"Yeah, I didn't actually think that entirely through." She tapped her upper lip.

"Alright everyone, that's almost the whole tour," Ms. Patton said. "On our way back, I'll show you the Oval, an area where a lot of students hang out on nice days. We'll be passing the cafeteria if you want to stay for dinner instead of going with me back to the dorm."

"Wanna get dinner?" Jenna asked.

"Sure." This was the second person I'd be eating with this week. I hadn't seen Mack at lunch today, so I'd eaten alone. But that was the norm, and this was different.

Everything was different now, including me. I didn't want to overdo it, but I was excited for the future for the first time in a long time.

Jenna and I scanned into the college cafeteria and wove through the tables to get to the serving areas in the middle of the round building. We met up at the end of the salad bar after getting our food. It was pretty crowded so we went all the way to the back and then started heading over toward a few empty tables.

I heard my name amidst the clamor of the cafeteria. I looked around until I spotted Mack waving at me, his black hair looking windswept. My heart did a stupid little dance.

We were already practically at his table. "Hey." I tried to sound calm and collected, but I was panicking. Who would I sit with?

"You can sit here if you want." He motioned at the empty seats.

I was being an idiot. We could all sit together.

"Awesome." I set my tray down and Jenna set hers down next to me.

"I'm Mack," he said.

"Oh! You're Mack. I'm Jenna." She put her palm on her chest as she said her name.

"Have you heard of me?" Mack asked, looking bemused.

I was blushing, of course, but I couldn't think of anything to say. Some guy a table over barked a laugh, and we all looked for a second, interrupting the awkward moment. But I was still worried about what to say.

"Nic was just talking about the people she's met so far," Jenna said matter-of-factly when we turned back.

Okay, good. That was a not humiliating explanation.

"Got it," Mack said.

I looked at his tray. His plate was empty, and napkins covered it. But it didn't look like he was planning to go anywhere, so that was a good sign. Like he actually wanted to talk to us. Or me, since he'd called my name.

I couldn't believe he'd called me over. This was amazing. Sam would be so impressed with me, even all the way over there in Scotland. I was going out of my comfort zone, and it was paying off, just like she always said it would.

Mack leaned back in his chair. "So I guess the obligatory question I have to ask you, Jenna, is where you're from."

"Oklahoma City," she answered while partially unwrapping a burrito encased in foil.

I started stirring my spaghetti to spread the sauce better before taking a bite.

"Ah, a townie. The other question that's fun to ask is, why'd you come here?"

She laughed. "Well, it wasn't totally to get away, if that's what you're asking. I didn't mind a change, but I'm planning to go into environmental science."

Mack nodded. "Nice."

I wondered how her poetry interest fit into that. Maybe she wrote poetry about the environment.

Of course, by that logic, I should be making art that dealt with gender since that was always on my mind, but I hardly ever did. Maybe I should. Would it help me figure things out?

"And what about you two?" Jenna asked. "Why'd you come here?" She took a bite of her burrito.

Mack smiled and crossed his arms. "I didn't want to be stuck in a small town—Kingfisher—for another two years."

Jenna looked at me and raised her eyebrows.

I finished chewing, suddenly conscious of the fact that I was eating a messy food with people I didn't know that well. I hoped I didn't look like a pig. I reined in my thoughts and said, "Basically the same thing, get out of small-town Emerson. I do well enough in math and science, but I'm not really interested in either."

"Half the kids here came to get away from where they grew up," Mack said.

Jenna nodded and turned to me. "What is it you want to do?"

"Art." It was weird to be sharing so much with people I barely knew. Three hours ago, I didn't even know Jenna existed. "I draw and stuff."

"Oh, that's neat," she said. "I can't draw for crap, but I write plenty of bad poetry."

"I doubt it's all bad," Mack said. "Though it is true that most professional poets didn't do their best work when they were teenagers."

Jenna laughed and wiped her fingers on a napkin.

"But you should see Nic's stuff," Mack continued. "It's great. Show her, Nic."

I blushed at the compliment. It was nice when people thought your work was good. I had learned the hard way last year that someone complimenting your art does not mean they want to date you, so I tried to tamp my excitement down.

I pulled my phone out and got to the art folder in my

photos and set the phone on the table. "This album has all of it."

She started scanning through, oohing and aahing along the way. "These are so cool, Nic! I'm not usually into traditional fantasy art—so sexist, you know—but I've grown up reading fantasy and used to play D&D with my brother until he found better people to play with. I really like this. It's good. Your dragons and people feel alive."

My face was still warm from my last blush, otherwise I probably would have blushed again. I was ridiculous. I remembered I needed to acknowledge the compliment. "Thanks."

"See what I mean?" Mack asked.

"Definitely." Jenna finished the album. "What are you going to do next?"

I'd taken a bite—eating while you were trying to have a conversation was a pain in the ass—so I raised a finger so she'd wait until I was done. "I don't know. The art teacher has a really structured class, and we're supposed to meet with her to plan our customized curriculum, basically. I'm talking to her tomorrow. I'm considering working on pen and ink and maybe acrylic painting, but I want to see what the teacher says. She says she will help me develop a portfolio so I can apply to art school. So I'm going to follow her lead. She might give assignments, I'm not sure."

"Well, I, for one, am excited to see what else you come up with," Mack said.

"Me too," Jenna said.

I smiled, embarrassed at the unexpected abundance of friend support. This was so weird. Usually, it was just my mom and Isabella and other artists who might be interested. But I wasn't complaining. "There's also something else really good. She told us about this mentorship program with a local artist that we can apply for, for next semester."

"That sounds cool," Mack said.

"Yeah." I had looked the artist up and she was really versatile, like Ms. Mangal had said. She painted in watercolors and acrylic, but she also did a lot of loose charcoal sketches, which were just so engaging somehow, despite their simplicity. I thought she was mostly a painter, but she had shared a lot of her prep work in some of her blog posts, and she did that mostly in pencil, charcoal, or ink.

"You should totally apply," Jenna said.

I nodded and then took a bite of spaghetti to get out of saying anything. I was feeling self-conscious again. Now that I'd told them, what if I didn't get accepted? They'd know about my failure.

Jenna dropped what was left of her burrito on her plate and covered it with balled-up napkins.

I wasn't done yet and took another bite while Mack asked Jenna about her classes.

"Yeah, junior year is mostly the same for everyone," he said. "Senior year is when you get to take all the specialized electives."

"What are you taking?" she asked.

My ears perked up at this while I continued working on my spaghetti. I hadn't managed to ask this question yet, and I was desperate to know the answer.

"I'm finishing up the calc 3, electronics, organic chemistry, computer science 3, robotics, nuclear chemistry, and of course English and history." He had a slight grimace on his face as he listed these.

"Wow," Jenna said. "That's intense. What are you planning to major in in college?"

I was really curious about this, too.

"I haven't decided," he started, "but I'm leaning toward computer science or computer engineering. You all know you don't have to take eight classes senior year, right?"

"Really?" Jenna said.

"Yeah, you can take a free period—but I couldn't decide between these, so I did them all. I may drop organic chem, though."

I already knew I wasn't going to take all those super-advanced classes next year. I finally finished the last of the spaghetti and leaned back.

"Want to get ice cream?" Mack asked us.

"Where?" Jenna said, at the same time I answered, "Of course I want ice cream."

Mack pointed to a station by one of the side exits. "It's even free once you've paid to get into the cafeteria. The best kind of ice cream."

"Let's get over there yesterday," Jenna said.

We cleared our trays, put them on the racks, got our ice cream, and left for the dorm.

Three of us. Me and two friends. I was in shock. Normally I'd be hiding somewhere alone instead of hanging out with people I liked. What else was going to be different this year?

I was sitting at the art table waiting for class to start when my phone vibrated. I pulled out my phone and saw Sam's drawing of a castle I'd put in the phone for her number. Yay! She was home from school and finally had a chance to respond to the IM that I'd sent last night. I'd told her about Mack and Jenna and how things were already different here.

Sam: thats great!

Me: i knew youd be impressed. im way braver. and no disasters so far.

Sam: i knew you could do it, even if you didnt think you could. but starting in a new place is easier

Me: yeah

The classroom bell chirped a one-minute warning.

She said some stuff about her boyfriend, the same one she had when I visited her in March. He was nice.

Sort of like Mack. Was it crazy of me to think of him so much, or to be using him as a reference point?

The bell chirped again so I signed off, and then Ms. Mangal told us to continue on our projects for this week, which was to make a piece of art related to our summer. My appointment with her for semester planning was at the halfway point of class. I didn't know what to expect. She went to the table right behind us and called Jacob for his appointment. He was probably the only boy at the school not wearing shorts. He'd worn jeans every day this week. It was kind of odd.

The rest of us got started on the assignment. I hedged and was drawing Linlithgow Castle in Scotland, which I'd visited with Sam. We'd both loved it. So, it was from a vacation, just not one over the summer.

That trip had been such a revelation for me. It showed me that other places are not the same as where I grew up. In Glasgow, nobody insta-judged me, and they even seemed interested in what I did in my spare time. They were impressed with the art I showed them, and nobody asked why I wasn't drawing delicate flowers like people back in Emerson did. Although there were a lot of really cool things on that trip—castles and more—I'd never forget sitting around in that tiny living room of Sam's friend, just chatting like everybody was worth knowing, including me. Everyone in Emerson evaluated you in terms of how you could benefit them—improve their social standing, date them, whatever —but in Glasgow, everybody just kind of looked at me as a fellow human.

The lesson—that things were different outside of Emerson—seemed to be holding up here, too, even though I hadn't left Oklahoma. It wasn't perfect here, but it was a little better. Sophia, in particular, seemed to be annoyed I wasn't something other than what I was, and OAMS had its fair share of jerks, but not as many—a lot of other people here were different.

I got back to the Linlithgow drawing. I sensed movement and looked up. Rachel had stopped next to my table and was studying my drawing, which was still in the light sketching-out phase.

She didn't say anything but pursed her lips and went back to her desk.

What in the world? Why would she care about me, or my drawing? It looked like she didn't approve or something.

I really couldn't even interpret the look. Was it disgust? Usually I could suss that look out no problem, since I'd seen it so many times in Emerson. There was maybe some of that, but it felt like something else was going on.

Ms. Mangal called my name, so I grabbed my sketchbook and laptop and sat next to her. There was a subtle floral aroma that emanated from her.

"Let's see some of your art, Nic," she said, bringing her hands together in a silent clap.

I double-clicked the art folder on my computer. Ms. Mangal had said the computer was better for viewing art than phones.

"Oh, I see you like fantasy art," she said.

"Yeah, that's kind of my thing." I hadn't brought up any

pictures yet, so it was just thumbnails that were visible at this point.

"Very nice work. You're clearly comfortable in pencil, too. Let's see some of these up close."

I pushed the computer closer to her, thinking she could look through them herself.

"No, it's your computer and your art, so you drive. You don't have to show me everything, but let's look at some of your favorite pieces." She sounded genuinely excited about seeing my work and tapped her fingers together. "I really want to get a sense for your range of skills and your favorite subjects. We'll look at these for a few minutes and then move on to the planning."

I nodded, not entirely sure what to show her. I decided I'd go in reverse chronological order. "I've been working on some other stuff in my sketchbook over the summer, but this was the last major piece I did." I double-clicked on the celestial leopard in the middle of a big yawn that I did in May.

"Oh!" she said loud enough that a couple people looked over, before getting back to their drawings. "I didn't realize those spots were different until it was bigger."

Instead of regular leopard spots, I'd made them stars and moons. I didn't even know why—it was just an idea I had at the time and I ran with it. Otherwise the leopard looked totally realistic. I was actually working on this drawing when I got the letter that said I'd been accepted to OAMS, so I was especially liking it right now.

"This is neat," Ms. Mangal said. "Creative, and well-executed. You even accounted for the angle of the spots in the shapes. Good work."

I blushed. My brain always sort of panicked when people complimented me. I mumbled, "Thanks," and showed her the dragon drawing next, explaining why the paper was brown from that jerk's coffee.

She shook her head in disgust at the damage, but admired the drawing. "You teenagers always surprise me. Often in a good way, and sometimes in a bad way. You are complicated beings, aren't you?" She winked at me.

"I guess so." I kept going, showing most of my major assignments from art last year.

"I like that you've tried different media, but I can see you're most comfortable in pencil. Pencil's fine, but I'd love to see you push yourself out of your comfort zone. Let's see your sketchbook."

I opened it up to the beginning, thinking that she was right. I still needed to move out of my comfort zone, even though it was scary (by definition). But I'd pushed myself before, in coming here, and in going to Glasgow, so it could obviously turn out fine.

The earliest stuff was actually some of my sketches prepping for the dragon drawing. I moved through the pages slowly, and she kept nodding.

"I really like your sketch style," she said. "There's a good sense of movement in them, which can be hard for newer artists to capture."

I nodded, again embarrassed. "This is my sister," I said when I got to a few I did of her over the summer.

"Oh nice. I love her smile there."

Looking at Isabella made me miss her, and I felt lost for a moment. It hadn't even been a week, but it was weird not seeing her every day. My heart ached. I missed her hugs and her funny opinions on her classmates.

"Yeah. So that's it for my current sketchbook."

"Okay, great." She rested her arms on the table and said, "Let's talk about the skills you want to develop. First tell me if you have any thoughts yourself, and then I'll share mine."

And there was the self-doubt. What if I chose wrong? It would be a wasted opportunity. "Uh." I tried to mentally regroup. I'd had an idea earlier, and now I couldn't think of it. Crap. "Oh! I just remembered. I was thinking pen and ink. It feels like that is kind of a natural step from pencil?"

She nodded energetically.

I continued, "And maybe painting? I don't know. I do like pen and ink with watercolors, but I think watercolors are hard. I've never painted." I shrugged. "That's basically what I was thinking."

"I absolutely agree on the pen and ink. I think you will like it, especially if you are considering going into sequential art, or other types of illustration. Black and white can be so striking in any context." She raised a finger to emphasize her next point. "I also think it's smart to start painting if you never have. We always start students with acrylics because they are easier to work with, fast-drying, and significantly less messy than oils."

I nodded, both nervous and excited about these things.

Ms. Mangal smiled and continued, "I think these two things will be a great set of skills to develop this semester. Next semester, we can see if you want to adjust anything, or stick with these."

My stomach was fidgety because possibilities were popping up everywhere. This was so great. It was getting real. I had these images of amazing ink dragon drawings in my head.

Ms. Mangal talked about the projects for the semester and how I would be going through several processes before starting the actual final drawing. I'd be doing three ink drawings, about five weeks each, and one acrylic painting, due at the end of the semester. She told me she'd come up with a prompt for each of the ink assignments and email me. The painting would be a still life.

She made a note in her notebook.

"There was one other thing," I said. The bell sounded right then.

"Yes?" She looked up from her book.

"I am interested in the mentorship program you mentioned."

"Oh, great. We're out of time today, but I can talk to you about it next class. We have some time before the applications are due."

So that was that. I grabbed my sketchbook and laptop, and headed out, more excited about my art than I'd been in a while. I was going to get so much better this year.

By Friday night, I was worn out. After dinner, which I'd eaten alone—I hadn't had any meals with other people except last night, but that was okay—I was sitting in my room. Like, literally just sitting at my desk, not sure what to do. Sophia had packed a bag and left, so she was probably one of those kids who went home on weekends.

Then I remembered something Ms. Mangal had mentioned in class earlier—we could spend time in the studio outside of class hours.

I gathered my stuff up and got up. On my way out I looked at the poster Sophia had put up on the wall. Some kind of tree diagram. I looked closer. It was a tree of evolution, showing the beginning of life at the base and lines branching off for plants, invertebrates, etc. It had pictures of an animal of each type filling up the space. Humans were at the top.

Okay, so she was into evolution. Even if she wasn't the best roommate, at least I hadn't been paired with a religious nut who was going to regale me with tales of Jesus riding a brontosaurus. I couldn't imagine living with somebody who constantly tried to convert me or something.

The RA working the desk called the security guard so they could unlock the art room for me and logged that I was going there. I was amazed at how easy this was going to be.

I went to the classroom building to wait. After about ten minutes, a grizzled-looking older woman in baggy jeans came into view.

"Hi, dear. You want into the art room?" Her voice said she'd smoked for a long time, but it was friendly. "Let's go in the back way."

I followed her along the side of the building, catching a whiff of smoker scent. The sun was only starting to go down, so there was plenty of light. It would be dark when I went back to the dorm.

"So you're an artist?" she asked as we neared the corner.

"Yeah. The desks in our rooms are really small, so it's hard to work there."

"I bet. I've seen those rooms. They are small. And there's two of you in there. Since my husband left, I've come to really value having my own space."

We turned the corner and she stopped at a white metal door, pulled a keycard on a cord from her pocket, and scanned it to unlock the door. She pulled it open and stepped inside. It was pretty dark in there until she hit a light switch.

"Yeah, I had my own bedroom at home," I said. "It's different here. I can't say I'm a fan of that part of living here."

She smiled and motioned for me to follow her. "This way. But you kids are all so talented. So smart with the math and science, and now they're bringing in artists, too, with more coming next year."

I followed her inside before I recognized where we were. The art room was right there. "Yeah, it's kind of intimidating to be around so many smart kids, actually. I'm not quite at their level."

"Oh, I'm sure that's not true." She scanned her card for the art room door and kicked the doorstop under it to keep it open. Then she hit the light switch. "Just so you know, the outer door is going to stay locked. You can leave the room door propped open while you're in here, but make sure to shut it when you leave so it will lock."

"Okay."

"I hope you enjoy your evening." She checked to make sure her keycard was hooked onto her belt. "Goodnight, dear."

"Thank you so much." I was excited to get started on something, even if I didn't yet know what I was going to work on. She left and then I dumped my stuff on the table I always sat at. I took my sketchbook out of my bag and grabbed a pencil.

I got to work on the castle drawing from class, finishing it.

Which meant I had to find something else to do. I twirled the pencil as I considered the first project Ms. Mangal had emailed. It was to show an animal doing something human—obviously, I was doing a dragon. I worked on thumbnails, which Ms. Mangal had explained were very small and rough idea sketches, focusing on composition.

I checked the time. Already after nine, so I set an alarm

for 10:15 to make sure I'd be back by curfew. I worked on more ideas for the assignment.

I checked my phone again a couple minutes before the alarm was going to go off. I started packing everything up and headed over to the dorm. I was walking along the concrete path toward the front entrance when I looked up and saw Mack coming from the other side of the building. My heart skipped. I hadn't seen him since Thursday night. He waved.

When we reached the door—at the exact same time— he said hi and asked what I was up to. I told him I'd been in the art room, drawing. Where had he been? I was so curious, but too chicken to ask.

"Can I see what you drew?"

A wave of elation washed over me. It was an overreaction, but I just loved that he wanted to see. We went inside and sat on one of the boxy couches in the main lounge to look through the sketchbook.

I explained the dragon project, and walked him through my brainstorming. "I was finding it hard to come up with ideas at first. So I tried to think of things that people do that are inherently funny. I came up with karaoke, dancing, Twister. Maybe a human and dragon interacting somehow. Or a dragon putting on southern makeup."

He laughed at that. "Would they use some kind of paste to smooth over the scales? How thick is foundation?"

I laughed. "Goth makeup might be pretty funny, too."

"Show me what you have."

I handed him the sketchbook and we looked at all of them. There was a dragon pushing a shopping cart at the grocery store. One working behind the counter at a Quik-Trip. Working the newborn room at the hospital. And a few more—feeding cats at a shelter, walking a bunch of yippy dogs, driving a car through a Taco Bueno drive-thru. Teaching preschool. Working the Subway counter. Pushing a cart of books in the library. I had drawn sketches for each of them.

"The hospital nursery is the best," he said.

"Yeah." I loved that he liked that one, since it was my favorite, too. I'd only drawn the dragon standing in there, not really doing anything. "I had a couple ideas—I could either show a close-up of a dragon tucking in one baby, or show lots of babies with this dragon in the midst of it all, maybe another dragon or human in the background."

"All those ideas sound great. I can't wait to see the final version." He scooted forward and put his hands on his knees. "Alright, I think I'm going to do some reading and go to bed."

We got up and headed toward the girls' side of the dorm together, which still confused me. "Is your room not upstairs?" I finally asked.

"Mine's in the hall back here." He pointed to the hall that led from the front to the girls' lounge.

"Oh, okay." I was desperate to know why, but it was kind of obvious that he wasn't telling me. Was there a reason? I thought I shouldn't ask.

We got to the stairs and he headed toward the hall. "Talk to you later."

"Good night."

Even if I didn't know that much about him, I did know that he seemed to genuinely like me. I was making a real friend, and it felt amazing. Maybe things were only going to get better.

~

Saturday morning, I slept in and then did some reading for physics before heading to the cafeteria for an early lunch, since I'd missed breakfast. Afterward, in hopes of something interesting happening, I decided to sit in the main lounge and read the book I'd taken with me. Someone was watching TV—one of those shows where they say how much your antiques are worth—but not loud, so it was fine. The blinds on the windows behind the TV were raised so the sun was shining in.

I was nervous, sort of inviting social interaction. Or at least the possibility. People were coming and going, but it was still relatively calm downstairs. I sat there cross-legged on the couch, against the cream-colored side wall. The couch sucked, though—it was incredibly uncomfortable, and the fabric was coarse and this ugly mustard color. I had the book open but I was also keeping an eye out.

Which is kind of funny, since I totally missed it when it happened.

"Nic."

I was so startled that I jumped. I looked up and Jenna was standing across the room, in front of the third-floor girls' fridge, holding a coconut water.

"Hey. How's it going?" I asked. Her hair looked wet and I stupidly asked, "Did you just take a shower?"

She laughed. "Yep. Lazy Saturday. Well, sort of. I studied a bunch this morning."

"Yeah, me, too. I'm not sure how I'm going to do here."

"Yeah. It's definitely intimidating. You want a coconut water?"

"Uh, sure." I'd never had it before so I hoped it was good.

She grabbed a second one and maneuvered around the other couches to sit down next to me. "Here you go."

I took it from her and we twisted the caps off at the same time.

I took a sip. Oh, wow, this was really good.

"Oh nice, I love your shoes," she said.

"Thanks." I looked down to see I had on my black-and-white checkered Vans, which I was very fond of.

"How many colors do you have?"

"Only three, but I actually want every color. I love Vans." I'd already worn all of mine this week.

She laughed. "They have a nice aesthetic, but I'm more of a Chucks person. I like the white toe box. But I only have two pairs."

We both looked down at her hot pink Chucks.

"Nice," I said. This was such a random conversation, but it was fun.

"What are you reading?" she asked.

I held the book up. "Wheel of Time. Rereading it. Book nine."

"Isn't that kind of boring and conventional?" she asked, giving me the side-eye.

Well, that made me feel stupid. "I like it," I said defensively. "Have you read it?"

"Sorry, I didn't mean to offend you. I've read the whole series, too. I love all speculative fiction, but I kind of got sick of the traditional Western European-inspired stuff, with all its white and cishet characters. I've sort of branched out."

"Into what?" It was awesome that she was interested in this kind of stuff. I almost didn't recognize the word "cishet" when she said it because I'd only ever read it.

"Come to the library with me and I'll show you some cool stuff, if you haven't discovered it yet."

I was confused. "I thought they didn't really have popular fiction?"

"Not the college library." Jenna laughed. "The public library. It's not far from campus."

"Ah, okay. Sure." I'd love to see what else was out there. "That sounds great. Are you going now?"

"Yep."

That's when I noticed she had a canvas tote with her. "Let me go up and get my backpack."

"Sure, I'll be here."

I raced upstairs and grabbed my backpack and threw my book and wallet in. This was amazing—I was going on a social outing that had happened organically and wasn't engineered by someone else, like all those failed attempts at finding me friends that Sam had made before she moved last year.

Jenna was by the front desk when I got back downstairs.

"We're both going," she said to the RA.

"Name?" the girl asked me.

"Nic Summers."

"Okay, got it. Don't go anywhere else."

We had to check out to go anywhere off campus. I didn't know how much they monitored us, though.

We headed out, the heat slapping me in the face the second we were out the door, and I followed Jenna's lead as we went around the back of the dorm.

"Are we going to be able to get cards?" I asked.

"I already have one because the library is part of the OKC system, but hopefully you can, too. Maybe with your student ID? Otherwise, you can check stuff out on my card."

"Cool."

"Also, there's a small used bookstore, further away, but still walkable. They buy your books and give you credit. We can go some other time if you want."

"That would be great."

I hadn't even been here a week and I was going on a weekend *social outing* with a *friend*. It was a miracle.

I needed to not think about it. Just try to be in the moment.

"Okay, so what else have you read recently?" Jenna asked.

I started listing the various series I'd read and she nodded along, obviously familiar with everything.

"Out of curiosity, what was your first series?" she asked.

"Harry Potter," I said with a laugh. "Yours?"

"That was number two for me. My first was the Warriors series."

"That cats one?" We reached the edge of campus and waited at a crosswalk.

"Yeah, I devoured that stuff. But then my cat got really sick from cancer, and when he died, I couldn't read the books anymore, so I moved on to Harry Potter. The rest is history. Though I still cried every time Crookshanks showed up in the story."

We were on a pretty busy street, with pickups and SUVs flying by, and on the other side was a gas station and a row of shops—a dry cleaner, nail salon, a Subway, and a coffee shop. Then further down to the right was a church. Every corner around here had a church or a McDonalds.

"Rowling's opinions on transgender people has made me love the series less," Jenna said, "but I'll never not love it."

I didn't want to admit I didn't know what she was talking about. I'd have to look into it. I could just ask, but instead I asked, "Where's the library?"

"Basically two blocks straight ahead, though the blocks are kind of long."

The light turned and we crossed, passing the QuikTrip.

The road narrowed into a residential neighborhood. The heat was starting to get to me, with my entire back soaked against the backpack. I realized I hadn't put sunblock on like I usually do when I go outside. Crap. I'd been so caught up in the social moment that I forgot. Now I was going to be pink for days.

"So I'm guessing you haven't read any N. K. Jemisin?" Jenna asked.

I shook my head. "I don't know him."

"Her," Jenna corrected. "She is incredible. You have to read her Broken Earth trilogy. It's seriously what got me started on reading different stuff. She's Black. Her world is radically different from ours but she still explores race and gender in a powerful way. It's amazing—like, it totally opened up my reading world."

"So you like her, then?" I teased.

Jenna laughed. "You might say that. But seriously, that's what you should read first."

"I'm game. I like what I've been reading, but it is predictable."

"Well, you are *re*reading the series," she pointed out.

"True. But I mean predictable in the bigger picture. I did read the Poppy War series, and the YA *Children of Blood and Bone*, and those were really cool." The YA novel pulled from western African tradition.

"Oh, yeah, I liked that one, too. There's a lot more coming out in YA that's based on different cultures."

We talked about some of those and I started pointlessly fanning my face. "Man, it is freaking hot."

"I know," she said, staring up at the sky. "A breeze would be nice, wind-comes-sweeping-down-the-plains state."

That made me laugh. When I was in Scotland, one of Sam's friends starting singing that song when I told them I was from Oklahoma like Sam. It was so awesome that things were going well here, too.

We reached the end of the current block and looked to cross the street.

Up ahead, we could see a freakishly ornate mailbox at the curb, several houses away. All the others were your simple wood post with a metal mailbox, but this one was solid and painted blue, with decorative metal covering the top.

"Wow," I said.

"Yeah. Wonder what's going on with that? It looks like horns. And is that a tail?"

My brain had trouble processing what it was seeing. It looked like some kind of animal with a thick tail pointing toward the house. We both watched it as we got closer, and gradually I saw we were right. Once we reached it, without saying anything, we both stopped and stared at it.

"This mailbox is a statue of a blue dragon," I said, stating the obvious. But it needed to be said out loud.

"My mind is blown. I am struck speechless."

The box part was basically the dragon's head. You flipped down the front part of the snout to open it. The lower part had front legs holding the body up, and the tail curved up with the tip pointing back. There were even scales hinted at with an outline of darker blue paint. I had literally never seen anything like it and was equally dumbstruck.

"No one will believe this," Jenna said. "I think this calls for a video." She opened up an app on her phone and handed it to me.

"Ready?" I asked.

"Yep."

I started filming, and she said, "You guys!" And then she

motioned at the mailbox and put her arm around the dragon like she was posing for a picture with a celebrity. "This is my future! Okay, that's probably enough."

I stopped the recording and handed the phone back. But I also had to get some pictures of it myself. I was going to draw this for fun. I took a video while walking around it so I could get it from all angles.

Jenna was still fiddling with her phone, and once she finished, we got going again.

"I wonder if these folks are book people or movie people," Jenna eventually said.

I laughed. "Imagine a normal family moving into that house. What to do about the mailbox? My mom would be weirded out."

"True. Mine, too. Pretty awesome, though."

"I know." After some more walking, we neared another intersection, and I could see what had to be the library—a tan single-story brick building with a parking lot surrounding it. I was getting excited. Maybe Jenna was right about this author. It was always cool to find somebody new, especially when they had more than one book out.

Once inside, the AC chilled my skin, and Jenna closed her eyes in relief and said, "Ahh, finally."

We surveyed the area to get the layout and then made a beeline for the fantasy and sci-fi section.

"Okay, first let's get the book you have to try."

I followed her to the J shelves and she pulled off a book called *The Fifth Season*, holding it to her chest and closing her eyes. "I love this series so much."

"I can tell." I took it when she handed it to me and started reading the back.

Jenna backtracked to the A's and started working her

way through the shelves. "Have you read this one?" She held out a gigantic book called *Jonathan Strange and Mr. Norrell*.

I shook my head. "That is a seriously large tome."

"I know. It's worth it. It's still European white dudes, but it's different. Kind of alternative historical urban fantasy."

I started looking myself, recognizing a lot of the series I'd read—Sanderson, Martin, Eddings. But I was really curious about this new stuff.

"Here's another one you should read." She held up *The Priory of the Orange Tree*. "It's like a feminist *Lord of the Rings*. Also doubles as a barbell."

"You aren't kidding—that thing is monstrous." But it also sounded kind of cool. "Okay, I'll take it, too. But I'm sad to say, this is probably enough. I know I'm not going to have as much time to read here."

"Yeah, this is a good point." She continued searching and pulled off a sci-fi I hadn't heard of and another fantasy.

We headed over to the circulation desk, where they were able to give me a card—and welcome me to town—and we checked the books out and left.

"Do you want to hit up that coffee shop by the QT?" Jenna asked.

"Sounds perfect to me."

We trekked back, gaping at the dragon mailbox some more, crossed to the next block, and finally walked through the QT parking lot and entered the cool coffee shop.

We studied the menu and I looked at the prices, deciding I should start drinking coffee because it was the cheapest. I got to the register first and the guy said, "What can I get you, sir?"

I froze like I always did when this happened—way too often—but Jenna said, "She's not a guy, idiot."

"Oh, sorry." He didn't really look sorry, but at least he

said it. Usually, people just pretended like nothing had happened. "What can I get you?"

"A medium coffee, thanks." I paid, avoiding eye contact because I didn't want to see him notice my flaming cheeks. I waited for Jenna to order, and then we picked a table.

When they called my coffee, I picked it up and took it to the station with the creamer, only to discover that the coffee was all the way to the top. I did like coffee, but there was no way I could drink it black. I wasn't sure what to do, but I ended up pouring some out to make room for the cream. Then I sat down, flustered.

Jenna was laughing at me. "You have to tell them to leave room for cream."

"I have no idea what I'm doing," I said, shaking my head. I didn't show my gender right, and I didn't know how to order coffee.

"Well, to be fair, I only know that because that's how my mom orders it, and she loves coffee."

We got settled in for some casual reading. She convinced me to start the Jemisin book, and I was pretty much immediately sucked in, forgetting all about being misgendered.

After the prologue and a couple chapters, I got up to go to the bathroom. When I came back, I glanced out the window, and there was Mack across the street, walking on the sidewalk that ran along the edge of campus. He was heading away from the intersection.

My heart fluttered. Where was he going all the time? I was so curious.

But then I noticed a group of girls who looked familiar going toward the intersection in the direction of the church.

Rachel and some of her friends. Ugh, I was glad I wasn't out there.

She could be going to do her Young Life thing. So not for me.

As Rachel's group approached Mack, he looked up and put his head down again. But then the group slowed down and it looked like Rachel might have said something to Mack because he looked up, but then away again, and as they passed each other, he sped up and kept going faster.

"What in the world are you staring at?" Jenna finally said, because I was still standing there staring out the window.

"Uh, something weird. So Mack was walking down the sidewalk, and then Rachel and some friends passed him." I explained the odd exchange.

"Who's Rachel?"

"This unpleasant senior in my art class. She's also president of the art club I got roped into being the secretary of." I sat back down and opened up the book, setting the library receipt on the table. "I wonder how they know each other."

Jenna shrugged. "Maybe just because they're all seniors."

"Yeah, you're probably right. I always make everything a big deal."

She smiled. "I can relate. You want to leave in a half hour? We could go straight to the cafeteria. I'm starved."

"Sure."

A coffee and a little bit of co-reading was a nice cherry on top of an enjoyable afternoon, barring being called sir. Still, a social afternoon. I couldn't wait to see what would happen next.

～

Jenna and I had gone straight to the cafeteria after the coffee shop, and we were still talking about books while we ate.

Out of nowhere, I heard "Hey" from behind me, and Mack sat down next to me.

"Oh, hello!" Jenna said, caught off guard, mid-sentence.

Mack laughed and then looked at me. The eye contact made my heart flutter.

"Hi. And wow, Nic, you are very pink."

I flushed, the heat I was already feeling on my cheeks from the sun now kicked up a notch. "Yes. I forgot to put sunblock on."

"Oh, he's right," Jenna said. "I hadn't noticed. At least you'll get a bit of a tan."

I laughed. "That's not how it works for me. I will stay pink for several days, sometimes even weeks, and then it will go back to pasty white."

"That's unfortunate," Jenna said. "But Mack, you're lucky —you probably don't burn at all."

Mack's skin was darker than ours.

"Mexicans can burn," he said. "Just not as fast as you two. But that's hilarious you're going to stay pink. I'm going to have to tease you about it."

"Great," I said, weirdly looking forward to this. Also, I liked having more info. I just wanted to know every single thing about him.

"Were you all studying somewhere?" Mack motioned to our bags that we'd dumped on the table. He patted his pizza slice down with a napkin to get rid of some of the grease, and then took a bite.

"We went to the library," I explained. "Like, the public library. Jenna is expanding my horizons."

She nodded. "There's more to fantasy and sci-fi than culturally regressive white, heteronormative European-style people." She folded her used napkin and placed it on top of another one.

Mack grinned. "You are so right. But I still find it a little hard to find sometimes. Which is a bummer."

"Have you read the Broken Earth Trilogy?" she asked, sounding hopeful.

"No, but I have heard about it. She won three freaking Hugos in a row with that series. It must be great."

I hadn't known that, but I did know that the Hugo was a major award given for speculative fiction.

"I adore it," Jenna said. "I've got Nic reading the first one. What do you think so far, Nic?"

I finished chewing the last bit of my stir-fry. "Mack's conclusion seems accurate. I'm about a hundred pages in."

"I'm in," Mack said. "What's the first book called?"

"You know what we should do?" Jenna said.

We both looked at her expectantly.

"We should form a book club. We can start with *The Fifth Season*." She turned to Mack. "That's the first book."

That made me sit up straighter. Sam and I had talked about books before, but I had never been part of an actual book club.

"I love this idea," Mack said, taking another bite of pizza. He had two gold studs in each ear, something I was just noticing now for some reason.

"Me, too," I added, a rush of happiness coursing through me. Were things going to keep getting better?

"They have the ebook and audiobook at the library," Jenna said to Mack. "And I'm sure they could pull the *book* book from another library if you wanted it."

He stirred his soup—one the joys of the cafeteria was that you could have soup and pizza, or stir fry and garlic bread if you wanted—and said, "I'll figure it out. When should we plan to meet to talk about it?"

Jenna nodded. "It's long-ish, and we're busy. Let's say two

weeks, so Sunday after next. If it works, we could try that cadence going forward."

Mack and I agreed, so it was a plan.

"I need your phone numbers," Mack said.

Just as I pulled my phone out, it chimed with an incoming text. It was from Isabella so I opened it to find a picture of me holding her when she was a baby. I was about seven in the picture, and for some reason I had a sailor hat on.

"Who's that?" Jenna asked.

"My sister and me." My hair was long under the hat, and I was wearing shorts and a t-shirt, like always. I didn't really look like a girl back then, either.

"Let me see," Mack said.

I held the phone out so he could see.

"Cute," he said.

I felt a little thrill, which was stupid because he was probably talking about Isabella, and even if he did mean me, it wasn't the same as saying it about me now.

We all exchanged phone numbers—now we were officially friends. I felt a twinge of something inside—genuine happiness, maybe? It was real.

Pulling my phone out reminded me of the video I'd taken. "Mack, you should have seen this mailbox we saw on the way to the library." I started pulling up my photos.

"Oh, my God!" Jenna said. "But don't show him. That is something you need to experience in person for the first time, if at all possible."

"Yeah, that makes sense," I said.

He grinned. "I think I know what you're talking about. The blue dragon?"

"You've seen it?" Jenna asked, incredulous. "And you never told us about it?"

"I've only known you for four days," he said, laughing. "It wasn't top of my mind. But yeah, I've passed it on my walks. It really is something, though. I stopped and stared at it the first time I saw it." He nodded. "It got my attention."

"Where do you go all the time?" I blurted out before I could stop myself.

His expression didn't change despite my worry, but he shrugged and said, "I just like to walk. The campus gets boring."

I felt stupid for asking and didn't say anything else, but Jenna said, "Well, I, for one, am disappointed. I was proud of our discovery."

Mack laughed, making the corners of his eyes crinkle. "I felt that way when I first found it. But one of my best walks ever was the one where I saw the guy getting his mail in a full cosplay getup."

"No way!" Jenna and I said at the same time, which made us all laugh.

"What was his costume?" Jenna asked.

"I'm pretty sure it was Gandalf." He nodded thoughtfully.

"Wow," I said. "I wish I'd seen that, too."

"Yeah." Jenna leaned back in her chair and crossed her arms. "Seriously. I may have found my future sugar daddy."

Mack and I cracked up.

Then he finished off his pizza and said, "Ice cream?"

"Definitely." I was kind of bummed because this meant this social time was almost over.

But I consoled myself with the fact that there would be more to come.

≈

I was sitting at my desk Sunday afternoon, reading for chemistry, when my phone rang. Home. It was weird to not be there, to be somewhere completely different.

"Hi, Mom."

I missed my family, but I did not miss the town of Emerson at all, or all the crap that went on at Emerson High.

"Hi, honey! How are you doing?"

"I'm fine." I was more than fine. My life had completely changed, obviously for the better. I pulled down one of the figurines, an orc, and fiddled with it.

"It's so strange with you not being here. I wasn't supposed to have to deal with this for two more years!"

I started to respond in agreement, but then I heard Isabella say in the background, "I want to talk to her!"

"Okay, okay," Mom said. "Here you go."

"Nic! I can't believe you're not here. It's so horrible. Now it's just me and Caleb. Yuck."

That made me laugh.

"Don't talk about your brother that way, you two," Mom said. Half-heartedly. She got it.

I didn't miss our brother at all. He was really hateful right now, especially to me. He was a year younger than me and was just a total douche to me all the time. It was one of his friends who had destroyed my giant dragon drawing.

"What's going on, Iz? How's middle school?"

"It's good. There's more kids at the school than elementary school. And we have to go to a different classroom every hour. But I like it."

"That's great. Are all your friends still there?"

"Yeah." She chatted for a while about her old friends, and a new friend, and some cute boys who hadn't been cute in fifth grade.

"You want to know something?" I asked.

"What?"

"I have two friends already." I worried that saying this out loud might ruin whatever good luck streak I was on.

"Who are they?"

"One's a girl named Jenna. She's really funny and likes the same books as me. And the other is a boy named Mack." My chest warmed when I said his name. I pictured him laughing at something last night at dinner. Now my heart pinched. I had no control over that thing.

"Is he cute?" Isabella asked. Of course she did.

"I think so." I blushed when I said it. I totally thought that.

"Are you going to go out with him?" Her voice was high with excitement.

"No! I don't know. I don't want to jinx it. I'm trying not to think about it."

"Nic, you have to put yourself out there." She sounded serious.

I had to be the only sixteen-year-old in the history of humankind getting dating advice from an eleven-year-old. Talk about making me feel like a loser. Enough of this.

"So my art class is really cool. The teacher is showing me how real artists work, planning things out rather than just sitting down and starting a drawing like I usually do."

"What does that mean?"

I explained the planning and rework I was supposed to do. Isabella also liked art, but she wasn't that serious about it. I think she often did it just because I was doing it. Would that change when she got older, like Caleb? Isabella had always sort of hero-worshipped me. I tried not to think about the fact that that might go away some time.

"Neat. Oh, okay. Mom wants to talk to you."

"Love you, Isabella."

"Love you!"

Mom came back on. "Did I hear you have a boyfriend?"

"No!" God, moms. "I just have two new friends. One is a boy."

"I'm pleasantly surprised, that's all."

"You don't have to be surprised. Thanks for the vote of confidence." This made me feel like a loser for a second, until I remembered it wasn't how things were anymore. They'd changed.

"No, that's not what I meant. I just know how shy you are, and it's hard to meet people when you're like that. It was the same for me, honey. Tell me about your friends."

I told her about Jenna first, adding that she was from Oklahoma City. "We went to the library yesterday and I forgot to put on sunblock, so now I am very pink."

"Oh, Nic, you need to always wear sunblock." She was in definite Mom mode.

"I know, it came up spontaneously."

"Does it hurt? Do you have aloe vera?"

"Yes, and no, but it's fine. I'll deal."

"Okay, honey. Tell me about your other friend."

I told her about Mack, trying to keep my voice from betraying my feelings. Then we talked about Mom's work— she was working as a server at a sports bar-type restaurant right now but was looking for something that paid better.

"Enough about me," she said. "Tell me about your classes."

I went through the list, and then told her about the art stuff, which was obviously the most interesting to me. She thought the mentorship sounded great.

After I wrapped up, she told me she was going to get my dad. While she was getting him, I wondered how she'd take it if I ever did decide to come out as nonbinary. I knew she'd try to be supportive. I knew Isabella would be, too. At least for now.

Dad got on the line and I had a quick chat with him—he basically asked about my classes and that was it—and then Mom got back on the phone.

"You have to call us every Sunday, Nic," she said. "Let's plan for three."

"Let's FaceTime!" Isabella called in the background.

"We can do that, honey," Mom said.

"What if I'm doing something at three?" I asked. I didn't like being on a schedule for this.

"At least text so we can change the plan."

"Okay." That was better. It's not that I didn't want to talk to my family, but I might have other things to do.

I could hope.

I was sitting at my art room table waiting for class to start. I glanced over at Jacob, who was reading a graphic novel. When the first bell chimed, he put it down and I happened to catch the name N. K. Jemisin on the cover. Wow, she wrote comics too? It looked like a superhero book. I'd stayed up too late reading her book last night. I was barreling through it because it was so interesting. Some people have amazing imaginations. I could never create a whole, complex fantasy world like that.

It occurred to me that I should talk to Jacob and ask if he'd read her other stuff. We had never truly talked before, despite sitting next to each other every day in art and physics.

Before I could work up the nerve, the starting bell

chimed and Ms. Mangal went to the front of the room and clapped her hands. Some people were already working on their own projects—she'd finished all the individual meetings last week. She said she'd be walking around to see our progress and she started with me.

"Ready to start ideation?" she asked with a smile, her floral scent surrounding me.

I explained that I'd already done some thumbnails. She looked at them but said she wanted me to do some more ideation.

She started explaining, telling me to start with a mind map with "dragon doing human stuff" at the center.

"You can start with the thumbnails you've already done, all branching off of the center node with each idea."

She didn't sound annoyed that I'd done the thumbnails already.

"Then you try to generate different ideas off of those ideas. The basic approach is to come up with original ideas, take each base idea and modify it in some way—make it bigger, stretch it, cut it wide open, divide it into parts, duplicate it, and so on. Almost any action verb will do."

I nodded, both motivated and intimidated by this approach. What if I couldn't think of new ideas?

She said the main thing here was to do something that was out of the ordinary in order to come up with an original idea. Like, take something normal and twist it to make it different.

"This is the kind of thing that could inspire you to go somewhere else, totally new and unique. Work on each idea for a while, instead of jumping around. Also, you want to iterate—try one thing, and then the next logical thing, and then the next—so it's not taking just one step. But you can always come back to the beginning."

I nodded. I wasn't entirely following all of this, but I tried to run with it. I was picturing a mess with all these nodes coming off the center one.

She pointed to the corner. "Go grab a big sheet of butcher paper off the roll. It's much easier to work big. Once you've got it big, you can take a picture and shrink it or scroll around it and so on."

"Okay, thanks." I worked for a while, and then I sensed movement on the other side of my table. When I looked up, it was Rachel, not Ms. Mangal making her rounds. She was looking at me through narrowed eyes.

This made me nervous. I worried about what she would say. We'd hardly had any interactions, but she always made me feel this way.

"Are you sure you want to be spending time with 'Mack'?" She made air quotes around his name.

What in the world? I was still nervous, but now I was confused, too. "Yeah," I said slowly. "Why wouldn't I? He's nice."

"*He's* nice? If you say so." She snorted and went away.

I looked over at Jacob, still totally confused, and he had a funny look on his face, too. He didn't say anything, but it was obvious that the whole thing was weird to both of us. I gave him a half shrug and looked back at my mind map.

Now I was even worse off, all distracted. I was already dealing with my frustration in developing it because I wasn't full of ideas most of the time, and the stuff I was coming up with wasn't great. But now I kept running Rachel's words through my head.

Did she like him? Was she trying to warn me off? It was so odd.

Was she saying he wasn't nice? He didn't seem like the kind of person to go out of his way to bully somebody or anything. And what about that exchange between them I'd seen on Saturday. They did know each other, I was sure.

Ms. Mangal was making her rounds, and eventually she got to me again, the last time for today.

Even though I was distracted, I liked how she did seem really invested in me already. She knew I was serious. But then I wondered if she was just helping me because I really needed it. I didn't think that was it, however. I bet teachers liked it when students weren't there just for an easy A. But I was worried she wouldn't think my work was good enough. Because I didn't think it was. This was hard.

"Okay, let's see what you've got." She set her mug on the far corner of the table and leaned over to look more closely at some of my nodes. She said I should keep going tomorrow, working on branching off of some of the nodes furthest from the center.

"After that, you'll do some research for reference photos. I doubt you'll get to the value study this week, which is fine. I'm excited to see what you come up with."

"Okay." I hoped she wouldn't think less of me, but I wanted to figure out how to be better at this. "This is actually kind of hard."

"Yes, it is." Her voice was soft and sympathetic. "But the thing is, you don't need every idea to be good—for this assignment, you just need one of them to spark your creativity, and then you've got the beginnings of a nice piece of art."

That did seem true. It's not like anybody looking at a piece of art would know anything about what went into creating it. And I normally erased a lot, sometimes large areas, when I would realize the composition wasn't right. It might make my life easier if I planned more.

"What's your favorite idea so far?" she asked.

"I thought of a dragon working in the baby room in the

maternity ward." Please let her like this one. I wanted her to think I was decent at this.

"That's fun. You could go a lot of directions with that. What are the babies—humans or dragons? You could play with that, among other things."

"Yeah, I was thinking if there were baby dragons there, they could be flying around, causing trouble."

She smiled. "That could be fun. Keep working on that one and see if you can develop ideas to branch off of it. Two more, at a minimum."

I nodded and she moved over to talk to Jacob. I glanced over to see what he was working on and only then saw that he was doing a mind map, too. He must be serious about art, as well. I didn't think anyone else had been assigned mind maps.

In the last ten minutes of class, I got to work, but I didn't get far with all the weirdness with Rachel running through my head. I would have to think about it tonight in order to be productive tomorrow. I wanted to finish this part up and get started on the drawing.

Jenna and I were standing in the middle of the food court in the student union Monday evening. We planned to study in the booth room if we could find seats, and otherwise go over to the library. But first—food. There was a deli I'd never heard of, a Sbarro's, a Taco Bueno, a Subway, and a Starbucks.

"I'm going to get something at Taco Bueno," Jenna said.

"I'll do that, too." I hadn't really thought about the fact that I'd have to spend money, especially having bought the coffee Saturday. The truth was, I didn't have a lot. It just hadn't come up before now because room and board with the cafeteria was covered by the state. My parents had put some on my student account, but I needed to watch it. My stomach twisted. What if we came here a lot? Would I run out of money?

We got in line and I studied the dollar menu.

It wasn't super busy yet, but there was still that roar of many voices in a large room. The floor was off-white tile and the store fronts all had green walls with white trim around their branding. OIT school colors.

I would have to pay attention to what I was spending and maybe skip food sometimes if we didn't go to the cafeteria.

Jenna yawned, which made her nose ring move as her nose scrunched up.

So of course I yawned in response.

"Man, I hate being tired all the time." she said.

"I know. I'm not getting enough sleep, either. My room-mate gets up really early and turns the light on so she can do her makeup. I had no idea how long makeup took. At least, not everyday makeup."

"I do really basic stuff and spend about five minutes. I figure, it's not my wedding, I'll just look like me."

I laughed. This was a really different world from Emerson. Would I have been a different person if I'd grown up in Oklahoma City? Impossible to know.

But then it occurred to me that I already was a different person. And there was still plenty of time to change even more. I didn't have to be the same as I always had been. You can't change the people around you, but you can move your-self to a different location, which is exactly what I had done. Sam and I engineered this with purpose.

It was working so far, and I finally had faith that things

were going to get better for me. I had to make sure I didn't throw opportunities away.

But something else was on my mind, now and all the time. Would things stay great if I came out as nonbinary? It was a scary question.

I adjusted my backpack straps. I'd brought two text-books with me and it was freaking heavy.

We moved up and were now second in line. The skinny boy in front of us ordered six tacos and a burrito, and Jenna and I looked at each other in surprise. She whispered, "Where is he going to put all that?"

"Maybe his stomach is an organic bag of holding."

She giggled and the guy moved out of the way and she went up to the counter. She ordered a couple things and I looked again at the dollar menu. When it was my turn, I ordered a bean burrito and we moved over to wait. I got some salsa and onions at the little salsa bar they had. Jenna got two little cups of jalapeños. "Yum," she said.

"I love their salsa."

She popped a jalapeño into her mouth, which surprised me and I said, "Spicy stuff, huh?"

"The spicier the better. I love getting Indian and Thai food at five stars, or whatever their max is. They never believe me when I order. Most white people can't take it. You know, it's spicier than potatoes with a sprinkle of salt."

"Oh, don't forget the green beans with bacon." I'd never had Indian or Thai food, which was embarrassing. I was so unworldly. But it wasn't my fault. My parents were the ones who had me growing up in Emerson. I wondered if they'd ever had Thai or Indian food. I told Jenna I'd never had either and her eyes went wide.

"We'll have to remedy that."

The person behind the counter called out, "Fifty-two," and the skinny boy picked up his loaded bag and left.

"I half want to follow him to see if he can really eat all that," Jenna said.

I smiled conspiratorially. "We totally should."

"Fifty-three," the person called. Someone else called my number, and we grabbed our bags and headed toward the back room. What the dorm mom had called Booth Forest.

It was even louder in there. The tall, dark wooden booths rose up in front of us. I followed Jenna as we snaked through the aisles.

"This really is kind of like walking through a forest," she said.

"I wouldn't know. I tend to stay indoors."

"Me too. But my older brother is all into nature and used to drag me along on hikes when I was younger. I was always worried about rattlesnakes and whatever, and finally one day I voiced my concern."

We turned a corner and still didn't see any empty booths.

Jenna continued, "He laughed at me and said we wouldn't find them wherever we were at the time, and I was like, 'You know where else you won't find rattlesnakes? My bedroom.' And I never went with him again."

The image of a small Jenna saying this was funny. I pictured her as a snarky ten-year-old, hands on her hips. I bet her hair was long back then. "Yeah, inside, the only wildlife you have to worry about is spiders."

She shivered. "I hate those things."

We turned another corner and spotted an empty one.

"Score!" Jenna said.

We dropped our backpacks and food on the table and sat down. Jenna unzipped her yellow backpack and I noticed she had a patch on it that said "Out of Breath Hiking Society."

I laughed. "I love your patch."

She looked at it and smiled. "My brother got it for me, on account of what we were just talking about."

"Yeah, I can see that."

She pulled out a couple notebooks and then said, "Oh, my God. Look." She pointed at a booth diagonally across from us. Skinny boy. He was reading from a textbook and I could see one wadded up wrapper.

"Well, he ate at least one of them," I said.

"Can he do it? I'm not sure."

I pulled my burrito out and opened it so I could pour the salsa inside. I was hungry so I took a big bite and a bunch of the salsa ran down my hand. "Crap. I didn't get napkins. Did you?"

"No, sorry."

I wiped my hand off as much as I could on the paper and then got up. I walked right past the guy's table. There were four wadded up wrappers. I couldn't believe he'd eaten them that fast.

I hurried to find napkins, cleaned off my hand, grabbed enough napkins for both of us, then headed back.

I slid into the seat and leaned forward, unable to keep the grin off my face. "He ate half of them already!"

"Oh, my God. That is hilarious. He should bottle and patent his metabolism and sell it to all the women of America."

"No joke. Many would buy it. I would get a job just to buy it."

She grinned. We started eating and were quiet for a while.

But then Jenna said, "Oh, I was going to ask—how is the Jemisin book?"

I had to finish my bite of burrito first, but then I said, "It's so good. I love it. I'm going to have it done this week. But I'll probably forget everything if we have to wait another week to talk about it."

"Maybe take notes or something? I don't know. I've never done a book club before."

"Me neither."

"Where are you at in the story?" she asked.

We talked about it and she was excited because something really interesting was about to happen. I couldn't wait.

"This is part of why I'm tired all the time. I keep staying up late to read, and then Sophia gets up so freaking early and makes no effort to be quiet."

"That's frustrating." She looked thoughtful as she wadded up her last wrapper. "My roommate's okay. We seem to have schedules that work fine together. I'm glad. It's hard enough sharing a room for the first time."

"I wasn't sure what to expect. She doesn't seem to like me, though. I'm not sure exactly why." I shrugged. "But whatever. I'll survive. She went away over the weekend, too. Maybe I'll get lucky and she'll go home every weekend."

"Why do you think she doesn't like you?"

I remembered move-in day and how she'd been such a snob. "She seemed really annoyed when we first met, and she went out of her way to avoid me. Plus she always gives me these looks. And if you liked somebody, wouldn't you at least try to be quiet when they were asleep?"

"I don't know. Some people are selfish."

"True. Maybe it's not personal." But I was still pretty sure it was.

"Yeah." Jenna nodded. "So what are you working on tonight?"

"Pre-calc." I was kind of dreading it, and I felt a twinge inside, thinking about it, but I needed to get started because it was due Thursday.

"Me, too. I wonder if we have the same assignment. Who's your teacher?"

I thought for a moment, trying to remember his name. "Dr. Lanford."

"Same here."

We pushed our trash to the end of the booth and pulled our stuff out. The syllabuses were identical.

"Great," she said. "This is perfect."

This made my chest warm. It was perfect. We got started, and soon had worked our way through the first problem set, helping each other a few times and figuring out one problem that seemed stupidly hard but had a trick to it. Homework with a plot twist.

"Two more to go," she said with a sigh.

"Blah."

"Let's get at it."

She had more energy than I did, but if she was going to work on it, so was I. This was now a joint effort. It might stay that way, too.

Wednesday I was back in the art classroom, Jacob quietly parked next to me. I was researching reference photos on my computer for my new project. I'd done more thumbnails yesterday and picked one. It would have the dragon in a corner of a room with a bunch of bassinets. Ms. Mangal said

I could work on the major parts of the composition and play with the background.

She liked the full room view because she decided it was an opportunity for me to learn two-point perspective, which I didn't even know was a thing. She was going to give me some one-on-one lessons later this week. I hoped it wasn't too hard. Pre-calc and physics were providing enough challenge for me lately.

I was googling dragons, looking for some examples of ones standing up, more humanoid. I started collecting the best ones in a folder and dropping them in a Word doc. I also kept reliving lunch, where I'd seen Mack.

Just then, some quiet laughter came from the front table, and it was Rachel and her table partners quietly cracking up at something.

I hoped it had nothing to do with me. I knew I was being paranoid, but Rachel really got to me.

I got back to my document, trying to keep my heart rate down as I kept thinking about lunch. Mack was almost never in the lunch room, but today we'd eaten together. And the cool part was that he said we should have dinner together, too. I'd texted Jenna to see if she wanted to join us for dinner, even though I sort of didn't want to—which of course made me feel like a piece of trash. But she'd texted that her dad was going to visit her most Wednesdays and take her out to dinner, so she couldn't come tonight. My joy made me feel pretty bad. I could enjoy tonight, but I wasn't going to be able to keep him to myself all the time. Besides, I genuinely liked Jenna. I just needed to get used to it being the three of us.

As much as I tried not to, I had to acknowledge to myself that I definitely had a crush on Mack. I wasn't sure if he possibly felt the same way. I was literally the worst judge of this. I'd made a huge mistake early last year in thinking that this boy in my math class liked me. He had not liked me at all. I'd made a fool of myself by going to his house to get an eraser of mine that he'd stolen in class, because I'd stupidly thought he was flirting with me. I barely escaped total humiliation. Luckily, he, his brother, and his friend, who was also in our class, were the only three that knew about it.

But then something even weirder happened with this guy Sam and I were friends with, who also drove us to Key Club meetings. I'd really liked him for a long time, and I thought he might feel the same because of the way he was always looking at me more than necessary in the rear view mirror when Sam and I were in his car. Even Sam noticed it, and I was really excited, but I wasn't brave enough to tell her I liked him.

And then he'd asked *Sam* out. So. Definitely not interested in me, after all. At the time I was devastated. My heart was totally battered by those experiences, so I wished now that I didn't like Mack so much. I was going to try to keep things reined in in case he didn't feel the same.

Which was the most likely scenario.

But lunch was great. He was making fast progress on the book we were reading, too. I was going to tell Jenna we should move our book club up to this weekend. It was going to be fun talking about this with other people. Especially these people.

I had a decent collection of standing dragon images now, and had started looking for hospital nurseries. Babies really were not my thing, so this felt weird. I still managed to collect some good references and dumped them into my document.

I also couldn't help but notice that newborns aren't that cute. They looked like animated yams or something. I was only one when my brother was born, but I remember when my parents brought Isabella home. I instantly loved her, even though she was wrinkled and pink. Though to be fair, she got cute pretty fast.

This was going to be an interesting drawing.

My mind wandered to what Mack and Jenna would think of it. Would they think I liked babies? Who knew? I couldn't wait to see what I came up with myself, actually. I loved the idea of working in ink.

Now I had to look for actual baby pictures. I thought of how cute Isabella eventually was as a baby. I should look at our family albums for some of those. I'd just avoid pictures of me. Looking at myself as a baby always weirded me out. That was innocent me, who knew nothing about how crappy the world could be. It was before Dad's friend had messed with me. That asshole.

I'd definitely fit the bill of the ugly baby as a newborn, even though I'd also turned cute for a while.

But that was clearly a short-lived phase.

I shifted my thoughts back to the task at hand, continuing to look for images of babies.

Soon enough, class was over, and I saved my doc again and closed my laptop to pack it up.

"Did you get everything you need?" Ms. Mangal asked me.

"Yep."

"Great. Tomorrow will be all about perspective. It'll be fun."

I smiled and turned to leave, looking forward to learning more about it.

But I reached the door at the same time Rachel did, and she looked at me and asked, "Are you really sure you know who Mack is?"

This made me instantly shut down again, self-doubt firing from all directions. But then I recovered in time to say, "What are you talking about?"

She flounced off without answering. What was her deal? Was she trying to warn me about something I needed to know?

Not possible. Mack seemed to genuinely like me and be interested in the things I did and thought.

Plus, how did she even know I was friends with Mack? Was she spying on me? She must have some other agenda. But what?

Mack and I had finished our dinner Wednesday night but were still chatting. He was already almost as far into *The Fifth Season* as I was, and we were comparing our thoughts on what was going on. There was one thing I'd figured out that he hadn't gotten to yet, and I was excited for him to get there.

"Are you going to finish this before Sunday?" he asked.

"Oh yeah, definitely, at the rate I'm going. Probably by Friday night. I'm flying through it even though it's long and I'm busy."

"Me, too." He wadded up his napkin into a tighter ball. "I find that when I'm reading a really good book, I somehow find more time than I normally have. Because you've still got to get everything else done. Do you think we should move the book club meeting up to this weekend?"

"We should. I'm really looking forward to talking more about it."

"Same here." He raised his eyebrows. "Ready for ice cream?"

My life had totally changed since getting here, and I was still in a constant state of mild shock. But yes, I was ready for ice cream.

"Of course," I said with a smile.

We stashed our trays and then deliberated over the ice cream choices. Eventually, we decided to get each other's favorite, so I left with chocolate chip cookie dough, and he had mint chocolate chip.

"This isn't terrible," Mack said.

I laughed and ate some of mine.

"What do you think of yours?" he asked as we stepped off the sidewalk into the giant parking lot we had to cross. Then he intentionally bumped my shoulder, and the backs of our hands brushed.

He intentionally bumped my shoulder. My shock launched into outer space. My heart was immediately racing as I tried to figure out what that could mean. It had to mean something.

I carefully followed him as we wove through the parked cars.

Sam was the only other person who had ever touched me like that. So maybe it was just a friend gesture?

Well, it certainly was going to be something I obsessed over for the next who knew how many weeks.

"So?" he prompted me. I hadn't answered his simple question.

"It's good." I tried to think of something nontrivial to say. "At least we both agree on the chocolate chip part."

"Yeah." He looked over at me, studying my face for a second. "I want to start calling you pink panther."

I groaned. "It's horrible."

"Is your skin still hot to the touch? Isn't that what happens when you get a bad sunburn?"

There was this small part of me, much braver than even the new me, that wanted to tell him to try for himself. But instead, I reached up and cupped my cheek with my free hand. "Nope, it's cooled off. Just looks pink."

We'd reached the end of the parking lot, so we stepped onto the grass and were soon at the dorm front door. We stood outside to finish our ice cream.

After licking his fingers clean, Mack opened the door and I followed him in.

"Oh, hey," Jenna said. She was standing near the desk.

"Did you just get back?" I asked.

"Yes, and I'm beat."

"We wanted to talk to you about the book club," Mack said.

"Okay, sure. Let's talk. Let's sit down first, though. I love my dad, but he wears me out." She headed into the lounge area and we followed.

She fell onto the nearest couch and leaned back with her eyes closed. We sat on either side of her.

"So," I started, "we're both really far into the book and think we could meet this Sunday instead of waiting until next week."

"Really?" she said, opening her eyes and looking first at me, and then at Mack. "That fast? I'm impressed. But sure. Why not. Let's meet at Booth Forest. What time works?"

"I have to call home some time that day, but I'm open other than that," I said.

"How about two?" Mack asked.

"Works for me," Jenna said.

"Me, too." I couldn't wait for this. Both to finish the book and to talk about it with my two new friends.

"Oh, wow, Nic," a voice said from beside us. It was Rachel, all disdain. "I really thought you'd listen to me about 'Mack.'" She put air quotes around his name, the way she had in art class.

My hackles were up and I was right back to my old Emerson self, frozen and unable to react, with my heart racing in a bad way. And this wasn't even about me—it had to be about Mack. Whatever she'd been hinting at would be coming out now.

"And *Mack*"—she put air quotes around his name again —"Are you trying to corrupt the young?"

"What are you talking about?" Jenna asked with enough contempt to equal Rachel's. "And who are you, anyway?"

But Rachel ignored her and looked at Mack again. "Or should I say Kenzie, like I did for years?"

"Shut up, Rachel," Mack said, but he looked smaller and like he was about to disappear into the couch from sinking so far back.

I was still unable to speak, but the air was charged and I knew something really bad was about to happen. Was already happening. Rachel looked at me and said, "You should know, Nic. Kenzie and I played with Barbies together when we were little, though even back then *she* always picked Ken."

I looked at Mack, who looked minuscule now and was staring at the floor.

"You're a girl?" I stupidly blurted. I had such a crush on him. Did that make me bisexual?

Rachel barked a nasty laugh and I instantly realized what I had done.

Mack's head jerked up and his eyes flashed. "I am not a fucking girl." Then he heaved himself off the couch and stormed off without looking back.

What was *wrong* with me? I'd just made a horrible,

horrible mistake, hurting someone I really did care about, whatever his birth certificate said.

"Jesus, Nic," Jenna said with disgust. "What is your problem? Did you not know?"

"I—" I couldn't even go on. No, I hadn't. Had it been obvious? Why had I not noticed?

Jenna shook her head and got up. She left without saying anything else.

I looked at Rachel, whose smug face showed how pleased she was with how this had all gone.

It was then that I knew I'd permanently ruined two friendships. Somehow it took Rachel's gloating to realize it.

I had just ruined everything, and now I wanted to die.

How could I have said that? How could I not have guessed he was trans? I stumbled toward the stairwell.

"Where do you think you're going?" called a voice from behind the front desk as I was almost through the doorway.

I stopped and looked back.

A blonde RA I hadn't seen before had narrowed her eyes at me, obviously suspicious. She thought I was a boy.

"What are you talking about?" I asked. "I'm going to my room."

She started to say something, but I turned and fled upstairs, taking myself to the bathroom where I stared down a toilet, convinced I was going to throw up from the roiling in my stomach.

I had called Mack a girl, and this lady thought I was a boy. Why was everything with gender so messed up?

Tears were flowing freely and I was trying to stay quiet, but I couldn't avoid the sniffling.

I deserved to get misgendered after what I'd said to Mack. The fact that that had made me feel like shit only increased my guilt, because Mack must be feeling even worse than me. I'd said the absolute worst possible thing to him.

Only a week and a half here, and I'd just destroyed the best things that had ever happened to me with three stupid words. There would be no recovering from this.

In the morning I remembered that I had pre-calc homework due and I was so glad that I'd finished it Monday night. I was also supposed to read something for chemistry and hadn't, but I couldn't bring myself to really care. I'd catch up later.

Last night I hadn't known what to do when I got back to my room, and I was totally unproductive. I was completely destroyed and never even changed into my pajamas. I just cried and cried, so much that I was shaking.

So this morning I woke confused and with a slight headache, and then remembered. And all the horror of what I had done came rushing back in. I almost gasped from the realization—yet again—that I'd ruined everything. I wanted to die.

All morning, I obsessed over what I'd said and how Mack must hate me.

How could I have been such an idiot?

I mean, in both ways—how could I not have noticed that Mack was trans? And then how could I say something so stupid to him?

But I'd never met a trans person before, so maybe it wasn't too surprising that I reacted wrong. But why did it have to be such an important person that this happened with?

Besides, even though I'd never met anyone transgender

before, I absolutely knew better—he was the one who got to say what gender he was. I knew that. He must really hate me.

I didn't think Jenna hated me, but she was obviously disgusted with me, which was almost as bad. I should have been used to that, though. That's what I'd grown up with. Everybody at Emerson was disgusted by me for having the gall to be a girl but not be feminine.

By the time I got to art, I was still in a bad place.

And now I was supposed to work with Ms. Mangal on perspective. This was going to suck because I wasn't going to be able to concentrate. I tended to shut down when things were really bad, losing the ability to speak or even react. And right now they were bad again, for the first time since getting here.

Rachel and Lily came in after me, and Rachel gave me a big smile as they walked past.

I hated her. I had to consciously release my fingers from the fists that had instinctively formed when I saw her.

After class got started, Ms. Mangal told me she'd get to me in about ten minutes and she met with someone else. I looked through my reference photos some more and tried to do some rough sketches of my dragon caretaker, but I ended up doodling jagged lines.

I was still trying to figure out why I'd said what I had to Mack. I think it was all because I had a crush on him. I'd had that stupid reaction because, since he was at least considered a girl when he was born, I thought it might mean I was a lesbian.

There was a part of me that found this confusing. I mean, it was hard for me. I was born a girl, with all the typical parts. Could I really just say I was something different, just because "girl" felt so wrong for me?

This was the whole problem with the binary, and the way other people felt like they had the right determine your gender.

I had no trouble thinking of Mack as he/him, but there was that tiny vexing part of me that wondered how he could just say, "I'm a boy," and have it be true. I mean, I thought my problem came from the fact that you can't do that with most things. I mean, I'd love to look like a model, but I can't just say, "I'm thin," and expect people to behave as if I were thin. Wouldn't that be nice.

So why was gender different?

But it *was* different, and I knew that. But that one stubborn, brainwashed part of my mind wasn't sure.

I wondered if Mack was doing anything medical related to transitioning. I think that holdout part of my brain thought that would change things a little. I hated myself for that part of my mind.

How did I convince it that Mack's belief about himself trumped any beliefs anybody else had, including me? Only he really knew himself.

This was disconcerting, because if I really was going to come out as nonbinary, I would be expecting everyone else to overcome their resistance to the binary, too.

This was so confusing.

"Ready, Nic?" Ms. Mangal said, jerking me out of my tangled thoughts.

I looked down at the sketchbook I had in front of me. I'd mindlessly covered an entire page with jagged doodles.

"Uh, sure." My voice was shaky. I really was emotionally destroyed.

She pulled up a stool on the side of the table and set down some rulers, a triangle, some paper of various sizes, and artist's tape. "You don't sound so convincing. Are you nervous?"

"No, I'm okay." Not really, but I would never say anything, especially with Rachel in the room.

"So, you said you are pretty comfortable with one-point perspective, right?" Ms. Mangal asked.

This made me nervous. "I've never heard it called one-point, but I think it must mean the one point on the horizon in the middle of the page, with everything disappearing into the distance along lines from each object."

I guess one-point was like my point of view in life. I'd only looked at Mack from one side—through my own perspective, not his.

"Yes, that is correct. The important thing is that it only works for objects that have a flat plane facing the viewer. As soon as that object is rotated to one side or another, that plane no longer faces the viewer. Instead it is just an edge— a vertical line—that faces the viewer. This is when we use two-point perspective."

"Okay." I was pretty sure I knew what she meant, but after she drew an example for each type, I was certain. It was like if you were looking at a house from an angle, from the side but a bit in front of it. It's how in the real world, you could see two sides when you were looking at almost anything squarish.

I was self-absorbed, even though I tried not to be. I would need to make more of an effort to try to see things from other people's perspectives.

Ms. Mangal drew another example, showing how there were two vanishing points for the angled house, on the right and left sides of the paper.

"The vanishing points can often be off the paper in two-point," she said.

I must have looked as surprised as I felt. Of course they were off the page. Why wouldn't this be complicated—everything else in life always was. Why couldn't I have gotten more social experience before coming here? Maybe I wouldn't have said something so dumb if I had. I really didn't have much actual knowledge about transgender people. This was partially my fault. I couldn't pretend like it was as simple as never meeting any trans people in my small town. I should have tried to learn more, especially since I'd wondered if I might be trans myself in the beginning of last year.

"This is what we use the scraps of paper for." She showed how to attach them to the paper I was working on and create the horizon line and two vanishing points.

This basically made sense, but I suspected it would get more complicated.

Her demo with a cube wasn't too hard to follow, with the converging lines going to each vanishing point.

"One of the things that is hardest about this is knowing how far along the converging lines to end the object. As you move back in the picture, repeated items will get smaller."

It made me think of how I felt smaller, now that I was even further away from Mack, metaphorically and physically.

"Our instincts aren't great at knowing how much smaller," she continued. "I will teach you the grid technique. For now, I want you to draw a few cubes in one- and two-point perspective. Try a cylinder in each, too."

I nodded and she got up, clapped her hands quietly, and said, "I'll be back around in case you have any questions."

"Okay."

Now I was left to my own dark thoughts again.

I grabbed the paper she'd been using with the vanishing

points off the sides of the paper and started working on a cube, but then my mind did its thing again.

I really should have texted both of them yesterday. I hadn't known what to say, so I hadn't reached out. And I guessed that it was too late now. My stomach hurt from the despair I was feeling, and I wondered if anything was really salvageable at this point. I had texted Sam to see if she could talk after I was done with school, but she hadn't responded yet. She might help me figure out if I could do anything.

I hoped I was wrong and I could fix this, but I wasn't going to kid myself.

I got more and more antsy as the afternoon wore on, and as soon as my last class was over, I raced back to my dorm so I could text Sam.

I obviously needed to text Mack and Jenna, but I was completely clueless about what to say. I'd messed up so bad by saying such an idiotic thing, and then by not texting immediately afterward. Or least the same evening. I'd frozen and couldn't do anything.

And if I couldn't convince my whole brain that Mack was a boy, then I didn't deserve to be his friend.

I dropped my backpack on my desk chair and flopped down on the bed. Sophia wasn't there, thank God.

I texted Sam, asking the universe to make her available.

—*What's up?*— she responded.

Thank God.

—*I really messed up and need your help to try to fix things*—

—*What happened?*—

God, I'd have to tell her. —*So I found out yesterday that Mack is trans. I had no idea, and my first thought when I found out was to wonder if I was bi because I'd been attracted to a girl—*

—*He's not a girl*— An image of her judgmental face was solid in my head.

—*I know, but in the moment that is what my brain did, and then it made my mouth do something even worse—*

—*Oh no. What did you say?—*

I paused. I didn't want to tell her. But I had to. —*I said you're a girl?—*

—*Oh God, Nic—*

—*I know. I want to die—* I truly did, all over again. I felt sick and my tear ducts woke up.

—*What did he say after that?—* she asked.

—*He just said he wasn't a girl and left—* My stomach twisted at the thought of how bad he must have felt in that moment. And all because of me.

—*Yeah. What did you do next?—*

—*Well, Jenna was there and she was disgusted by me and left too. I went to my room and did nothing for hours—* I didn't need to tell her I cried for most of that time.

—*Did you text them yet?—*

—*God. I'm horrible. I didn't know what to say, and then it was today and now it's been too long and it's even worse and I still don't know what to say. Help—*

—*Nic, come on. Why don't I call you? We can figure something out—*

I agreed and answered as soon as it rang.

"I can't believe you didn't already text them," she said.

I closed my eyes and pressed on my forehead. "I know. I hate myself right now."

"Why did you even say it in the first place?" She sounded a tad impatient.

This made me open my eyes again. This wasn't the

normally supportive Sam I knew. Probably because I was completely at fault here, and I'd done a terrible thing. But really, she couldn't condemn me any more than I was already condemning myself. My stomach was in knots before I was able to finally say, "I don't know, it just slipped out. I've never known anybody who was trans, and I didn't notice anything that made me think he was, and I guess I'm confused by it and I don't know. I don't know."

She was quiet for a moment. "So actually, maybe I'm being harsh. I know several trans people here. But it's not the same in Oklahoma. It's new to you. It does take some getting used to. And if you really had no idea, I can see how it would have caught you off guard."

I didn't say anything, but it made me feel a tiny bit better. But still, a single tear fell from the corners of each of my eyes.

"I'll be honest," she started. "I don't know if you can fix this, but it's possible, and you won't know if you don't try."

Please let it get fixed. It was bad enough to look at a future without my two new friends, but it wouldn't be just that—they might be enemies. Or at least, people who hated me. Things might be as bad as they'd been at Emerson.

"What should I do?" I didn't even try to hide the desperation in my voice.

"Well, obviously you need to text Mack. Start off by saying you're really, truly sorry. Be convincing but don't go on too long. Tell him how you know he's a boy, and how you've never met anyone trans and you were surprised."

"Okay." This made sense. And it was all true.

"I think you should also tell him something personal that he might not know—make yourself vulnerable. Something that will mean something to him. You've struggled with gender, too. He might still be mad, but he might also forgive you. Don't be surprised if he doesn't respond right away. It doesn't mean he won't eventually forgive you."

"Okay. What should I say to Jenna? She thinks I was horrible to say it. Which obviously I was."

"I don't think you need to apologize to her. Just tell her you regret it. You might even text Mack first and see what he says, in case he responds right away. Or at least tell her you've reached out to him. You know people respect people who own their mistakes more than when they don't."

I pressed on my forehead, eyes still closed. She was right, but I was so worried I'd make things worse.

We sat there silent for a moment until Sam said, "You know I'm right."

"Yeah, I know." Even though I was worried, I did feel a little lighter because now I had a plan.

"My guess is it's going to be fine. Open up to him. It shows trust and makes people like you more."

I thought about how I did that with Sam when I was visiting her in Glasgow. I'd never told her about being sexually abused, and when I did she turned out to be so supportive and really helped me see some things differently. In a better way. I didn't know why I hadn't done that earlier. "When did you get so wise? Are Scottish people just smarter?"

She laughed. "No, but they definitely sound smarter than Americans when they talk. I still love the accent."

"Yeah, me too."

"Go write your text, Nic. Stop stalling."

She was teasing when she said it, so it made me smile, but she was right.

"Okay. Thanks for your help." This was still going to be so freaking hard.

"Let me know how it goes. Don't worry if you don't hear back right away."

"Okay." My stomach was working itself into a knot again because I was really going to have to do this. And I couldn't possibly know how it would turn out.

"Talk to you later, and good luck!" Sam said.

"Thanks." After I hung up, I realized I'd never asked anything about her life. I could be such a selfish jerk sometimes.

—*I forgot to ask, how is Donald?*—

—*He's good. We're going to a concert tomorrow. A Glasgow band I haven't heard of, but he swears they're good*—

—*Cool. I will probably hang out in the art room again and work on my drawing*— I wondered when I'd ever go to a concert. It wasn't something I'd been able to do yet.

—*That sounds fun, too. Ttyl! Let me know how things go*—

Okay. Now I had to do it. I was nervous again. But I was still holding my phone, so I opened up the text screen. I didn't put Mack's name into the recipient field yet because I wanted to compose it first. An accidental premature send would be horrible. I needed to be very careful with what I said. This was basically my one chance to at least start fixing things.

I thought about it.

—*Mack*—

God, this was going to be painful.

—*I just wanted to tell you I'm so sorry for what I said. And I'm sorry it took me so long to text you. I felt so stupid and terrible and figured you hated me and there was no point in texting you because you probably wouldn't read it and it wouldn't change the horrible thing I said so it would change nothing.*—

Phew. That was a load off, but it wasn't a good enough apology.

—I am a horrible coward. But I finally realized it didn't matter if it would change anything for me, I owed you an apology no matter what. I hope you read this, because even if you never talk to me again, I want you to know I am truly sorry.—

I read over what I had so far and remembered what Sam said about explaining a little.

—I know you're a boy. I always thought you were and so I was really surprised to find out you were trans. I've never known anybody who was before, and I've always been a little confused about how it works, so in my shock my brain did a stupid thing and my stupid mouth didn't stop it. I wanted to die as soon as it was out.—

This was okay, but I didn't know if that would make him feel any better. I thought of what Sam had said about being vulnerable.

—It's especially frustrating to me that I would make this mistake because I am one of the few people around who also is unusual in my gender. I spent most of last year confused. Kids at school have always called me an ugly lesbian, and I used to hate it, but I wasn't sure. I didn't think I liked girls, and I knew I wasn't like other girls, but I didn't know how. I even thought I might be trans. I did a lot of research and came to the conclusion that I am gender nonconforming. I don't think I'm trans. I don't feel like a boy. But I don't feel like a girl. It's a hard thing to explain, but you know that. It's just what you know about yourself.—

I stopped and looked over it. Then I added one more thing.

—So I am sorry, and I hope you forgive me, but if you can't I understand.—

I typed his name at the top until his number popped up, and I sat there one more moment.

Send.

I stared at the giant green text bubble it was in. The first text I'd ever sent him, and it was a mile long.

I felt sick. And the more that I stared at it—he wasn't responding yet—the more I wondered if it was really enough. I had been honest, but it didn't feel like enough. I mean, I could tell anybody this stuff, really. It occurred to me that there was one thing I could tell him that would both really explain why my brain did what it did and also be a huge risk.

—I wanted to say something else. There was a real reason my mind did that, and it's not as simple as I said. This is really hard for me, but I think you deserve the truth. I said I was questioning myself last year. It's still not resolved. I have wondered if I was bi. I've never liked a girl that way before, but it's a question constantly on my mind because the only good friend I had was a girl and I liked her a lot, just not like that. But every time I like a girl at all, I wonder if I like like her. I don't think that's happened yet. Here's the part that's really hard for me.— I swallowed in fear over what I was about to do. *—I really like you. A lot.—* Oh, my God. This was terrifying. *—I've never told anyone that before. But because I liked you, and when I found out you were trans, my brain suddenly wondered if that meant I was bi because I was attracted to someone who was considered a girl before. So that's why it popped out. I am an idiot. I'm sorry. You must hate me—*

Swoosh. It was sent before I could chicken out.

Now I was sick to my stomach.

And I hadn't even texted Jenna yet. What was I going to say to her? It wasn't really a big apology for her, more of an explanation.

The only real explanation was the last thing I'd just told Mack. I steeled myself and wrote up another version of that and sent it to her, also mentioning that I'd apologized to Mack, wondering if she'd respond either.

I would just have to wait and see what would happen next. In the meantime, I really needed to work on some chemistry homework, but I had no idea how I was going to concentrate enough to get it done.

Friday night, after a lonely dinner, I grabbed my computer and sketchbook and headed over to the art studio after getting the front desk to call the security guard.

Mack hadn't responded yet, and I was still heartbroken. How could I have ruined everything so fast?

At least Jenna had responded. She'd basically said it was okay, it was only Mack who'd been hurt. She said she kind of understood since I hadn't realized he was trans. She had guessed, so it wasn't a surprise for her. So at least that wasn't ruined. But I worried that she would always think less of me for it, even if she was being nice to me. And she hadn't suggested dinner or anything, so I didn't know if that would go back to normal, either.

The guard was walking up the sidewalk. She smiled when she was close enough to recognize me. "Hello, dear. You're quite the hard worker, aren't you?"

I caught a whiff of cigarette smoke as she got closer, which usually kind of grossed me out, but I liked this woman so I tried to ignore it.

"I guess. I love art and I've had a stressful week so I'm hoping this will relax me." I followed her around the side of the building and she scanned her keycard to open the door.

I hit the light switch and she went to unlock the studio door. "Here you go, sweetie. Good luck relaxing."

"Thank you." I dropped my bag on my table and listened for the exterior door to shut.

I got my supplies and some practice perspective drawings from my cubby, picked up some rulers, and went to get some of the butcher paper so I could do more practice sketches before making real attempts in my sketchbook.

I stared at the blank sheet. My mind, of course, went to Mack. Was he out walking like he usually was? Had he read my texts? Would I see him when I went back to the dorm tonight?

So many uncertainties. I closed my eyes and pressed my fingers to my forehead. I didn't think it was possible to regret saying words more than I regretted mine.

But would he even show up on Sunday to our book club? Would Jenna? I really needed to get cracking on the book to finish it in time. I'd be spending a lot of tomorrow reading.

But now I needed to work. It would distract me and keep me from obsessing.

So, I did have a good understanding of one-point perspective. But the dragon drawing needed two-point.

I needed to remember to apply this multiple-point perspective to my life, too. Always try to look at things from other people's viewpoints.

I drew the bassinet that would be closest to the viewer in the bottom right of the page, trying to make it look right based on intuition. I had practiced more and even learned the grid system today from Ms. Mangal. It was very useful—you could basically measure how far back to go based on all the different lines you had to draw. But it was also complicated.

Just like life.

I sighed and finished the first bassinet I'd started on.

With it drawn, I grabbed the ruler and drew lines out from the edges of it way off to the left and right. Where the two on the left intersected, that was that vanishing point. Same for the right. Then I drew the horizon line between them.

All set up.

Now for the grid. I closed my eyes, took a deep breath, and inhaled slowly. My mind went to Mack again and I felt queasy. I hoped he was okay. I mean, it wasn't only hurt feelings. It was deeper than that. It's like I denied who he was with three stupid words. I'd read more about being transgender online last night after sending the texts, and misgendering somebody was really bad. And my text said something about him being a girl before, which is wrong— he was never a girl, he was just treated like one. I hoped he could forgive me.

Deadnaming somebody was also really horrible, and that was what Rachel did when she called him Kenzie. He shut down as soon as she started up her whole thing. He must have known what was coming and sank into himself the way I do. He'd always been so confident every other time I was around him.

I needed to focus. I opened my eyes and got to work.

It was painstaking, but eventually I had the imaginary plane over the tops of the bassinets all measured and marked, so I would know how big to make the other bassinets.

This really was great, if incredibly tedious. Honestly, I'd never known art could be so much work. But I got it—this was how professionals would do things. And that's what I wanted to be.

My phone dinged so, of course, I instantly grabbed it.

A text from Mack. My mind was racing so it took me a

second to comprehend what I was seeing. All he'd said was
—*thank you*—.

Okay, that was something, right? This was good, I was
sure. He'd acknowledged my apology and accepted it. That
was step one. Nothing else good could happen without this.

Was he going to send another text?

I forced myself to draw out the bassinets on the page,
making sure to leave enough spacing between them to allow
for a humanoid dragon to fit in there. I wasn't currently
drawing actual bassinets, but instead rectangular cubes—
whatever those were called—that represented the shape of
the bassinets.

My phone stayed frustratingly quiet. But still, that was
okay. It took him a day to respond in the first place. I would
have to give him time. The worst thing I could do would be
to pressure him.

I knew this, but it didn't remove the desperation from
my heart.

Still, I worked my way through all the bassinets in the
room, in pencil. They were looking pretty good. I thought I
had the angles right. I would show this to Ms. Mangal on
Monday and hopefully she would agree that it looked right,
and I could start the real drawing.

The alarm on my phone went off, shocking me, and then
I was doubly shocked at how perfect the timing was. I had
fifteen minutes to get back to the dorm.

I started putting everything away and again wondered if
I'd run into Mack if he was coming back from a walk, like I
had last week.

I hit the light switches on the way out and walked back
to the dorm.

No Mack.

What was he doing right now? I was desperate to know. And if he'd be there Sunday.

And would I even have the nerve to show up myself? Emerson me wouldn't, but maybe OAMS me would. I steeled myself. OAMS me would show up.

By late afternoon on Saturday, I hadn't heard anything more from Mack. Jenna had replied saying we were fine, but she was just going to spend the weekend focusing on some homework she needed to get done.

So I still had no idea if they'd show up to the book club tomorrow, but I continued working my way through the book, alternating an hour of homework and an hour of reading all morning until lunch, and then again after I got back. I'd be finishing tonight, and I was making good progress on my homework, too. I was numb, but it was good to be focusing on something other than my problems.

Texting them had taken a load off my shoulders. Or part of it, anyway. And hearing back from Jenna was a huge help in lessening that load.

Sophia had apparently gone home again this weekend, which was great. I loved having the room to myself. I was going to ask for a Bluetooth speaker for Christmas so I could go without headphones when she was away.

At a few minutes before five, I realized I was hungry, so I threw on my red Vans, grabbed the book, and headed out for the cafeteria.

It was still pretty hot out. I walked across the parking lot, remembering how Mack had bumped my shoulder when we were crossing it coming back from dinner Wednesday night. And how the backs of our hands had brushed. I'd gotten my hopes up, only to have the disaster occur a few minutes later.

I wove between two giant pickups and wondered again what Rachel's deal was. Why did she apparently hate Mack? Why would you torture someone like that and enjoy it? In the first art class, she'd made a big deal about the pronouns, insisting that hers were obvious. Which was true. She'd probably always felt like a girl, her whole life.

I couldn't imagine what it was like to really feel like you knew who you were. I'd always felt disconnected from who I was, even though it was such a fundamental thing about being alive. I was sure if you didn't feel like I did, or like Mack did, it was probably really difficult to understand. To know you are somehow wrong in your own body. It probably was a little weird.

But the more I'd thought about it, the clearer it had become that he really was a boy. That holdout part of my brain was in the process of giving in.

I stepped up on the curb and crossed the strip of grass to get to the sidewalk that led to the cafeteria. I pushed open the door and realized I'd forgotten my ID so I couldn't scan in.

Crap.

I went up to the cashier and asked if there was any way I could get in without it.

"What's your name, young man?"

I flushed but I wasn't feeling bold enough to say anything about the mistake. "Nic Summers."

She typed in a few things and then looked back and forth between the screen and me several times. "You're not a young man."

"No."

She pressed a button and motioned for me to go through the turnstile.

I did, and tried to forget about the annoying misgendering. I headed over to the pasta bar after grabbing a tray. The place wasn't busy yet so there wasn't a wait.

I usually got spaghetti, but this time I decided to branch out and chose bowtie pasta. Why did even this tiny change feel like a big deal? I was completely messed up.

While I scooped the pasta onto my plate, I could smell the hint of olive oil that was on it, and I moved along to the sauces. They had regular marinara, meat sauce, and an Alfredo. I was still feeling like I needed to do something different, so I put all three sauces on different areas of the plate. Why not?

Even though I was all messed up, I actually felt a little better. At least not despondent anymore. I was going to finish the book. I'd made great progress on my homework. Jenna at least would probably show up for the book club tomorrow. My entire life was not ruined, after all.

After grabbing two pieces of garlic bread, I moved along to the Coke fountain, where I had to wait behind a couple of nerdy college guys. It really was a bit weird to be sharing a campus with older people. I wondered how often girls at OAMS ended up dating college guys here, and how often that caused trouble.

It wasn't going to happen with me, but maybe other girls. Or maybe I should just say girls. I was pretty sure I wasn't one, so I shouldn't be including myself in that.

I grabbed a clear plastic cup and chose the cube ice over the crushed ice, then filled it with Coke. I picked up silverware at the end of the line and found a quiet spot around the corner away from everyone.

Would I see Jenna or Mack tonight? It might be best if I didn't, so we could wait until the book club. Assuming they showed up. I was still convinced Jenna would, but I shouldn't be so confident. She hadn't said anything about it in her text. And she was really mad at me, even if she said things were okay.

There was nothing else I could do now. Texting more would be too much. I needed to give them space.

So I pulled the book out and took a bite of garlic bread before starting on the pasta.

One of the nice things about library books is that you can spread them open on a flat surface without dealing with the guilt of breaking a spine. One of the downsides of reading while eating is that you get pasta sauce on the pages. Sorry, library and next reader.

After I finished the pasta, I kept reading to finish off the chapter. When I was done, I skipped the ice cream because it so reminded me of Mack. I wasn't ready for that, with things still being in limbo. That ice cream would taste like guilt and regret.

I was still desperate to know what would happen with him. I really hoped he would show up tomorrow, but I was trying to convince myself to not expect it.

We'd see. My slightly good mood had faded, and now I was less certain even Jenna would show up. Plus, how awful would I feel again if Mack didn't? I was nervous again, and would be until three tomorrow afternoon.

Sunday morning I got up and dutifully worked on more physics homework. I had managed to finish the book last night, so I just kind of powered through the homework, only thinking about Mack and his silence every five minutes or so.

When I finished the physics problem set, I needed a break and decided to learn more about being trans and all the rules around it. I got out my computer and started googling. This reminded me of the night I dug through all the gender stuff online and figured out I was gender nonconforming. I went down rabbit hole after rabbit hole, but I eventually came out with what I thought was a better understanding of life as a trans person.

Not that I was an expert. But it gave me a lot to think about.

In the midst of all that, I also thought about the book club. Every minute that passed took me closer to three o'clock.

I didn't know what would happen. My world had shattered, all because of my own idiocy. I knew there were plenty of people who would have done the same, or even been aggressive about it, and not felt bad at all, but I didn't want to be that kind of person. I understood where Mack was coming from on a personal level, in a way most people didn't.

At one thirty, I called Mom. She answered and we switched to FaceTime, and there was Isabella. I guessed Dad was watching TV but would come in at some point.

"How are you, sweetie?" Mom asked. "Do you have a big social life now?"

I had to focus not to close my eyes in response, as I was overwhelmed with emotion. But I didn't even know. God. "It's just a book club."

"How's your boyfriend?!" Isabella asked.

My stomach twisted. "He isn't my boyfriend." I wasn't

even sure he was anything at this stage. And it was all my fault.

"Is your book club with your new friends?" Mom asked at the same time Isabella said, "Why not?"

"Yeah, we read this new fantasy book. It was really good." I wasn't going to answer my sister.

"I'm so glad you found your people." Mom had a big smile on her face, obviously genuinely pleased. "It makes me feel so much better that you're settling in so well. Maybe this really was the best thing for you. I wasn't sure before, but now, I think so."

"I think it's good." I told her more about the art class and how I was learning to be more like a professional artist.

I tried not to think about the fact that art, this thing I loved so much, also put me in such close proximity to evil Rachel.

"Cool!" Isabella said. "What is your next drawing?"

"I had to come up with a drawing of a dragon doing something a human would normally do."

"A dragon!" Isabella said. "You love drawing dragons."

"Yeah, so I came up with all these different ideas and decided to draw a dragon tending to a baby in a hospital nursery." The absurdity made me smile a bit.

"Baby dragons?" my sister asked.

"Nope. Baby humans."

Isabella looked confused and Mom said, "*You're* going to draw babies? I never would have thought this could happen." She laughed. "You are a new person. But I'm really excited for you. Who knew that sending you to a science and math school would mean you'd be developing your art skills so much? I hope this helps you achieve your goals."

That was Mom, being her ever-supportive self. She kept

on. "How are your science and math classes going? Are they challenging?"

"Wait a minute," Isabella said. "I'm still stuck on this dragon thing."

"It's supposed to be incongruous. That's the point. I think it will be funny."

"Okay," Isabella said, clearly unconvinced.

"So anyway, about my classes—it's a matter of putting the time in, I think."

"I want to hear more about your friends, Nic!" Isabella said, her eyes bright. "Especially Mack!"

There went the stomach twisting again.

"Yes, me too," Mom said.

Fine. "Well, we all like reading fantasy. Mack is a senior and he's taking a bunch of hard classes. He wants to do something with computers in college. Jenna is a junior. She has a nose ring. They're both really nice." And they both think I'm an idiot, or a jerk, or a loser, or something. It hurt talking about them.

"That's all very generic," Mom said.

"Well, I don't know what to tell you. We often go to the cafeteria together." Or, we did. I had no idea if we would start again.

Mom laughed. "Okay, if that's all you're going to give us, fine. I'm glad things are going well, though I have to admit, you don't sound as happy as I'd like."

Of course she would notice. "I'm just tired. I'm still adjusting to the workload, so I've been staying up late. I'll get used to it and it will be fine."

"Isabella, go get your dad," Mom said.

"Are you really okay?" Mom asked, after Isabella had left the room.

"Yeah, it's fine. I did something stupid this week and I'm not sure if it's going to change things."

"Okay, honey. You know if you need to talk, we can talk more than once a week."

"Thanks." I knew she meant well, and although she did know things about me, she didn't know everything, and I didn't think she could help.

"Hi, Nic," Dad said, his face appearing on the screen.

"Hi."

"Everything going well?" he asked.

Isabella popped up between him and Mom, grinning like a loon.

"Yeah, it's good. I'm learning a lot."

Isabella started making funny faces, crossing her eyes and sticking her tongue out.

"That's great. You know I'm really proud of you, challenging yourself."

"Thanks." Then when my sister pulled her nose up with her thumb, I laughed and said, "That's a great look on you, Izzy."

My parents both looked at her as she said, "Isabella. But you're allowed one mistake a month."

"Sorry," I said. What a month of mistakes I was having. "Is that a calendar month?"

"Yes." Her face was back to normal, and she was smiling.

"Oh, man, it's only the third."

"You're going to have to be careful."

Dad tousled her hair and looked back at me, also smiling. "I love you, Nic. Have a good week and I'll talk to you next week.

Dad disappeared and Mom said, "I think we'll let you get back to your busy life, honey."

We all exchanged I love yous and I hung up. I let my arm

drop, as it was tired from holding the phone for so long. I closed my eyes and thought about stuff. My mom would never understand why calling Mack a girl was so bad. Adults just didn't get these things.

But I knew better, so the guilt was still heavy in my stomach. But it was less than an hour until the meeting. Where I'd find out if things were salvageable or not.

At a quarter to three, I left my room and headed over to the student union, book in hand. What else should you bring to a book club? I had no idea.

Then my mind went right to Mack. Was he even going to show up? I thought Jenna might, but didn't know that for sure, either. My stomach was in mild turmoil and my pulse had quickened from thinking about all this.

The sun was beating down, making me move slowly even though I wanted to get there already.

When the building came into view, my heart beat even faster.

I continued along, wiping sweat off my forehead. Finally, I reached the back door, which led into Booth Forest. I checked the time. Two minutes to three. I made a request of the universe in my mind—*please let everything turn out okay* —and opened the door.

The roar of all the voices hit me. Would we even find a booth if either of them showed up? I passed through one aisle of the room, looking at faces, and didn't recognize any. So I wove through the other aisles and didn't see them, but there were some open booths, so that was a good sign. The universe was at least setting things up to go well.

I ended up at the other entrance to the room, on the

food court side. It might be nice to get a drink. But I wouldn't stay here by myself if no one else showed up, because I only had the book with me, so I decided to wait.

"Hey," I heard from close by.

I turned. Mack. My heart leapt and I couldn't keep the smile off my face, or keep myself from saying, "You came."

"I did." He held up his Kindle, a small and maybe uncomfortable smile on his face. "Stayed up late last night to finish."

His black hair was looking especially good today, even spikier than normal. Light from one of the fluorescent over-head fixtures was glinting off the earrings in his left ear. He had on a Star Wars t-shirt, showing R2-D2 and C-3PO. I liked everything about him. I don't know how I could have doubted who he was. It was obvious he was a boy.

"Well, I, for one, am glad you're here," I finally said. I didn't know what else to say. Also, it seemed like he should be the one to direct the conversation. I had already bared my soul, so he had all the knowledge, and I knew very little about him.

"Did you want to get something to drink?" he asked.

"Sure. Do you know if Jenna is coming?"

"I'm assuming so. We can keep an eye out for her while we're in line."

I nodded. "Starbucks?"

"Sounds good."

We headed over there, getting in line behind three people.

There was a slightly awkward silence, which he broke by saying, "So, you like me, huh?"

My heart lurched and I panicked. I had not expected him to come out and say it. "Um." I looked at him. He didn't look like he was being mean. He still had that sort of smile on his face. It wasn't entirely convincing. But I didn't think it was fake, either.

I felt raw, like he knew everything about me, both good and bad. I'd opened up to him more than anyone else besides Sam, who I'd known for years before I let her in that much. I tried to quiet my frantic brain down and watched him watch me in silence until I finally said, "I guess."

He nodded. "Nobody's ever liked me before."

Okay, this didn't feel as horrible as I was afraid it would. Still, I didn't know where the nerve came from, but I said, "I can relate to that. Nobody has ever liked me before, either."

"Well, I like you." He smiled again but this time it looked shy. "Even if you do still look like a lobster."

I stared at him in shock, his words reverberating in my chest. "You do?" How could we even be having this conversation after everything that had happened? The line hadn't moved; it looked like the person at the register was ordering for an entire soccer team or something.

"At least, before Wednesday."

"Oh." My heart sank. I *had* ruined everything.

"But your text, I think it did make me feel better. I had wondered if you also were kind of questioning your gender. I guessed you were, but I didn't think we had known each other long enough to bring it up. But I assumed you knew about me."

My emotions were swirling all over the place and tears welled in my eyes. He'd mentioned the sunburn thing, which felt like a good sign for friendship, but maybe not anything more.

Crap, I didn't want to cry. I wasn't even upset right now, because it sounded like it might not be over. I was just so overwhelmed.

"I didn't," I finally said. "I mean, I hope it's okay to say, but I can kind of see it now. Your voice isn't very deep, and I guess there are other things, but when I first saw you, I read you as a boy and never reevaluated." I had to wipe a tear from each eye. It was impossible to be subtle with that crap.

"I love that," Mack said, averting his eyes. "That actually sort of makes up for what you said."

"I'm so sorry about that." My voice was thick and more tears rolled down my cheeks. I was going to be a mess in a minute. I wiped my eyes again. "I'm sorry, I just get overwhelmed sometimes and it makes me cry."

I was terrified by how much he knew about me now. I thought I could trust him, but you never knew for sure.

"It's okay. I believe you. And I also know what it's like to be surprised by something." He sort of patted my shoulder while I wiped away more tears.

"I hate crying. One time I cried in fifth grade math class because the teacher called on me and I didn't know the answer because I was completely confused by non-decimal based systems. But I couldn't stop crying, and she sent me to the bathroom, where it only got worse because I kept looking at my puffy, tear-stained cheeks in the mirror. I was so embarrassed and knew I'd have to go back into the classroom and everyone would stare at my red eyes."

God, I was rambling now.

Mack smiled. "I won't stare at your red eyes."

That made me laugh. He didn't seem to be judging me for going on about nothing. "Okay, good."

Finally the line moved forward.

Mack looked back toward Booth Forest. "Have you been watching for Jenna?"

"No, I forgot. I'm terrible." I figured that the conversation we were having about how we liked each other was over. I didn't think either of us were brave enough to continue on that topic.

"Me, too."

I checked my phone to see it was already five after. "Maybe she's found a booth or something and is wondering where we are."

The line moved forward again and someone showed up at the other register. We were next. We were both quiet. What was he thinking about? Technically, he hadn't said that he still liked me, just that he *had* liked me. I didn't know what to think.

After ordering, we watched the entrance to Booth Forest while waiting for our drinks. No Jenna yet.

Once we had our drinks, we headed over and managed to snag a booth. I walked around to see if Jenna was anywhere, but she wasn't. So I returned and sat across from Mack.

"I really loved this book," Mack said, pointing to his Kindle.

"Yeah, me too. I'm so glad there are two more in the series."

"Hi!" a voice said, and I turned to see Jenna.

"I'm sorry I'm late," she said. "Do you mind if I go get a coffee?"

"Go ahead," Mack said.

She dropped her book on the table and headed off.

"I don't know when I'm going to make it to the library to get book two," I said.

"They're open until nine some days, six on others," he said.

"Great. I can go over after class one day." I hoped Jenna would go with me.

Just then, she reappeared with a hot drink from Starbucks.

"That was fast," I said.

She held up her cup as she slid into the booth next to me. "Drip coffee."

"Don't tell me you are drinking it black," Mack said.

She smiled. "I'm a badass."

We laughed and I pulled my book toward me and took a sip of my tea.

"So, how do we do this?" Mack asked, touching his Kindle.

"I have no clue," I said. "I think it's on Jenna because it was her idea." I grinned at her, so glad that she didn't still seem mad at me.

"No pressure," she joked. "So, I'm not entirely sure. Did either of you mark pages or lines?"

"I highlighted some things," Mack said.

"I didn't," I said. "I should have used those little flag things. I am unprepared."

"No worries," Jenna said. "Maybe we should start with general impressions, anyway. So, what did you guys think?"

We both said we loved it, which made us all laugh. But it got the conversation started. We talked about it overall, and some of the major things that happened, and Jenna told us which ones were going to come up as important in the future books. We talked for over an hour about all this, and it was so much fun to talk about a book I'd read, to dig deep into some things, and to find out things that other people thought were interesting when I'd glossed over them. Sam and I had done that some, but never in such depth.

After that, we went through Mack's highlighted lines and talked about each of those. I hadn't really noticed, but there were some powerful lines in there. I usually just missed stuff like that if I was enjoying the story and kept charging ahead.

As we seemed to be wrapping up, Jenna asked, "Do you want to do this again?"

I said, "Yes," as Mack said, "Definitely."

"Book two or a different series?" she asked.

Mack and I looked at each other, apparently reading each other's minds. "Book two," we said in unison.

Jenna laughed again. "Book two it is." She turned to me. "When are you going to get it?"

"I was thinking tomorrow after school."

"I can come with you."

"Cool." This was so great. Things were going to get back to normal. I just had to avoid saying stupid, hurtful things in the future.

"Are we aiming for next Sunday?" Mack asked.

"Let's see where we are later in the week," I said. "I do need to make sure I'm getting all my work done. It seems to be getting more intense."

"Yeah, that happens." Mack arched his eyebrows.

"Alright," Jenna said as she slipped out of the booth and stood up.

Mack and I followed her out the back door. As soon as we were outside in the heat again, Mack asked if we were going back to the dorm.

We said yes, and he asked if I'd mind taking his Kindle while he went on a walk.

"Sure," I said. Another one of his mystery walks.

He smiled at me. "Thanks." Then he turned and headed off.

Jenna and I started walking toward the dorm.

We hadn't gotten far when she bumped my shoulder and said, "Nic, I was late on purpose. Aren't I awesome?"

That surprised me. "Did you know he was going to be there?"

"Yeah. I texted him. I told him I didn't think you really meant to hurt him, and that you felt really horrible. I wanted to give you some time to chat before I got there."

"That was sort of awesome." It was also kind of sweet that she'd even thought of that.

"So did you guys talk it out? Everything seemed cool by the time I got there."

"Yeah, we did. He told me that the fact that I'd thought he was a boy and never questioned it sort of made up for my stupid reaction."

She laughed. "I can see that."

"Can I ask you a question?" We turned a corner on the sidewalk.

"Sure."

"How did you figure out he was trans?" I asked.

"His voice made me wonder. It's pretty high for a boy. Not obviously a girl's voice, but close. But it was really his hands. They're not very masculine."

That was interesting. "I don't think I ever really looked at his hands."

"I have known a couple of trans people before, though they were both girls, so it was different. But it wasn't out of the realm of possibility for me. I guess you said you'd never met any trans people before."

"I've never met anyone who isn't straight and cis. Or at least that doesn't present like that." That was the first time I'd used that word out loud, and I was sort of proud of myself.

"You probably have and just didn't know it. People who weren't out."

"Yeah, my town wouldn't have been supportive, that's for

sure." A slightly bitter laugh escaped me as my anger flared at how horrible people there had been to me. I wiped sweat off my head more forcefully than necessary.

Jenna didn't comment on any of that and instead said, "Things are different in bigger cities. But if OKC is better than some small Oklahoma town, imagine how New York, or San Francisco, would be. It would be like the dream."

Was she uncertain about her gender or sexuality? She'd never mentioned it, but she was clearly interested in it, based on her reading selections. I wasn't going to say anything about it. This kind of stuff was too personal. You didn't ask, you just listened.

We approached the corner of the parking lot for our dorm and continued on the sidewalk.

"Are you hungry?" Jenna asked. "I just realized it's well into dinner time."

"Oh yeah. I'm actually starving, now that you mention it." I'd been so fixated on everything else that I hadn't even noticed.

She veered right and I followed. We were going to have dinner together. Things were going to get back to normal. I hadn't realized how tense I was until I noticed it was gone. That tension had been in my body since Wednesday, and now I just felt my normal levels of anxiety again.

Now I would wonder if Mack still liked me or not, and if anything would come of that.

The next day was our first critique in art class, and I was sitting at my table, next to Jacob, before class started, nervous. Especially because Rachel would be there, and who knew what she'd say. Or what I would say to her, for that matter. I did not get what her deal was. I still didn't know how she knew Mack, even though it was obviously from before OAMS. She was from the Tulsa area and Mack was from a small town, so it didn't make a lot of sense.

Ms. Mangal started class after the bell chirped by clapping her hands. "Okay, our first critique. We're going to be critiquing our first assignment, the summer or trip piece I had all of you do. We'll do these for each of your final project submissions, so Every five weeks."

Doing this that often sounded horrible.

She continued, "Remember that this is a *critique*, not a criticism session. We are trying to help each other grow as artists, not tear each other down. Each artist will stand at the front and display their piece on the easel. They have two options. One is to basically say nothing other than to tell us the name of the piece if it has one."

That seemed easy enough.

Ms. Mangal kept going. "The other option is to explain the goal of the piece, what you are trying to accomplish with it. We start by all going up to view the piece up close before sitting back down. Then we go around the room and identify things we like about the piece, things that are particularly successful in achieving the goal of the piece, if we know it.

"Then we will discuss opportunities for improvement. During this time, critiquers should avoid making complicated suggestions. Instead, focus on why you think something doesn't work. You are allowed to provide example suggestions to illustrate your point, but keep them short. Remember, you are not trying to get the artist to make the piece you would have made in their place—it is and will remain the artist's work. During all of this, the artist receiving the critique should not speak unless directly asked a question."

The idea of having to answer questions about my work while standing at the front of the room was horrible. Even if they were saying nice things. How would I would take compliments? Would I believe them, or think they were being fake, or grasping at straws? I didn't know these people well enough to trust them.

This really was intimidating. Though now that I was thinking about it, it might be interesting to see other people's work. I assumed that the kids in here were better artists than those at Emerson, since Ms. Mangal had said people here were taking art because they really wanted to. You didn't come to OAMS if you were looking for easy A's.

"And remember," she continued, "as the artist, every-thing critiquers say is their opinion only, and you are not obligated to change anything based on their reactions. However, if several people are saying the same thing about your piece, you would be wise to seriously consider what they are saying. Remember that what you have in your head may or may not have made it to the paper or canvas."

She clapped her hands again. "And with that, let's get started. Go get your pieces and we're going to go around the room to take turns, starting with Rachel."

Most of us got up and headed over to the cubbies, where we grabbed our work. Rachel smiled at me while I waited for the crowd to clear to get to my cubby. I raged inside. That was the fakest smile I had ever seen in my life.

We all returned to our tables except for Rachel, who confidently stood next to the easel beside Ms. Mangal's desk, her work displayed on it.

The piece looked like a concert, done in colored pencil.

Once everyone was seated, Ms. Mangal said, "Okay, Rachel, tell us about your piece, or tell us to start."

"So this summer, I went back to Houston to stay with friends for several weeks. We saw General Yorke in July. So I drew what it looked like from the crowd."

That was a rock band that was sort of up-and-coming. I liked them and it surprised me that Rachel did, too.

"It's called *View*," Rachel continued. "It was a great concert in general, and a good trip to my true home, since we moved here less than two years ago."

That was a revelation to me that I felt in my chest. She kept going on about the concert, but I was fixated on the fact that she was from Houston. She seemed to know Mack when they were both a lot younger—back in Barbie days—so did that mean that's where Mack was from? How did they both end up in Oklahoma? Because Mack had told me he was from a small town here. That was why he'd come here, to get away. It must have been quite a shift to go from living in Houston to a small town in Oklahoma, especially if you were trans.

"Okay, thank you, Rachel. Everyone go up and have a look at her piece. Feel free to bring a notebook to take notes. But you only have a minute since we have to get through everyone today."

I slid off the seat and realized I hadn't heard anything Rachel said after the Houston bit. If she'd talked about the goal of the piece, I had no idea what it was. I hoped that didn't matter for when I had to say something about her work.

We crowded around it and I avoided looking at Rachel's face.

The drawing wasn't bad, but sort of flat. The perspective was off. It should have been two point, because the view of the stage was off to the left, so the stage should be rotated some, but she drew it like it was straight ahead. I probably wouldn't have noticed if I hadn't been heads down in learning perspective lately. Otherwise it was fine. She hadn't used very bold colors, but she did a good job of suggesting people in the crowd without obsessively drawing every head. The band looked fine, but they were the part that really looked flat. Not that I was criticizing, as drawing people who really looked alive was still hard for me, despite what Jenna had said about my own art. I didn't always succeed in that. Giving two-dimensional renderings life was hard.

Ms. Mangal had us all sit down and asked Emily to start since her seat was next to Rachel's.

Her comments were kind of generic, but Lily said she liked the color scheme Rachel'd used, with mostly pastels in the crowd and bolder colors for the band. I hadn't noticed that, but she was right. Ms. Mangal had everyone talking pretty quickly, going around the room fast, so it was my turn too fast.

My stomach was fluttery with nerves, but without looking at Rachel herself, I said, "I like how the crowd was drawn, where it's mostly suggested with a few more detailed heads drawn to make it clear what it is. My opportunity for improvement is the perspective. It feels a little off, and you might look at drawing the grid first before drawing in the details."

That sounded okay. I didn't look at Rachel during this, either, just her drawing.

Emily didn't want her piece critiqued, so Lily went next with hers, then the other girls at the front tables. Finally it was Jacob's turn. He'd done a comics-style rendering of a baseball game, looking from behind the pitcher to see the batter, catcher, and umpire. But the bodies were all exaggerated. It was good.

But this meant I was next. The dread was heavy in my stomach. We made it through his critique, and then it really was my turn.

I headed up there with my drawing and put it on the easel, my hand shaking. I liked the drawing, but this was terrifying. Then Ms. Mangal asked me to start.

I took a deep breath to try to steady myself. It did not really work, but I had to start talking. "This is from a trip, but not over the summer. I went to Scotland to visit my best friend in March, and we saw a lot of different things, but my favorite was this castle in Linlithgow."

I paused for a second, both feeling my current fear but also remembering the magical feeling of being in those ruins, and how much Sam and I had bonded on that trip, deepening our friendship even though she was now thousands of miles away. I wasn't going to tell them that, though, because that was too personal.

"Does the piece have a name?" Ms. Mangal prompted.

"Not really."

"Do you want to tell us your goal, or anything else?" she asked.

"I guess I just wanted to remember the trip and that castle specifically."

"Okay, thank you, Nic. Everyone, please view it."

I stood there awkwardly, staring at my feet, the dread of what they were going to say keeping those feet heavy and locked in place.

Of course Rachel went first. What would she say?

"I think this is a strong drawing. It looks realistic, but there is a gentleness to it that really fits a ruin, I think."

Well, that was really nice. I looked at it, and I knew what

she meant. I hadn't thought about it, but she was right. Sometimes my marks were a lot bolder, with stronger outline, but this one had a lot of blending and subtle changes from one surface to another.

Then Rachel said, "For the improvement opportunity, I also think you could have used a wider range of values. Some darker darks would be nice. You could still do it on this drawing."

Okay, my heart was racing, but that wasn't bad. Part of me wondered if she was really so terrible, then I remembered what she'd said to Mack. This was just a performance for Ms. Mangal.

Lily liked the detail on the stone, and then said that the next part wasn't really a critique because she couldn't really find anything to improve, but she pointed out that I could try doing a new version of this drawing in pen. She said she loved ink drawings of ruins.

The others said they were impressed by how realistic it was, the way the fountain looked so amazing and they could imagine it back when it was working. Jacob said he thought the composition was interesting, because although I'd centered the fountain horizontally, it was lower on the page so the second story of the passageway around the courtyard was really visible and interesting.

So by the end, I was wrung out, but my ego wasn't really battered like I'd expected it to be.

Did that mean I was a real artist? Maybe this was something I really should be doing.

I should keep putting everything into my art, because in that moment, I knew it was going to pay off. I could do this.

PART III

A DRAGON IN THE BABY ROOM

Monday night, Mack, Jenna, and I were sitting in the cafeteria after dinner, still talking even though we'd finished eating ages ago. It was like the whole horrible thing had never happened last week.

Thank God.

And I knew I was lucky for this. Thank you, universe.

"Oh, hey, what's the plan for the next book?" Mack asked.

Jenna looked at me. "Broken Earth Book Two?"

"Sounds good to me," I said, "assuming we can get it."

"We could go tonight," she said.

I nodded, making tracks in the remaining green pea soup sludge in the bottom of my bowl. "I can't spend much time there, though. I have a bunch of crap to do. This place is no joke."

"Yeah, me too," Jenna said, sighing, which echoed how I felt about it. She pulled out her phone. "I'll make sure they have it. It's the one called *The Obelisk Gate*, Mack."

"Okay, great," he said.

"Are you coming with us, Mack?" she asked.

He yawned. "I can walk that way with you, but I'm going to keep going once you go in."

"Cool." I was still curious about these walks of his, but I was starting to think there wasn't any secret destination. He might just like to walk. But if that was the case, why did he always have to do them alone?

Jenna was looking at her phone, scrolling. "They've got it on the shelf."

"Great," I said. "Should we go?"

"Probably." She tucked her phone in her back pocket.

We put our trays up and headed toward the ice cream station, dithering over our choices and somehow I ended up getting French vanilla. We walked out into the evening heat, the outermost layer of our ice cream immediately starting to melt, so we all scrambled to eat enough to keep it from dripping all over our fingers.

"So we had our first art critique today," I announced as soon as I had control of my ice cream and we were in the parking lot. I'd been hesitant to bring it up because it might involve talking about Rachel, but it turned out that I did want to talk about it.

"How'd it go?" Mack asked, tilting his head to eat some of his chocolate chip. The sun glinted off the studs in his right ear.

"That sounds intimidating to me," Jenna said.

"Yeah, I was so nervous at first, to the point of feeling queasy." I could even feel some of those nerves now. "We had to take our work and put it on an easel at the front of the room and stand there while we talked about it. Not my favorite thing, but people were mostly nice. It ended up not being as bad as I expected."

"What piece did you show?" Mack asked.

I explained about the trip to Scotland and showed them the picture on my phone, which they both thought was good.

"I'm so impressed you got to go to Scotland," Jenna said.

"Yeah," Mack said. "We went to London when I was six, but I hardly remember it." He laughed. "Though I do remember that we went to Stonehenge and I cried because we couldn't get close enough to actually see it properly."

"You can't get close?" Jenna asked, eyes narrowed in confusion.

"No, you are so far away. They want to protect the stones. You used to be able to go up there and walk between them and stuff. I think I heard that some tours let you, but not the majority."

"That seems like a bummer," Jenna said. "So do they tell you how to do better, in the critique?"

"Yeah, but we're supposed to not really criticize." We stopped at the crosswalk, waiting for the light to turn so we could cross. I felt like such a rebel since we hadn't told the RAs we were leaving campus.

"Got it." Jenna took in some of her ice cream. "I've always been scared of that. I could never let somebody read my poems."

"It sounds intimidating," Mack said, just as the light turned. We all stepped into the street. "It seems like your work is really close to you. How could you listen to anybody else's opinion on that?"

I nodded. "It does feel a bit like somebody driving a stake through your heart."

We finished crossing and headed into the neighborhood.

"You know what's coming up," Mack said as we started down the long street that would lead to the library.

"We have to take a selfie," Jenna said.

We all laughed. The dragon mailbox. A picture with all of us and the dragon would be awesome.

"Dr. Tolstoy scared the crap out of us all in electronics today," Mack said.

"What happened?" Jenna asked, which was good since I was dealing with a mouthful of ice cream. Almost done.

"We were in the middle of a lab and Logan's lab partner left the room for a minute. Logan fell asleep, and Tolstoy had a rolled up magazine and slammed it down on the desk, right next to his head."

Jenna and I both cracked up.

"Logan jerked his head up and made this little shriek. It was pretty funny. But it was also weird because Tolstoy is normally so nice. He must have been having a bad day. And Logan doesn't normally sleep in class. A perfect storm. But I don't think anybody will be sleeping in class again."

We were halfway to the dragon mailbox. I finished my cone and licked my fingers clean. Then I had to wipe the sweat off my forehead. Good old Oklahoma in September. It always seemed like summer should be over, but it wasn't yet.

"We're almost there," Jenna said, her voice giddy.

Just as we reached the mailbox, Mack and I smiled at each other, which made my heart flutter. He asked, "How are we going to do this?"

We all looked at it, trying to figure out how to take the picture.

"You go there," Jenna said to Mack, pointing to one side. Then she directed me to the other. We tilted our heads in and I managed to hit mine on the dragon.

"Ouch."

Jenna laughed. "Careful over there."

Then she got sort of in the middle, in front of it but off to the side. "Crouch down."

She held her phone out and we could see that we weren't quite all in the frame. "Squeeze in."

I'd never actually taken a selfie with friends before. Sam and I didn't really do that sort of thing.

Was I really becoming the kind of teenager who took selfies? This seemed crazy. How could I be a stereotype? I was supposed to be a freak.

I kind of liked being different. It was part of my identity. What did it mean that I was normal in some things?

Jenna angled the phone differently and took the shot.

"Hey!" somebody shouted from behind us. We all turned to see the owner of the house standing in the doorway. "Scat," he said, waving us off.

We jumped away from the mailbox and hurried away, giggling like idiots.

Once we got a couple of houses down, we stopped, still cracking up.

"It's actually a good shot," Jenna said.

We all crowded around it to see, still grinning.

"This is great," Mack said.

It was. I was smiling a little, something that didn't happen often in pictures of me. Mack was also smiling, though less subtly like me. Jenna, on the other hand, had on an enthusiastic smile.

We started walking again while she fiddled with her phone, posting it on all her social media.

The heat was already melting my good spirits from the photo. We kept trudging along, finally reaching the intersection with the library. As we stood across the street from it, Mack said, "Okay, I'm going to head off. Have fun at the library. Don't pick up too many books. Remember how busy you are." He squeezed both our shoulders and took off down the street.

We crossed and were soon in the building, the glorious AC chilling my skin. We went straight to the fantasy section and found the book, and then we perused the shelves a bit. There was nothing like standing in front of a bookshelf. So many possibilities.

Just like in my new social life. Anything could happen.

The next day was our first real art club board meeting, so I got there at four thirty with a notebook and pen. Rachel, Emily, and Lise were already there, sitting at the front left table, and Ms. Mangal was sitting at the desk at the front of the room, colorful mug next to her. Rachel heard me come in and turned to look at me. I slunk to my regular table.

Rachel was still staring at me, a big, fake smile on her face. "Oh, come on, Nic, sit up here with us. No need to hide." She pointed to the table next to her.

Everyone was looking at me now, so I moved up.

"You didn't bring your computer?" Rachel asked in this exaggeratedly alarmed tone.

My stomach lurched. Of course I should have brought it. I was supposed to take notes and post them to the club's page. "I ..."

"It's okay, Rachel," Ms. Mangal said. "Nic, you can hand-write your notes and add them to the site later, or maybe someone can lend you their computer."

"Unfortunately, I need mine for the meeting," Rachel said, this time with an exaggerated frown on her face.

What was her problem? She wasn't sorry. She was

enjoying herself. Everything about her face and body language was fake right now. Was every interaction we had going to be this big performance?

Then Lily walked in, backpack slung across her shoulder.

She said hi to the room and sat next to me, nodding perfunctorily.

"You can handwrite your notes, Nic. It will probably be easier to write them directly on the site, but you can decide for next time."

I nodded, feeling stupid. It didn't take much to take me back to how I was at Emerson. I was bolder here, but it wasn't foolproof. But I opened my notebook and clicked my pen to get ready.

"Alright, let's get started," Ms. Mangal said. "Rachel, you're up."

Rachel stood up and headed to the front of the room, her open laptop in her hand. Ms. Mangal sat in a chair off to the side.

She looked at me, that fake smile plastered on. "Don't forget to record attendance and the time we start. Okay, everyone, I'm calling this meeting to order."

I recorded everything and listened as she started talking about the fundraiser.

"Are you all fine with the chocolate bars again?" she asked.

Lily said, "I don't want to do the door-to-door thing."

Me neither.

Rachel nodded. "I don't love it either. Do we have other thoughts?"

Lily had done some research on some alternatives so we reviewed those. I jotted everything down.

"Do you want to do some additional research on alternatives?" Rachel asked. She was bossy—a natural for the position of president. "We don't have to decide right away. But we do need to make sure we can order the stuff by whatever deadline they have. You might remember, we start in mid-January and go through the end of February. So, Lily, do you want to own doing some more research and bring that info back to us next meeting?"

Lily nodded. "Sure."

Rachel turned to me again. "Oh, and Nic, make sure to record Action Items."

I must have looked confused, as I didn't know what that meant.

"Basically to-do items for people," Rachel explained. "Anything that someone needs to do outside of the meeting."

I nodded and put a star next to the note about Lily doing research.

"Okay, on to the fun stuff. The mural." She brought her hands together, fingertips touching each other. "I did call the children's hospital, and they are interested in us doing a mural. They have a twenty-foot-long wall, the standard eight feet tall. I asked them if they had anything specific in mind, and they said not really, but they do obviously want to approve the idea first, and then the design." She walked behind the desk to the whiteboard and uncapped a blue pen. "So what I'd like to do today is throw around some ideas for themes or high-level concepts. We don't have to decide tonight, but I'd like to do some brainstorming. Anybody have any ideas?"

There was that moment of silence that always follows a question like that. But then Lily spoke up. "What about something with flight? Like, metaphorical flight."

"I like that," Rachel said, writing the word "flight" on the board. I also noted this down.

And then of course my mind went to dragons. We could do a cutesy dragon, not serious, dangerous ones like I usually drew.

"We want it to be something inspiring," Lise said. "I think flight is good for that. But we could also go more abstract, like joy. We could show dancing and music and happy people."

Rachel and I recorded that.

"Yeah, and I think we need to paint mostly children, not adults."

Lily and Lise agreed with that.

"We should also make sure to have a diverse cast," Emily said.

"Definitely." Rachel wrote that word on the board. "What about animals?"

"We could do a couple of kids riding a dragon," I suggested quietly. But then I hedged, "Or a dinosaur. You know, flying. Like, cartoon-style." Then I wrote down my own suggestion.

"Cartoon dragons are fun," Lily said. "We can do all sorts of bold color combinations."

I was a little surprised—somebody else liked my idea.

Rachel didn't look pleased with Lily, but she dutifully wrote down 'dragon,' 'dinosaur,' and 'bold color' on the board.

"Kids love all that," Emily agreed.

"We've got a lot of space," Lise said. "We can do other types of flight. A kid flying a plane, a hot air balloon, a helicopter, maybe even a paraglider. We can make the whole thing cartoon-style, so the kids are all way out of proportion to the mode of transport."

I glanced over at Ms. Mangal, and she had a small smile on her face. I wondered if this was not how these conversations usually went. We were making some real progress on an idea.

Rachel stood back and looked at the board. "So I think we've got a great start. One thing we could do if we want, is to each pick one of the things and draw our own version. Then you can send me pictures of those and I can start piecing them together in Photoshop to see how we could arrange everything, and consider size and stuff. I can post a version of that to our site. We can share it with the whole club for feedback."

"Is that good for everyone?" Rachel asked.

We all nodded in agreement.

"So why don't we plan to get everything to me by our next meeting and I'll start working on the mock-up. Then we can do a more detailed drawing and I'll share it with the hospital. In the meantime, I'll contact them with the basic idea and make sure they like it. Who wants to do what vehicle?"

"I'll do a hot air balloon," Emily said.

"I'll do a dragon," I said.

"Don't make it too fantasy," Rachel deadpanned. "Stay cartoony."

"I know." I sounded weak. I didn't know why I couldn't be braver around Rachel. I had regressed. Maybe not completely, because I doubted Emerson Nic would have even suggested the dragon.

"What about you, Lise and Lily?" Rachel asked.

Lily answered first. "I was thinking it might be fun to do a unicorn with a kid riding it, running fast, hair and tail flowing behind them."

"That sounds good," Lise said. "I can do a helicopter, I guess."

Rachel nodded. "So I'll do a plane. And we'll see where this goes." She held up a finger. "One thing before we get to officer reports. The t-shirt. Let's send out a request for designs from the whole club in October. Anybody disagree with that?"

"Who's going to send out the information?" Lise asked. "And do we need to decide on rules and stuff?"

Rachel nodded. "Good point. Let's do just the front of the shirt. It will be cheaper. Do we really need any other rules besides whatever the printer has? I can look those up."

Nobody said anything.

"Might I suggest something?" Ms. Mangal asked.

"Sure," Rachel said, and we all looked over.

"It should include the name of the school and the words 'Art Club' somewhere on it. You might specify that it can include a rendering of a tangible thing, like a palette, which I've seen before, or be entirely lettering. To give people ideas."

"That sounds good to me," Rachel said. "Did you get all that, Nic?"

There was that sickly sweet smile from her again. Ugh.

"Yes."

"Okay, now let's do officer reports. We'll start with the VP Membership."

Everyone went through their reports. When it was my turn, I said I'd get the minutes up on the site tonight or tomorrow.

Rachel wrapped things up after that and after the meeting was officially over, she came over and said, "You really should try to get those notes up tonight." She had this totally fake-helpful tone going on, and I was annoyed. Then she continued. "Speaking from experience, you'll forget a lot of context if you wait."

"Okay, sure. Thanks." I grabbed my notebook and slid off the stool.

"And make sure you're careful who you socialize with." She spun on her heels and headed out of the room.

What was her freaking problem? I couldn't believe I would have to spend this much time with such an evil person every two weeks. Plus the art classes themselves. I didn't know how I was going to handle this. But for the moment, I was looking forward to dinner with Mack and Jenna. They were supposed to be waiting for me in the dorm lounge.

These were good people who'd have my back, even if Rachel was trying to make my life a pain.

Wednesday night, Jenna was with her dad again, so it was just Mack and me for dinner. I had big plans for what I was going to ask Mack, so I was nervous. But I still got myself two slices of pepperoni pizza and got settled into a table away from the biggest crowds.

I took a bite of pizza and wiped my hands on a napkin. I couldn't see where Mack was, so I thought about what I wanted to bring up. Last night, after the art club board meeting, I'd told Mack and Jenna about Rachel being kind of shitty. Mack had shaken his head and looked like he might say something more, but changed his mind. Jenna said Rachel was a bitch, and we went on to talk about something else. But I wanted to know what Mack was going to say. So tonight I planned to ask him to tell me what had happened with her. I still didn't even know how they knew each other.

I was tapping my fingers on the table and staring at them moving against the faux wood grain table top, sort of mesmerized by the rhythm, when Mack showed up and sat down.

"The stir-fry line was so long. And somebody tried to cook with the sesame oil, which didn't work too well."

I instinctively smiled at his presence. "They need instructions." I needed to figure out how to bring Rachel up. But I should probably not bombard him right away.

"They do."

I took another bite of my pizza and stared at Mack's plate, with a heaping pile of noodles and saucy vegetables, steam rolling off the top. He stuck a fork in, twisted it to wrap noodles around it, and brought it up to blow on it.

For some reason, I was fixated on his lips.

I didn't know what my deal was. I was distracted, but I also clearly had it bad for him. Staring at his lips? Get a grip.

I focused on my own greasy food.

"I'm glad I met you and Jenna this year," Mack announced. "I figured it would be another year of being pretty isolated."

"You didn't have friends last year?" I asked, genuinely surprised. I realized I shouldn't be, because he didn't seem to have any senior friends, but he was so easy-going and friendly, it was weird.

He laughed, a hint of bitterness to it. "Rachel."

It was like a pot of gold had been dropped at my feet.

I knew what I wanted to ask, but I couldn't go straight there. "Did she tell people not to be friends with you?"

"Kind of. People were a little weird when they found out

I was trans, but then she spread some rumors about me." He frowned, looking off into the distance for a moment.

I kind of wanted to ask what the rumors were, so I could hate Rachel more, but that might lead us down a rabbit hole away from what I really wanted to ask.

"How do you know her, anyway?"

He leaned back, looked up, and rolled his eyes toward the ceiling. "Oh, man. What a history."

I just took another bite of pizza and watched him as he brought his head back down and rested his elbows on the table. The place was bustling, people moving all around us. But it still felt like we were in our own bubble.

"So, our dads worked together at this oil company, even before we were born, in Houston. Our parents were really good friends." He had a faraway look in his eyes when he said this. "Then we came along, and then her younger brother, and we all grew up together. So that was before I really figured out who I was—I mean, I obviously always knew something was different, but honestly, I just kind of ignored gender. Thinking about it made me uncomfortable. My parents didn't obsess over gendered toys so I had all sorts, not just ones for girls. I was into Lego for a long time, and my parents stopped buying dolls when I was really young because I never played with them. I only played with super-gendered toys at Rachel's house. She had a huge collection of Barbies. So that's what she was referring to the other day."

Just the mention of that horrible moment, with my big, stupid mouth, made me sick to my stomach. I wanted to ask him when he came out, but he was already talking a lot more about himself than he usually did, so I didn't want to push my luck.

So I said, "Something changed?"

"Yeah, I mean, at that point I disliked dresses, but I could largely ignore what I was wearing as long as I wasn't restricted. Everything changed when I hit puberty, and that was when things became clearer in my head. I felt betrayed by my body, and that everything was wrong. I started dressing like a boy and my mom eventually didn't fight it, just bought me boys' clothes. It was surprising to me how much more comfortable I was in boys' clothes. I hadn't realized quite how *un*comfortable I'd been until I was comfortable."

I nodded. I also remembered when I started refusing to wear dresses.

"But that was when everything started changing with Rachel's family. They did not approve of the new me. Although our parents were friends, they were really different in one key way—Rachel's family is all Southern Baptist, and my parents are actually atheists. Even my mom, despite growing up in the Catholic Church."

"Wow. Do they talk about it with people?"

He snorted. "You know how well that goes down around here. So no. I mean, her parents knew they didn't go to church, but that's all they knew. But it's weird, because her parents weren't always that way—before we were around, they were always going out drinking and partying and stuff. But they got more religious after they had kids."

I interlaced my fingers, totally engrossed in this story.

"So when I came out, Rachel's parents flipped out. They couldn't believe my parents were 'letting' me do it." He made air quotes around the word. "They stopped hanging out, and I never saw Rachel except at school. She was a bitch to me there, making my life a hellscape when I was anywhere other than inside my house. My parents were pretty good about it, even though I think it still surprised them. They'd always assumed I was just a tomboy." Mack shrugged.

I nodded so he'd keep going.

"But Rachel's parents couldn't let it go. They reported my parents to the state under that new fucking law that says parents can't support their trans kids."

"Oh, my God! Are you serious?" I could feel how wide my eyes were. I hadn't even thought of that. "That's just evil."

Mack nodded, a pained look on his face. "In order to avoid prosecution and still allow me to continue the treatments I was doing, they had my mom's sister legally adopt me. She lives in southeast Oklahoma, so I ended up here. It's actually a lot easier on everyone for me to live near OKC, because the doctor isn't miles and miles away."

I was really rather speechless. How could anybody be so hateful? Rachel was being a total bully because of her own Baptist-branded hate.

"Anyway, I don't usually talk so much. Sorry." He looked down at the table, obviously feeling the weight of everything he'd shared.

"I'm glad you told me. I'm sorry that happened to you. I'm also glad that Oklahoma hasn't copied Texas with that law yet."

"Right? Give them time. But I'll be eighteen by then, so it won't matter for me, just all the other kids that come behind me." His face was pinched. "I hate them all. These asshole politicians who don't know shit about any of this."

"It's horrible. Why do people have to be like this?" I was worried for myself, too, if I ever came out as nonbinary. These people would hate me, too.

"I know. I mean, I hate politics, but it seems like so many conservative people think they should be entitled to decide how other people should live their lives, like there's only one way, and it's the one they like. And they're out to punish people who don't live like *they* want. All while claiming they are for freedom."

"I know. I've seen that punishment mentality myself, growing up in a small town and not performing my gender the way they want." It was so nice to be here, where there wasn't constant bullying like back at Emerson High.

"Yeah. People suck. And more liberal people are like, You do you. I'll just judge you quietly in my mind."

That made me laugh. "That's true. Everybody judges everybody, I think."

"Yeah, I think it's human nature. But what makes us civilized is choosing not to act on our lizard brain instincts."

I laughed at the lizard brain comment. "Still, I would have thought it would be better in a big city like Houston. I mean, it already seems better here."

"It was, but then Rachel went out of her way. Life's mission and so on."

I nodded, feeling bad for Mack, but also emboldened by the fact that he trusted me enough to tell me all this. It gave me minor stomach butterflies.

We finished eating, which meant I had the last bite of pizza while Mack had most of his stir-fry to work through.

I crossed my arms and kind of absent-mindedly watched him, feelings swirling. He'd hinted that he kind of liked me. Did the fact that he'd shared all of this with me have anything to do with that, or was it truly just friend-level sharing?

He put his fork down and said, "So anyway, I guess that's why Rachel is being a bitch to you. To punish you for not making the kind of friends she thinks you should, and also kind of to punish me."

"Yeah, I guess I'm going to have to figure out how to deal with her. I'm not great at conflict. It kind of shuts me down."

"Same."

"Maybe she'll get bored."

Mack had just taken another bite and his eyes widened as he smirked while chewing.

"Not likely, huh?" I asked.

He shook his head.

"I guess it's time to put on my big girl pants," I said. "Big person pants. Whatever."

Mack nodded.

So the situation for me with Rachel wasn't exactly improved, but at least I understood what was going on. And I knew Mack trusted me. And maybe he even liked me enough that something could happen?

Was that really possible, or was this yet another of my pipe dreams?

Mack and I left the cafeteria, ice cream in hand.

My mind was still spinning with everything he'd told me. I'd known Rachel was horrible, but I hadn't expected it to be that bad. How could she be so brainwashed by her parents that she couldn't just leave Mack alone? If she didn't want to be friends anymore, fine—but to intentionally hurt him was crazy to me. I felt so bad for Mack. I also felt hyped up and closer to him than I'd been to anybody other than Sam.

We stepped off the sidewalk into the parking lot, heading back to the dorm. I wondered how I could keep Mack to myself for a while longer. Would he go off on one of his walks? Would he let me go with him if I asked? I had to do something. We were well into the parking lot when I finally worked up the nerve. "Are you going to go for a walk?"

He looked over and scratched his chin. "You wanna go with me?"

It was like my heart lit up. So much so that I didn't trust myself to speak. I nodded.

"Let's go."

He veered sharply off to the right and we were heading for the edge of campus, basically in the direction of the public library.

My heart wouldn't calm down. This was a huge deal. I didn't even know what to think.

We crossed at the light, me trying so hard not to skip as I walked.

Did it mean something that we weren't talking? I glanced over at him just as he did the same.

Then he shared the same shy smile. "So you never gave me your opinion of Barbies. Was young Nic a fan of Barbies, or team Teenage Mutant Ninja Turtles?"

That made me laugh, even if I loved that he was interested in what I was like as a kid. "I was actually more about Lego. I had Barbies, but I wasn't sure what to do with them."

"I always made mine have what I thought of as adult conversations. 'Did you mop the bathroom, honey?' Or, 'Burp the baby.'"

"Mine talked about jobs. I was glad when I could be 'generous'"—I made air quotes for that—"and give them to my little sister."

"I forgot you had a little sister."

"I definitely do. She's awesome, even if she is a total princess kid. She's eleven."

"Cool." The corners of his eyes crinkled up from his

smile. "I always thought having a sibling would be nice. Like an automatic friend."

I snorted, thinking of Caleb.

"What?" Mack asked. "Is that not a thing?"

"My brother Caleb is one of the biggest assholes on the planet. He's a year younger than me, so he is always in my space, laughing as his friends make fun of me or whatever. His friend was the one who poured coffee on my drawing." Out of nowhere came a feeling of rage. That *asshole*. I would never not hate him for that.

"Okay then. Not automatic friends." He shrugged.

"Yeah, no." We were getting close to the dragon mailbox again.

"Clearly even fake siblinghood doesn't last, either. When we were pretty young, Rachel and I called each other sisters even though she had a younger brother."

"That must have felt like such a betrayal, when she turned on you. Someone you've known your whole life. That's how it was with my brother, too."

"Yeah. It did—does—suck. When we were in elementary school we were so close that we used to talk about always living next door to each other when we were grown up." He had a small frown on his face.

I hated what Caleb had turned into. We had been great friends all the way up to middle school, when he figured out how uncool I was. "My brother regards me as a problem for his social life. He had to make it clear to all his friends—and everyone else—that he had nothing to do with me, so he just became this bully whenever anyone else was watching. The first time he did it, I was so shocked. We'd always been close before that."

"It's weird with it being family. Like with me and Rachel, once I'm away from her, I can avoid seeing her again. But your brother will always be your brother. That sounds pretty terrible."

He was so right. "Yeah, I don't know what will end up happening. My parents are so mad at him. He's just kind of a giant piece of shit right now. I'm not sure I'll ever forgive him."

The mailbox was at the next house and I couldn't help remembering the three of us taking that selfie. I couldn't believe how things were turning out here. How I was having a real social life, however small.

Mack knew I liked him and he was really letting me in. I wished I knew what that meant. But maybe I'd be finding out.

He looked over and grinned as we reached the dragon. "I will never not love this thing." He rested his hand on the snout as we passed it.

"I know. Jenna and I were dying—in the good way—when we first saw it."

"I very much prefer the good way of dying," he teased.

I laughed. "Yeah, of course."

We kept trudging along, accompanied by the sound of our shoes crunching acorns on the sidewalk. It was still hot, even though the sun was getting lower. The houses started getting further apart, and then we turned left.

"I'm going to show you a place I like to go," Mack said.

"Really? I thought you just walked."

"I do, but sometimes I need to get away, and stay there for a while."

This was going to be amazing. He wasn't just letting me in emotionally, he was sharing a kind of secret. I could barely keep the excitement in my chest.

After two more blocks, we turned right. We were still in the middle of the neighborhood, an old one with lots of giant oak trees. They did offer some shade, but the heat was everywhere. I sort of tuned into things more and started hearing birds, and the leaves rustling in the wind.

It was a little odd. I was usually in my head so much and kind of ignored the outside world. Probably because it had people in it that made me uncomfortable.

Three blocks later, there was a green space with a short brown fence separating it from the sidewalk. We walked through an opening in the fence, and I could see that it was a simple park, with a swing set in one corner. The rest was grass, lined with trees.

"This way," Mack said.

Curiosity piqued, I followed him across the park and onto a skinny dirt path in the back that I could only see when we reached it. We emerged from the trees into another, smaller, grassy area.

Mack stopped and I looked around some more. There didn't seem to be anything special about the area. I looked up, and although it was framed by trees, there was a clear view of the sky, which was less bright already. The birds were even more noticeable here.

"We're early, but this is a great place to watch the stars. Or just the sky in general."

I followed Mack's lead and lay down on the grass. I struggled to figure out where I should be, in relation to him, and ended up about an arm's length away from him. It seemed not too close, but still close enough for people who are friends.

I was guessing. Sam and I had never done anything like this.

But then I remembered that we sort of had—we would sometimes lie on her bed next to each other and talk. The difference was that I wasn't attracted to her.

This realization felt significant. I had never been entirely sure, always wondering if my attachment to her was more than a friendship. But given how I was feeling right now, that was all it was. Because being with Mack felt completely different.

Mack didn't say anything, so I just watched the sky as clouds shifted and everything got darker. Birds flew from one of the trees bordering the space to another one. A plane flew overhead, high above us. The scent of the grass was all around me, that fresh, very green smell I didn't spend a lot of time with.

"Isn't it peaceful?" he asked quietly.

I could feel him looking at me, so I turned. He was smiling, looking tranquil.

"Yeah. Is this what you do when you're gone?" My stomach was jumpy, since I still didn't really know what was going on, but Mack showing me this place was a huge deal.

"I mostly walk, but sometimes I come here when I have a need-to-chill emergency."

After he said that, I panicked and looked back at the sky. It had finally gotten dark enough that the stars were visible. And now the crickets were out, making their racket.

"Are you experiencing a need-to-chill emergency now?" I asked.

"Nope. I just wanted to show you."

This struck a chord deep inside. So many things were popping into my head—wanting to tell him how much I liked him, asking more questions about what it's like to transition—but I was kind of confused and didn't want to ruin whatever this was. "I love it," I finally said.

"Do you know the constellations?" Mack asked.

"No, I never spend time outside." I laughed—louder

than I meant to—because it suddenly seemed weird to not know any constellations.

"Me neither, so I mostly make stuff up. I do know a few, including Orion and Draco, though."

"Where are those?" I asked. I'd at least heard of them.

"Only Draco—the dragon—is visible right now." He explained where to look until I could see it. I'd never noticed it before, but there was something enchanting about stars. Imagine living in a time where you had no idea what they were. It must have really felt magical, when all you knew was that, whatever they were, you couldn't touch them. I would never forget this constellation now.

"What are some of the others you've come up with?" I asked. I really wanted to know. What was this going to tell me about Mack?

"I've done this since I was little, so some are really dumb. But I found a mouse eating cheese over there." He gave me the reference point and the other stars and explained the shape, but I couldn't see it.

He scooted over until our shoulders were touching, which sent a shiver through me and got my crazy heart going again. But this way he could point more easily, even though my brain still wasn't working and I struggled to see it. I pretended I could, after a while, because I didn't know what else to do.

Then he showed me a woman laughing. He pointed and explained, and I could smell his soap, even over the scent of the grass. This one I eventually could see.

"Why is it a woman?" I asked. It was basically a person with an open mouth.

"Eh, probably because I was young and my mom laughed a lot more than my dad. He's cool, but doesn't have much of a sense of humor."

"Makes sense." It was weird how different moms and dads could be. Most dads weren't as involved. Or maybe moms were just more like control freaks. Mine wasn't bad, but Sam's was pretty annoying.

There was silence for a time, where the sounds of nature were all I could hear, and I looked at the stars some more to see if I could find anything myself. My spinning brain was not able to focus on the sky.

I pushed off a mosquito that had landed on my arm. I did not like this part of the outdoors, but I would brave the bugs to spend time with Mack.

"So, I gave you my story. What's yours?" He quickly added, "If you want to tell me. You don't have to."

I couldn't believe he wanted to know. I couldn't be wrong about how close we were getting. Both physically and emotionally.

"Well, where to begin?" I said, stalling because I didn't know what he was looking for.

"Start at the beginning," he joked.

I laughed. "Well, I've always struggled socially. I didn't seem to understand how things were supposed to work in the social world. And I've always been fat, and also taller than everyone—including most of the middle school teachers—until eighth grade. So I was a target. And I didn't know how to stand up for myself."

I paused. Was this what he was curious about? I looked over at him. He sensed it and turned to face me.

"But I guess it was middle school when things got really bad, because it was becoming more obvious that I wasn't doing 'girl' the way everybody wanted. The older you get, the less tolerant they are of tomboys."

"That's the truth," Mack said. "Did you ever think you were a boy?"

That cut right to the chase. "Not really. I was annoyed at the high expectations for girls and constant excuses for boys, but I never wanted to be one. But I didn't feel like I was a girl, either. That became really clear last year. There was an incident where I let these two girls give me a makeover, and I completely freaked out, I hated it so much. Like *really* hated it." I shuddered and glanced away, reliving that night. "And they posted it to social media so I was harassed about it at school for a while."

"Why did it bother you so much?" Mack asked.

We were still looking at each other, and normally I would be uncomfortable with eye contact for this long, but it felt nice here.

"I guess because it felt so inherently wrong. It's such an obviously girl thing to wear makeup to try to make yourself look like everybody else." I closed my eyes, remembering the horror of the makeover night, being paraded in front of all our drunk parents. "It was like I was going against my very nature. I've never liked girly stuff."

"So what did you do after that?"

"I started googling things. They always called me an ugly lesbian at school, and I was so confused about it all. I liked boys, but I still wasn't sure I wasn't trans. Gender nonconforming seemed to fit. It felt distinct from being nonbinary, the way I understood it, and I wasn't ready to go for that. I mean, they would have tortured me for it. I wasn't brave enough." Disappointment in myself rushed in. I was lying next to someone who had been much braver than me. He'd also suffered for it, but he probably felt more comfortable in his own skin than I did. I doubted he was confused like me.

"It's difficult," Mack said slowly, finally looking back at the sky, so I did the same. "Houston seemed like a decent place to come out, big enough and so on. But it wasn't. So I can imagine how that would have been in a small town here. They probably still would have called you a lesbian, and possibly 'it.' And maybe a devil-worshipper, too."

That made me laugh despite the fact that I was open and raw. "Yeah, I didn't even tell anyone, except my friend Sam." I remembered what Sam had said about being vulnerable. I was doing that here. I still couldn't believe how much I had shared with him.

"It would probably be safer here than where you were," Mack pointed out. Then his voice got sharp. "The real problem for me was that fucking law, not most people."

"Yeah. That law is horrible. But figuring out how to really identify has been on my mind a lot lately." I was jittery thinking about this. Why was it so hard to know yourself?

"I actually found a couple books—well, my mom found them for me—that helped me figure things out. There was one about being trans and one about being nonbinary. They're like workbooks, so I can't loan you mine, but I can give you the link." He pulled out his phone and soon mine dinged. "I sent you the nonbinary one."

"Cool. Thanks." The text came through and I looked at it. The book sounded great. Maybe it could really help me figure things out. I thought about getting my mom to order it for me, but I didn't want her to know anything yet. I had a little money in the bank that I could use.

"You should think about it. A lot of the students here don't really care. You don't have a Rachel. How would your family be about it? Other than your asshole brother."

I wasn't 100% sure about that. I thought Mom would be fine, and Dad probably wouldn't really care one way or another. Isabella I wasn't worried about. She'd be fine, but would probably ask a bunch of questions. Caleb would be Caleb.

"I think they'd be fine," I finally said.

"Well, you should think about it. The outside world isn't the most important thing. I mean, it matters and you have to think about it, and consider your safety, but it's most important to be true to yourself."

"Yeah." Now my mind was spinning like crazy again. I could still feel the warm spot where our shoulders were touching. Too much was happening.

We were quiet. I stared at the stars some more, trying to focus and see shapes, so when Mack reached over and squeezed my hand, it sent a shockwave through me. And he left his hand there.

He was *holding my hand*. My heart was exploding. I didn't even know what to do. Finally, my brain started working again and I squeezed his hand back.

We lay like that, still not saying anything.

I actually wanted to check the time on my phone. I was feeling like something had to go wrong, because too much was going right. But I had put it back in my right pocket after looking at the book, and my right hand was currently occupied.

This was an awesome problem to have. But still, I didn't want to get in trouble.

"Mack?" I finally said.

"Yeah?" He didn't let go of my hand and I was still up in the invisible clouds.

"Do you know what time it is?"

He laughed. "I have a pretty good internal clock. We've got time." But I could hear him pulling his phone out of his own pocket.

"Huh, it's later than I thought. We should get going. It's eight ten."

"Oh, wow. I didn't think it was that late."

We let go at the same time and sat up.

"We might have to truck it a bit," Mack said.

Truck it, we did. We went through the dorm's front door at eight twenty-nine.

"Barely made it, guys," the desk RA said.

Mack touched my shoulder. "See you later."

"Yeah." We stared at each other for a second, both smiling.

"You guys need to get studying," the RA said.

We both glanced at him, and I headed toward the stairs as Mack went down the hall.

This was the first day of my radically changed life. I'd *held a boy's hand*. What else was going to happen?

I woke up early the next morning, instantly happy. I couldn't believe what had happened. For the rest of the night after I got back to my room, I'd felt high. Or at least what I thought feeling high would be like.

I still didn't know what it meant, but I didn't think it was simple, normal friendship hand-holding.

I was giddy all morning, in the shower, in class, in the hall going from one class to the next. I didn't see Jenna or Mack, and I didn't know which one I wanted to see first. I was bursting to tell Jenna and see what she thought. But obviously I wanted to see Mack again.

I was still happy when I got to art class. The room was empty, so I assumed Ms. Mangal was in the back. I had beaten everyone else there and was standing in front of my chair when Rachel came in with Lily and Emily. My hackles went up the second I saw Rachel. She was a monster. And I worried that she would somehow know what happened with Mack last night and harass me.

Which was stupid. Nobody knew except me and Mack.

She stopped next to my table while Lily and Emily sat down at one of the front tables, engrossed in a conversation. Rachel held her head high like she was thinking about how great she was. Then she looked at me, totally down her nose.

"Are you trying for the mentorship?" she asked.

I panicked. What was she going to say about this?

"Yes," I said carefully.

She looked toward the back room, presumably to make sure Ms. Mangal was still out of earshot. "You know you don't have a chance, right? Lily's better than you and she's a senior."

I felt queasy. I didn't care what she thought, personally, but she was probably right. But I had no idea what to say, so I just took my sketchbook out, dropped my backpack on the floor, and sat down.

But Rachel wasn't done. "They're not going to take two people from OAMS." She looked at Lily, who was laughing at something with Emil. "Isn't that right, Lily?" Rachel said loud enough for her to hear.

Lily looked back, still smiling. "Oh, definitely."

Had they planned this?

Rachel gave me a smug smile and went to her seat.

A minute later, Jacob arrived and took his seat. We accidentally made eye contact before we both looked down. We still had never spoken, except for those muttered sorries in physics the first day. I was still awkward. Even if I thought things had changed. I would never not be awkward. I hated being me.

Ms. Mangal came out of the back and greeted us all, making me feel better. It was nice to have some people on my side. Although she never really showed it in an obvious way, I knew Ms. Mangal saw through Rachel. And I suspected most art teachers liked the more serious art students better than the dabblers or easy-A-ers.

There was a burst of laughter and I turned to see the rest of the students coming through the door.

I looked over at Lily, and my gut twisted. Rachel was right. Should I even bother applying?

We got started on our work and Ms. Mangal made the rounds. Of course, I was having trouble focusing because I kept thinking about Mack. When Ms. Mangal got to me, I was dying to ask her about the mentorship, but it had gotten quiet and I didn't want Rachel or Lily to hear.

I worked on the dragon drawing for the mural, trying different configurations for one in flight. Then I made some progress on the nursery drawing, despite my wandering focus, and eventually time was up.

My heart lurched Thursday after classes when I came in the front door of the dorm after classes. Mack was passing by, a sparkling water in his hand that was presumably from his fridge in the main lounge. He saw me and I swear his whole face lit up and his eyes looked brighter than normal.

"Hey!" he said as he stopped.

"Hi." I knew I had a stupid look on my face and I didn't even care.

"I'm going to skip dinner tonight because I've got a paper

due tomorrow that I've been seriously avoiding." Okay, he was also grinning stupidly. "So I'm going to be holed up in my room. See you tomorrow?"

Disappointment burned through me. That sucked. But he wasn't happy about it, either. "Oh, okay. Jenna and I will miss you."

"Heh. You'll do fine without me."

I laughed nervously, wondering if he knew we were going to spend the whole dinner talking about him and analyzing last night's events. Because that was what was going to happen.

He was still smiling. "Well, I'd better get to it."

I nodded. "Later."

We went our separate ways but maintained eye contact until I was in the stairwell, where I took the stairs two at a time because I was so energized by seeing him.

Once in my room, I flopped down on the bed, butterflies going wild in my stomach. Sophia was packing her big backpack.

"Are you okay?" She kind of looked at me sideways as she pulled out her duffel.

That was weird. She almost never talked to me. "Why?"

"I don't know, you're lying around, and you look different somehow." She loaded some of her textbooks into the duffel.

"I'm good. Thanks." I was curious enough about why she was packing her bag on a Thursday night. "Are you going home?"

"Okay. Yeah, I have a doctor's appointment tomorrow." She zipped up the duffel and was out of the room with a trailing "See ya."

I could lie around and daydream as much as I wanted tonight.

But now I didn't feel like that. I got up and sat at my desk. I pulled out my pencils and sketchbook and started roughing out more ideas for the mural dragon. It needed to be cartoony, so not a lot of detail. At this point, I basically just needed a line drawing. I had a few ideas but the best one was a dragon in flight, chubby around the middle rather than all sharp edges, in order to get the cartoon effect. I'd work on this more later, but it was at least a starting point.

Then I wanted to do something more personal. I googled until I found a nice image of a couple of people holding hands, and then a zoomed-in shot of the hands. So I sketched that out, remembering what it felt like—it was like nothing I'd ever experienced before. I really thought he liked me. I still couldn't believe it.

And oh, my God, I wanted to talk to Jenna about it. Because I needed to know if I should do something next, or wait and see what he did. There was still that tiny doubt, that we were just close friends, not that he wasn't interested in going out.

I couldn't believe I was actually thinking I could soon be going out with somebody. This was way more promising than it had ever been with Zack back in Emerson. All those times he'd stared at me in the rearview mirror had me and Sam both convinced he liked me, but then he went and asked her out. And because I'd never told her I liked him—I was way too guarded, even with my best friend—she'd said yes. It had been so horrible, I'd thought I was going to die. I'd wanted to.

I wondered what Zack was up to now. Leading on some other innocent girl?

But this was different. This wasn't just looks, or even only words—this was actual touch.

I was dizzy from thinking about it.

I looked back at the drawing and started filling in the details on the hands. One of them was wearing a charm bracelet, so I was detailing that, doing one charm at a time. There was a cat, a butterfly, a chess piece, an elephant, and a cow. The random combination made me laugh as I worked on shading the elephant.

What was Mack doing right now? I wished I'd asked him what class the paper was for. I wanted to know if he was thinking about a book, or a historical event, or whatever.

I really needed to ask more questions about other people's lives. I almost never did. I was kind of self-absorbed. It was embarrassing to think about, but I couldn't just snap my fingers and be different.

Right now, I really wanted to know if Mack was thinking about me. Was he having trouble focusing?

I hoped so. Because I was. My cheeks were hurting from smiling so much. I told myself to stop staring dreamily at my bookshelf and to get back to the drawing. I was going to work on the fingernails next.

Mack had short fingernails. I knew this because I'd actually *felt his hand last night*.

It was unbelievable. And I had a feeling it was only going to get better.

～

Jenna and I left the dorm right after five, and I was totally bouncing on my feet. I didn't know how to start.

"Chang fell asleep in English today," Jenna said. "I was so offended for Ms. Kaur."

"That's rude," I absently said. How could I bring it up?

We stepped off the curb into the parking lot.

"I know. And in English? I don't understand people who don't like reading."

"Yeah." I was thinking about Mack's hand, and staring at the sky, and how awesome that all was.

"Earth to Nic." She waved a hand in front of my face.

I couldn't stop myself. "Mack took me to his secret hiding place last night and we held hands!"

"Oh, my God, really?" She turned to me wide-eyed.

"Yes!" I quieted my voice. "Sorry. I don't mean to be so excited."

"Don't apologize. That's awesome." She sounded genuinely excited for me. "Who took whose hand first?"

"He did."

"So what happened?"

We were halfway across the parking lot, heat pouring off the cars as we passed them. "So, after dinner, he basically invited me to go on a walk with him. He said he really does just walk most of the time, but he has this cool spot in a park he sometimes goes to. It was past the library and down another road. But we got there, and there's a small opening in the trees and brush at the back of the park, and we went through there and there was a clearing. I really think most people don't know it's there." And now *I* was one of the few who did. It felt amazing. "He said we should lie there and stare at the stars."

"That's great. Staring at the stars together is so romantic."

I laughed, because obviously it was. And it made me so happy. I continued giving her all the details. I was at the part where he was talking about the books about gender that he told me about when we scanned into the cafeteria. I'd ordered it, so now I'd be checking my mailbox every day.

"I want to hear everything else," she said. "But I'm starving. Let's meet back up."

I didn't want to have to make any decisions, so I headed over to the pizza section and got a couple slices of pepperoni.

I grabbed a Coke from the fountain and sat at our normal table. My leg was bouncing so much that I hit the bottom of the table and my Coke almost fell over. I caught it and some spilled on my hand, and Jenna appeared right as I was stupidly licking the side of my hand to get the Coke off it. So, obviously, I felt like an idiot, but it didn't stop me from launching into the rest of the story.

After I finished, she said, "I think this is all very good. He must really like you. Not that I'm an expert. I've never held anybody's hand before." She laughed. "Well, my mom's. You know."

I nodded, still grinning, and picked up a slice of pizza that was already getting cold.

She wiped her bowl of broccoli cheese soup clean with a piece of bread and started in on a salad that looked good. It had chickpeas and lots of green peppers.

"I should ask how you are," I said. "I forgot how to be a person because I was so excited. Sorry."

She laughed. "No, I get it. We see each other all the time, anyway. Nothing exciting has happened in my life since I saw you last, which is fine. I'm too busy to worry about extra stuff."

"Yeah. That's true. I'm just going to have to figure out how to make time."

She nodded as she worked on her salad.

But I wasn't done, after all. "So even with all that's happened, I don't know what to do next. Should I do something, or see what Mack does next?"

She rocked her head back and forth while finishing her mouthful of salad. "If I were you, I'd wait for Mack. Because I wouldn't be quite one hundred percent convinced I was interpreting things right. But if you are, maybe you could do something."

I grimaced. She was right. "Yeah, I am not that confident. I don't want to mess things up."

"So I guess you should make yourself available and be enthusiastic about any move he makes, or suggestion, or whatever."

I nodded. What kind of move might he make? Would I freeze up? I was still weird about touch, although hands were clearly fine.

"I think I'm kind of freaked out." I took a bite of my pizza, imagining things. Would he try to kiss me? What if he did? What if he did it in front of other people? I probably wouldn't like that.

Oh, my God. There were so many unknowns here. I was stressing out. I had to stop my leg from bouncing again.

Jenna looked at me and smiled. "It will be fine. It will be great."

I flushed, embarrassed that she read my mind so easily. "I hope so. I just don't *know* so."

At the beginning of art class the next day, Ms. Mangal talked some more about the mentorship. "Who's interested in applying?" she asked the room.

Lily and I raised our hands, but then Rachel looked back at me and arched her eyebrows, which made me drop my arm.

Dammit. I didn't know what to do. Why did I never

know what to do? Other people didn't seem to have this problem.

"Everyone get started on your work. I'm going to print a packet of information about applying for the mentorship for those of you who are interested."

I got to work on my dragon in the nursery drawing. I'd made a lot of progress on it. I was proud of it. I may not know crap about boys, but at least I knew art.

I'd finished the bassinets a week ago, and since then I'd drawn the front windows—it was like someone was looking into the room from the other side of the glass. And I'd drawn the background, with some big machine—I didn't know what it was, but it gave the image some authenticity. Then there was a desk, and I'd added a nurse sitting there, watching the dragon, which I'd also drawn, in the front right as planned. This was all done fairly lightly in pencil, because I was going to go over it all in pen.

But first I needed to start adding the details. I was working on the dragon's scales when Ms. Mangal showed up with a packet of papers.

"Here you go, Nic."

"Oh. Thanks." I took them even though I wasn't going to fill them out. There was no point. But I didn't want to tell her that. I didn't know what she'd say.

"Just have a look through everything and let me know if you have any questions. It's due November first." She smiled at me, making me feel even guiltier about not telling her I wasn't applying.

"Okay." I smiled awkwardly. She didn't need to know yet.

I got back to work on the dragon scales. And then I realized I hadn't thought of Mack for the last ten minutes. It was amazing.

But it was only because I was so torn about the mentorship application. It was a distraction.

And now that I was thinking about him again, there was no stopping it. I hoped he'd be able to have dinner tonight. I was curious how Jenna was going to act around us. I hoped she wouldn't reveal anything about our conversation. I didn't think she would on purpose, but she might say something accidentally.

But what could she really say? He already knew I liked him. I didn't need to worry. Besides, Jenna was not a blabbermouth.

I was staring at the wall behind Ms. Mangal's desk. I shook my head to clear it, and looked back at the drawing. What else could I do to make this interesting?

It needed to be good. Everything I did for the next two years had to be good, because I had to get into a good art school, and I'd need a strong portfolio to do it.

I remembered the charm bracelet I'd sketched yesterday. I should give the dragon a charm bracelet. That would be interesting.

What sort of charms should it have? A dragon egg, for sure. Probably a baby (a human one, that is). Maybe a book.

Mack liked books, I thought. Just like me. What was he doing right now? I didn't know his schedule by heart. How could I find out?

I tapped my pencil while I was thinking, and Jacob looked over.

"Sorry," I muttered.

"It's okay." He said it so quietly I barely heard.

But then we both realized something at the same time.

"We just talked," I whispered. This felt like a major breakthrough, but also ridiculous.

He smiled, which made his eyes scrunch up. He obviously thought it was funny, too. "Yeah."

And then we both looked away, but a milestone had been achieved.

I glanced at what he was working on. It was a superhero of some type, but I didn't recognize it. It looked like a battle scene, but I couldn't quite see what the superhero was battling.

I'd see the final version when we did our critiques.

I looked back at my paper.

I still had to figure out what the other charms should be.

A stethoscope! That was perfect.

I was on my way with this drawing. I just had to not mess it up when I was working in pen. I believed in myself in this.

Even if things didn't work out with Mack the way I hoped, at least I could still draw. But I had a good feeling.

Friday night, Mack was able to make it to dinner, and he, Jenna, and I left the cafeteria after a long discussion of the second Broken Earth Trilogy book. I was a bit behind, but we had more than a week before the next book club meeting, so I'd be good.

Being around Mack was hard. My stomach was in a constant state of heightened butterfly activity.

"I have found the book we should read next," Jenna announced as we neared the parking lot. "Or after the third book."

"What?" Mack asked, eyebrows raised slightly. Today he had on a blue t-shirt with a TARDIS on it.

"It's called *The Black Tides of Heaven*, and it's by a nonbinary author named Neon Yang. It's also the first in a series, and it's pretty short, which is a plus for busy students like us."

"Fantasy or sci-fi?" Mack asked.

We stepped into the parking lot, full of cars like usual.

"Fantasy, I think," she said. "But Yang used to be a molecular biologist, so they've got a great perspective. Maybe there's some actual science, too. I don't know."

"I like the short part," I said, and they both laughed.

Jenna nodded. "Yeah. It will be a nice break."

She wasn't being weird around Mack like I had been worried about. She was much more emotionally in control than I ever was.

We'd sort of spread out walking, and I'd fallen a tiny bit behind Jenna. Mack waited a second and then he was next to me and taking my hand.

My heart nearly exploded. Our fingers intertwined. This was even better than I remembered.

We'd fallen far enough back that Jenna turned around. When she saw us, she smiled and turned back around.

"Are all the books in the series out?" Mack asked. It was good that he was speaking because I'd lost the ability. The fact that I could even understand him was an achievement. My mind was scattered.

"Yeah. There are four books. It's been called silkpunk, which sounds cool."

"Nice," Mack said. "Does that mean it pulls from East Asian history and lore?"

I couldn't get over this. We were *in public*. Other people could see us.

And I was okay with this.

"I think so," Jenna said. I hardly paid any attention while she talked more about what she'd heard about the author.

We had to weave between the cars, which meant Mack and I had to turn sideways in order to keep holding hands, but we did and that was also great.

My stomach was still jumping all over the place when we got back to the dorm, still holding hands. A few people spotted us and did double takes, but it was nobody I really knew well or anything. We all headed into the lounge to see what was on TV.

There was nowhere to sit, and they were watching some reality show, so not my thing. But all of those people were seeing us holding hands.

I was starting to feel weird, though. I wasn't sure I was entirely comfortable with everyone seeing us together, all of us in this small space.

"Guys, I think I'm going to go upstairs and read," Jenna said, yawning. "If I don't fall asleep first."

But then I had a thought. My brain was finally functioning again. "Before you go—do you guys want to meet up to study at the library or Booth Forest this weekend?"

"Sure, I'd be up for that," Jenna said as Mack nodded. "Sunday? I have some stuff I want to do tomorrow."

"Sounds good to me," Mack said. "Two o'clock? Then we can get dinner after?"

"Sounds perfect." Jenna waved and disappeared up the stairs.

That left just me and Mack. He said, "I should go to my room, too. I do have some stuff to do tonight, otherwise my weekend will be too busy."

My heart sank, but I knew it wasn't personal. We couldn't go to his room, and the only lounge we could use was full, and I was still uncomfortable with the PDA inside our own dorm. So I nodded. "Okay."

"Lunch tomorrow?" he asked.

We picked a time and I said I'd text Jenna, and we walked back toward the stairs up to my room. When we got there, we smiled at each other for a while—he had really dark eyelashes—until the front desk RA cleared her throat. We both glanced over as she glared at us, then instinctively dropped our hands at the same time.

"See you tomorrow, then," Mack said. He sounded excited by the prospect.

"Yeah. See you." I headed upstairs, the stomach butterflies coming right along with me.

I was so glad Sophia wasn't there. I could lounge in private and think whatever thoughts I wanted.

I was looking forward to dreaming some more, to see if those could come true, too.

Saturday morning, Jenna was doing something and decided to skip lunch, so it was just Mack and me. I didn't know if she was leaving us alone on purpose, or if she really had something to do. I felt guilty about how happy I was we were going to be alone, because I didn't want to be one of those people who abandoned their friends for a boy.

I tried to forget about that and waited patiently near the front door, staring at the hall Mack would come out of.

"Hey," he said, suddenly appearing in my view.

I started. "Ack." He'd come from the opposite direction, where the fridges were.

Mack laughed. "I was seeing how much water I had left. I need to get some more."

"Okay." My heart was beating faster from the surprise, and it didn't slow down because now we were going to be walking together and I wondered if he'd take my hand.

"Let's go," he said, pushing the door open, letting some of the heat in. I followed him out, immediately roasting.

"Are you starving? Do you want to go for a walk first?"

I wasn't starving, except for more time with Mack. "A walk sounds great."

He glanced over at me. "Do you have on sunscreen?"

I laughed. "Okay, *Mom*. Sometimes I do remember to put it on in the morning. Today was one of those days."

He chuckled and headed right at the sidewalk instead of his normal left.

"This is a change," I said.

"Yeah, there's some cool houses this way. No dragon mailboxes, though."

"Oh, too bad." I didn't really care. It was time with Mack. The trees that were scattered along the street moved in the mild wind, the rustling sound providing a now common backdrop for my time with Mack.

He hadn't taken my hand yet. Did I have the nerve to grab his hand myself? I absentmindedly wiggled my fingers, as if warming up.

No, I did not. Not yet.

"I assume you seen the sundial," Mack said.

"The giant one over by the library?"

"Yeah. That's the one." He looked over at me and we made eye contact. I forced myself to not look away and it was one of the hardest things I'd done in a while. It was terrifying and exciting at the same time. It felt so intense.

I finally broke the contact and so I could formulate words and answer. "Jenna and I saw it on the campus tour Ms. Patton took us on."

"I really like that thing, for some reason. Actually, I know why." He looked back at me.

"Why?"

"I like thinking about early scientist types. Like Archimedes and Newton and Darwin and those guys. And how their tools were rudimentary but they still managed to make so many discoveries and stuff." He shrugged, maybe feeling self-conscious at the kind of nerdy admission.

But I didn't think it was nerdy at all. "I can relate, actually. I love Leonardo da Vinci, myself. He was an inventor and a scientist, and on top of all that, an amazing artist."

We were approaching the gym, one of the many buildings I had never visited since the tour. Some guys emerged and started walking toward us.

"Definitely," Mack answered. "One of the things I like to think about is what they would have done if they'd lived now. Science has gotten weird because now there is so much to know and it takes forever to learn it all, and people have to specialize so much. Not so in the old days, when they all did everything. Even if it was crazy. Back then, health care was still based on humors or whatever."

I laughed. "And using leeches to bleed you to health. Oh, my God. When I first heard about that, I freaked out. I'm so glad we don't live then."

"No joke."

The guys from the gym passed us and one said, "Freaks."

God, I was never ready for that crap.

"Assholes," Mack muttered.

Then he sped up even more. He already walked faster than I normally did on my own, so it was a bit of an effort to keep up with him. Unfortunately, it made me sweat even more than the heat alone did.

I wanted to hold his hand more than anything. I didn't know where the urge came from, but it was stronger than my fear.

Screw those assholes.

I reached over and our hands bumped—I had the angle totally wrong—and there was this awkward fumbling, but eventually we were holding hands again.

"That was smooth, Nic," he teased.

I flushed, but it still made me laugh because I knew he wasn't being mean. "Maybe we should practice more."

Where had that come from? Was that flirting? Oh, my God. Who was I?

"Perhaps," he said, his smile in his voice.

We turned toward the library. I was still thinking about the fumbling, but I couldn't get over how good it felt to hold someone's hand. His was warm, and he was gripping my hand firmly. Not tight, just comfortably firm, like he meant it. I guessed it was like a handshake. I once shook someone's hand and it was limp, and it was a terrible experience. You wanted some firmness there. This was the same.

Man, I was rambling. It was good that it was only in my head.

We soon got to the sundial and stopped to look at it. Or Mack was looking at it—studying it, really.

"How long has this been here?" I asked.

"I don't think it was ever used for real," Mack teased, squeezing my hand.

Which made my heart squeeze in sync. But I recovered quickly. "Ha."

"Let's see if we can find a date." He moved over to the right, dragging me by the hand.

We stopped at a small stand with a plaque.

He pointed to a spot on the bottom: 1982.

"I think that's the year my mom was born," Mack said.

"My parents were around there, too."

"I still think it's cool," Mack said.

I looked closely at the thing. It was about ten feet in diameter, and the part that sticks up was, like, four feet tall.

"Okay, enough of this," Mack said. "Let's go."

We continued north until we were off campus and in an old neighborhood I'd never been to before. Pretty much as soon as we entered, there were so many trees that you could hardly see the sky. The intensity of the heat was slightly calmed under them.

"I love these houses," Mack said wistfully. "They feel cozy. Like you could imagine being in there on a crisp fall day, reading a book and watching the leaves fall out of the corner of your eye. But watch the sidewalk."

I looked down and saw that it was uneven, even in the distance, corners sticking up and so on. And then there were the cracks.

"How's the mentorship application going?" Mack asked.

I frowned in disappointment at the thought. "I don't think I'm going to apply. Lily's applying, and she's better and a senior. I doubt they'll take two people from here, so it seems like a waste of time to apply."

"What?" He looked over at me. "That's crazy. You should still apply."

I avoided his gaze. "I don't know. It's pretty involved. You have to write two different things and prepare a portfolio."

"I think you should do it."

"Maybe." I still didn't think I would. Rachel might be a horrible person, but I thought she was right about this.

We walked in silence, swinging our joined hands. It was hard to say exactly how I felt. Comfortable, wanted and valued, understood.

There were big trees and smaller houses that seemed to be nestled amongst all the greenery. The heat was a contrast, but still, Mack was right—it felt cozy. I wondered if that's how my life would be when I was grown up. Would I buy a little house like that? Would I suddenly develop an interest in gardening?

Would Mack still be in my life?

I had no idea what the future held, but for the first time in a long time, I felt good about it.

～

"I'm so dreading this physics test," Jenna said, swinging her sticker-covered purple water bottle as we trudged along in the heat on Sunday.

"Yeah, same here," I said.

We were meeting Mack, who was out walking.

Jenna sighed and adjusted her backpack. She had a new patch on it, a heart-shaped view of a bookshelf. "I actually feel like I'm learning stuff, I just don't think I know it well enough for a test."

"I know. Like, doing the homework is fine. But keeping it all in your head is another matter."

"What are you working on?" Jenna asked as the doors slid open and we passed the threshold into the air conditioning.

"Pre-calc, physics, and I have to do some reading for history."

"I'm all about the physics today." She played with the loose straps of her backpack as we got to the elevators.

I was hoping to get enough done here so I could spend some time with the gender identity workbook that had arrived yesterday. I hadn't started it last night, other than doing a really quick flip through.

"So, random question," I said. "I've been wondering. Did it hurt getting your nose ring?"

Jenna smiled. "I wish I could say I was totally stoic. But yeah, it hurt, and I instantly had that about-to-pass-out feeling, so the lady had me lie back. I didn't pass out, though. Thank God. I would have never heard the end of it from my brother if I had."

I grimaced. "I'd probably be a total wimp."

"Are you thinking of getting one?"

"No, I'm not cool enough for that. I like yours, though."

"I think it's the nose ring that *makes* a person cool," she said quietly, like she was passing along a trade secret. But she was smirking at the same time.

It made me laugh.

Then she yawned, which made me yawn, and we both laughed right as the doors of one of the elevators opened.

Some college girls—perfectly made up despite the fact that it was Sunday afternoon—stepped out. We got in and I pressed the third floor button.

"Are you excited to be seeing Mack again?" Jenna teased, bumping my elbow.

I, of course, blushed. "Yeah."

"I'm glad it's working out. I think it's good for both of you."

I was still blushing furiously and couldn't think of anything to say. I glanced over and she was grinning at me, which made me smile back.

The elevator made a small ding as it stopped, and the door opened.

My face still hadn't cooled off by the time we saw Mack at a table near the back of the open area, which made it worse because that was embarrassing.

He looked up and saw us and waved, a big smile on his face.

Almost of its own volition, my mouth went into a smile of its own.

"He's happy to see you," Jenna said quietly, leaning close to me. I still couldn't answer, but it did seem that way.

He was still smiling when we got to the table, a light faux-wood four-seater, and I sat down in the chair next to him. Jenna sat across from me.

"Hey, guys," he said, looking first at Jenna and then settling on me.

We grinned at each other like idiots until Jenna laughed. "You two are so cute."

That jerked me out of my trance and the smile fell off my face, simply from shock. I looked at her. I was cute? This was not something I ever thought would be said about me.

Mack had looked away, too, and pulled a red spiral notebook out of his bag. "What's the plan."

"Ugh, physics," Jenna said.

I told him my plans, and Mack gave us some of his senior wisdom on the first physics test, which amounted to, You'd better know those formulas backwards and forwards.

Jenna's head was in her arms on the table and she groaned again, which made Mack and me laugh.

"I've got a major electronics lab to write up," Mack said. "I guess we'd better all get to work."

Jenna lifted her head and squinted at the bright light overhead. "Fine."

We got started, but then I was too distracted to study and decided to work on the dragon for the mural instead, so that's what I did.

After a few minutes, Mack lightly tapped my foot with his. When I looked at him, he grinned at me again before getting back to his lab.

This new situation was unbelievable. I wanted to enjoy

it, but this little part of me was still cautious. Everything could come tumbling down. And that would really hurt.

I tried to wrap that part of my brain in imaginary tinfoil.

Things were going to be good.

Or maybe I would crash and burn.

In art class a few days later, I started inking the dragon drawing, working in the character in the top middle, behind the desk. I had a scrap of paper under the side of my palm to avoid getting oils from my skin on the paper. There were only nine days left before the in-class critique, and I wanted to get it done early in case I had to redo the whole thing. I'd finished the final design and pencil line drawing yesterday. Ms. Mangal had given me these Micron pens of different widths for inking it in, and I was trying to figure out which to use where. I decided to go with the smallest to start with, and I could go back over some of the lines in the thicker ones. I'd then go back and erase the pencil, which I had done very lightly on the paper.

The room was quiet as everyone worked on their projects. I glanced over at Jacob's work, which was a super-hero action scene, with a caped and masked character jumping off a building toward a winged character. Even though I'd never gotten into superheroes, it looked really good. He obviously knew what he was doing. There was some interesting perspective going on there.

I got back to my character and wondered if I should have not gone with such a stereotype for the grumpy nurse. Like, made it a male nurse or whatever. Even though I hated the rules about gender that society enforces, I had much of the same brain programming. The binary still felt real to me. I'd started the book Mack had recommended, but I hadn't gotten very far. The first part was basically just setting the book up—how it was organized, how I should use it, and so on. I was going to work on it some every night.

Whether I regretted my choices or not, the nurse was going to be a grumpy woman. I was going to ink her in first, and do the desk after her. I decided to do her face now, even though I was dreading it. If I messed it up, I could redo the drawing and start over.

The idea of redoing work didn't exactly appeal, but at least it was a possibility, unlike redoing things in real life.

I capped the smallest pen and studied what I'd done so far. The hair didn't look bad. Adding thicker lines would give it some texture. But the face was going to be tough. Hopefully I could do this.

I decided to start with her left eye.

My pen hovered over the spot. God, eyes were hard. You had to get the curve just right, and it wasn't an obvious shape.

Okay, I knew I could do this. I positioned my elbows comfortably on the table.

Suddenly, Rachel laughed and it totally messed with me. Was it about me? I still wasn't free from that victim mentality that was such a constant in Emerson.

I capped the pen again and put fingers to my forehead, eyes closed.

Rachel and Lily were talking about something, but at first I couldn't tell what.

Then Rachel asked Lily, "How's your application coming?"

Oh, no. The mentorship. My stomach roiled. I still didn't know what to do.

Lily told her a little about it, complaining about the

artist statement and talking about how it was hard to pick pieces for the portfolio.

This was so horrible. Even Lily was intimidated by it, and she was so good. I had no chance.

Finally they were all talked out, and they got back to working quietly. I tried to mentally quell the queasiness in my stomach and looked back at the woman's face.

All I had to do was put the pen down in the corner of her eye and trace the thin line I'd done in pencil to the other side of the eye. It wasn't rocket science.

I uncapped the pen and placed the nib on the paper, and carefully moved it to the other side of the eye, pulling the pen away and looking.

It was fine. Phew. Now I just had to do the rest of the eye, and then the next one, and then the mouth, and then the nose. And the ears. Argh.

I closed my eyes for a second. I could do this.

I drew the lowest line at the top of the eye. It looked good. Nothing wrong at this stage.

I'd do the right eye next to make sure I got them symmetrical.

It was just a matter of doing it. And I knew I could.

Maybe I could do the mentorship application, too. My heart said yes, even while my brain was firmly in the No camp.

Jenna and I were sitting in the library meeting room, ready for our book club meeting, when we got a text from Mack on our group text.

—*You guys mind if I add someone new to the group? I met a guy*—

My hackles went up. Jenna looked at me, and I could tell she wasn't any more excited by the idea than I was.

—*Who?*— she asked.

—*His name is Jacob. He says he knows you, Nic*—

I looked at Jenna in surprise. Jacob? This was probably not horrible. "There's a Jacob in my art class. He reads comics and does his own superhero comics."

"Well, a lot of those people read other stuff, too. What's he like?" She sounded almost excited.

I smiled, thinking of our first ever exchange a few days ago. "We are always awkward around each other. We've only ever talked once. He's quiet. You know how it is, two shy people together."

Jenna laughed. "General pretending each other doesn't exist."

"Exactly."

"So what do you think?"

Mack pinged us —*Guys? He's read the book*—

"I guess it's okay?" I mean, Jacob seemed nice. Maybe he'd just sit here in silence, too.

Simultaneously, Jenna and I responded that it was fine.

—*Awesome*— Mack replied.

"How'd they meet, though?" I wondered.

"Yeah, I'm curious, too."

Not two minutes later, I saw Mack—and Jacob—walking between the stacks toward our meeting room. Jacob had on jeans, like he always did, even though it was so hot out, and he was wearing a Marvel t-shirt. Mack had on his gray cargo shorts and a blue striped shirt. They were both smiling, and Jacob looked more animated than I'd ever seen him look before. I also hadn't realized how short Jacob was—Mack had at least two inches on him. But together, they just looked like a couple of boys without a care in the world. That didn't stop me from feeling such affection toward Mack that my heart hurt a little.

I was embarrassed by the Mack-inspired smile stretched across my face, but there wasn't anything I could do about it.

I watched him—smiling like me—and Jacob approach. Mack opened the door.

Jacob smiled and waved at me.

"Hello!" Mack said.

Jenna and I both said hi in response.

As they came into the room, Mack said, "Jenna, this is Jacob. Jacob, Jenna. You and Nic already know each other."

I awkwardly waved back at Jacob. I didn't know what to say. "Hi" didn't occur to me until it was a beat too late.

Mack sat next to me and Jacob sat next to Jenna. Mack bumped my knee and we stared at each other.

I felt self-conscious. What would Jacob think? He didn't know me or Mack well—would he be surprised by this?

"So you've read the book?" Jenna asked Jacob.

Jacob nodded. "A while ago."

"Cool, cool."

Mack faced the others and said, "He was downstairs last night, reading something I hadn't seen before, and we got to talking."

"My roommate was doing squats and lunges and stuff," Jacob explained.

Jenna laughed.

"And then I ran into him near the cafeteria today, so I invited him," Mack said.

Jacob raised his eyebrows and nodded.

It was weird having him here instead of seeing him in the art room, but I found I didn't mind.

"So what was the book?" Jenna asked.

"Last night?" Jacob asked. When Jenna nodded, he continued, "*Three Parts Dead* by Max Gladstone."

"Oh, I've heard of that," I said. It was about a necromancer and a dead god and sounded really interesting. "Is it good?"

"Yep," Jacob said.

"Great," Mack said. "*The Obelisk Gate*?"

"Right," Jenna said. "So, I guess first impressions to start."

"Well, I loved it because it was awesome," I said. It was kind of weird—there was a new person in the group, but I was still comfortable around my friends, instead of forever awkward around people I didn't know well.

Mack and Jenna laughed and Jacob smiled.

"Same here," Mack said.

Jenna said, "Well, obviously I agree, but let's get more specific."

"I like how complex everything is," Jacob said.

"Yeah," Jenna agreed. "There's all these different threads and some of them get explained in this book, but not everything, and so I'm dying to know. Which means I have to start book three right away."

"It makes me think of life," Mack said, bumping my knee. "Like there's always more stuff to know about people."

"You only get some info and have to wait for more," Jacob said.

He wasn't wrong. And now I was curious to see what I'd learn about Jacob. And also what else I'd learn about Mack. I couldn't wait.

∼

Monday morning, I got to physics early and was doing some final touches on the mural dragon design because we were going to be talking about it in the art club board meeting tomorrow. I wasn't paying much attention as people were coming in. Then a rustling sound next to me made me look up, and there was Jacob, putting his stuff down in the spot next to me.

"Hey," he said.

"Oh, hey." Even though it had caught me off guard, it made total sense that he would sit next to me now, since we'd finally broken the communication barrier. "I wonder if Dr. Jones will see that you're present since you're not in your official not official seat."

He laughed. "Let's hope so."

Dr. Jones was writing some stuff on the board in green marker, some of the formulas we were going to be tested on soon.

"What's that for?" Jacob asked, pointing to my sketchbook.

"The mural that the art club is doing at the children's hospital."

"I was thinking it wasn't really your style. You're more of a realism type, not stylized and cartoony."

"I know. It was hard for me." I slid it over so he could see it better. "Do you think it looks okay?"

He studied it for a moment. "I think you should make the wings bigger, and more rounded on the edges, since this is for kids. Little kids can sometimes be scared by the dumbest things."

"Yeah, good point."

Dr. Jones cleared her throat and glared at me and Jacob. Apparently class had started. We both looked down and I closed my sketchbook while we gathered our notebooks.

She started the lecture and we dutifully took notes. She was talking about acceleration. Although I thought it was pretty neat how all of these formulas could all be derived from just one of them, it wasn't entirely intuitive. I was getting increasingly nervous about this class.

Jacob was scribbling away, taking way better notes than me.

I realized I'd missed copying part of what Dr. Jones was now erasing. I leaned toward Jacob. "Did you get that last thing?"

He showed me his page and I finished it out in my notebook and took a deep breath.

I needed to pay more attention in here. Actually, what I needed was to pay all my attention, every last drop.

I hoped I could manage it.

I intentionally got to the art club board meeting right on time because I didn't want any extra time with Rachel. But when I got there, Ms. Mangal wasn't around, and so I sat down quietly, hoping Rachel wouldn't turn around and see me. My heart raced with dread at the thought of dealing with her crap.

She was talking to Emily, and Lily and Lise were chatting. They were all at the front tables. Then there was me in the second row, like normal. At least nobody had noticed me.

Lise was talking about getting more members, even kids who weren't taking art here.

I thought of Jacob. He had talked a lot more than I expected on Sunday. And it turned out he was really smart

—he made all these really insightful observations even though it had been over a year since he read the book.

I should talk to him to get him to join the art club, too.

Then Rachel barked a laugh, loudly. And turned around and spotted me.

My face flushed and I didn't even know why. She just made me so nervous.

Where was Ms. Mangal?

"Oh, Nic, you're here," Rachel announced. Everyone else turned around.

"Where's Ms. Mangal?" I asked.

"She had to run and do something."

Why did she have to do it right now?

"So I saw you with Mackenzie the other day," Rachel said.

"If you mean Mack, then yes. We're friends."

"Normal friends don't go around holding hands." She had this ugly smirk on her face.

My blush deepened.

God, why did she have this horrible effect on me? Why couldn't I be the awesome New Nic around her, not lame-o Emerson Nic? I shouldn't care what she thought. I couldn't stand her and didn't value her opinion, but still her comments made me feel like a loser. I didn't know what the others thought of me or Mack. I guessed they believed Rachel's crap.

Everyone else was looking, probably waiting to see me admit this "transgression" of holding hands with a freak, or whatever Rachel had spun it as.

"I'm not sure what your point is." I tried to keep my voice as level as possible.

Rachel moved off her seat and leaned on my table. "You know you can't trust her." She emphasized the "her."

My gut twisted in rage. I couldn't keep the hate out of my voice, even though I stayed calm. "Now I really don't know who you're talking about."

Lise said, "Come on, Rachel."

Right then, Ms. Mangal breezed in. "So sorry, you guys." She clapped her hands together as she headed toward the front. "Finished! We can get started."

I glared at Rachel. Why couldn't she let it go? Why did she think Mack recognizing who he really was had anything at all to do with her? He didn't betray her by starting to transition. That was entirely for him.

She's the one who chose to unfriend him because she didn't like who he was now. It was her parents who had gone after him and his parents—Rachel should feel bad about that. They ruined a long-term friendship with bigotry.

Why couldn't everyone see that?

I'd started going through the gender identity workbook a few days ago, and it was making me question things. What would she do if I came out as nonbinary? She'd definitely have a problem with it.

Oh, shit. Emily was talking about the bank account balance and crap. I was supposed to be taking notes. I scrambled to get going on those. Hopefully, I hadn't missed anything really important.

Though really, I seriously doubted anyone ever went back and looked at the minutes. I think the main thing was to get action items out of them. And I didn't think anything had come up yet for that.

Lily started talking about what she was doing to advertise the club, and she said Lise had some ideas about getting new members, so they were working together and so on. I typed my notes dutifully, trying to focus on everyone in the meeting, but that didn't keep my mind from heading straight back to Rachel, like her shittiness was a magnet for my thoughts.

At least when we got to the mural part, I was able to share my drawing, and everyone else had theirs. We were supposed to send a digital version to Rachel so she could put it all together, with some help from Ms. Mangal.

But every time Lily talked, it reminded me of the mentorship, and I felt a little queasy from disappointment. I really wanted to try for it, but I didn't know if I'd feel worse if I applied and didn't get it, or if I never applied. But I knew Rachel was right. Lily was better than me.

Why did everything here revolve around Rachel?

I needed to rethink things. But I didn't know how to reprogram my brain.

~

Mack, Jenna, and I were downstairs Tuesday night, studying before official study hours started. We were at one of the tables in front of the windows. I glanced over at Mack, but he was intently reading from his electronics textbook and didn't notice. I wanted to stare, but I also didn't think I should stare. His hair was getting a little long. Just more of him to admire.

But I had to stop. I compromised by looking at Jenna, who was leaning back in her chair reading *One Hundred Years of Solitude*. She blinked a lot when she read. I felt a weird surge of affection for her, another oddball.

I was getting a jump start on my next drawing, even though the assignment didn't technically start until next Monday. This one was an illustration of a story in the public domain, but I had to put some kind of twist on it. The twist could be anything, so the first step was to pick a story. I pulled out my laptop and started googling.

Eventually I settled on Dracula as my character. But what could he be doing? I had no idea and wasn't feeling very creative today. So I went on a news site and started looking at headlines to see if anything jumped out. There was an article about a dog walker who stole a bunch of stuff from a client's house, which wasn't interesting on its own, but I loved the idea of Dracula as a dog walker. I could even make the dogs short haired, with visible bite marks, which would be funny. I had this image of Dracula, in long dark robes, with eight tiny dogs in a cluster dragging him along. And one big dog.

Okay, that was it. Silly, but fun. Why shouldn't art be fun?

I should really have been working on physics, but I wanted to play with the Dracula and dog-walking idea. So I googled Dracula to see lots of images of old-timey movies and stuff. Even though a different look might be more inter-esting, sticking with the classic vampire outfit would be extra contrasty with the dog-walking thing. I could have some people in the background dressed in regular, skimpy clothes to show how ridiculous his outfit was. Maybe a girl in a tank top and cutoff jean shorts.

I stared at my sketchbook, not loving any of my ideas. I wasn't officially thumbnailing at this point, just playing with concepts. But I'd run dry. I spun my pencil.

I wanted to make some progress since I didn't feel like doing physics right now. I was going to meet with Dr. Jones while she was here for office hours this evening.

I felt a gaze on me and glanced back to see Mack looking at me sideways, a tiny smile on his face.

That went straight to my heart, and I obviously smiled back.

"You haven't drawn anything yet," he whispered. I could smell his soap. I was pretty sure it was Irish Spring.

"I know. I'm thinking."

"I have faith in you."

We gazed at each other for a moment before he arched his eyebrows and nodded his head toward his textbook.

My stomach dropped a tiny bit in disappointment, but he was right. I needed to accomplish more than gazing at Mack.

I started sketching and had a few concepts on paper after the next few minutes. Then I was out of ideas and leaned back in the chair.

Mack and Jenna both looked up from their work.

"I need a break," he said.

"Me, too." I yawned.

"What ever happened with that mentorship?" Jenna asked. "Sorry. Random topic introduction."

My stomach twisted just thinking about it.

"You're frowning," Mack said.

"I think it's pointless because of Lily, and how she's better than me. She's also a senior. There's pretty much no chance two of us would be selected from the same school."

"Who says?" Jenna asked. "I don't buy it."

I continued frowning. I didn't want to bring up Rachel.

"Yeah, really, that doesn't sound right," Mack said, brow furrowed. "Why would they care?"

"Well, Rachel pointed this out to me," I said in a small voice.

"What?" Mack exclaimed. He pointed his finger at me, all animated. "Don't listen to her. She's just being a bitch for the sake of being a bitch."

"Yeah, if you think it's really true, talk to Ms. Mangal," Jenna said. "Besides, who says you wouldn't be the one picked from this school if there can be only one?"

There was a tiny lift in my heart. They could be right.

But I didn't know. I loved what they were saying, but doubt infused me.

"Nic, art is really subjective and personal," Mack said. He leaned into my shoulder a tiny bit. "You know this. And yours is really good. Just because somebody else is also really good doesn't mean the artist won't like yours more."

My shoulders loosened.

"I think you should apply no matter what, but talk to Ms. Mangal. I'm sure she'll tell you what Mack just did. Because he's totally right."

I closed my eyes and focused on the tiny bit of hope that was bubbling up inside. "But what if I try and don't get it? I'll be so upset."

Suddenly there was a loud sound and my eyes flew open.

Everyone on the couches in the lounge had turned to look, too.

"Shit, that was louder than I meant," Jenna muttered. She'd slapped her book on the table. Then she gave me this serious look, eyes all intense. "You just have to remember that we will always be rejected from things. Not trying means you have no chance. Applying gives you a chance, at least, even if it's small."

"She's absolutely right," Mack said. "My dad makes fun of her for it, but my grandma buys a lottery ticket every time she goes out. She says somebody always wins eventually, and there's no reason it couldn't be her—unless she doesn't buy a ticket. She says never to buy more than one play per ticket, because doubling a tiny, tiny fraction is still a tiny,

tiny fraction. But one ticket makes sense, because a tiny, tiny fraction is still a greater than zero chance."

Jenna and I laughed, and she said, "My parents call it a tax on the poor."

"It can be," Mack said. "But it's not the players with the nonzero chance philosophy who end up in the poorhouse."

"Probably not," I said. I was feeling even lighter, thinking about Mack having a grandma. She sounded cool, and I wondered if I'd ever meet her.

"Ten minutes, guys." The RA was going around. We had to officially start studying soon.

"I think I want to lie down to keep reading," Jenna announced, standing up. "So I'm going up to my room. See you guys tomorrow."

Once she left, Mack said, "What are your plans?"

"I've got to work on physics and chem. I'm meeting Dr. Jones later. You?"

"Still working on this electronics homework. But you distract me a little." He smiled at me.

I flushed with pleasure as a shiver went through me. This was so new.

"I should go upstairs, too. I need to prep for my meeting with Dr. Jones, but it's hard for me to concentrate when I'm with you, too." I felt a rush of terror at having shared something so deeply personal.

"Alright, then. Off we go." He had a big smile on his face as he stood up and held a hand out like I needed help getting up.

I laughed and took it, and then we stared at each other. It felt charged to me, and the corners of Mack's mouth were slightly turned up. I was pretty much speechless. He obviously wasn't going to kiss me here.

But maybe soon? I was pretty sure he wanted to. I still

felt like, if I was braver, I would just do it myself. But I was going to have to rely on him. It annoyed me that I was doing the whole "the guy has to make the first move" thing, but this simply wasn't in my skill set yet. Plus, if I were nonbinary, would that change things? What would the rules be then?

But it didn't matter. It was only Mack and me, and we'd do what we wanted. And I was sure he wanted to kiss me. Whenever it happened, I couldn't wait to find out what that was like.

I was waiting to talk to Dr. Jones about physics. She was helping another student so I was sitting one chair down, going through my homework so I could be completely prepared for meeting with her. I was nervous because I knew she didn't really like me, even though I didn't know why.

There was one problem I couldn't figure out how to start, but I had worked through all the rest as well as I could.

I didn't know the other student, but she was a senior. She was obviously in an advanced class, way beyond my baby physics. Would I ever get the hang of this?

Dr. Jones and the student both laughed about something. She obviously liked this girl just fine. What was her deal with me? Maybe it was because I wasn't good at physics.

At least I was doing well in chemistry and pre-calc. The other classes were fine. I even liked computer science. Our midterm project was to write a simple chatbot using loops to repeat things and conditions to choose different paths.

I started rereading the section we were working on in the textbook, hoping to glean something more this time.

Eventually the other student thanked Dr. Jones and left.

My turn. Oh, boy.

I moved over to the chair across from her, and she said, "Hello, Nicole."

I'd given up that fight. She refused to call me Nic. The last student must have taken Dr. Jones's smile with her when she left, because it wasn't there now.

"I was trying to do the homework that's due on Thursday, and I got completely stuck on one and was unsure about a few others."

"Okay. Show me." She looked down at my notebook, so I moved it sideways so we both could see it.

I showed her the first one I was uncertain about. Without looking at me, she drily ran through the goal of the question, the principles it was testing, and the approach to take. I'd done that one right, though she didn't seem impressed, judging by her flat voice.

The way she didn't look at me was nerve-racking. It was like she was pretending I didn't exist.

We continued on to the other questions and she said I'd done all of them right except one. She gave me some hints about that and told me how to approach the one I hadn't started.

So, even though I felt awkward, I said thanks as I stood up. Then I headed up to my room to finish them.

On the way, I got a text from Isabella with some dumb joke she'd heard at school today. It wasn't worth repeating, but it still made me smile. I loved my sister.

But I'd have to wait until next week to find out if I'd managed to do those last two problems right.

Even though this was the second time we were doing a critique, I was as edgy as the first time.

And then things got even worse when Ms. Mangal decided to start from the back this time. Which meant with me. I hadn't been expecting that.

Oh, my God.

She finished her spiel. "Please go on and get your artwork, everyone."

I got up, lead in my stomach nearly holding me in place. I had to stand back while everyone else grabbed their pieces, and Jacob muttered, "I can't believe we have to go first."

"I know." I was breathless from nerves.

Finally we got our stuff and both dragged our feet all the way back to our table, falling behind everyone else and delaying the inevitable. I glanced over at his piece. It was a comics multi-panel page, showing a fight between super-heroes. Most of it was black and white, but he'd colored the top panels. He'd used markers, too. He was really good. They pretty much looked professional.

"Nic, come on up," Ms. Mangal called.

Crap. There was no avoiding it.

My steps were heavy on the way up, but I set my dragon picture on the easel and pinned the corners with the magnets Ms. Mangal had for this purpose Then I stepped back while everybody looked at it. I stared at my feet because I couldn't bear to watch their faces. What if a look of disgust crossed over them?

Then everyone sat down and it was time to explain the drawing. I took a deep breath. Getting up in front of people was hard enough, but to do it so everyone could dissect your work was a whole other level of torture. But I had to do it. "So, the prompt was an animal doing something a human would usually do. I like dragons a lot, so I started thinking about different possibilities. And I don't even remember where this exact idea came from, but when you think about taking care of babies, you think of people who do that as being ... soft, I guess. Dragons are the opposite, so it seemed to fit the prompt." I stopped, nerves all energized. It was all I could do to keep from moving my hands and arms.

Jacob had to critique my piece first, and he talked about how interesting the perspective was, which I loved because I was especially proud of that aspect. It was my first ever two-point perspective drawing.

Other people commented on the ink work being surprisingly clean, and liking the detail, and how different strokes were used in different areas. But my favorite was when we got to Lily.

She said, "I like how it makes it obvious that the dragon is an outsider. But it's like they're doing the best they can at something important, even though maybe they don't belong. I respect and like them for that."

That was the first thing anybody had said that wasn't about the technical aspects of the drawing. Jacob's perspective comment was about composition, but Lily was talking about meaning. I hadn't even thought about that part, but I loved her point. It lifted my heart.

Lily's only suggestion was that I could do more with line weight. Which was a fair point, as I'd ended up only using two different pen widths.

Rachel echoed the comment about details, and that was about it, but she then said she thought it would be more interesting in color.

When we went around the second time for suggestions,

I was doubly nervous. But it ended up okay. Most people had only trivial things—there were a couple of spots I'd slightly messed up with my lines, but Ms. Mangal had pointed out that I could tweak it in Photoshop and fix those things. It wouldn't look quite the same, but that was one option.

By the time we finished, I was still rattled, but since the reception had been pretty good, it was okay. My body physically relaxed.

We went through the other critiques and then class was over. We put our work away, packed up, and filed out.

The first piece of art was done. I felt really proud of it, especially since it was my first time using pens. It was solid work, and it would be a good portfolio piece.

Either for the mentorship, if I was brave or stupid enough to apply, or maybe for when I applied to art school next year.

I really didn't know what I was going to do. This seemed to be a theme in my life right now. Was I going to figure out my gender identity? Where were things going to go with Mack? Would I have the nerve to apply for the mentorship?

Argh.

PART IV

DRACULA WALKS SOME DOGS

I'd brought my sketchbook to the study session with Mack, Jenna, and Jacob on the Saturday after the critique. We were at Booth Forest, with the hum of a hundred voices echoing off the ceiling. I was sitting next to Mack, so I felt like I was glowing. It was like induction charging—all I had to do was get near him. He was busy studying, but we'd stared at each other some, too. Jenna and Jacob were also both quietly studying. Jacob's laptop was closed next to his book, and I could see it was covered in Marvel stickers.

The table was full of textbooks, Taco Bueno trash, and giant soda cups, but there was enough room for me to spread my sketchbook open and work.

I started sketching versions of Dracula to get a feel for his look, using the reference images on my phone as guides. The main thing was the cloak.

I debated the bowtie. They were so dorky. But that could be a plus.

I was about to start my thumbnails, but I hadn't drawn

out the grid, and I really preferred to do that in pen. I rifled through my backpack and somehow I didn't have one with me.

I leaned toward Mack, boosting the charge through my body. He side-eyed me and smiled before I could even speak.

"What's up?" he asked.

Jenna and Jacob both looked up from their work. Jacob looked back down and Jenna took a swig from her water bottle.

I was so distracted by his mere presence that I had to clear my throat. "Do you have a pen?"

He continued to smile at me while he took a pen from his backpack.

I was goo inside.

"Here you go." He handed me the pen and our hands brushed because neither of us were looking. This made me blush.

"Thanks," I forced out. Then we both looked away and I stared hard at my sketchbook.

Oh, my God. If he didn't kiss me soon, I was going to die.

I turned the page and eyeballed the right size for the thumbnail boxes, making a grid of nine per page over three pages.

The stupid lines were wobbly because my hand was shaking. Ridiculous. I needed to get a grip.

I closed my eyes for a moment to mentally regroup. Then I looked up dog walkers and started sketching out my thumbnails.

After a while, something brushed my shoulder, and the touch was electric. Mack was leaning over.

"What did you draw?"

"So, this is Dracula as a dog walker. Or just Dracula and a bunch of dogs." I showed him what I had so far. There were a handful with Dracula running from a pack of dogs, and another few with him lying on a couch covered with small sleeping dogs. I'd also tried a couple with him just standing there, with leashed dogs pulling him in opposite directions.

"This is the best one," Mack said, pointing to the one where Dracula was about a third of the way in from the left, with one leash going off the page to the left, and a bunch of dogs pulling him to the right. "He's being pulled in all directions, something OAMS students can relate to."

That made me laugh. "Unfortunately, too true. I like this one, too. But I still have to do some more."

"Let me guess, you're avoiding physics."

I closed my eyes and sighed. "You are correct."

He gave me an affectionate grin, and then got right back to work.

I opened my physics book and started trying to read. It was hard to focus because I was so distracted by being close to Mack. I had to wait patiently (impatiently) for him to kiss me some time. Maybe Wednesday.

"I'm glad we're finishing this series up, because I can't wait to see what we read next," Jenna said after we all got situated at our next book club meeting.

"I know, but oh, my God, I want to talk about this one," Mack said, his eyes wide. "The whole stone people thing is so weird and original."

I nodded. "I know, I wasn't sure if it was really going to happen to her, or not."

Jacob piped up, "Right. It's like, will Jemisin really go there? And she did."

We continued discussing the wrap-up of all the stuff in the series. I loved talking about it, but I was fixated on Mack. I thought we were close to maybe kissing some time, but I didn't know for sure. There was pretty much no way I was going to be able to initiate that. So it would be entirely on Mack.

I was honestly getting impatient. I wanted things to go to the next level, even though I didn't really know what it would mean.

To stay engaged even though my brain was wandering, I talked about how I loved the storyline with the daughter. I liked how she was young and naive, and trying to make decisions with major consequences, all with the mind of a kid. I thought back to how dumb I was at her age, and said it was amazing things turned out okay in the book.

"Yeah, I know what you mean," Jacob said. "I was worried."

Jacob and I made eye contact and I remembered how we didn't talk for weeks, and it made me snort-laugh.

"What?" Mack asked.

"You guys have no idea," I said. "Jacob and I sit next to each other, at the same table, in art. Every day, since the beginning of the semester. And we're in physics together, too. And with the exception of the first day in physics, when we almost ran into each other, we never spoke until about two weeks ago, by accident."

Jacob smiled at that.

I continued. "And now he's here talking away and so am I. I guess my point is that shy people aren't shy in every situation. People forget that."

"It just has to do with comfort level," Jenna said. "It develops over time."

"Yeah," I agreed. "Everybody's always said I'll grow out of it. Maybe in certain situations, but I'll probably be shy even when I'm thirty."

Mack bumped my shoulder. "You never know, though."

Jenna nodded. "He's right. It's hard to predict the future."

"True." I picked up the book and flipped through the pages.

Jenna slammed her hand on the table. "Two words. And I know this was in the second book, but somehow we didn't talk about them enough for me. Boil bugs."

"Oh, my God," I said. "That was possibly the creepiest part of this series. Though the kirkhusas were also horrifying."

We debated the terrors of both. Boil bugs were these giant bugs that inject victims with boiling water and are positively horrific when they swarm somebody. Not survivable. Incredibly painful.

Jacob said, "I think the idea that the kirkhusas could go from being sweet pets to vicious monsters overnight, when the world changes the way it did, is awesome. I mean, I guess rabies can do that, but not to all of them everywhere, all at once."

"Yeah, it's like, things have already turned horrible, and now you're betrayed by even your pets." Jenna looked thoughtful.

"Kind of like what Essun's neighbors did to her," Mack said.

"My grandma has Alzheimer's," Jenna said. "She used to be the sweetest lady. Now she's a terror. It's hard to look at someone and know she's no longer the same person. But also sort of is."

The mood had turned serious and we all looked at other in silence. Then Jenna said, "Awkward! Sorry."

That made us all laugh.

"Yeah, so. I love how creative Jemisin is," Jacob said. "I appreciate it, as someone trying to write a story for a comic book. It's not easy."

"You're trying to write a comic book?" Mack asked, obviously surprised.

"Well, yeah. I have to have a story to know what to draw. Otherwise it would just be a sequence of fight scenes."

We all laughed again.

"You know you have to show us, you know," Mack said.

"It's weird that we've never asked before," Jenna said, her brow furrowed.

"Sure," Jacob said. "Why don't I just bring my tablet and show you some time. It's not good to look at it on a phone."

"It's all really awesome," I added. "But I also would love to see it all together. Have you been doing it in order?"

Jacob shook his head. "You know how much I love doing the fight scenes. I'm still working out what happens between them."

"That's hilarious," Jenna said.

Jacob shrugged, smiling. "I do have a rough idea of the overall story, which I can talk through when I show you. You all can tell me what you think."

"Sounds awesome, Jacob," Mack said. "Maybe you can grab it for dinner tonight. But now, we need to pick the next book. What do you guys want to do?"

"I have this book on my shelf I've been wanting to read, called *An Unkindness of Ghosts*," Jacob said.

Jenna leaned toward him. "Tell us more."

Tuesday evening, Ms. Mangal took some of us over to the hospital where we were doing the mural so we could clean the walls in preparation for starting the line drawing Saturday. She drove the whole board over there in a van. Then she prepped some buckets of cleaning solution and we got to work wiping down the walls.

I was worried that it might be rough working with Rachel, but she mostly left me alone. I guessed that maybe she had something on her mind, which was fine with me. The others were chatting amongst themselves.

Since I was taller, I was the only one who could reach the top part of the wall we needed to clean, so I had to follow behind the others after cleaning the smaller section that Ms. Mangal had originally assigned me.

After a while, I needed to use the restroom, so Ms. Mangal took me down the hall.

"How's your mentorship application going?" she asked as we reached the bathrooms.

"Uh," I said, brilliantly. Why couldn't I talk like a normal person? I mentally regrouped and made sure my voice was low, even though I could hear the girls talking at the other end of the hall. "I was wondering if I should even apply since Lily is applying?"

Ms. Mangal's brow furrowed. "Why wouldn't you?"

"Because she's better than me, and a senior."

"Oh, honey. She's not 'better than you.'" She made air quotes when she said the last bit. "You two have very different styles, but you're both talented and skilled. And the fact that she's a senior doesn't matter."

That was a surprise. "Really?"

"Yes. Nic, there's something you need to understand if you're going to become a professional artist. You will experience a lot of rejection. You'll have more rejections than acceptances, in all sorts of things you try for. It's hard, and you have to develop a thick skin. That's why we do critiques in here. It's important to learn to separate your work from you as a person."

"Okay." At least she wasn't saying this was easy to do. Because it was terrifying to me. I was dreading the next critique.

But she wasn't done. "The other thing you have to understand is that art is always subjective. Even among high-profile artists, you can rarely say that one is better than another. Some people prefer one artist's work, another prefers a different artist's work. It's the way of things."

I nodded. This part did make sense.

"So, I have no idea if Clee will like your art, or Lily's art, or some other artist's the most. There's no way to know. But applying will be good for you, even if you get rejected." She smiled and squeezed my shoulder. "Get that first rejection under your belt."

I laughed. "Already done that. Rejection is my middle name."

She smiled. "Nic, I really believe you've got a bright future if you want it. It takes work, but you don't seem afraid of that."

"Thanks." She really was on my side. But I had to get myself into the bathroom. I pointed at the door. "I better ..."

"Sure, honey. Go ahead. I'll head back."

I thought about it all through my time in the bathroom and the walk back to the wall. Maybe I should apply. She was right that a rejection wasn't the end of the world. And I did need to learn to start taking more risks.

It was still going to hurt, though. Every bad thing felt like the end of the world to me, at least at first. My mind was so overdramatic.

I was about to turn the corner when I heard some of the girls laughing. Then I heard, "She's as much of a freak as Kenzie." It had to be Rachel.

I stopped and tried to mentally regroup, feeling both shitty and mad. But there was nothing I could do about it. I turned the corner and acted like I hadn't heard anything.

I got back to work cleaning. The truth was, with all the bad things I'd experienced, even the ones I overreacted to, I'd always recovered eventually, so I should just go for it. I would do the application. Screw Rachel's theory.

Mack and Jenna both said they didn't buy it, and neither did Ms. Mangal.

Thinking of Mack and Jenna—and now Jacob— reminded me of how much my life had completely changed, despite the fact that I'd only been here a little over a month.

I'd been texting Sam updates, but we hadn't managed to talk in a while. She was impressed that I'd been able to turn things around after calling Mack a girl. The guilt at doing that coursed through me again. Sam had been right about being vulnerable, and taking a risk being worth it.

It was hard to keep Mack off my mind, but I looked back at the wall and continued my work. I'd see them all at dinner tonight. And then maybe I'd get started on the mentorship application.

A few days after the wall cleaning, I was sitting in the art room in my old Friday tradition. Mack had had to go away for the weekend for a family thing and had left before school even finished. I'd been thinking about the mentorship since Tuesday, but I hadn't started the application yet.

It had taken me, like, an hour to dig up the packet of info

Ms. Mangal had given me. It was buried under several notebooks on the shelf over my desk. Once I'd found it, I'd headed over.

I liked being in the room by myself again.

I wondered if I might ever bring Mack in here. I knew I shouldn't, so I wouldn't. Ms. Mangal wouldn't like it.

But I needed to keep my mind off Mack. I had work to do.

I opened the folder and began reading the requirements. There was a lot of info in it, including a couple of sample artist statements, a suggested outline for the essay, and a couple of different portfolios.

I glanced over the essay outline. We were supposed to talk about what we expected to get out of the mentorship. Then I read through the artist statements. I was pretty sure these were by high school students, but they honestly sounded like they totally knew what they were talking about. It made me queasy. How could I get to that point?

This was way too hard. But then again, Mack and Jenna were convinced I could do it. Of course, they hadn't seen the application packet.

So, it was intimidating. I didn't even know where to start. With the portfolio, maybe? It might help to know what I was going to submit before writing the other stuff?

Or maybe that was just me avoiding the hard parts.

But still. It wouldn't hurt to pick a few pieces as a starting point.

Definitely the dragon one I'd just finished. And I was going to include the Dracula one since I'd have it done before the application was due. If it didn't turn out well, I'd swap in another, older piece.

I started flipping through images in the art folder on my phone, copying stuff into a new folder to consider later.

There was a lot of good stuff in here, which made me smile. Sometimes I surprised myself. But I was really glad I was branching out into pen. All my good stuff before this semester was in pencil. Professional artists rarely worked in pencil. I needed to get out of my comfort zone.

I was so glad I'd met Ms. Mangal. This was way better than the way art was taught at Emerson.

I eventually made it through all my best work and had fifteen pieces in my folder. I'd look at them later, and ask my friends what they thought. For now, I'd do some more work on the Dracula drawing.

I was still working on the rough, so I could do the value studies. I'd gone with the composition Mack and I had liked. So I continued sketching out details for a while until I felt like stopping. I checked the time—just after ten, so I could pack up and be back at the dorm in plenty of time. I stuck the art and supplies in my cubby, stuffed my phone in my pocket, and grabbed my bag.

Once I was back in my room, blessedly alone, I started swiping through the pieces I'd put in the new folder on my phone, rejecting a handful. I was going to do some work in the gender identity workbook when I finished.

My phone dinged while I was still holding it, practically giving me a heart attack. But then my heart leapt. Mack!

He was checking in. It was the first alone time he'd had all night. His family had a strict no-phones policy at official get-togethers.

I hated not seeing him and not texting him, even though I kept asking myself if anything was ever going to change in our relationship. It felt a little stuck.

Would he ever kiss me?

～

The following Wednesday, Jenna was with her dad and Jacob had something else he had to do, so it was Mack and me at dinner. He hadn't said much so far. He was really quiet. Super low-energy.

I was telling him about what I was working on in art, talking about the drawing, which was coming along nicely. But I'd also started the acrylic painting I had to do this semester.

"Ms. Mangal's got me doing this still life." I dug out my phone to show him the picture. He leaned over and I could smell his soap.

"That's kind of boring. Did you have a choice?" He sounded distant, not as interested as he usually was.

"I know, and not really. I wanted to paint Isabella, but Ms. Mangal told me it wasn't a good idea to start with painting someone you care about because it would be frustrating when it doesn't turn out good. So a bowl of fruit it is."

Mack smiled but didn't laugh. Something was definitely off.

"Are you okay?" I asked. I didn't know why it took me so long to ask. But I totally was weird about asking people questions.

He looked over the panini he'd just taken a bite of, and set it on his plate. Usually when I caught him like that, he'd raise his eyebrows and rock his head a little, but this time he just pointed at his mouth.

"I know," I said. "Bad timing." But my question hung there in the air, because he obviously wasn't. At first I wondered if he hadn't slept well, but it was more than that.

"Well," he finally started, staring at his plate. He wiped his fingers on a napkin, leaving behind orange streaks.

I waited, taking a bite of my pizza to make it clear I wasn't going to say anything else.

"I got some really bad news."

My gut twisted for him. I knew it had to be serious. "Okay," I said after a pause.

"The hospital where I've been getting my T-shots was just ordered by our asshole governor to stop all treatments on minors. It's a new law."

"What?" I was shocked. I knew enough to know that that was his testosterone. Everything would change if he stopped getting it. "How can they do that?"

"You know what kind of state this is, one that runs on hate and forced conformity. You grew up here. You know."

"Yeah, but a law? Isn't that taking it too far?" As soon as I said it, I knew it was stupid. There were already laws about this, just not in Oklahoma yet.

"Come on, Nic." He was impatient, which made me grimace. "You know about the Texas law that caused my parents to have to give up custody of me. And you know about Florida's Don't Say Gay Bill and all the bullshit it involves."

It all made sense now. "And Oklahoma has such an inferiority complex with Texas. They're always trying to outdo Texas. Like with the abortion laws."

"Exactly. Texas passes an insane one, and then Oklahoma passes one even worse. So yeah, this is step one. I thought I was going to be okay. I turn eighteen in March. But no." He closed his eyes and pressed his fingers to his forehead.

He sounded completely and totally beat down.

My heart broke for him. I was almost afraid to ask, but I had to. But I still said it quietly. "What happens if you stop taking it until you turn eighteen?"

He opened his eyes and looked at me. "It would be a disaster for me." He closed his eyes and tilted his head back.

I wasn't sure, but he seemed on the verge of crying. I couldn't do anything except frown. Seeing him like this made *me* want to cry.

I didn't really understand how much the testosterone changed him because I only knew him the way he was now. Nothing like that would ever change the way I felt about him, but it was crazy that some hateful people could just arbitrarily decide things about Mack's body.

There really wasn't anything to say or do. I stared at my cold pizza. His eyes were still closed, so I took a bite, but it tasted like ass. I stared at what was left, which was most of the first slice. The second was untouched.

Out of nowhere came this sing-songy, "Break it up, girls. Break it up."

Rachel. God, I hated her.

Neither of us turned around, but I could feel Mack tense up. Still, we appeared to have a tacit agreement to refuse to acknowledge her.

"You guys are gross," she said, standing right behind us.

We still said nothing, and she and her friends went off. I really wondered what they thought of her and how she just wouldn't leave Mack alone.

"She's such a bitch," I said.

"I know."

Both of those laws were pure evil. And Rachel, too. Why do people who claim they are the party of freedom do everything in their power to take away people's freedom? People didn't even have the right to make decisions about their own bodies anymore. This was crazy. The world was going insane.

I felt so bad for Mack, but I had no idea what to do to help.

"Nic, they're coming for us." He sounded tired. "They want to stamp us out of existence."

I didn't know what to say to that. He was right.

I had no idea what it really meant for me or for him.

Rachel was blessedly quiet in the next board meeting, at least with me. She didn't even look at me, which was fine.

She went over the progress on the mural. We'd done a huge amount of the work over the past two Saturdays, and some of us had gone with Ms. Mangal to work on it on a couple evenings last week. But the plan was for us to finish it this Saturday.

I dutifully listened and took notes, forcing myself to ignore a few texts from Mack that were coming in, because if I read them, I'd totally tune the meeting out. I wasn't happy when Rachel talked about the fundraiser. They'd found something that was entirely online. We gave people a link to buy popcorn and cheese trays or whatever and it was delivered to their house, and we got a cut. But they'd probably be expected to go door-to-door. I just wasn't going to.

We also were going to open up the contest for the t-shirt design next week, pick the winner in December, and get the shirts in February.

Finally the meeting was over. I decided to stay and work on my drawing, but first I checked Mack's texts as people were leaving the classroom. He was complaining about a class and rambling about the book we were reading for our book club. I mostly agreed with him, so we went back and forth about that.

Then I told Ms. Mangal I was staying for a while, and

she was fine with it. She was going to be sticking around for a bit herself. She left the room, her favorite mug in hand.

I had Dracula done for the line drawing, and I was halfway through the third dog on the right. He was a Labrador, so fairly simple to do because he had no markings. I was tempted to leave the drawing and go back to my room now because I wasn't totally in the mood to draw, but I told myself I needed to be serious about my art. I should stay and finish.

I finished the Labrador and started drawing the Great Dane, which was so big that I'd had to make him the furthest back so you could still see all the others. Once I had him done, I did the Chihuahua and then worked on one that had super-long fur. I had no idea about dog breeds and I'd had to look them up for reference photos. There was also a Pomeranian, and the last one was a poodle groomed in that stupid way people did those dogs, with the balls of fur all over them.

This was totally something Jenna would make fun of in a really funny way. That made me smile.

"How's the application coming?" Ms. Mangal asked when she returned, coming by to see my work. "Oh, that's fun!"

"Thanks. I, uh, have the portfolio ready, and I've made some progress on the essay and statement." This was not strictly true. The portfolio was mostly prepared, but the artist statement wasn't ready and I hadn't even started the essay.

"Make sure to get it to me by next Thursday so I can give you feedback."

"Okay." I'd have to get to work. I did not like writing, and writing about myself was extra weird.

She headed back to the front and my phone dinged, so I

grabbed it. Mack asking when I was going to be there for dinner.

Crap! I hadn't been paying any attention to the time. It was already six so I was late, leaving my friends standing around waiting for me.

I jumped up and headed toward the back room to put my stuff away.

Then I texted Mack that I'd be there in a few and hurriedly put everything in my backpack. My panic didn't lessen the excitement of being about to see Mack again, and hold his hand on the way to the cafeteria.

"Bye, honey," Ms. Mangal said. "Don't forget that essay and statement."

I nodded, grabbed my bag, and raced out of there.

How in the world was I going to manage to get everything to her in time? Although that wasn't what was making me freak out a little right now.

Right now, I had to rush to meet my friends.

Wednesday night, Mack and I went to dinner on our own. Dinner itself wasn't particularly eventful. I had the usual charged feeling I got whenever I was around him, but the conversation hadn't been anything special. I was a still constantly analyzing everything he said to look for hints that he might be thinking about kissing me. We finished eating but didn't leave right away.

"I've got the essay almost done," I told him. "I'll finish it tonight and send it to Ms. Mangal tomorrow. She'll get it back to me Friday so I have the weekend to make changes."

"It's due Halloween?" he asked.

I nodded.

"What else is left to do?" He wadded up his napkin and dropped it on his plate.

"I've got a draft of the artist statement, miraculously, but I've got to make it better. But then I've got the other essay to do, and I want to do a final check over my portfolio, to make sure it really is my best work." I suddenly doubted if it was good enough.

He bumped my shoulder and said, "Let me see. I know I'm not an artist, but I can help you decide. If you want."

"Okay, sure." I had everything I had chosen in a folder so it was easy to go through each one.

"I'm including both drawings I've done for class this semester." I showed him the dragon nursery worker and Linlithgow fountain.

Okay, maybe these actually were pretty good. I felt a little floaty.

"These are all so good," Mack said, all intense. "You really are so freaking good. You know that, right?"

I flushed and my stomach flipped. All I could do was mumble, "Thanks."

Mack laughed. "You're too humble."

"I don't want to be arrogant," I explained. I fiddled with my napkin.

"You are so far from arrogant. It is possible to recognize you're good at something and be proud without being a self-absorbed douche."

I flipped to the next drawing, which was the celestial leopard, the one I'd been working on when I got the acceptance letter to OAMS last June. The letter that totally changed my life. I got dizzy thinking about how different things were now.

"I love this," Mack said. "It's so creative but still manages to look realistic."

"Yeah." I flipped to another piece in pencil.

"Have I ever shown you this self-portrait?" I asked him, holding the phone out for him. "It won first place in a contest at my school last year."

"That's awesome." He leaned in toward the phone, the familiar scent of his soap filling my nostrils. "It really looks like you."

"But funny story. About this." I wanted to tell him the whole messed up story about the original self-portrait I'd drawn that got me in trouble. "This was version two."

He cocked an eyebrow. "What was version one?"

Pulling my phone back, I leaned back and looked off into the distance. Then I started flipping through other images. "So, we were assigned a self-portrait in pastels or colored pencils. I'm terrible with pastels. But as I started working on it, I had an idea for something that would be really interesting."

I got to the image. It was a decent rendition of my face, but I'd drawn it with a hand pulling it away like it was a mask. Behind it, the "real" face was entirely black and deep purple with red eyes. I smiled looking at it. It really was pretty great. I still loved it despite the crap that happened after I drew it.

"Okay," Mack said, his eyes expectant.

I showed him the image.

"Oh, my God, that's cool!" He laughed. "Kind of terrifying, but in a good way, like horror movies."

"Yeah, I still really like it." It was hard not to get angry about what had happened. "But it got me in so much trouble. They pulled me out of class and sent me to the school counselor, and also called my parents and freaked them out, so that they sent me to the world's worst therapist, who was so detached from reality that he didn't think teenagers drank."

Mack rolled his eyes. "Adults are so clueless sometimes."

"Yeah." They totally were.

"Are you including this?" he asked.

"Should I? It might make me look like a psycho."

"It might be interesting to have both it and the realistic portrait, to show versatility and creativity. But ask your teacher to make sure."

That was a good idea. She'd be honest. She was more of a real artist, I thought, so she'd understand that it was just a piece of art.

"Let's go," Mack said. "Ice cream beckons."

I was disappointed. Were we going to go back to the dorm? Nothing else was going to happen?

We headed out, hand in hand. I consoled myself with the ice cream in my free hand. But really, I still felt energized being this close to him.

"We both have stuff to do tonight so we can't go far, but maybe we can walk around campus a bit, if you want," Mack said, immediately lifting my spirits and giving me the old stomach butterflies.

"Sure." Okay, so there was still a chance something could happen. It was almost dark already, so it would feel more private.

We headed in the opposite direction from the dorm, surrounded by the familiar white brick buildings.

As we neared a group of college guys walking toward us, they were being loud and rowdy, and then they all looked at us. I was instantly nervous. As they passed, one said, "Wassup, fags?"

Then another said, really loud, "I wonder who the girl is in that relationship."

My stomach dropped. Mack's hand in mine tensed, but he didn't say anything and we continued on like nothing had happened.

"Assholes," Mack said.

"Yeah." What else was there to say?

We kept going and I got the feeling he had a plan in mind, but I didn't know what.

Finally, he said, "Want to go to the Happy Hollow?"

I drew a blank and looked at him for a clue, which made him laugh.

"The sitting area built into the Oval," he explained.

Memories of the campus tour dawned. They'd built some seating in a sort of dug-out area in the middle of the grassy expanse. "Sure."

We headed in that direction, swinging our joined hands. I guessed we both were mentally telling those assholes off.

I finished my ice cream and started on the cone. Would there be college kids there? It was fairly cool and a boring Wednesday night, but I had no idea how popular it was. I hoped it would be empty. My stomach butterflies hadn't slowed down. It felt like something was about to happen.

We got close enough to the Oval to see that nobody was in the Happy Hollow, unless they were lying on the ground in the middle, which seemed unlikely. My heart sped up.

When we got there, I could see it was a pit dug into the ground, with stone seats along the side. There was nobody lying on the ground, so we took the steps down and sat on the lowest seats, hips almost touching. We were still holding hands. We were in a circle about fifteen feet across, dug about four feet into the ground, with two levels of seats around the whole circle.

Was this the moment? Did Mack have this all planned?

"We can see the stars from here, too," Mack said, and we both looked up.

Then I looked back down. The fact that there was room for people to lie down in the middle of this thing combined with my charged body made me wonder what people had done here. "Do you think people have ever gotten really happy in here?" I asked.

Mack laughed and bumped my shoulder, but he didn't pull away. "Probably."

Our shoulders were still touching and my body was on fire. Even though I was terrified, I turned my head toward his to find that he was looking right at me. Very close. Closer than anyone had been to me before. We stared at each other. He looked serious and intense, like he was trying to make a decision.

Was he going to kiss me? I wanted to lean forward, but I was so scared I was misreading this situation.

But then suddenly the fear was gone and we both leaned in at the same exact time. Our lips met and I thought my heart was going to burst. We sort of stayed like that, and we were both squeezing each other's hands, and Mack reached around and put his free hand on my shoulder. I copied him and wondered if I should do something else, so I moved my mouth a little.

Mack squeezed my shoulder and pulled back. I was smiling, and Mack looked at me intently for a second before looking off to the side. He dropped his arm so I let go of his shoulder, too.

Was it a bad sign that he'd looked away? I also turned forward. Maybe he was just overwhelmed? I was. Anxiety kicked in. How was I supposed to feel here? I had no real idea how it had gone. It definitely wasn't like a movie kiss.

He leaned back against the top step and I did the same.

We sat there a while until he mentioned one of his constellations and we talked about those.

"Do you want to get back?" Mack asked. "We both have stuff to do."

"Sure." I was hugely disappointed that that was it for tonight.

But I'd finally had my first kiss. I couldn't wait to tell Sam—she'd be proud. And Jenna. She'd be impressed, too. Hopefully the kiss was just one of many more to come.

Thursday night turned into a mad scramble on the mentorship artist statement and essay. I had not gotten to it at all Wednesday night, because I spent the whole time reliving the kiss with Mack and overanalyzing it, and then talking to Jenna about it until her intimidating and badass roommate came in, and then going back to my room and overanalyzing it some more.

I hadn't seen Mack all day and didn't know what to think. He'd sent me a text saying he was busy tonight. So, obviously, I was happy about the kiss. But there was this small doubt flitting around my mind. I couldn't put my finger on it. Maybe it wasn't the world's best kiss, but neither of us knew what we were doing, so we'd get better at it. So I wasn't sure what the doubt was.

But I didn't have time to dwell on it tonight. I had to get this essay done and emailed to Ms. Mangal tonight so she'd have feedback for me tomorrow. Plus the statement. It was a lot for one night.

I opened the laptop at my desk and stared at the jumble of words I'd managed to get down on the essay. I would have the weekend to make changes after feedback from Ms.

Mangal, but I needed to give her something that wasn't a piece of trash. I pulled down two of my favorite fantasy figurines—a ranger and a mage in a green robe. The green was such a nice color. These would be my muses.

It was so hard, because I wanted to get a million things out of the internship. How was I supposed to know what to mention?

Being flummoxed by this brought my mind back to Mack, which made my stomach go all fluttery. He'd skipped dinner tonight. What was he doing instead?

Focus, Nic. I had to think about this mentorship, not Mack. I decided to talk about how I was creating art in a more professional way with Ms. Mangal, and I wanted to get even more professional. And I said I wanted to deepen my skills in pen and ink. According to the provided outline, I should start the essay with a history of my art experience. That wasn't too hard. I explained how I'd just always done art, and went into how important it was to me. I went on a little about how it had sort of saved me at times when I was struggling in the real world.

Even though it was a little unsettling to put all my experiences of art and struggling socially in the computer, it all flowed pretty easily. It was funny how I'd never really thought about how interrelated my art and pitiful social life were, but how easy it ended up being to write about it. But it was also interesting that I was still loving art even though my social life had completely turned around. I even had a boyfriend, and we'd kissed! But my art was still such a huge part of my life. It was the most "me" thing about me.

So then I talked about how excited I was to find out about this mentorship, as I didn't have much experience with real artists and I thought I could learn a lot. I talked about my goals with pen and ink.

It was already eight when I finished that section. And I still had the artist statement to do. This situation was a mess. Of my own making, obviously.

I leaned back. Why didn't Mack just tell me what he was busy doing?

Stop it. I didn't own him. He didn't have to tell me everything.

I opened up the artist statement and made myself read one of the samples. It took three tries before I was able to focus on the first paragraph, but I did finally get back there. After reading the samples, I basically copied the structure of one of them for my own. The author talked about the things that mattered to them in the real world, and how that related to the art that they made. I said how important fantasy art was to people wanting to escape. That was the main idea. I didn't know what else to say.

I went back and read the essay. It was still a mess, but I thought all the right parts were there, except the conclusion. I threw something down for that and then saved both files and emailed them to Ms. Mangal.

Monday night, I was putting the full application together and writing the email to send to Clee.

I had spent the whole weekend working on the essay and personal statement. Ms. Mangal had given me feedback that forced me to rework a lot of it, and it took several rounds of writing the essay, then looking at the statement, before going back to the essay, and so on. It was helpful to take a break from one to work on the other, even though there was some overlap.

Mack had been MIA through the whole weekend. I

hadn't seen him at school today, either, which wasn't out of the ordinary, but not seeing him all weekend was. He texted that he had a family thing, but he usually texted me when he could throughout the day, so I didn't know what was going on. So it was just Jenna, Jacob, and me for several meals.

With my email open behind it, I flipped through the portfolio one last time. Everything was in a folder and I was going to create a zip file out of it.

I had two of my figurines on the desk again, hopefully acting as muses. One was the wizard in green robes, and the other was an elf warrior in very colorful garb. It had been fun to paint.

As I looked through the photos, I was struck by the fact that I really did have some nice work, but that just reminded me of showing Mack my portfolio last Wednesday. I couldn't stop obsessing over him. I obviously was getting really nervous about everything. I had first thought Wednesday's kiss was a good thing, but now I was wondering if it was a bad thing. I don't know how—he initiated it, so it's not like I forced myself on him. But maybe he wasn't that into it? I really didn't know.

And I didn't know how to find out, other than by asking him. Which wasn't happening. I'd been so happy and excited when I talked to Jenna Wednesday night that I didn't want to admit to her I was having doubts now. It would be embarrassing to have to say it out loud. And obviously I didn't know Jacob well enough. Plus he was a guy, and I'd feel extra uncomfortable talking to him about it. Talking about feelings was virtually impossible for me. I was getting better, but I couldn't become a whole new person overnight.

I created the zip file for the photos.

How long was this going to drag on with him?

I read over the essay and statement again, feeling nervous about everything I'd shared—how much was it going to hurt when I got rejected? I'd revealed so much about myself, which I rarely did. I told myself I shouldn't expect a good outcome, even though keeping my expectations low never actually worked—I still always felt terrible when I got rejected for something I wanted, like the world was ending. I wished I didn't always overreact.

And thinking about rejection had my thoughts going right back to Mack. Was that what was going on? Was I such a bad kisser that he couldn't tolerate me anymore?

I closed my eyes and tried to clear my mind so I could finish this email. I wanted to get this in.

I saved the essay and statement as a pdf like they'd asked.

I leaned back in my chair, feeling sick because Mack was still so much on my mind, and now I was really worried. I attached all three files to the email. I didn't need to write much in the email itself, so I said this was my application for the mentorship and left it at that. Then I was going to put her email address in and I couldn't find it.

My heart started racing and I went into a panic. I knew I was overreacting, but I was so frazzled by Mack and the last-minute status of everything, that I couldn't think.

It wasn't actually due tonight—I had until Wednesday night to turn it in. So I told myself to chill out. I sat back and tried to concentrate on my breathing.

I wanted it in tonight. I wanted it done.

I dug back through the original application materials I still had in the folder on my shelf, and there it was on the first page.

God, I could be such an idiot sometimes.

I typed in her email, checked it twice, made sure the three attachments were all there, and clicked Send.

Done.

I put my two muse figurines back on the shelf, again admiring the green I'd chosen for the robe. So pretty. Hopefully the muses had served me well.

Now I just had to wait for the rejection to come in to know how I'd feel about it. Ugh.

Mack finally texted that he'd meet us for dinner Tuesday. He was the last to arrive and smiled at me as he rounded the corner from his room to where we were waiting in the lobby, but it didn't seem to reach his eyes. He nodded at Jenna and Jacob, and took my hand. His grip on my hand was like normal. My whole body relaxed in relief.

Jenna pushed the door open and Jacob was right behind her, with Mack and me last. They led the way, having a conversation about a class they shared.

"How've you been?" Mack asked. "I'm sorry I've been out of pocket the last few days."

It was so good to hear his voice that I didn't care anymore that he'd gone missing.

"Good," I said. "I got the mentorship application in last night." I felt both further relief about this, and also tension for the rejection I figured would eventually come.

"I thought it wasn't due until tomorrow," he said.

It was sweet that he remembered. Maybe things were still good, and I'd been imagining a problem. Maybe he really was just busy with something that whole time.

"How have you been?" I asked. "How was your ... thing?"

We stepped into the parking lot.

"Oh, you know. Fine. My parents came up to visit me, so we hung out at a hotel in OKC and just ate out several times. I don't think my parents know what to do with me. But there was some good news."

My heart lifted. "Do tell."

"My aunt is going to come up once a month to take me to a clinic in Kansas so I can keep getting my T-shot."

"Oh, that's great!" I was so happy for him. This had to be a huge weight off his shoulders.

He nodded but didn't say anything at first. "But then there was some bad news. I'm afraid my dad's job might be at risk. My mom kind of hinted she was worried."

"Oh." Man. The world sucked sometimes. "Would that mean he couldn't keep paying for your treatments?"

"I don't think right away. But I remember the last time he went through a job search. It was bad."

We single-filed our way between a hatchback and a giant pickup.

Maybe I could make him feel better. "My, uh, parents are going through a tough time financially. My mom even had to go back to work, at this restaurant. They cut our allowances, so I hired my sister to clean my room so she'd have enough money to buy her monthly craft kit."

"You did that for your sister?" He looked over at me, a slight smile on his face, and squeezed my hand. "That's so nice."

I shrugged. "I didn't really need that much money most of the time. And after a while they were able to increase our allowance some, so she has enough. I guess my point is, usually things work out. Does your mom work?"

"Part-time, because she's working on her Master's right now, so I hope she won't have to stop that."

"Oh, wow."

We were quiet as we wove between parked cars. Jenna and Jacob laughed about something ahead of us.

Eventually, we came out on the other side of the parking lot and got back on the sidewalk, Jacob and Jenna still enjoying themselves.

I didn't know what else to say to Mack. I wasn't going to give him empty comforting words, because I had no way of knowing what would happen. I wasn't going to basically lie.

We didn't say anything, and I focused on the warmth of his hand on the cool night.

"I won't be able to do anything after dinner," Mack said as Jenna opened the cafeteria door. "I'm still trying to catch up from the weekend."

"Okay." I tried not to let the disappointment that coursed through me show.

Maybe everything with us really wasn't okay? Now I was nervous again.

We went inside, the roar of the voices immediately surrounding us, along with the stale smell of old grease. My stomach churned.

Jenna turned around and said, "Meet over there?" She pointed to the section we often sat in.

"Sure," I said.

Then Mack went off toward the sandwich area, Jacob went in the direction of the salad bar, and Jenna and I ended up heading to the pasta station.

"How's it going?" she asked, leaning in. "Is this the first time you've seen him since the ..."

I looked at her and she waggled her eyebrows, which made me laugh, despite the tension throughout my body.

"Yeah," I finally said. "He's being weird. I don't know what's going on."

We got in line, with about six people in front of us.

"I am of no help, sorry." Jenna picked up a tray.

I grabbed one, too. "Yeah, I have no idea, either. No experience in this department."

We edged forward as two of the people left.

"I guess you just have to see what happens. He obviously cares about you, whatever happens."

That sounded really ominous and made my heart race. Was she thinking it might be over? I hadn't really, truly considered that possibility.

She grimaced. "Sorry. I didn't mean to sound so dark. I'm sure everything is good. He had that family thing or whatever. I think his family life is complicated."

I wondered how much she knew. I wanted to ask, but I couldn't betray Mack's confidence, and I had no idea what he would want other people to know.

We finally got to the serving area and both grabbed plates.

I put a heap of pasta on my plate, way more than I meant to. But I didn't think I should put it back, so I covered it in red sauce, which made things worse. I didn't want to look like a pig, but it was too late now. I looked over to see Jenna put three small piles of spaghetti on her plate, and then a scoop of one of the three pasta sauces on each one.

When she caught me staring, she sheepishly said, "I'm feeling indecisive."

"No, I was just thinking I did the exact same thing the other day when I was feeling adventurous."

"Did it satisfy your need for speed?" She raised her eyebrows sardonically.

"I don't even remember."

We laughed. On the way to the table, we stopped at the drink station to get Cokes, then found Mack and Jacob.

"What is that monstrosity?" Jenna asked Jacob as she sat down, pointing to his plate.

Mack laughed, but it wasn't full of his normal energy. "Right? I already asked. Tell them what you told me, Jacob."

I looked at the plate in question after I sat down. I could see some lettuce, tomatoes, carrots, and celery, but on top of everything was every type of meat they had on the salad bar.

"It's not that big a deal," he said, probably embarrassed. "I like salads, but I need protein, or I'll get hungry later."

"Sure," Jenna said, still teasing him. "Deli meat drenched in blue cheese dressing. Mmmm."

Jacob smiled, but then he picked up his fork and stabbed some of the meat for a first bite. He raised his eyebrows. "Mmm for real."

Jenna laughed. They had a great dynamic, but I'd asked Jenna if they were a possible item, and she emphatically said no. I didn't know why.

"What's going on with your little pasta piles?" Jacob asked Jenna. "Like you should be talking."

She put her hand to her chest, pretending to be offended. "I didn't know what I wanted. This is the advantage of buffet-style, right?"

"Oh, my God," I started. "There're huge risks with mixing and matching food. One summer day I was hungry and I couldn't decide what to eat, and somehow I settled on a can of beef stew and some frozen burritos with salsa, and it was the absolute worst, foulest combination of foods ever in the history of human cooking. I haven't been able to eat beef stew since."

Everyone laughed, but I was grimacing at the memory.

"What did it taste like?" Jacob asked before taking another bite of his deli meat pile.

"It cannot be described. Like death." I shuddered. "But it was an important lesson. You have to be careful."

"Now I want to try it," Jenna said.

"Don't." I stuck my tongue out in disgust.

Mack glanced over at me, smiling, but then he looked away. He was distant tonight. I told myself it was probably the whole hormone therapy being at risk. Like, what if Kansas did the same thing? It was so scary.

The rest of dinner was kind of quiet. The conversation was uncharacteristically bland. I think everybody could tell something was up with Mack, even if no one knew what it was.

We held hands on the way back to the dorm, but parted ways at the stairs, and that was that. I'd built it up so much in my mind that I was on the verge of tears when I got back to my room.

I heard talking inside when my hand was on the doorknob. Just one voice, so I waited. Sophia was probably filming one of her videos. I leaned against the wall. I'd give her one more minute, and then I'd just go in there quietly. It was my room, too.

Of course, I spent the minute wondering what was going on with Mack. I really didn't know, and I especially didn't know how or when I'd figure things out.

I opened the door and she looked up from her phone, where she was probably editing the video she'd just recorded.

I sat at my desk. I was glad that Mack had solved his immediate problem with his T-shot, but it still seemed precarious. And I didn't know what else was going on with him. Would we kiss again soon? Or was this the end?

∾

Dinner with Mack and Jacob Wednesday night was fine. Things were mostly normal. Well, it was Halloween, so the wider population of the college wasn't normal, but within our group, it seemed okay. Mack held my hand on the way over and sat next to me, and Jacob sat across from us, and we talked about books. But through the whole meal, I was wondering what was going to happen with Mack.

The problem was that things seemed like the normal before the kiss. He was still not looking at me as much as before, and I hadn't seen him since dinner last night.

Mack finished his sandwich last, and tossed his wadded up napkin onto his plate. "Ready?"

He said it in general and then looked at me, but he wasn't smiling. He looked too serious. Was he still stressing about his family situation? Or was it about me?

It made my heart lurch, and I was confused all over again.

I was so queasy, I didn't get ice cream. Mack didn't either, and then as soon as we got outside, Jacob said, "I need to go to the library. I'll see you guys later."

It seemed on purpose. Like he thought—or knew— Mack wanted time alone with me.

That could be good, right? I watched Jacob walk off, my anxiety increasing with each of his steps.

I didn't think it was good.

I looked over at Mack when Jacob was out of sight and we hadn't moved yet.

"Let's walk," he said. He was looking off into the distance.

My heart was already beating hard, and the dread in my stomach almost kept me in place. But I followed him, and caught up as we headed south instead of toward the dorm. Once I was next to him again, he took my hand, which threw me off. Would he be holding my hand if something bad was about to happen?

I wanted to say something. I wanted to have a voice in whatever was about to happen. I didn't want it to just happen to me. But I couldn't think of anything to say because I had no idea what was in Mack's mind.

Leaves blew across the sidewalk as we followed it around the corner of a building, saying nothing.

A group of girls in sexy-whatever costumes passed us, laughing about something. Some people had dressed up at school today, but I didn't do anything. I was too stressed.

Those girls were having more fun than we were, for sure.

I'd never been over in this part of campus. There were some concrete benches a ways down, even further away from the dorm. One of those blue lights was across from the first bench, making it look a light blue instead of white.

We seemed to be heading there.

Now I knew for sure that this was bad. He should be talking to me.

We finally got to the bench, and Mack said, "Let's sit." He dropped my hand.

We sat, with a couple inches between us. He said nothing, and after a moment I stole a glance at him. He was studying his hands, with his fingers interlocked with each other.

"Listen, Nic." He stopped there.

"Yeah." It squeaked out.

"So. Um. I ... This is hard to say." He took a deep breath. "Uh, I figured something out about myself. I really didn't know before, but I do now." He stopped again.

What was he talking about? I didn't know what to say, but I had to say something, even though I felt sick. I came up with, "Okay."

"Listen. I, um, I really care about you a lot. So it's not you ..."

Oh, God. I wanted to puke. Here it came. I was hunched forward but didn't say anything.

He tensed his fingers. "I'm asexual."

My head jerked back at this, because it wasn't what I thought he was going to say. And I wasn't sure I knew exactly what he meant.

"I really like you a lot. I feel closer to you than I have to anyone else before. But I can't be your boyfriend."

Tears instantly welled in my eyes.

He leaned forward, elbows on his knees, head in his hands. "I'm sorry. It isn't you, I promise."

I closed my eyes and the first tears rolled down my cheeks. How could I get so close, only to have it taken away?

Mack sniffed. Was he crying? I glanced over. Now he was covering his whole face with his hands.

"Are you okay?" I asked, my own voice thick.

"I don't know. I feel so bad. I feel like I strung you along. I didn't know."

The tears were falling off my cheeks but I still needed clarification. "What does being asexual mean, exactly?"

"I guess it means I'm not sexually attracted to anyone." It was muffled because he was still covering his face with his hands.

Even though I was in mild shock, the next question was obvious. "How do you know it's not just me you're not attracted to?"

He dropped his hands and looked at me. "Because I like you more than I've liked anyone. I've never had a crush on anyone before, and I thought that's what this was. But it wasn't." He wiped both his eyes.

I had to wipe my own. "Okay." I didn't think I really believed him. It still stung so much.

If he hadn't been sure, why hadn't he told me? This was terrible, and I was kind of mad.

He looked down again, elbows on his knees and hands under his chin.

Why did he string me along? Shouldn't he have at least tried to figure it out before we got this far?

He sniffed.

It was obvious he was upset, too. Part of me wanted to reach over and put my hand on his back to comfort him, but I also didn't want to because I was mad at him. Also, I wasn't sure what the touching rules were now.

I wiped more tears from my eyes.

We were quiet for a bit longer, more costumed students walking by in front of us, one group super rowdy and obnoxious. We both stared at the ground when they passed, not wanting to invite attention.

I was still crying, but I was leaning towards being pissed right now.

Finally, I was mad enough to say something. "If you knew this was a possibility, why did you lead me on?"

"I don't know. I didn't think I was. I'm sorry."

That didn't make me feel better, but what would at this stage? "Okay."

We continued sitting there, both sniffing as we tried to get ourselves back to normal.

"You know something, Nic?"

That didn't sound good.

"You should always be true to who you really are. Don't try to fit some mold other people define for you."

What was he talking about?

I didn't say anything, and he continued. "Don't be afraid

to really ask yourself who you are, and don't let society's bullshit expectations influence your understanding." He sounded a little angry.

Was he talking about being asexual? I kind of wanted to ask, but I also didn't. That seemed to be the theme for tonight.

"Okay?" he prompted.

"Okay, sure," I said, exhausted. I could barely hold myself upright.

"Do you want to go?" he asked quietly.

"Okay." I tried to stand, but I felt glued to the bench. But Mack was already standing, so I scooted forward and pushed off the seat.

My feet were lead all the way back.

My new life was over. There was no more mystery with Mack, but things were no longer perfect.

We didn't talk at all—and there was definitely no hand-holding now. When I got to my room, I texted Jenna to text me when she was back from dinner with her dad. She said it would probably be another hour, but she would. In the meantime, I was going to be crying.

I tried to compose myself as much as possible and knocked on Jenna's door, still sniffling even though I had mostly stopped crying at that particular moment. But I was sure my eyes were totally puffy. She opened the door.

"What's wrong?" she asked, her eyes wide with surprise.

I immediately burst into tears and she grabbed my shoulder and pulled me in. She guided me to her desk chair and sat across from me in her roommate's. Thank God the roommate was out.

I had to wipe my eyes as more tears fell, and I concentrated on not sniffling too much.

"What happened?" Jenna asked, her brow furrowed in concern.

"Mack," I started, more tears forming at his name. I closed my eyes and pressed on the bridge of my nose.

"I mean, I guessed. Did he ...?"

I opened my eyes to see that she was still looking at me, still looking concerned.

"He broke up with me," I finally said.

"Man, I'm sorry," she said. "I was worried. He's been different these last few days. What did he say?"

I dropped my elbows to my knees and rested my face in my hands. "He said he's asexual. He feels really bad and wants to stay friends."

God, it hurt to say. He liked me, but he was just one more guy not attracted to me. Here came another round of stupid tears I had to wipe away.

"Oh," she said, her voice higher pitched from surprise. "I would not have guessed that."

"Me neither." I thought again about how it might actually just be me. Maybe there was somebody out there he would be attracted to, but he hadn't met them yet.

I sniffled like an idiot. I could usually cry pretty quietly, but not entirely in silence.

"That really sucks. I mean, it really does. I'm sorry." She paused before saying, "You might want to be careful with that information. It's kind of Mack's thing to share."

This shocked me and I stared at her, mouth open because I couldn't breathe through my nose.

She held her palm toward me. "Sorry, I didn't mean you'd done something wrong telling me. We're all friends.

But he might not want everyone to know, you know, outside his friends."

I nodded. "You're right."

"I won't say anything about it to him." She paused, frowning in sympathy. "This really sucks. Are you going to try to stay friends?"

I tried to imagine it. Us going to dinner, studying together, talking about books. It would be hard to go back to the way things were before, because before I thought I had a chance with him, and now I knew I didn't.

I wiped my nose on a tissue from a box on Jenna's desk. "I don't know. I want to, but it will be really hard."

"Yeah, it will be." She was quiet.

I kept wiping my eyes. I couldn't seem to stop crying. Would Mack even eat with us now? What would happen with Jacob? Mack had brought him into the group, so if Mack didn't come with us for dinner, I didn't know if Jacob would, either. I would miss him. Would we still talk in class? But Jacob and Jenna got along really well, so maybe he would.

"Everything is all messed up now," I said miserably.

"Not everything. We'll definitely stay friends," Jenna said, putting her open palm on her chest.

My heart lifted for a millisecond. "Thanks." Maybe the best thing that had happened to me since coming to OAMS had fallen apart, but it wasn't the only good thing.

I should try to remember that.

Jenna's door opened and her roommate—a tall, slim Black girl who always had a basketball in hand when she wasn't in class—marched in. She glanced at me.

Jenna jumped up out of the girl's chair.

"You can stay," the roommate said. "I'm grabbing books and going downstairs to study." In addition to being actually athletic, she was also the junior class's go-to person for physics help, and she'd often hold court in the girls' lounge during study time. I found her intimidating, but she was obviously the kind of person you couldn't help but look up to.

Jenna moved out of the way and sat back down after the girl left.

"I should go, too," I said, seeing it was after eight thirty. "I need to at least try to study."

"Yeah, same here. But are you sure you're okay?"

I thought for a second. "No. But I don't think any of my teachers will care that he broke up with me."

She bobbed her head sideways. "Yeah, probably not. They always trivialize our lives."

"Yeah, I know."

She grimaced. "I am really sorry about Mack. Let me know if you need anything."

I nodded. She sounded like she meant it.

I stood up and wiped my last tears away, hoping I could make it back to my room before the next round of crying. I at least wanted to have my back to Sophia before I started again, if she was in there. But I really did need to study, so I hoped I could keep my shit together enough to get things done.

Even though it felt like my life was over, not everything had ended. I needed to be able to stay here. Going back to Emerson was not an option.

～

When I got to art class the next day, I sat down next to Jacob like normal. He looked over and said hi, then continued looking at me. I gave him the best smile I could muster.

"Are you okay?" he asked quietly, not looking at me, but leaning over so nobody else would hear.

I turned toward him but didn't say anything. I wasn't entirely sure what he was asking.

He turned his head to face me, looking uncomfortable. "I heard about ... you know. Mack."

I had to look away because now there was that familiar burning behind my eyes. I could not start crying now. I'd been doing so well all day.

I frowned and shrugged, glancing back at him. "I guess not really."

He nodded. He looked awkward, like he didn't know what to say, but at least he was being nice.

At least we could stay friends even if we didn't continue hang out a lot. My heart ached at the idea of not hanging out with him or Mack anymore. More about Mack, but still. And would Mack and Jacob hang out together? Without me? I didn't like that idea, even though I rationally knew it was none of my business.

And what if Mack ended up being attracted to Jacob? I still wasn't convinced it wasn't just me.

I needed to stop thinking about it. "I should go get my drawing," I told Jacob.

"Me too." He got up and we went to our cubbies, grabbing our stuff and heading back.

My heart nearly stopped at a new thought. "How did you find out?" I asked him as we were getting situated at our tables.

"Huh? Oh. Mack told me."

I relaxed. I was worried it was in the rumor mill or something.

He gave me an awkward smile before looking at his drawing.

So I looked at my own. I had the basic line drawing sketched out really lightly, but I was still shifting things around. Dracula was about one-third from the left side of the page, taking up most of the vertical space. He was wearing a long cape with a pointy, upturned collar, and his teeth were showing.

Had anyone ever broken up with Dracula? If they had, it probably wasn't because they were asexual. God.

Get a grip, Nic. I pressed my fingers to my forehead and closed my eyes for a moment to mentally regroup.

When I opened them, I focused on the drawing. One of Dracula's dogs was pulling off to the left, with the leash going off the page so you couldn't see the dog. Then there were six dogs of different sizes, all pulling off to the right, straining against the leashes Dracula was barely holding onto.

I glared at the ceiling until the fluorescent lights were too bright.

Okay, the drawing was looking pretty good. Dracula's quandary was pretty funny.

But it also was familiar. I was being pulled in a couple of different directions about being friends with Mack. Most of my dogs were desperate for me to stay friends. But there was one that was like, It's too risky. You'll get hurt again.

I tried to make myself focus, and closed my eyes again for a second to reset. I hadn't decided on the background or where Dracula even was standing yet. I was thinking he might be standing on a sidewalk, with the one dog pulling toward the street and the others starting down an alley. So then there would be people on the sidewalk walking. I could have someone, or a few people, staring at him. He'd be blocking the sidewalk with the leashes, so I could do something with that.

But I didn't feel like doing anything, even working on this thing. I let my head fall and stared at the table. How could Mack have just let me think he was into me like that?

I mean, I guess I knew he really wasn't sure, but why didn't he tell me that? Why let me think everything was great? As much as my heart hurt, there was still some anger roiling in my belly.

And then for some reason, my mind went to that cryptic thing he'd said at the end, about being true to yourself. Was he trying to tell me something more?

He probably was, but I still wasn't in a receptive mood.

I looked over at Jacob's drawing. He was further along on his line drawing than I was. He'd rotated it counterclockwise while he worked on something in the corner, so I could see the whole picture well. It was his regular superhero, this time in a fight scene with a caped villain. The superhero was blocking a hit from some kind of rod the villain had. But Jacob was so good at capturing natural movement that it was obvious he wasn't only in a defensive position—you could tell he was about to go on the attack, based on the clear power in his legs.

"How do you do that, Jacob?"

"What?" he asked without stopping his work.

"Capture movement like that. They're about to leap off the paper."

Now he stopped and looked at me. "What are you talking about? Yours do the same thing."

"I don't think so. You're so good at this."

"If you're not as good at it, which I'm not saying is true, you just need to practice more. I've drawn, like, a million fight scenes." He arched his eyebrows before getting back to working on his piece.

I nodded. "Yeah, you're probably right. I usually draw

people who are still. But I did a drawing of a dragon fight last year. I should take a look at that and see if it's as good as yours. I doubt it."

"I bet it is."

I liked the idea that you could need to defend yourself but still be in a position of power. It was actually a little like the dragon drawing in question. My dragon was battling another, bigger one, but she was rising from behind the mountain, totally in control of the situation.

I wished I was in control of my life. It felt like I had no control at all right now.

But that wasn't quite true. I suspected it was on me to decide whether to stay friends with Mack. That might determine what would happen with our friend group. I had a lot of power I didn't want right here. I was supposed to talk to Sam after school today, so maybe she could help me figure out how to handle things.

~

Friday night I went to the studio again. I was working on wrapping up the Dracula drawing again, and still obsessing about Mack.

And it didn't help that the RA working the desk was one of the really rude women. When I went up to the desk, she said, "What, you going to ask for a special room, too?"

What did people get out of saying shit like that?

I tried to shake it off, but it didn't help my mood or confidence. Nothing more had happened with Mack, but Jacob still came to dinner with Jenna and me the last two nights. I was glad Mack was staying away, because I was still mad, in addition to being depressed about it. It was easier to just not have to navigate interacting with him. When Sam and I talked yesterday, she agreed that Mack and I needed some time away from each other, but she thought we'd be friends again. She didn't have any specific advice for how, though. She said there was a good chance that he'd be waiting for me to make a move—like invite him to dinner or something. I hoped she was right, but I wasn't sure how that would work—or how I'd handle it.

I glanced down at the paper. I was working on the background. I'd drawn a person looking at Dracula in surprise, and then there was street and buildings. There was also a guy across the street, walking on the sidewalk.

Despite being mad at Mack, I still missed him so much. It was almost like I missed him more because of all the future time I wouldn't be spending with him.

So as I drew in details on a passing car, I obsessively went over Wednesday night. I had to make myself relax my hold on the pen as I drew. I was still trying to figure out what Mack meant with that last thing he'd said. About not letting society's stupid expectations define who you really are. And being true to yourself. Was he talking about himself, or me? Or both? He'd sounded so serious when he'd said it.

It abruptly occurred to me that he *was* talking about me. I think he knew I was nonbinary even though I hadn't admitted it to myself yet. I'd been distracted, and focused on other things lately. Maybe he knew because he had gone through something so similar, for longer than I'd been thinking about it for myself.

I knew what to do. I was going to finish off the gender identity workbook tonight after I got back to my room. I was close to the end. Whether Mack was telling me to be true to myself in this way or not, I was going to do it.

I worked on the car some more, and focused on the fact

that I did still have good friends. I just needed to figure out how to get over Mack so I could be around him again.

I finished up the car and packed up, butterflies in my stomach in anticipation of working through the book.

I made sure to hit the light switch on my way out and let the door close.

It usually didn't bother me, but tonight it felt creepy in this dark hallway all by myself. This would be the perfect spot for a murder.

This thought freaked me out and had me hurrying to the side door, and I kept scurrying once I was outside, too. I was rushing so much that I wasn't paying attention. Suddenly, I realized Mack was heading toward the dorm's front door from the other direction, and he'd already seen me.

I jolted to a stop. He was going to be more prepared than I was, because I was panicking. I wasn't ready for this. I made myself keep walking.

We kind of looked at each other as we got to the front door at almost the same time. My heart was racing like crazy.

He opened the door and held it for me. He tried to smile, but it was a big fail. "Hey."

"Hi." I couldn't hold the eye contact. It made my eyes burn with looming tears. But that anger in my stomach flared up. I walked through the door and he followed me in.

"How are you?" he asked as the door fell shut. He sounded nervous.

I stopped and turned around to face him, so many emotions swirling inside. Sadness, anger, and a little confusion—what should I do about him? "Fine. You?"

"Okay."

Then we were silent and stared at each other. I could

feel myself blushing at the awkwardness, and I hated that there was a desk RA staring at us.

"Well," we both said at the same time, which was even more embarrassing, and he sort of grimaced.

"So, I, uh, am gonna go back to my room," he said.

I nodded, still fighting tears, and turned and raced up the stairs, trying to get to my room before I started crying again.

I got back to my room and dropped my bag on the bed. I pulled the gender identity workbook off my bookshelf. My hands were shaking from the aftermath of seeing Mack. I was totally rattled. But I wasn't going to let this keep me from figuring things out.

I pulled my desk chair out and sat down. You write stuff in the workbook, so I had to sit up to work on it. This was probably the main reason I hadn't finished it yet, because I usually read lying down.

I tried to calm my hands and opened the book. There were three sections, and I'd already gone through the first two. They were kind of "woo-woo," so I hadn't done every exercise, but I did a lot of them. It mostly covered thinking about stuff, like how you viewed yourself and your gender in your childhood and so on. But this last section was called exploration, and I was hoping I'd really have an answer by the time I finished it.

I cracked open the book, my heart skipping as I considered what I might be finding out soon. What if I figured out that I really was nonbinary? Would I do something about it? I honestly wasn't sure. Obviously, I could be brave in some things, but not all.

What would Mack think if he found out I was nonbinary? Would he hear it from someone else? Or would I tell him? I had no idea what the future held, and it was scary. I might not even be nonbinary.

The first chapter in the last section had this long questionnaire in it, asking how you felt about certain things, especially your body—like height, facial hair, feet and hand size, and voice. I dutifully filled out most of them. It was kind of interesting, because a lot of them I hadn't really thought much on. I was lucky because I didn't have any overly feminine traits. I mean, I guess I had hips and my chest wasn't small, but I didn't have a particularly high voice, or delicate hands or whatever. I knew that being tall contributed to all the times people mistook me for a boy.

They also asked how you felt about your name, and that one I was pretty sure of—I didn't think I would change my name if I came out as nonbinary. I kind of liked my name. At least the short version. I might want to legally change my name to Nic instead of Nicole.

Ugh, I hated Nicole. So they were onto something after all. I'd just found a workaround.

I kept going. The next chapter explained the different labels related to gender identity. The section on gender nonconforming, which is what I'd settled on last year, also covered gender diverse, gender variant, and gender creative. It made it sound like it was more about bending the rules, like maybe you sometimes feel one way, and other times another. That wasn't me. Last year I'd thought about it in terms of kinship. And I figured out I wasn't a trans boy because I'd never felt kinship with boys. But I didn't really feel kinship with girls, either. I'd just kind of accepted that I was one. I'd never felt like a boy, so I just assumed I was a girl. I didn't know any better, so I'd accepted the binary.

I wondered how it had been for Mack. It was confusing to feel like neither—what would it have been like to actually feel like a boy? How certain was he? And how do you know? It seems so tricky.

And what was he doing right now? Was he thinking about me?

I shook my head to clear it.

The book then explained gender dysphoria, and how it was basically just anxiety and depression and stuff that comes from the way you feel about your assigned gender. The next section was on the nonbinary identity, and my heart sped up again as soon as I saw the heading.

This had to give me the answer.

But man, there were a lot of labels here. Most of them I'd heard of, but others were new. Some of them were for people who felt like both binary genders, or even all the genders, either all the time or sometimes, where others were about not having a gender at all. The last ones made the most sense to me. When I read the entry on "agender," my stomach jumped. I'd obviously been thinking about that term for a while, but it was starting to feel more right. It basically meant that I felt like I didn't have a gender at all, like it was completely outside my experience.

Mack would probably be proud of me if I came out as agender. I think he'd been hinting at it for a while. But that was not why I was going to do it. This was finally about finally understanding myself. Being totally honest and digging deep.

Still, I already missed him so much, it made me queasy. That combined with the excitement I felt reading this book made me feel totally off.

I kept going. There was a list of things that could indicate a person might feel comfortable identifying as nonbinary. One of them was wishing there was no such thing as gender and wanting nothing to do with it. That pretty much summed my feelings up, but I said yes to a lot of the other questions, too.

There was also a list of problems nonbinary people would face. Basically, it amounted to how much society was stuck on the gender binary. Then it covered stereotypes, and I had to write down stuff about myself that might be gendered, like hobbies, behaviors, and physical presentation. So many things about me were things people I'd grown up with considered "male," like my interest in fantasy art, or just fantasy at all, really. I thought a lot more girls liked fantasy since Harry Potter, but hardly any other girls in Emerson cared as much about dragons as I did. And I mostly wore guys' clothing and shoes, even though they were really more unisex. You'd definitely never catch me in a form-fitting women's t-shirt with those skimpy sleeves. Not with my chubby arms.

A knock at the door jolted me out of my head.

"Nic, lights off." The dorm mom.

I looked at the time. It was after midnight. They walked around the building looking for rooms with lights on.

"Okay," I called.

But I wasn't done. I turned the light off and shut the blinds. Then I pulled my comforter off the bed and sat back at the desk, pulling the blanket over my head and desk so I could keep working from my phone light.

It was awkward, but I could make it work.

I went on to the next chapter, which was about finding other people to learn from. I needed my computer for this, so I grabbed it and tried to get the blanket over it. It was a pain.

Why did they care how late we stayed up on a Friday night? They were so controlling. It was stupid.

But back to the book. I was supposed to go online and find videos or posts about being nonbinary to see what made sense to me. But this wasn't easy—I had to try a bunch of search terms before I started getting good results. Finally, I found some helpful videos and blog posts, so I opened them in different tabs and started going through them one by one.

For the book, they wanted me to write down some of my reactions for four of the things I'd found, so I dutifully did that.

The book also wanted me connect with other people online, like through groups or whatever. I still felt weird about that, even though it did make a lot of sense. I just had so much trouble trusting people, even in virtual spaces. But I was supposed to be doing this right, not jumping into things blindly, so I signed up for a couple of groups on Facebook for nonbinary people. I had to fill out some questions on being nonbinary, so I mentioned I was just coming out as nonbinary, and I hoped that was good enough. I doubted I'd be approved tonight.

The last thing I was supposed to do with that chapter was work on connecting with other people in real life. I couldn't see that happening, beyond my friends.

And who knew if I'd ever talk to Mack again. I closed my eyes against the pain in my heart at that thought. How had that gone so wrong? My eyes burned, but I didn't want to start crying. A couple tears escaped, and I was able to stop. I had shit to do.

So I turned to the next chapter, which talked about listening to your gut. I felt like I was doing that, and my gut was in love with the term "agender." It felt so much more accurate than "girl" ever had.

It was obvious that this part of the book was meant to be done over some time, not all in one night, but I was impatient. It was time for me to decide.

But I already had. I *was* nonbinary. I was agender. I knew it. And now it was time to figure out how to tell people. If I was brave enough. My stomach was all over the place, excited to have finally figured it out, and terrified of talking to anybody about it.

But I should at least be able to tell my family and my friends. I had my family call Sunday, and I would have to figure out when to tell Jenna, first among my friends.

But *first* first, I had to talk to Sam. She'd help me see if there was anything I hadn't thought of. I'd text her in the morning, so hopefully we could talk tomorrow.

As soon as I opened my eyes on Saturday morning, I felt different. Not like a different person—I was still me, had always been me—but I understood myself better. I made more sense. I was agender.

It was an amazing feeling. For so many years I'd felt confusion about something so basic. I'd always hated gender, but I never knew I could just recognize that it had no part in who I was. So my hatred made sense—it came from some stupid, archaic binary system being forced on somebody who exists outside of it.

I unplugged my phone from the charger and texted Sam.

—*Can you talk today?*—

It was only eight thirty, so I didn't know what I was doing up. It had been after two when I'd finally gone to bed.

I guess I was bright-eyed and bushy-tailed—as my mom would say—for my new, more self-aware, existence as an agender person.

Another thrill went through me.

But I was impatient for Sam to answer. I wondered what she was doing.

While I waited, I decided I'd do some work in my sketchbook. I didn't think I could concentrate on anything too difficult.

I played with the idea of the background in the Dracula drawing, which I still hadn't finished.

It was clear that there needed to be someone else in the background, looking on at Dracula about to lose the plot.

Then it struck me—I should include two or three people and make them all gender neutral, so no one could tell what they were.

That could be sort of fun, to see how other people inter-preted them, applying that stupid binary. They'd probably just assume they were all guys, since apparently men were the default and women were the deviation.

So stupid.

My phone dinged—finally.

—*Sure, what's up? Are you busy now?*—

My heart sped up as I typed that now worked and asked her to FaceTime. I was about to tell someone for the first time. It made sense that it would be Sam. She'd been such a fixture in my life over the last few years. I FaceTimed her.

"What's up?" she asked, looking like her happy self. "I'm glad you called. We never talk enough!"

"I know. For some reason it's hard to remember to call, even though I think about you all the time. It was so much easier when we saw each other at school every day." I was suddenly tense, thinking about what I was going to say. It would go fine. I looked away from the screen.

Sam laughed. "Now we're thousands of miles apart. But you look nervous. What's up?"

"So, I wanted to talk to you about something." I'd mentioned to her that I was sort of exploring my gender identity before, but I hadn't gone into detail. It was hard to form the words. "So, I finished that gender workbook last night. And I've finally figured it out. What I am, I mean."

"Awesome! What did you decide?"

There was a knock on my door. "Crap, there's someone here."

"You have to tell me what you decided before you answer that!" Sam said.

"Agender." I sat up as the knock sounded a second time.

I opened to door to find Marisa.

"Hi, Nic," she said, all fake sweetness and light. "I just needed to talk to you about last night."

"What?" I had no idea what she was talking about.

"The light. You were up past lights out."

I stared at her a second. "Okay, I'm sorry. I was reading and didn't notice the time. As soon as Ms. Patton knocked on my door, I turned it off."

Was she going to lecture me about this?

She fake smiled. "I know. It's just, next time make sure to pay more attention. Maybe set an alarm. It's really important that you get enough sleep. Teenagers never do, and it makes life harder."

"Okay. I'm actually on the phone with somebody. I'll make sure to get my light turned off in time from now on. I'll get enough sleep."

"Okay, great." She fake smiled again and turned to leave.

Thank God. I resisted the urge to slam the door, and shut it quietly.

I raced back to the bed and grabbed my phone. "Oh, my God. My RA is horrible."

"Is it more exciting than coming out as agender?" She raised her eyebrows at me.

"No, it's stupid. Coming out is way more important."

"Anyway, I think it makes so much sense." She nodded, looking thoughtfully off to the side. "I'm happy for you."

"Yeah, there are a lot of other labels that just don't fit, but that one makes the most sense."

"Yeah. I can see that."

I was sort of out of things to say at that point. When I didn't say anything, Sam said, "So what does it mean, from a daily life standpoint? Are you going to use they/them pronouns?"

My body quivered at the thought. "Yeah. I think so. Though I am scared."

"Yeah. Some people won't do it."

"I know. I'm not sure what I will do. Or how I will tell people. And the school. I don't know if I'll tell them."

"Are you not going to try to get your own room, like your friend? What about your roommate?"

I hadn't even thought of all that. "I don't know. I kind of think I don't want to make a big deal of it. But I have no idea how my roommate will be about it."

"It's a big decision. But so is deciding who to tell, and when. Are you telling your family?"

"Yeah, I think so. I can see how that goes. If it's bad, at least I won't be there." I frowned. I hoped it would go fine.

"It won't be bad. Your parents are nice. And your sister's the best."

"You're right." I knew she was right. "But you never know with a hundred percent certainty."

"True." She grimaced in sympathy.

"So what's going on in your life?"

She laughed, but it sounded uncomfortable, and she looked away again. "Nothing as interesting as yours, that's for sure. I think Donald may be getting bored with me. Which is a bummer because I still like him. But I think if we break up, I'll still stay in his circle of friends. I'm pretty sure I'm entrenched enough."

"Oh, that sucks. Why do you think that?"

"I don't know." She paused and took a big breath. "It's more a feeling than anything definite. He just seems less engaged when we're together. I don't know. It's hard to say exactly why."

"Ah. Well, unfortunately, I cannot give you any advice. I didn't even know my boyfriend wasn't attracted to me at all. Obviously I'm no expert." I'd tried to make a joke of it and now I felt like I wanted to puke.

"That was not your fault, Nic. It's not his fault either. It also totally was not personal. Though I do think he could have handled it better."

I was obsessing again, my mind whirring. "I think it was the kiss. That's what ruined everything."

"Maybe, but what would be the point of having a boyfriend if you never kissed? You're not asexual." She paused for a second, her brow furrowed. "Are you?"

"Definitely not. I've had lots of crushes on guys I have nothing in common with, so it wasn't like I just wanted to hang out with them and draw or something."

"Yeah. I didn't think you were, either. You were just very private about that stuff."

This was a definite reference to the thing with Zach, the

guy I'd liked who she ended up dating because she didn't know I liked him. I finally came clean about that when I visited her in Scotland.

"Yeah," I finally said after we'd stared at each other awkwardly for a moment. But I didn't want to think about Mack anymore. "What are you doing today?"

"Just staying in. Practicing my oboe, probably. Drawing some. Donald is down in England on a family thing—or at least that's what he told me." She sighed. "I hope it's true."

"Me too. Maybe he's just going through a mid-relationship crisis."

"A what?" She laughed.

"Like a mid-life crisis, but in a relationship."

"I love it." She was smiling, which was good to see. "We should all start using that term."

"You have been together a while."

"I guess. But neither of us is *forty*. Can you imagine?" She looked horrified at the thought.

"Oh, my God, what would we look like, all wrinkly. Would we have gray hair?"

"Right? I mean, but also, what will we be doing? Will we have kids?" Her eyes widened at that thought. "Do you think you'll have kids?"

My own eyebrows rose in surprise. "That's a good question. But you know that's never been a dream of mine, or something I've ever envisioned for my future."

"Me neither. I'm usually thinking about the things I'm going to accomplish, not about being married or whatever."

"I don't think either of us is destined to be a soccer mom."

"Especially not you," she said pointedly before laughing.

"Oh, you're right. I guess I have a lot to learn about what terms to use now." I really did. I would have to do some research on this. "I mean, I guess I'm Isabella's sibling now, not sister. And my parents' child. It's weird. Soccer parent doesn't have the same ring."

"Everyone will get used to it. It just takes time."

"Yeah."

"I have faith." She sounded full of wisdom.

"Me too, I think. This just feels so right. But I guess I should get going. I have so much homework this weekend."

"You know you work too hard," Sam said, jokingly pointing her finger at me.

"I have to do well enough to stay here for the art class. Ms. Mangal is so much better than any other art teacher I've ever had. But, oh, my God, physics is killing me. That one scares me."

"Well, good luck. It's so great that you've ended up in this cool art class. I never would have expected it." She turned serious. "I'm so glad you went there."

"Me, too."

"Okay, Nic. I'm glad you called. Was I the first person you told?"

"Yeah."

"That makes me feel really good." I could hear the smile in her voice. "I'm so glad we're still friends."

"Yeah, same. Thank you for always being such a good friend. I think you saved me in Emerson." For some reason, I was on the verge of crying. For once, not because of Mack, but because of Sam. Crying when you're happy is so stupid.

She laughed a little. "You would have figured things out."

"Maybe," I countered. "Talk to you later."

We hung up, and I wiped my eyes.

Now one other person knew I was agender. It was weird

to think that only two of us, of the eight billion people in the world, knew this.

I'd be adding to the count tomorrow, because I was definitely telling my family.

But I was going to be nervous all day today and tomorrow about how it was going to go.

And soon I'd be opening it up to more people. How were people going to react? Was I going to have any problem with people here? What would it be like when I went back to Emerson?

I was really nervous before my Sunday family call. I would to tell my family on this call. It was going to be hard, and I had no idea how they would react. I didn't think it would be a problem, but sometimes people could be weird when they were surprised. But there was no other way to do it. Well, I could email, but I trusted my parents enough to tell them face to face. Well not face to face, exactly, but at least in real time.

And of course there was Isabella. I was pretty sure she would stay supportive, but I was kind of paranoid that I would suddenly be just too different for her, and she'd turn on me.

No, she wouldn't. She was the best sister.

Still, I was lying on my bed, stressing. My stomach was overly active, but there was also this little part of me that was excited. I was really going to do it. I was going to be brave enough to really tell the world I wasn't who they thought I should be. And this was step one—my first time telling the people who had known me longest.

I had begged off lunch because I was too scared to tell

anybody here yet. I wanted to see what my parents said first. If it went badly, I could always back out and leave it there.

The phone rang, and I stared at the screen. My mom's number.

My heart was racing by the time I answered it, after the third ring. "Hello?"

"Hi, honey," Mom's voice said.

"Hi, Nic!" Isabella called, probably standing right next to Mom.

"Your sister says hi," Mom teased.

"I heard. Put me on speaker."

"Nic, they picked my drawing to display on the bulletin board!" Isabella said.

"Which one is it?" I asked.

"The one of the unicorn with the rider. I sent it to you."

"That's great. It was a good drawing. Maybe you'll become an artist, too. You just have to practice a lot."

"Who has time for that?" she asked, all disdain.

Mom and I laughed.

"Okay, maybe you won't become an artist. You can be whatever you want."

"I know," Isabella said.

"So what's going on in your life, Nic?" Mom asked.

No way I was telling her about Mack. I hadn't ever told them we were officially dating. And now Mack and I weren't together, and maybe we weren't even friends. My insides twisted. Last week, I'd decided I would tell them about Mack today, but obviously everything had changed.

Besides, the agender thing was way bigger. A shudder went through me. This was going to be so hard.

"You there, sweetie?"

"Oh, yeah. Sorry. I've just been busy with school. You know, lots of homework. Physics, and math, and pre-calc. It's a lot. And my current drawing is almost ready to start inking." That wasn't true, but who had control of verbal diarrhea?

"That's nice," Mom said. "Is this the Dracula one?"

"What dogs are you drawing?" Isabella asked, excited. She'd always wanted a dog and our parents always said no.

I listed all the different types and she giggled at the Pomeranian.

"Well, we both want to see it when it's ready," Mom said.

"I can send you a picture when I finished the line drawing."

"I can't wait to see it," Isabella said.

"What else is going on?" Mom asked. "Are you still meeting your book group?"

Oh, that hurt my heart. Were we? I had no idea what was going to happen. We had pushed it back an extra week because the book we were reading now was really long, so it wasn't until next weekend. "Um." I needed to act normal. "Yes. Still meeting. The next one is next Sunday."

"That's great. I can't believe it's already almost Thanksgiving!"

Oh, wow. That meant I'd go home for a few days. I'd have to see my stupid brother. And it would be after I'd come out.

Which, thinking of that, I still needed to do. But my nerves were all over the place.

"We're going to come Tuesday evening to pick you up," Mom said.

"Okay. We can talk more about it later." I took a deep breath. I needed to do this. I'd decided, and even though I was scared, it was the right thing. It was who I really was. I'd been so focused on Mack until last Wednesday, now it was time I really focused on me.

"Are we going to have the cranberry sauce this year, Mom?" Isabella asked.

"Just like every year, honey. Straight out of the can. You know your dad likes it."

"Maybe I'll try it this time," Isabella said.

Mom and I laughed, but mine sounded off because I was so nervous. I was on the verge of sweating.

"Mom?" I said.

"Yeah, honey?"

Should I have her get Dad? I suddenly wasn't sure. I hadn't planned this part out. I had imagined telling only her and Isabella.

I decided I'd stick with them for now, and Mom could tell Dad. I wasn't sure how he'd react. It seemed easier to do one at a time.

"What is it?" She must have sensed I was nervous.

"I need to tell you something." There, that was a start and I couldn't back out now without looking stupid.

"Okay," Mom said, a strain in her voice making her sound worried.

"So I, uh, figured something out about myself."

"Okay ..." she said, stretching out the A. At least she was paying attention. She could tell it was a big deal.

I took another deep breath. "I figured out I'm nonbinary."

"Really?" Isabella said. "You know, that makes a lot of sense."

"What does that mean, exactly?" Mom asked, her voice overly chipper, like she was putting on her Very Supportive Mom hat. "I've heard about it but don't know much."

"It means I'm not a girl or a boy. And I want to use they/them pronouns instead of she/her." My stomach was in turmoil, but part of it was excitement because I was saying it out loud again. Sam was one person, but now I was really making it happen.

There was silence while she processed what I'd said.

Isabella spoke first. "Dana in my class is nonbinary. But the teacher won't use the right pronouns, and some kids make fun of them."

Which was exactly why I didn't even seriously consider it when I was living there. Things were just different here. Not hugely different, but enough. "That sucks, Isabella. Thank you for using the right pronouns for them."

At least, I thought things were different here.

"Okay," Mom said. "Does this mean you're gay? I heard something last year."

"No. God, Mom. You overheard somebody making fun of me, that's all. I'm not gay or straight now because I'm not a girl or a boy. But I like boys. That's who I like."

Okay, now that was some real turmoil in my stomach. That was a lot of information to throw out there.

"Okay, honey." She sounded confused. But she obviously was trying, because she then asked, "What do we need to do?"

"Just use the right pronouns when you talk about me. And don't call me your daughter anymore. Call me your child." I felt a sudden wave of elation that I was doing this. "Or progeny," I joked.

They both laughed. Mom said, "You're so funny, Nic. I'll stick with child."

"Okay." I was smiling at this point, still feeling good. "And you have to tell Dad. No point with Caleb as he won't do it."

"He needs to know, too," Mom said. "He has to stop being such a turd."

I laughed and Isabella went into hysterics. I almost

couldn't believe that she had called her own son a turd, but seriously, that was exactly what he was right now. I still couldn't believe how close we had been when we were younger, and then how it changed overnight.

"Do you want to tell Dad yourself?" Mom asked. "He's in the den. If you want, I can tell him. But I'm going to go out there so you can at least say hi."

I felt good coming out, but it wavered. "You tell him."

She walked out to the den and we said hi, and I told him how school was going, and then Isabella—who had only just then stopped laughing like a crazy person—asked Mom for the phone because she had a secret to tell me. She took the phone off to her room and told me about the two boys in her class that liked her, and how they argued all the time over who could sit next to her at lunch.

It made me smile, because Isabella and I couldn't be more different. Apparently, I was turning people asexual, while she had boys fawning over her. But I still loved her so much. She was the best sister. I guessed that she would probably be the one in the family to make sure they all used the right pronouns. She was loyal like that.

But now I had to see how it was going to go here. I was feeling good, but it could all come crashing down if something went wrong.

Monday, I stood in front of an easel working on my acrylic painting, the still life with a bowl of plastic fruit. My mind was still spinning with the fact that I'd come out as agender to my family. And the simple fact that I had figured out who I was. It was invigorating to finally feel sure about it.

When I first got to class, I'd wondered if I should go for it and tell Jacob. But that was too risky, since the others might hear. Plus, I thought I really should tell Jenna first, or at least at the same time.

I was working on the painting to get it out of the way. I wasn't loving painting, but it was okay. I was not good at it, so it wasn't as satisfying as drawing. But I was ahead on the Dracula drawing, so I figured I should work on this.

I'd painted the background of the still life a sort of dusty red for the tablecloth and a pale cream for the wall. The bowl was made of wood, but I wasn't really going to try to reproduce the grain. That was beyond my skills in paint at this moment.

I was obsessing over telling Jenna and Jacob. And Mack, though I wasn't sure how to do that should. Should I even tell him at all? Or let him hear it from somebody— maybe Jacob? I could ask Jacob to tell him. They still talked.

I did a base layer of yellow for the banana, which also had brown spots like an actual banana would.

A wave of sadness washed over me. How was I going to get over Mack? This was so much worse than the guys I'd had crushes on last year. Even the one I'd thought liked me back, but who'd apparently preferred Sam.

That still stung, actually. I frowned, unable to forget the moment she'd told me he'd asked her out. I'd really thought he was close to asking *me* out. What a nightmare that had been.

But I was glad I'd told Sam how I'd felt in Scotland. It made her feel bad, but it was good practice for me to be more honest with my friends. That vulnerability thing.

I mixed some red for the apple, spreading the paint out on the palette more than I'd intended. I needed to be more careful. There was only so much room on this thing.

My phone vibrated. I pulled it out and saw a text from Isabella. —*I'm so glad you told us yesterday*—

My forever loyal little sister. I texted back. —*Me too. But what are you doing texting in the middle of school?*—

—*Dentist appointment. I'm with Mom*—

—*Before or after?*— I asked.

—*After*—

—*Back to school, then*—

She just responded with a bunch of frowny faces.

I put my phone away and got back to my paint. This palette had an airtight lid and would keep the paints fresh for, like, weeks, from what I understood.

What had painters done in the old days?

Actually, they didn't have the problem of paint drying because they used oils. Those took ages to dry. I had no interest in oils. Too complicated and messy.

Sort of like my life.

Would it always be this way? Would I ever really go out with someone? For longer than a week?

I realized I'd been sitting there, paintbrush an inch away from the canvas, for a while. I forced myself to focus and paint in the apple. There was also a plum and an orange.

I checked the time. I only had fifteen minutes left in class, so I wouldn't get far. I worked on mixing an orange and a dark purple for the last two pieces, and got the base coats done on those. I'd be able to come in and add to them all tomorrow.

Would I have told anyone else about being agender by tomorrow, or would I still be obsessing in my head? I didn't know what would happen at dinner tonight.

Or, I didn't know what I was going to do, because this was about actions I was going to take or not, not things that would just happen.

Tuesday night, Jenna, Jacob and I were studying in Booth Forest, the table full of wadded up taco wrappers.

I hadn't told them yet, but I still felt electrified with my new understanding of myself. My brain kept going, *I'm agender, I'm agender, I'm agender*.

I wasn't quite sure why I hadn't told them. It had gone fine with Sam, and with my family, and I knew my friends would be fine with it—probably actively supportive, if I needed it.

I stared at my physics book, but I was trying to figure out why I hadn't told them. I was also trying not to think about the fact that I was going to have to see Dr. Jones for office hours tonight. She seemed to dislike me, and I still didn't know why.

The reason I hadn't told my friends probably came down to my problem trusting people. I'd known my family and Sam for years, obviously. But even though I felt so close to my friends, they were still new friends.

I thought of what Sam had said when I'd messed up so bad with Mack, about making myself vulnerable. I trusted Mack and it turned out fine. I knew Jenna and Jacob were good people, too, but there was still that hesitant part of me.

Should I go out on a limb, and trust them more?

I looked over at Jenna's spot at the table, next to me. She had her chem book open and a couple different notebooks, some with chemical structures drawn all over the place. Across from us, Jacob was working on calculus.

I looked back at my physics book, but soon found myself staring at Jenna's water bottle, parked between us. It was covered in book-related stickers, ones that said "I love reading" or showed stacks of books with a coffee cup on top.

I hadn't been able to study properly since I'd figured things out Friday night. I really needed to get myself in order, as I had homework and tests coming up.

If I told them, it might clear my head.

I glanced again at each of them, heads down in their work. I probably shouldn't interrupt, but I decided I was going to anyway.

"Um, guys?" I said, utterly lacking in confidence.

They both looked up from their books, at me.

"I, uh, wanted to tell you something." My hands were shaking. I knew I could trust them, but maybe my body didn't know.

Neither of them said anything.

"So ... I'm agender. I decided it was time to admit it to myself on Friday night."

"Cool," Jenna said. She smiled. "I'm glad you figured it out."

"Did you know?" I asked, surprised.

She held her hands up. "No, that's not what I meant. I just mean, I'm sure it wasn't easy to figure it out, and you must have thought about it a lot."

Jacob nodded like he knew what she was talking about.

"Yeah, that's true," I said. "I started really thinking about it over a year ago." I looked at the wooden bench behind Jacob's shoulder. There was a knot there.

"What pronouns are you going to use?" Jacob asked.

"They/them. But I'm not sure how that's going to go here."

"Well, I'll make sure everybody around does it right," Jenna said. Jacob echoed her.

That made me smile. "Thanks."

See, I knew they'd be supportive. Sam was so right about putting yourself out there, but just being smart about it.

They were both still looking at me, curious expressions on their faces. "Well, I don't need any more of your time," I joked. "We can get back to work. I just wanted you to know."

"Got it," Jenna said as Jacob nodded. Then they both looked back at their books and continued with their homework.

So I looked back down at my physics book, but my brain was still all charged up. Now I was wondering how things were going to go with other people. Who else would I tell? Who else should I tell? I didn't really know. Did I want everyone to know?

Should I make sure somebody who was a big gossip found out so it would spread fast?

I really didn't like the idea of being the topic of conversation. But that would be unavoidable.

This was going to be a weird few weeks. Maybe if things got crazy, they'd die down over Thanksgiving.

Without a doubt, I was walking into unknown territory.

And when would I tell Mack?

For the Dracula critique, I wasn't as nervous as before, but Jacob and I looked at each other and grimaced when Ms. Mangal said she would start with me this time. I thought she'd switch the order, but she must have forgotten and no one said anything.

I headed up to the front of the room and talked about how this drawing was mostly meant to be fun, again putting two things together that don't go together.

I decided to wrap things up. "I don't know a lot about dogs, but I thought it would be fun to do a bunch of different types, so I spent some time on Google to find some interesting ones. So that's what this drawing is about."

I stood back while everyone came up with their notebooks to look at the drawing up close. Rachel didn't look at me, which I was glad for. Jacob smiled at me while he waited toward the back of the pack around the easel.

I wish Jacob and I had talked sooner. It was dumb that we wasted all that potential friendship time. Dual shyness was crap.

I glanced at him again. He was kind of cute. His skin was fairly light brown, light enough that you could see a spattering of freckles across his nose and cheeks. For some reason those freckles charmed me.

Was this a sign that I was moving on from Mack? I didn't think I really was interested in Jacob, just that it was hard not to see him as cute. Maybe it was because I liked him so much as a person. I didn't know.

I needed to stop thinking about that. It was confusing.

I looked at Lily, who was one of the ones nearest to the drawing now. She was looking closely and squinting and I couldn't wait to hear what she was going to say.

Finally, everyone was done and they went back to their seats.

Jacob had to start, and he said he really like the overall composition, and the leash that was off the page was intriguing because the viewer could imagine whatever kind of dog they wanted. His opportunity was that the range of values could be greater. This was a problem I always had. He was right. I'd heard this on the last one, too. I never leave enough light areas, so it was mostly middle-dark areas with some really dark spots. Once you put ink down, you can't really take it up, so you can always make something darker, but not lighter.

Someone said that they liked Dracula's facial expression, which was nice because I still struggled to do faces when they were small. Lily said the cross-hatching looked really good since I had done it with a fine pen. Then she said that it might be interesting if there were more activity in the background, to add to the general sense of chaos in the picture.

I kept my face neutral when we finally got to Rachel. But all she said was that she thought the dogs looked good. Then I got nervous again because this was the part where she could totally say something passive aggressive.

"I can't tell if the people in the background are men or women," she said, clearly annoyed.

Mission accomplished, you dumbass. I kept a straight face and nobody else said anything. That was it.

My turn was over and Jacob was up. His was so good— his superhero fighting his villain. It honestly looked like they were actively in motion. I hadn't done very many drawings like that. After our conversation, I'd looked at the dragon fight drawing. It was pretty action-y—not as good as Jacob's, but they did look like they were in motion. I should do more like that to get better, like he said. Maybe for the final drawing. This was the one that had to be a self-portrait, but of me doing something I wouldn't do. Dancing or something. I could not imagine myself ever dancing. Not happening.

I'd have to think about it over the weekend and decide on some options to thumbnail on Monday. It could be another fun one, or I could make some sort of statement like I'd tried with the previous one. Whatever I did, it could be fun. I was really getting the hang of this art thing.

PART V

NIC SALSA DANCING

Monday I sat in art class, thumbnailing different ideas for the self-portrait. Some of the ideas I'd had involved me in a prom dress, me dancing, me playing golf or another sport—basketball, maybe—me as a princess, either Disney or wearing a tiara, me riding a horse, me shopping, and me in a beauty pageant. I was sketching out these ideas, trying to see what I liked.

One thing I was struggling with was whether to represent myself as I really was—agender—or to feminize myself in the typically female activities (like wearing a dress or something like that).

The room was really quiet today for some reason. I glanced over and Jacob was also thumbnailing, but they were too small for me to really see what was going on in them.

He must have sensed me looking because he gave me a smile before getting back to work.

So I did a few versions of each of my ideas, trying to

stretch my imagination. I did more of the dancing ones, with a pretty hilarious one of me grinding with somebody. I'd be too embarrassed to show that to people. There were a lot of different types of dancing I could do, though.

I set my pencil down and sat upright on my stool. I couldn't imagine myself ever dancing—it wasn't even something I did in the privacy of my own room—so it fit the bill.

But then a flash of Mack flew across my mind. Would I have danced with him if we'd continued dating? Like at prom or something?

I really couldn't imagine the answer to that ever being yes, but who knew. Maybe we'd have done it as a joke. My heart skipped a beat at that crazy thought, like it could have happened.

It would never happen. I got queasy, thinking of Mack like that again. Would I ever be completely over him?

I went back to my computer for more ideas. A salsa dancing image showed up as I dragged my fingers along the trackpad.

That one could be interesting. There was a lot of stereo-typical passion in that type of dance, and it was very gendered, all of which made it even less likely I'd be doing it. I started digging deeper into the salsa dancing idea, and continued googling.

There sure was a lot of leg showing on the women salsa dancers. The dresses tended to fly all over the place.

But it would be good practice for drawing fabric, which was still difficult. It would also be good for trying to capture action like Jacob did so well.

So I added some more thumbnails based on the different positions in the images.

But I still had to decide if I'd be in a dress. Or I could

even be the guy in the couple. Or I could just be an agender dancer doing the woman's moves.

The dress would be interesting, so I decided to go for that, but instead of wearing the high-heeled dance shoes they wore, I'd be wearing my Vans.

I'd decided it, then.

Me salsa dancing in Vans with ... who? I had to figure out who the partner would be. A guy, another nonbinary person, or what? I'd see what happened when I got further along in my composition development.

But definitely it wouldn't be Mack.

I was downstairs in the dorm lobby waiting for Jenna so we could walk over to the library for our book group.

This girl who I didn't know, other than that she was a senior, came out of the stairwell and stopped and looked me up and down, which made me turn my head slightly in confusion, or self-defense, I wasn't sure.

I didn't know why she was looking at me, as I was my normal self—jeans and a t-shirt, my purple Vans on my feet.

So I looked back. She was in a yellow halter top and white shorts, a full face of makeup, and I'm sure people thought she was cute. She looked girly to me, so it was unlikely this was a friendly gesture on her part.

"Are you trans?" she asked.

"No, I'm agender," I answered without thinking. Though I did know that a lot of non-binary people identified as trans, but I knew what she was asking, and it wasn't about the subtleties of gender identity.

The girl said, "Huh," but she didn't leave.

The fact that I'd just said that to a stranger was both

thrilling and terrifying. I wasn't even sure why I'd done it. Was it because she caught me off guard, or was I doing this now?

Jenna came out from the stairwell. When she walked over to me, the other girl turned and went off toward the TV area.

"Who was that?" Jenna asked.

"I have no idea, but I just told her I'm agender." I grimaced, unsure now.

"Oh, wow. I guess you're going all-in then. Good for you."

I nodded, but my heart was racing now from concern over what I'd done.

Jenna squeezed my shoulder. "It'll be fine. Let's go."

I nodded, trying hard to believe her. We headed out.

Outside it was really starting to look like fall, with the leaves changing. The trees were covered in orange now instead of the green of a few weeks ago. My life had also changed dramatically in the last three weeks. I'd gone from having my first boyfriend, to getting dumped, and then coming out as agender.

"How's physics going?" Jenna asked as we passed the next building.

"Ugh. I don't want to talk about it." I really didn't. I was so stressed about that class.

"Okay, topic change, then. Are you looking forward to Thanksgiving?"

"Not really. My parents and sister will be fine, but my brother will be an asshole about it. He won't use the right pronouns, for sure, and will make fun of me any time my parents aren't around."

"That sucks," Jenna said, growling. "For me, I just love turkey. And the sliced crap from the deli doesn't cut it."

That made me laugh. "I'm personally a fan of corn and mashed potatoes. Don't really like turkey."

We were past the gym, getting close to the end of this path.

"Wait up!" I heard from behind us.

Jenna and I both stopped and turned around. There was Jacob, jogging to catch up with us.

"Hey," Jenna said. "What's your take on Thanksgiving food?"

He laughed, and we continued on our way, talking about the absurdity of canned cranberry sauce and the correct ratio of pumpkin pie to whipped cream.

By the time we got inside the library, we had established that turkey gravy was generally superior to brown gravy, but it didn't hold a candle to sausage gravy.

"Biscuits and gravy," Jacob said, rubbing his belly as we waited for the elevator.

When we got close to the room, we could see that Mack was already in there. My heart sped up. I had no idea what I was going to say. I would have been stressing about it all the way here if we hadn't been talking about food.

We kept walking toward the room and Mack waved at us. He was looking right at me, but his face was unreadable.

Finally, Jenna opened the door and we all said hi. I was feeling shy again, and I sat in the spot diagonally across from Mack. Jacob sat next to him, which left Jenna next to me.

"How are you all?" Mack asked.

"Good, good," Jenna said.

Jacob said, "Same."

They all looked at me.

"Good," I finally muttered, feeling awkward. I didn't want to be like this. I wanted things to be back to normal.

Maybe I needed to do something big, go out on another limb.

"So, Mack," I started. "Um, I wanted to tell you that, well, I'm agender. I'm going to be using they/them pronouns from now on."

Mack smiled, looking genuinely happy. "Oh, wow. That's great. I'm glad for you. I know you've been thinking about it for a long time. It's good to be true to yourself. You know I think that's important."

He looked thoughtful for a second before continuing. "So actually, since we're being honest with each other, I should tell you all that I have realized I am asexual. I didn't know before, but I figured it out."

Jenna nodded. Jacob looked reflective.

"What, did Nic tell you?" Mack asked.

I grimaced. "Sorry, I was upset. Jenna told me not to tell anyone else."

"I didn't know," Jacob said. "I wonder if it might make life simpler, really."

Mack laughed. "Well, maybe long term. I can't say it's been uncomplicated so far."

He looked at me sheepishly, which made me blush. It was awkward to have everyone thinking about my love life. My failed love life.

Jenna put her hands together. "Well, if we're all sharing, then I can add to it. I'm gay."

"Really?" I said, truly surprised. How could I have had no idea?

Mack laughed at me and said, "I thought so."

"Me, too," Jacob said.

Jenna smiled at them. Then she nodded, looking amused. "Nic, you don't always pay the most attention."

"Oh," I said. But oh, my God, she was right.

"It's okay, I'm just giving you a hard time." She patted my shoulder.

"No, you're right. It's stupid. I always expect people to recognize my differences as being fine, but then I assume other people are like everyone else. Sorry."

Jenna laughed and Mack and Jacob smiled.

"I guess since it's a confession party," Jacob said, "I'm gay, too. Or maybe bi. I'm not quite sure about that."

"Called it," Mack said. "In my head, at least."

"Same," Jenna said.

"Well, you guys will be gobsmacked, but I had no idea," I said. "I'm over here, still being totally clueless. Sorry."

Everyone laughed.

"So, like, how long have you guys known?" I asked, looking at Jenna and then Jacob.

They looked at each other and then Jenna said, "I've been pretty sure for a while—or at least, I knew I didn't like boys that way. I actually thought I might be asexual too, or grace or whatever, because I'd never really liked any girl in real life. Just famous ones."

"What does grace mean?" I asked. Mack and Jacob looked confused, too.

"It's from the way people abbreviate asexual as ace. So grace is gray asexual. It means you're mostly asexual but rarely you might be attracted to someone. Just very few people."

"Oh." I immediately wondered if that applied to Mack. I stole a glance at him, and he looked contemplative, like he was wondering too. It kind of made me feel sick, thinking that there might be somebody else out there that Mack would be attracted to.

But there was nothing to be done about it. I knew this, but it was hard to convince my heart, which still ached.

"So who are your celebrity crushes?" Jacob asked, to kill the awkward silence.

"Ah, if only Taylor Swift and I could meet in real life, it might be a beautiful thing." She sounded wistful.

"She's too old for you," I pointed out.

"What are you talking about?" she scoffed. "This is fantasy. But anyway, I finally have found someone I do like in real life."

"Who?" Mack and I both said.

"I'll never tell. She's a senior and I'm sure she's totally straight, but at least it tells me I'm not asexual." She looked at Mack. "Not that I'm saying it's a bad thing. It's just that I wasn't sure, and now I know."

"You've just given us a mystery to solve," Mack said. "Who is it?"

"Don't," she said. She wasn't mad, but she obviously meant it, and Mack nodded in acceptance.

We all looked at Jacob, since it was his turn.

"Uh, I've known since middle school. At least about being gay. The bisexual thing came up more recently. Nobody here." He nodded. "So yeah."

"I guess we're not getting details from you," Jenna said.

"Nope."

Jenna nodded. "I guess we're like OAMS' LGBTQ Dream Team."

"With a big emphasis on the multiple meanings of 'Q,'" Mack said, a sardonic expression on his face. "And don't forgot the 'A.' Or at least a plus."

"Yeah," Jenna said, and Jacob and I both smiled. We might not be questioning as much anymore, though.

We were all quiet for a moment.

"So, uh, should we talk about the book?" Mack asked.

Jenna nodded. "Let's do it."

I was feeling so weird. I'd shared something personal, and now I knew so much more about all my friends.

It made me wonder, what was going to happen next in my crazy new world?

∼

Monday wasn't the greatest. After lunch, I headed into the bathroom. I pushed open the door and two senior girls were in there, talking.

"You can't be here," one said. "This is the *girls'* bathroom."

"Yeah, and you're not a girl," the other one said. "Apparently."

I just stared at them. The first one was wearing a white skirt and black fitted t-shirt and the other had on jeans and a lacey shirt, and of course both of them had on full makeup. Nobody would look at them and wonder what their gender was.

Unlike me. But I didn't want them to wonder—I wanted them to not care.

I went in anyway and into a stall.

One of them made an annoyed grunt. "Why do people have to do that? What's wrong with just being a girl?"

I fumed. Nothing was wrong with *just being a girl*—if you actually were a girl. I wasn't. The physical stuff was genetic error. I knew in my mind who I was, even if these girls couldn't understand that.

They eventually left. I waited until I knew they were gone to leave the stall and wash my hands.

The rest of the day, people were staring, and I got a few snide comments. It wasn't as bad as it would have been at Emerson, but still. Not great.

After school, I was sitting at my desk in my room before dinner when Sophia came in.

I turned and we nodded at each other, and then I could hear her moving around the room and dropping her backpack in her desk chair. But I kept working on my chem homework.

"Nic?" she said.

My pulse quickened. Was she going to say something bad? "Yeah?" I didn't turn around, but that was normal for us.

"So, I heard you're agender today."

I closed my eyes as my heart sank. "Yeah." Everybody must know by now. But this was scary, with Sophia. Was she going to try to change rooms? There had been a lot of looks in the halls today, and some rude and nasty comments, but nothing too terrible, besides the bathroom thing. But now it was my roommate talking about it.

"Can you, like, explain how that works?"

That surprised me because she didn't sound like she was mocking me. I turned around and she was leaning against her desk, looking at me.

"Are you being serious?" I asked.

"Yeah. It seems strange to me, but a lot of things do. And things are a lot different here from home." She shrugged. "I just want to understand."

"Okay." I shifted in the chair so I wasn't twisted so uncomfortably. She was also from a small town, so I knew what she meant. "So, agender means I don't feel male or female. Gender isn't something I feel at all, and I hate when people think I am either a girl or a boy."

Her brow was furrowed. "How do you ... know?"

"It's hard to explain if you don't feel this way. But basically, I don't feel any connection to being female, even though I have all the physical stuff that goes with that. All the unpleasant stuff."

She nodded. "There's some of that, for sure."

"But my dislike for my period or whatever is much stronger than the normal irritation most of you all feel." I flushed from talking so frankly about this.

"And you're not trans? You don't feel like a boy?" She was clearly trying to understand, but I could hear confusion in her voice.

"No, I've never felt like a boy. I get called sir a lot and I hate it."

"Some people are saying Mack turned you this way."

A flame of rage rose up in me. They couldn't even allow me enough of my own power to know myself. I gritted my teeth.

She continued, "But I said you aren't just a blind follower. This doesn't seem like something you'd do on a whim."

It was nice that she'd noticed that about me. "It's not. I'm not a trans boy. But the word trans can be used for nonbinary people, too."

"So what is nonbinary?" She sat down in her chair, her knees to the side so she could continue looking at me.

"Nonbinary is more like an umbrella term. It covers a lot of different labels, including agender. But some people feel like both genders at different times, or even the same time, and stuff like that, and nonbinary covers that, too. Basically anything that allows for more than only male or only female all the time."

"Okay. I guess I don't really understand what it feels like, but I guess that all makes sense. It's a lot, though."

I bit my bottom lip. I wasn't sure what this conversation

was really all about, but she seemed genuine enough, and interested in learning more.

"Does this mean you use those other pronouns?" she asked.

"Yeah, I use they/them."

"So how does that work exactly?"

It was weird having her looking at me like she was really interested in this conversation.

"You know how when you don't know the gender of somebody, like a stranger or a hypothetical person?" I asked.

"What do you mean?"

"Like if I said, Do you know who your teacher will be next year? Will they be nice or not? And how that sounds totally normal."

"Oh yeah," she said in a slightly high-pitched voice. She obviously was kind of amazed by that. "You're right."

"That usage has been in English for hundreds of years."

"Huh."

I had to finish explaining. "So basically, you use that phrasing when talking about nonbinary people. At least if they use they/them. Some people use other pronouns."

"Okay. Well, thanks for explaining it to me."

"Sure."

She looked away and turned back to her desk.

But I was curious.

"Sophia?"

"Yeah?" She turned back toward me.

"Why ... do you care? I thought you didn't like me." Look at me being brave.

"Oh, I like you fine." She waved her hand dismissively before cocking her head to the side. "I mean, I was unsure at first. You know I'm from a small town. Things are different here. I always knew there were some stupid things about people in Oklahoma, like how they think evolution is something you choose to 'believe' in." She made air quotes. "I think it's so stupid that people think evolution and Christianity are incompatible. I mean, maybe God created this awesome, self-sustaining system so he didn't have to micromanage the whole planet."

I was so surprised by this turn of conversation.

"I don't really believe that. I'm not really into religion in general."

I had to make an effort to not laugh since she'd totally read my mind. "Me neither. But it is an interesting perspective."

"But anyway, I guess what I'm saying is, my eyes have been opened, and I'm trying to cancel out all the red state training I've had growing up in a small town here." She nodded thoughtfully.

I heard my phone ding. Jenna asking where I was.

Oh, crap. "That's really nice of you. Thank you for trying to learn. I'm late meeting my friends." I stood up.

"No problem. See ya later." She turned back around at her desk and I raced out of the room.

So much for chem.

On the stairs heading down, I wondered if I'd be running into anyone else who would comment in some way on the day's news. I hoped I could handle it.

When I stepped out of the stairwell, Marisa was sitting at the reception desk. She shook her head and rolled her eyes.

And, there it was. People could really suck.

I wondered what would be next. I honestly didn't know if I was handling it right or not. What did handling it really even mean at this point?

Tuesday, I went into the art room right after class and worked on my self-portrait. The art club board meeting was starting in a few minutes. I was dreading more contact with Rachel. I don't think she'd heard before class yesterday, but she'd stared at me in class today.

I tried to put her out of my mind. I was sketching some Vans in preparation for the salsa dancing drawing. I worked for a few minutes before the other board members arrived.

Ms. Mangal came out of the back. She had on jeans today, which was unusual. Usually she was in a skirt of some type. "Let me run to get my tea, everyone. Be right back." She breezed out of the room.

Rachel came over to my table, looking pissed off. She leaned forward, palms on the table.

"What?" I said, trying to sound confident.

She rolled her eyes. "So Kenzie finally got to you, huh? She turned you into an even bigger freak than she is. You're not even a person anymore—you're an it. And now you're even *uglier*." She spat the last word.

I stared at her, processing the montage of emotions going through me, moving from shame to rage fast.

I'd had it.

"You really are a piece of shit, Rachel. You think Mack is a freak? You think I'm a freak? You think I'm uglier? Uglier than what—some plastic doll blindly following her parents' prejudices? Why do you think you get to decide how some-body else should live their life, or even *who they are*? You don't dictate people's opinions. You are *nobody*. I don't care what you think, and *nobody* cares what you think."

Seeing her shocked, silent face felt good for a second— I'd never really fought back before, and she obviously wasn't

expecting it—but then I teared up, which fucking under-
mined the whole thing. I wasn't sobbing, but I was having to
wipe away flowing tears.

I refused to look at the rest of the girls, who were dead
silent.

But then I heard Lily. "Rachel, you really crossed a line
there. Why can't you just leave them alone? What is your
freaking obsession?"

The next thing I knew, Lily side hugged me. "Most of us
don't think like her. Nobody knows what to say. People are
wimps. Including me."

My heart swelled at the support, but of course—because
I'm a fucking weirdo—that made me cry more.

She let go and patted my shoulder. I wiped some more
tears away and raced into the hall, where I almost ran into
Ms. Mangal.

"Nic? Are you okay?" Her look of concern was as grati-
fying as her support always was.

"I'm fine," I muttered. "I need to go to the bathroom. I'll
be back in a minute."

I raced down the hall to the bathroom and pushed the
door open. I stared at my red, puffy cheeks in the mirror,
eyes glistening with more tears. And then it occurred to me
that I was in the girls' bathroom. I'd asked Mack yesterday
what he did for the bathroom, and he said they let him use
the staff bathroom. So I asked at the front desk, and they
gave me permission, too. But I hadn't even thought about it
this time.

I'd just won an argument, and I couldn't even enjoy it
because I was so stupidly sensitive. I thought of what Lily
had said, about how she basically regretted not speaking up
sooner. That did feel good.

Sometimes I really hated feelings. They seemed more

trouble than they were worth.

Lily really had never been anything but nice to me. Rachel had basically manipulated me into thinking Lily and I were rivals, and I bought into her crap without questioning it. I didn't know why I was only figuring this out now, but as my friends had pointed out, I could be pretty oblivious.

God.

I wiped away additional tears. I often assumed the worst about all people, just because some people were horrible to me. I was getting better, but I had a ways to go.

But right now, I had to get my shit together because I needed to get back to the classroom. They couldn't start the meeting without me. I wiped my tears away, hoping they'd be the last. I got some toilet paper from a stall and patted my eyes dry. Then I took a deep breath and left the bathroom.

～

Mack came to dinner with the three of us Wednesday night, and I was nervous because I hadn't seen him since Sunday. We had been texting, but not a lot—not like before—and I had told him yesterday that something had happened with Rachel, but not the details. So it wasn't surprising that it was the first thing he brought up.

"Details!" he said jokingly enthusiastically as we all stepped off the curb into the parking lot. "I want the details about this Rachel thing."

Jenna laughed. "Yes, Nic, give us the deets!"

"You already know them," I said drily. It was weird being around Mack when he was this animated. It had been a while, since before. "But okay, I'll tell you, Mack. She referred to you by your deadname and said you'd 'gotten to me'"—I made air quotes for this—"and turned me into an even bigger freak. Then she said I was an it."

"Well, that's horrible and makes me feel like crap," Mack said, seemingly taken aback. "But I know this turned out bad for Rachel, so tell me more."

I went over everything I'd said back to her.

"Nice." He bumped my shoulder. "You got brave. What happened then?"

That shoulder bump was both good and bad, and I had to tell myself to focus. I told him how Lily jumped in, and what she said about Rachel being obsessed. It was nice that other people could see it, too. "The best part was that she used the right pronouns."

"Nice," Mack said.

"I think that's my favorite part," Jacob said.

"Yeah. *Some* people here will be nice about it," Jenna said. "Some people are decent human beings."

"Key word there is 'some,'" Mack said.

We squeezed between two big pickups.

"Yeah, it's true," I said. "People are bothering me less than they were on Monday. I guess things are only interesting for so long. I'm sure there will continue to be the occasional barb, but hopefully not too bad."

"Yeah," Jenna said. "I hope so, too."

"So, there's one thing, though. My dad is really worried about what might happen to me. He's afraid I'm going to get beat up." He'd called me yesterday to tell me this. I hadn't been expecting it.

"Your dad?" Mack asked. "Isn't he pretty oblivious?"

We got back on the sidewalk.

The fact that he knew that made my heart pinch. None of my new friendships were at the same level as Sam and me, but I really thought they could be.

"He generally is," I acknowledged. "But there is a nonbinary person at his work, and they've explained some things to him. I guess when he found out about me, he asked them questions. They apparently gave him a lot of info. They got beat up one time in Tulsa and said they have been in some other scary situations. He said there's a hate crimes case for the time they got beat up, but they don't think the police will really do anything because they were shitty when it happened. It was this person and a trans woman friend that it happened to."

"Oh, man," Mack said. "Were they beat up bad?"

We'd reached the front of the cafeteria, but we stopped to keep talking.

"He said they said two guys came out of a bar and stopped it. My dad's coworker was worried at first that the new guys were about to join in, but they helped instead. But the friend's nose was broken and they both had broken ribs. The attackers ran off, but the two guys from the bar knew who they were, so they stuck around to tell the police."

"Jesus." Jenna sounded freaked out.

"That shit's scary," Jacob said.

"It probably wouldn't be a bad idea to take a self-defense class, actually," Jenna said. "We all should."

Mack was frowning, but he nodded. Jacob's mouth was tense.

I felt bad. "Sorry, I didn't mean to kill the mood and stress you all out."

"No, you're right," Mack said. "It really is something we have to take seriously. I'm going to talk to my dad. Maybe he can pay for a self-defense class for us. I bet he would."

"I would absolutely do that," Jenna said.

Jacob and I both said we would, too. Since my parents were worried, maybe they could swing paying for it.

"Have you all heard about the clothing bans?" Mack asked.

None of us knew what he meant.

"They really are coming after us, and it's not just me. It's all of you too, even if you stay exactly as you are. They are talking about banning cross-dressing, which would apply to you—Nic and Jenna—since you're not always dressing like they think girls should. It's all in these drag bans that are in play. They are truly evil."

"Really?" I was shocked. "How would that work?"

"I have no idea. It's probably one of those things that they would just use when they felt like it. Like, a woman in cargo shorts with a lot of makeup on might get left alone, but they'd go after you."

Me? I looked at Jenna and she looked stressed, too.

Mack kept going. "Maybe they'd have a minimum length that women's hair had to be, I don't really know. I'm sure they'd have a heyday writing up these rules."

We were all quiet, but then Jacob said, "And all the book bans. They want to pretend that we don't exist. Both people like all of us, and people like me and my family. Like history didn't happen."

"Yeah, those are such bullshit," Jenna said.

I nodded.

Mack made a grunt of agreement. "Should we go in?"

Nobody said anything as we scanned in and split up to get food.

When we regrouped at the table, Jenna said, "Let's talk about something happier. Have any of you started the new book?"

She'd suggested a book called *Phoenix Extravagant*, supposedly in my honor. It was about a nonbinary artist. It sounded pretty good to me, but the library didn't have it so I had to ask my mom to buy it for me, and she had to wait until tomorrow—payday—to buy it. I didn't want to bring this up, so I said, "Not yet," and left it at that. I wouldn't get it until she picked me up on Tuesday.

I was glad we'd moved on. I didn't want to think about violence and self-defense and laws against us, so I listened to the three of them talk about the beginning of the book, and got genuinely excited about reading it.

Even though it was still hard to be around Mack, I was glad we were all back together. I just hoped things stayed good. And that I could continue to be around Mack without suffering too much—and eventually not at all.

"You do understand the consequences of this decision, right?"

That was Mr. Matthews, the school counselor, with his opening line for my first counseling session on Thursday. They'd made me come by after my last class.

I glared at him, instantly pissed. Adults are so stupid sometimes. Did he think I just decided on a whim to be agender? Like, Oh, you know what? I've never been agender before. Let's see what that's like!

Moron.

"I'm aware."

"I'm not sure that you are. Have you really thought this through?" He was behind a desk, leaning back in his chair with his fingers tented. His generic short brown hair was clipped really short, and he had on a white button-up shirt, a couple of pens in his pocket.

How stupid did he think I was? I mean, maybe kids in more liberal places could try on different identities. But this wasn't something anyone here would do without under-standing what they would face. Why would anyone choose to do something that most people wouldn't understand and would think weird, and that would make other people want to erase or even kill you?

So I didn't say anything.

He blinked several times, and from the thin line his lips made, I guessed he was annoyed at me.

What did he expect? He started off attacking me and accusing me of making the most important "decision" I'd ever made in my life without any thought.

"Okay, look," he said. "I want to help you. A lot of time teenagers have really strong feelings. It can be useful to have a sounding board and talk things through."

What a jerk. "Look, you're obviously going to try to convince me I'm not agender. You are incorrect. Nothing you can say can make me forget who I am. I don't see how anything good can come out of these meetings."

He studied me, clearly still annoyed. "We still need to have them. I'll see you every week on Thursdays after school. But you can go now, if you promise to really think about this."

"Sure, I'll give it lots more thought."

What an ass.

All the kids with cars at the school had already left, but I was waiting downstairs at the end of one of the couches with my duffel on the floor in front of me, along with a bunch of other kids. My mom and Isabella were supposed to arrive soon. Isabella had texted to say they were in Okla-homa City, so, like, twenty minutes away.

Lots of kids were talking and I felt like an outsider, like I always did around large numbers of people, but I didn't care as much as I used to. I wasn't a total social pariah, I just needed to find the right people to socialize with. I was reading, anyway, so it didn't matter that I wasn't socializing at the moment.

So I was shocked when I heard my name said enthusiastically right in front of me.

"Isabella!" I said. "You're here."

"Obviously," she said, half crawling over the arm of the sofa to hug me.

I hugged her back, then I stood up with my bag. We headed to the reception desk, where Mom was checking me out.

"Hi, honey!" she said, meeting me with a hug, too.

"Where's Dad?" I asked.

"Your brother is grounded and we couldn't leave him alone this long. But you're all checked out. Ready?"

"Yep." I held up my duffel and we headed out to the car.

"Shotgun," I called before we even got close.

"Oh, man," Isabella said. "Fine."

I tossed my bag between the second row of seats in the minivan and Isabella sat behind Mom. Once we were all situated, Mom backed out and we were off.

Isabella started chattering about school and her art teacher, who was new at the school and apparently cool.

Isabella continued, "We're doing collages right now, cutting up magazines and construction paper to make stuff. It makes me feel like a kid again."

Mom and I both laughed and I turned around to look at Isabella, who was grinning. She knew she was funny.

"So what's your collage of?" I asked. "Does it have a theme?"

"It's about expectations. A lot of the magazines the teacher has are ones like *Vogue*, so there are lots of pictures of women dressed in nice clothes. But there are also some hunting and fishing magazines, so I've been cutting the heads off and mixing them up, matching them with wrong bodies and so on. Sometimes they're not the same size and it looks weird, but whatever."

"That sounds neat," I said. I wondered if she was doing it because of me. She probably would like *Vogue* magazine when she was older, but she knew it wasn't my scene. I pulled up my art folder on my phone and handed it to Isabella. "Look at my most recent stuff."

"Dracula! And dogs! Hilarious." She looked through everything and laughed at all the silly ones.

"You should draw me," she said when she handed the phone back.

"Sure. I'll do it this week."

"You sound happy, Nic," Mom said.

"Yeah, I guess." I wouldn't go too far with that.

"Is it the school?"

"I don't know. I finally have friends. I like them. We have a lot in common. But things are just easier here. People leave me alone more." This was so true. I was dreading being back in Emerson. I'd have to avoid going out.

She nodded. "That's good. Can we talk about your gender?"

Oh, this was going to be a pain. "Okay."

"Honey, you know we will support you no matter what. But Dad and I are really worried. Is it possible for you to just know this about yourself but wait until you are somewhere else, another state, somewhere safer, to tell other people?"

Irritation flashed inside me. "Why?" I knew why, but I didn't care that much.

"Dad explained it to you. You are putting yourself at risk, and I want you to be safe."

I glared at the dash. This must have been planned. I was sure Mom had told Isabella to keep quiet for this conversation.

"Look, I assume you're going to leave Oklahoma for college and go somewhere more progressive, and although I am sad at the thought, I'm asking you to wait until then to do this."

This time it was anger that flashed in me. "No way. I've spent my whole life not being who I am, and it's made me constantly uncomfortable and depressed. This is the first time I feel like I'm really me. I don't think I could go back, even if I wanted to. Which I don't. And everybody at school already knows."

Mom sighed. "I was afraid you'd say that. Okay, honey. We will support you. Maybe don't talk about it when you're out in public. You are probably safe at the school. Do you feel safe?"

I looked out the window at the cows we were passing. "Yeah. Some kids are being mean about it, but most just ignore me. Some people have been cool about it."

"Okay." She sounded resigned. I hope she wasn't going to bring it up again over the break.

Now I didn't know how this was going to go at all. I had been planning to avoid Caleb, but now he was grounded, so he'd not only be around, he'd be pissed about it.

I was probably going to hole up in my room. I'd just have to see.

~

Sunday night, we were all back at the dorm so we went to dinner together. At first I wasn't sure if Mack would come. I'd texted him that we were leaving at five but he didn't respond. Jenna, Jacob, and I were about to leave when he came rushing around the corner from his room, looking harried and rubbing his eyes. He looked cute.

"Were you asleep?" Jenna asked.

"Maybe," he said, running his hand through his hair, shorter than last week.

We laughed and left.

It was still hard to see Mack, even though my brain had accepted that the rejection wasn't personal. But I still regretted that I had wasted so much emotional energy on him when it was never going to happen.

It still stung, and I was suddenly sad. I had to weave between two ancient beaters. I wondered if they parked next to each other on purpose.

As we fell into step, I glanced over at Jenna and noticed that she also had gotten a haircut. It was short again and even spikier. I wondered if I should cut my hair off. Having long hair didn't prevent people from thinking I was a boy. It was also boring because I never did anything to it.

Jacob and Mack were talking about a series they were watching on YouTube, featuring a family of Black superheroes. This was obviously exactly up Jacob's alley, and he was the one who'd gotten Mack watching it. Jenna and I weren't interested—neither of us cared about superheroes.

"You're zoned out," Jenna said to me just as some idiot revved an engine one row over.

"Yeah, sorry." I'd been in la-la land, pondering hair changes.

"I wasn't saying anything." She laughed. "I'm tired. Not the best way to feel the night before classes kick back in."

"Just don't stay up late," I told her.

She snorted. "You're full of wisdom."

"Always," I said as we stepped back out of the parking lot and onto the sidewalk. There were other people heading to the cafeteria, too. Some OAMS kids and some college students.

I wondered if Jenna had seen her brother over the break. And then I realized that I never asked her questions about her life, despite all the things she asked me. It was part of that whole being oblivious thing.

"Did you see your brother? Are you guys still close?" There, I asked something.

"Oh, yeah, he came home this time. He usually doesn't at Thanksgiving, but he's going to be in Europe over Christmas. So yeah. And I wouldn't say we're close, but we do get along. He's not like your brother."

Some more people heading to the cafeteria came around a corner and got behind us.

"That's cool. I don't know what I'd do if I didn't have Isabella. Ugh." There I went, making it about me again. I had to stop. "So does your brother feel the same about your family's favorite movies as you?"

She laughed as she reached for the cafeteria door. "Yep. We usually play card games. Our parents tolerate it as long as we're in the same room."

It looked like we got in right before a rush. The place was filling up fast by the time we met back at the long table we'd picked, sitting near the end.

Jenna asked how our breaks were, so we each went over ours. One of Jacob's brothers was temporarily home from Germany, where he was doing something in the military. He sounded pretty happy about it, because this was the brother who got him into comics and he was Jacob's biggest art fan.

"He bought me this shirt," Jacob said, motioning to his blue t-shirt with Black Panther on it.

We all made approving noises, even Jenna and me, since we were nice.

When it was Mack's turn, he started with, "Oh, my God. My dad loves parades so we always have to watch the Macy's parade thing. So boring."

"At least you had that flan," I pointed out.

"True."

"You had flan for Thanksgiving?" Jenna asked.

"Yeah, tres leches pumpkin flan. It's awesome. Christmas, too."

"You should bring us some after Christmas break," Jenna joked.

"Maybe," he said. "But I might eat it all before you get any."

We all laughed.

Mack raised a finger. "Before I forget, I did want to mention that my dad is looking up self-defense courses we might be able to take. I'll keep you all posted. But let's not think about that. Jenna, you're up."

She listed all the boring old movies she'd had to watch with her family. "I mean, how many times can a person watch *Back to the Future* or *Ferris Bueller's Day Off* in their lifetime?"

"I've heard of *Back to the Future*," Jacob said, "but what's the other one?"

"Oh, my God," Mack said. "Parents love that movie. My dad sat me down once when I was twelve and made me watch this, but he said I was not to copy any of the behavior in it—it was just for entertainment."

"Okay ... so?" Jacob said. I was with him—I'd never seen it.

Jenna started explaining. "So this disobedient kid gets in trouble in class all the time, and he convinces his better-behaved rich friend to 'borrow' his dad's Ferrari or whatever it is, and they go on a joy ride while skipping school. The movie is all about how much havoc they cause and how close they get to damaging the car, which has the friend insanely stressed out, but they end up getting the car home safe. The end is kind of funny, though."

Mack laughs. "It is."

"So ...?" Jacob says.

"They know that the friend's dad is going to know they took it because of the extra mileage they put on it. The guy's super anal. Ferris has the bright idea to put the car in reverse to drive the mileage back down—"

"Um, what?" Jacob asks, dumbstruck.

Jenna and Mack both laugh. She continued, "Yeah, exactly. They manage to prop it up and put the car in reverse with something on the accelerator so the tires are just spinning backwards in the air. But then it falls off the blocks and goes shooting out the back of the garage, which, unfortunately, is like twenty feet off the ground in the middle of a forest, so it's very much not a good thing."

Jacob laughed.

So then it was my turn, and I started with, "Okay, guys, I did a thing?"

They all looked at me and I couldn't help but grin. I pulled up a photo on my phone and put it in the middle of the table so they could all see it. It was a drawing I had done of all us, using the selfie we had taken with dragon mailbox.

"Oh, my God!" Jenna said. "That is awesome!"

"I wondered what you were going to do with that picture," Jacob said. Since he wasn't in the original photo, I had texted him for a picture of himself over the break.

Mack was laughing and zooming in on part of it.

I had drawn the selfie as-is, and then added a thought bubble coming off the dragon's head. Inside the thought bubble was a picture of Jacob laughing. It had turned out exactly as epic as I knew it would.

"This is so cool," Mack said. He picked up the phone and they passed it around while I started in on the rest of my break.

"My brother called me an it and Isabella raged at him in my defense. Then she and I hung out some more, and I drew her while she read."

"Your sister sounds awesome," Mack said.

"She really is the best. She's actually made me kind of rethink how I view people. I sort of had an epiphany over the weekend."

"Why, because she's a good person despite living here?" Jenna teased.

"Sort of, actually. I mean, it was always confusing to me how she could be all girly and still like me. I always judged 'normal' girls and basically looked down on them, mostly in retaliation for how they were my biggest bullies. But I realized things aren't that simple."

"Yeah, everything is complex," Mack said. "Especially here, where things are so red. Yes, the politicians hate us all, and the authority figures judge us harshly for not conforming, but not every individual person agrees with that."

"Right," I said. "And while the girls who were so mean to me were all 'normal' by my definition, not every normal girl made fun of me. It's stupid—I should have figured this out a long time ago. I even made friends with this girl in my art class last year, and she was super-petite and feminine, and I still thought she was the rare exception."

I felt bad about this. I mean, I was pretty self-absorbed. I was a little ashamed. But I really did think I was getting better. I was definitely more self-aware than I'd been at the beginning of the semester.

"You should cut yourself some slack, Nic," Jacob said. "It's hard to notice all the people not saying anything when the bullies are at it. And I don't mean their friends standing right next to them—those assholes are implicitly saying the same stuff—but the people outside their circle. We don't even see them in those moments."

"You're totally right. I also found my seventh grade yearbook while I was home and even though it was a bad idea, I ended up going through it and reliving that shitty year." I'd flipped through the pages, seeing all the people whose faces I had X-ed out. It was actually kind of painful to look at, but it was also a little cathartic because I could see how far I'd come.

"Man, seventh grade was bad for me, too," Jenna said, grimacing and shaking her head.

"Sixth for me," Jacob said.

"I think middle school is the perfect breeding grounds for behavioral shittiness," Mack added.

It made me chuckle. "I think you're right. But to Jacob's point, it occurred to me that between all the cute girls whose faces I'd scratched out in the yearbook, there were lots of other cute girls who never did anything to me. And I studied their faces and tried to remember who they even were, and came up totally blank. So obviously not every apparently conventional person is horrible."

"Yeah, some people just aren't brave enough to let their differences show," Jenna said.

We all nodded, because that was the truth.

I was glad I'd found some other people who were brave in that regard, like me, even if we struggled in all sorts of other ways socially. Despite what my parents thought, the only way I could be comfortable was to be myself, even if so many people didn't approve. I wanted to be out with my agender status. I was afraid before, but not anymore.

The last Saturday before we left for Christmas, Mack texted me to see if I wanted to go on a walk with him.

At first I wondered if he meant all four of us, but we'd literally never done that. Walking was Mack's thing. I'd just been a rare lucky invitee.

He laughed at my hat and gloves when I met him downstairs.

"What?" I said, pretending to be offended. "It's freezing out."

"Let's go," he said, still smiling. He had on jeans and a sweatshirt and that was it. It was only forty, overcast, and there was the typical wind. It was his frostbite to get.

As soon as we were outside, I asked, "Are we going somewhere specific?"

"No. Let's go south today, though."

"Okay, sure." I was pretty sure south was toward the library. After we got going, I saw that that was right.

Since we'd established the direction to go, there was now this awkward silence. He must want to talk about something. But I wasn't sure if I should ask. It felt like forcing the issue.

"Um, you must wonder why I invited you," he said, grimacing a little.

"Yeah, it crossed my mind." We were passing the gym at this point, basically heading toward the library.

"Sorry, that sounded ridiculously formal." He put on a

fake British accent and said, "You must wonder why I requested your illustrious presence for my afternoon ambling."

This made me laugh. "I'm not sure if I'm laughing at what you said, or how bad your British accent is."

When I stole a glance at him, he was smiling, but he looked nervous, or at least uncertain, which made me nervous.

But then I decided to be brave. "Is something wrong?"

"No, not really." He exhaled, his breath a big cloud in front of his face. "I guess I just wanted to tell you again how sorry I am for that stupid shit I did to you. I was really selfish to not be up front with you."

I didn't say anything because I was busy reliving those horrible feelings I'd had after we broke up.

He held his hands up and said, "Not that I'm stupid enough to assume it was that big a deal to you. You seem totally fine, except I do feel like we're not like we were before."

I was so deep in the memories that I was on the verge of tearing up. I couldn't risk talking, but I did nod, unsure if he'd see it or not. That whole before time he was talking about was me thinking he might be interested in me, and me being so excited and enthusiastic about that. I don't know how it would have been if I'd never liked him like that.

Besides, I still liked him, but it wasn't such an overpowering thing now—now that I knew it could never happen. I was feeling queasy. Revisiting this stuff was bringing everything back, all the bad feelings.

We turned the corner around the library and kept going past it.

Finally, Mac said, "Please say something, Nic."

"Okay." But what to say? "I appreciate that you feel bad.

It was really terrible for me, because I sometimes build things up to be really good, so then when they go bad, it feels *really* bad. But that's not your fault."

"I should have told you I was trying to figure things out. I didn't think of it this way at the time, but I totally used you. I'm so sorry."

"Yeah, you did, kind of. But I do understand it wasn't malicious. It still hurt, though." I glanced over at him and he was frowning and nodded.

This was so weird, just walking along a sidewalk baring my soul. It took me years of knowing Sam before I really did that with her. I didn't know if it was Mack or me who made the difference. Maybe I had grown, and learned to trust people more. The right people.

"I know. I just felt—feel—so connected to you that I thought it might be real attraction, because I've never felt like that before. I've never had a crush on anyone before, and I thought that might be what it was." He spoke quicker than usual. "I know I've kind of told you this, but it was so new that I thought it was different this time."

That really was flattering, but still hard. "It's really difficult for me to talk about this stuff, but I feel really connected to you, too."

"It's hard to be vulnerable," he said.

"That's exactly what my friend Sam told me—that I needed to be more vulnerable with people I felt like I could trust. I have a hard time trusting people. But I glommed right on to you." I wondered why I did that. I did have a tendency to fixate on people sometimes, but I honestly didn't know what would get me going on a particular person.

He laughed lightly "It wasn't like that. I wanted you around."

"I know. But I know I can be intense."

"People are more interesting when they have feelings, you know."

"Well, that's good." I was feeling almost dizzy from this conversation. We stopped at a crosswalk, waiting for the light to change to cross the street and step off campus. Across the street was a shopping center that surrounded the block. I'd never been here or into the neighborhood on the other side of the shops.

But I was going to say what was on my mind. "The thing that keeps picking at me is that you might not be asexual. You could be grace and just not be attracted to me."

"I don't think so. I like you so much, but it's not physical. I don't know how else to explain it. But when I first met you, I felt something, and when I thought you liked me, I loved that. No one has ever liked me before, and I think I lost perspective there." He bumped my shoulder. "I am so sorry. I want to hold your hand again. I miss it."

I was near tears at this point. "I don't think I can handle that right now."

And the shoulder bump threw me. He hadn't touched me since the ill-fated kiss. Maybe we really could get back to normal? I didn't know.

"Okay." He was obviously disappointed, but he wasn't going to push it.

We walked in silence. I tried to process everything and calm my queasy stomach. As painful as this was, I was glad he had told me all this. It meant he really did care about me, even if it wasn't in the way I wanted.

"So when do you hear about the mentorship?" Mack asked.

My heart lurched. "Next week." God, this was going to be stressful, waiting to hear.

"I'd say I'm sure you'll get accepted because you're so good, but I know that's not how the world works. I sure hope you do, though."

I nodded, grimacing. "Yeah. Me too."

"Do you know what day?"

"No, they just said the week of the nineteenth."

Mack bumped my shoulder again. "I hope it's early in the week so it doesn't drag on."

"Yeah."

The walk sign appeared so we started crossing the street.

"We should meet over the break for another book club instead of skipping it," Mack said.

That threw me. "Like, in person?"

"No, no, like on Zoom. I'm going to be in Texas, anyway."

"Oh, with your parents?" I wondered how complicated things were with the whole weird custody thing. I should ask about that some time, because I was curious. But it didn't seem like the right time.

We continued along the road on the side of the shopping center.

"Yeah. My aunt's coming down too. So are you interested in meeting? Not Christmas Day, but maybe New Year's. We have to be back that next day. But at least we could squeeze one in."

"Definitely. I'm going to create a group chat so we can talk about this. And keep in touch over the break. I missed you all over Thanksgiving." Never in a million years did I think I would be in a position to create a *group chat*. It occurred to me that I had no idea how to do this. Google, here I come.

"We texted over Thanksgiving," Mack pointed out.

"I know, but this will be easier if we're all on the same chat." I wondered if he was against it, or if he was just making conversation. I would have felt more self-conscious about it if I was Emerson Nic. But I was a different person now, and it didn't matter as much.

"True."

He was just talking, not really meaning a lot.

"We should pick the book," Mack said.

We continued talking about book options as we walked past the shopping center and into a neighborhood. It seemed like we were done with the heart-to-heart part of the walk, which I was fine with. I was still feeling raw, but I did think it was a good conversation. Mack obviously really did want to stay friends, and even though it would probably always be a little hard for me, so did I.

I really wondered what next semester would bring. And this next week, with news on the mentorship.

By lunch with Jenna and Jacob on Monday, I'd already been checking my email obsessively all day, hoping for one from the artist.

So when an email did come in and the screen showed the word "Congratulations," I fumbled the phone when I tried to pick it up, nearly dropping it. But then I got my email open and there it was—I'd actually been accepted!

"Did you get in?" Jenna asked, responding to the wide-eyed expression of shock that must have been on my face.

"Yes!" The word shock was not sufficient for how I felt. "I can't believe this!"

I checked the email to make sure my name was the only one on there and it was. She had addressed it to me, so it must be real. This was the biggest thing that had ever happened to me, and I could hardly think. My brain was frozen. My whole body was frozen.

"That's so awesome!" Jenna had on a huge smile. She was obviously genuinely happy for me.

Jacob also was smiling and he gave me a high five, which I almost missed because I was so dazed.

I texted everybody—my mom, Sam, and Mack.

Only Sam got right back to me, with a bunch of confetti emojis. Mom was probably working, and Mack was doing whatever it was he usually did during lunch. He worked with a teacher or something.

I was still flying on a cloud when Jacob and I walked into the art classroom. Rachel was in her seat at the front table, and I thought, Ha, you were so wrong. Jacob sat down but I went to tell Ms. Mangal, who I found in the back, talking to Lily. My footsteps faltered at the sight. I didn't want to say anything in front of her, but then I saw she also had a big grin on her face, and when they both noticed me, I couldn't remove my own grin.

Lily asked, "Did you get accepted, too?"

We'd both been accepted. Rachel had been wrong in every possible way, and I'd believed it for months. I was so glad that was over. I smiled. "Yeah."

Ms. Mangal clapped her hands, the silver bracelets she was wearing on both wrists clinking together. "This is wonderful! I'm so excited for you. Clee loves working with students who are talented and work hard. Can I tell the class about your successes?" She looked back and forth between us.

I nodded and Lily said, "Sure."

I felt so ridiculous having ever believed Rachel about anything. She was obviously so full of it. Being a junior didn't matter. Lily being really good and from the same school didn't matter. They'd accepted both of us. I was reeling.

"Congratulations, Nic!" Lily said as we left the back room.

"You too!" I said, sounding more excited than I normally did. I was wired.

I got back to my table and told Jacob that Lily had also been accepted.

"That's really cool," he said. "Rachel always made it sound like that was impossible. Shows what she knows. Maybe I'll apply next year if she offers it again. You'll have to tell me what it's like."

I dropped my bag on the floor and fished my computer and sketchbook out before taking my seat. My hands were shaking. "Definitely."

Other kids started arriving, sitting in their spots at the front tables.

"I'm really happy for you, Nic." Jacob smiled at me. "I'm also really glad we started talking. I was admiring your work from over here, not knowing what to say."

"Same," I said.

My head was spinning with what the mentorship would really be like. Spending almost all day Saturday doing art with a real, professional artist.

I'd know in less than a month.

I didn't think I'd ever been more excited for anything.

"So, here we are, last day before Christmas break," Mack said ceremoniously at dinner Thursday night. We had a full day of classes and finals on Friday, and we leaving right after, so it was going to be crazy that evening. "Let's toast."

Jenna laughed. "Yes, let's."

We all held up our plastic cups of Coke and Mack said, "To our continued success as the resident queer contingent."

We all laughed and tapped our cups against each other's.

I started to set mine down but Jenna said, "Oof, no you don't. Drink first."

"Oh, yeah." I took a sip of my Coke. There was a time when I would have been embarrassed for not knowing what to do after a toast, but things had changed. I had changed. I couldn't believe how much. I was a totally different person.

"When are you leaving for Arizona?" Jenna asked Jacob.

"Saturday morning at six-freaking-a.m." He took a bite of his taco.

"Gross," Jenna said.

"It's a good taco," he protested, covering his mouth.

"Not the taco," Jenna clarified. "That's way too early."

Jacob nodded emphatically. He finished chewing and said, "Normally we would leave early tomorrow afternoon, but since my brother also has school, they can't get here until five, and they decided it was too late. So six a.m. it is. My dad is hardcore about planning these long trips. No possibility is unconsidered. Even my visit to the barber on Sunday is planned down to the minute."

We laughed. Jacob's hair had gotten a little longer, but I thought it still looked fine. But I wasn't exactly an expert on hair.

I was almost finished with my second pepperoni pizza slice, and I was still feeling navel-gazey. I liked these people so much, even if I did still like Mack a little too much. But I'd literally never had a group of friends before.

I started thinking about next summer, and then I noticed Mack looking at me, while Jenna and Jacob talked about who knows what, because I was so down a rabbit hole in my head.

"You look deep in thought," Mack said.

"I guess I was just thinking about how hard summer is going to be, being back in a small town with no friends." I could feel my mouth in a frown. These were not pleasant thoughts. I'd just have to stay in the house all day.

"Don't start fretting about that yet. It's months away. Just try to live in the moment."

"Oh, come on, Mack. Fretting is my secret hobby."

"Not so secret," he teased.

Jenna laughed. She and Jacob were looking at me now.

"I guess I'm a heart-on-my-sleeve kind of person." I still didn't have the best control on my emotions, much to my chagrin.

Jacob shrugged. "You kind of are, but it's not always easy to read exactly what emotion you're feeling. Just that you're feeling something."

"He's right," Jenna said to me. "I didn't totally know how to read you at first."

"Huh." I guess I hadn't made friends in so long that I forgot it took a while to get to know someone. I only knew that Sam could read me pretty well. Although she did miss the whole thing with that guy I liked who she ended up freaking dating, so maybe they were right. "I do have trouble trusting people."

"Yeah," Jacob started. "When you have thoughts and beliefs that aren't popular, sometimes it's risky to be too open."

Everyone nodded. He was not wrong.

"Well, anyway," Jenna said, "I think our little group is solid. I trust you guys."

"Doesn't that term bother you?" Mack asked.

"You guys?" Jenna asked.

"Yeah," he answered.

"A little, but it's so common, even I forget," Jenna said. "Besides, I've heard you use it."

He cocked his head to the side in acknowledgment.

I pondered this. "It doesn't bother me, but you are right, it should. The obvious alternative is 'you all,' but you have to say it slowly and carefully or else it'll sound like 'y'all,' which is, obviously, unacceptable."

"God forbid we sound like people from where we're from," Jacob joked, which made us all laugh.

But Mack was right. I hadn't thought much about it before. Why did everything have to be gendered?

"On to something less controversial. When does your mentorship start, Nic?"

"The first Saturday after we're back." I smiled thinking about it.

"That's so awesome," Jacob said. "I'm jealous."

"You should apply for next year," I said. I wanted to share this good feeling with everybody. "I wonder if she does them in the fall, too. Maybe you could apply for that. I'll ask when I'm there."

He nodded. "Thanks."

"Oh!" Jenna suddenly said. "I just remembered—Nic has never had Thai or Indian food. I promised them that I'd take them out for both at some point. You guys in?"

Mack and Jacob both said, "Sure," at the same time, which made us all smile.

"It's a plan," she said. "Next semester. Are you excited, Nic?"

"Yeah. I hope I like it."

"It will be fine." She bumped my shoulder. "Don't fret."

Mack looked at me. "Are you going to try to get your own room downstairs for next semester?"

I'd been thinking about it. "I don't know. I'm kind of scared to ask."

"You should," Jenna said. "They need to recognize your identity."

They were right. "Who ... should I ask? How did you do it, Mack?"

"We talked before I came here. Your parents will have to formally request it from Ms. Patton, but at least give her a heads up tonight. Can your parents talk to her tomorrow? They could officially request it then."

"Okay. I'll talk to her when we get back. And I'll tell my mom to talk to her tomorrow." Now I was nervous. I was really going to be forcing the issue now.

"I hope they aren't assholes about it," Jenna said. "I don't have a lot of faith. But you have to at least try."

"I think if your parents are insistent, it will happen." Mack shrugged. "That's what happened with me, at least."

I sighed. "That's not great. My parents are not the forceful type. At least Sophia doesn't have a problem with me." I couldn't keep myself from frowning.

"Her 'red state training' comment still both cracks me up and is awesome," Jacob said.

"Yeah, it is," Jenna said. "I'm just glad she's not going to make your life hell. Imagine rooming with Rachel."

She and I both shuddered, and she stuck her tongue out in an expression of disgust.

Mack laughed and then asked, "So what's everybody taking next semester?"

We talked about our upcoming classes and the semester in general. That carried us back to the dorm where we went our separate ways to study for our last finals the next day.

We all had at least one. Mine was in physics, and I did need to study, but I actually felt okay about it. I'd been studying a lot these last few weeks, and things were starting to click.

I was more nervous about the final critique, since I had put myself in a traditionally gendered role and attire. I hoped I didn't get any weird comments.

Less than twenty-four hours before I'd find out. This time tomorrow I'd be in the car heading back to Emerson, where who knew what annoying stuff Caleb would do.

I'd survived my physics final—I thought I'd done pretty well, actually—and now Jacob and I were nervously waiting for art class and the critiques to start.

"I can't decide if it's worst to be first or last," he said.

I groaned. "They both suck."

Jacob nodded. "I think you are right."

Ms. Mangal came out and clapped her hands. "All right, let's get started. Rachel, you're up."

Rachel's colored pencil drawing was of a flower. She explained that she was desperate for spring. It looked decent from several feet away, but when I got close, it didn't have any life in it. I think it's the hardest thing in art—to make it look like the subject of the artwork was caught naturally. It's what I was hoping to have accomplished in my own piece this time. Well, every time, but especially this time since the characters were actively in motion.

I wrote some notes and took my seat. I said something about the color being nice and that I thought the background could have been developed a bit more for my positive and negative points.

Lily's piece was amazing, as always. She'd done another

portrait, but this one was a younger boy and his dog. The kid was hugging the dog and he had a big infectious grin across his face. It was beautiful. I felt like I knew the kid, she'd captured him so well.

I loved how she worked in markers, too. There was this inherent looseness in the medium that she used so well. I was admittedly jealous.

I really struggled to come up with an opportunity for improvement. Like, I couldn't legitimately see anything I thought she could do better, so I said that and then some crap about how she could work bigger.

Jacob's drawing felt like the perfect thing for the last day of the semester. It was his superhero standing over the body of the villain. This was where he was starting to wrap up the story, the beginning of the end, as it were.

Finally, it was my turn. I was nervous as always when I first got in front of the class. I was afraid of saying anything too honest, especially with Rachel staring me down like she was. She was probably thinking of all the horrible things she wanted to say about my work but couldn't because Ms. Mangal was right there.

"So the prompt for this assignment was a self-portrait of me doing something I'd never do. There's pretty much no way you'd ever catch me dancing, especially in front of people. When I was searching for images, the salsa dancers stood out as being especially in contrast to who I am, because they're stereotypically so intense and passionate about the dancing or whatever. I would never dance, but I also would never wear a dress, so making myself the traditionally 'female' dancer"—I made air quotes around "female"—"made the most sense to fulfill the no-way-would-I-do-this criteria. So this is what I came up with." I glanced around and clocked an annoyed look on Rachel's face. Good.

I watched as people came up to study it, trying to read their expressions, most of them looked bored, honestly. Lily and Jacob were the only ones who looked like they cared.

Rachel said it was "interesting" and then made some comment about how it would be better if the other dancer were clearly male. Ms. Mangal and Lily gave her looks, and she didn't say anything else, so that was nice.

The next comments were not very interesting, but then Lily said she could feel the movement in the piece, which made me so happy I couldn't help but smile. She then suggested some stuff I could have done with the lighting that might be worth exploring. I made a note because she was much better at lighting than I was.

I wondered if we'd be collaborating at all during the mentorship. Maybe I could learn from her.

Jacob's comments were also nice. He said I did a good job on the clothing and said he loved the Vans that the dancers had on. His suggestion was that I might look for an even more dramatic moment in the dancing, like with my character with her head thrown back or something.

I thanked everyone and took my piece back to my desk. Last critique of the semester, done. And it had gone well.

"Thank you everyone for your great work this semester," Ms. Mangal said. "You are welcome to leave any of your work in your cubby, but you are also free to take it home. I'll get my comments on your work to you this evening. Have a great holiday break."

Jacob and I looked at each other. "Are you taking your stuff?" he asked.

"I don't know. I sort of want to hang it in my room, but I

feel like it's important to keep it protected, since I'm being more serious about everything now."

"Yeah, I have these portfolios I keep all my work in to keep it safe. You can flip through them and see everything and so on."

The bell chirped, indicating we needed to get our stuff and get out of there. I went with him while he got his, but I decided to leave mine for now. I'd see if my mom would buy me some kind of sleeve or something to put them in so I could hang them on my walls in the dorm.

We walked out together into the hall and went our separate ways with a simple "see you later." Just three more classes and I'd be free to go.

My mom was going to talk to Ms. Patton about me getting my own room when she got here to pick me up. Ms. Patton had been nice about it last night. She'd said no promises, but it obviously wasn't a No.

But then I'd be heading home with her and Isabella.

The problem was that home was a place I didn't want to be. I felt like OAMS was my true home now. It was where I'd found my people, even though we were in a state where they were making hurtful laws based on hate for people like us. They still felt entitled to punish us for not being like they wanted us to be. All while claiming to be the party of freedom.

But I shouldn't think about that. Things were really good for me right now. And maybe they would only get better, with my mentorship starting in a couple weeks. I would try focusing on the positive, because now there was a lot of it in my life.

What a difference moving to a new place had made. This year had been amazing so far, despite a few bumps and misgendering incidents, and I was already looking forward to coming back to school.

For the first time in a long time, I was excited to find out what would happen next in my life. The next chapter was less than two weeks away.

THE END

* * *

Thank you for reading *Uglier*. Please consider leaving an honest review. They help authors immensely.

If you enjoyed *Uglier* and haven't read *Ugly*, make sure to check it out to find out what Nic's life was like before OAMS.

To keep up with Kelly's books and to find out when the next book in The Art of Being Ugly comes out in 2024, join Kelly's newsletter, which you can do at kellyvincent.net.

ACKNOWLEDGMENTS

This book would never have been finished if not for the help of my critique partners and beta readers. Thanks to Shari Duffin, Stacia Leigh, Karrie Zylstra Myton, and Anne Shaw for their always honest and valuable feedback of work in progress, and thanks to Gwen Sharp, Vicky McDonald, Debra W., and my ever-supportive mom, Kathy Vincent, for their help as beta readers.

BOOK LIST

A lot of books were mentioned in this book and they are all real. Nic and Jenna talked about the Harry Potter and Warriors series, as well as books for school: *Pride and Prejudice* and *One Hundred Years of Solitude*. But here's a list of the more unconventional speculative fiction the group discussed and/or read, in no particular order:

- The Broken Earth series by NK Jemisin
- *Children of Blood and Bone* by Tomi Adeyemi
- *Jonathan Strange and Mr. Norrell* by Susanna Clarke
- *The Priory of the Orange Tree* by Samantha Shannon
- *The Black Tides of Heaven* by Neon Yang
- *An Unkindness of Ghosts* by Rivers Solomon
- *Phoenix Extravagant* by Yoon Ha Lee
- The Poppy Wars series by R. F. Kuang
- *Three Parts Dead* by Max Gladstone

I highly recommend checking these out if you're looking

for something fresh and new. There are many more great diverse and LGBTQ+-friendly books being published now both by traditional publishers and indie authors, and it helps encourage them to make even more of them when people snap them up.

Preview of Book 1, Ugly

If you enjoyed *Uglier* and haven't read *Ugly*, the first book in The Art of Being Ugly series, keep reading for an excerpt to get you started!

PART ONE: ALL YOU NEED IS A MAKEOVER

The school hall was as packed as ever, but one boy was weaving through kids, heading right toward me. He shouted, "Give me five, bro!" and slapped another boy's raised hand.

I needed to stay out of his way, so I leaned against my locker and waited for him to pass.

Then he careened toward me. "Put five right here!" he said, hand in the air and grinning like a maniac.

I tentatively raised my arm, and then his face fell.

"Oh. I thought you were a guy."

Someone else barked a laugh behind him.

The high-fiver dropped his arm, and I realized I was still holding mine half up like an idiot, so I let it fall, just as the laughing guy said, "She might as well be a guy. She's a big lesbo."

I blushed fiercely, and they both cracked up and moved on like it was nothing. I stood there stupidly, wanting to sink into the floor. I looked around and heard a couple of snickers.

I grasped my books to my chest and headed toward class.

Why did everybody have to say all that stuff? I was aware that I didn't dress all girly—it just felt wrong, and I couldn't have done it if I'd tried. What was wrong with wanting to be comfortable? So what if I liked jeans and unisex t-shirts. So-freakin'-what?

I lifted my head to navigate around a corner, squeezing past a group of girls who didn't mind at all doing their makeup and wearing cute clothes. I made sure not to look too closely, lest I get some kind of snark.

God, I hated this shit.

And I didn't think I was a lesbian, anyway. But everyone acted like I was. How could everyone else know something about me that I didn't know myself?

Later, in math, Mr. Martinez was going on about algebraic expressions, an x here, a y there. He was writing on the whiteboard in blue. I was trying to pay attention because I was actually interested. I'd hated geometry freshman year and was glad to get back to algebra. I had my notebook out and was copying the latest expression down when I saw Carlos's hand shoot over and grab my white eraser.

I looked at him. His fingers closed around the eraser, and his eyes twinkled.

He was cute. He had light brown eyes and wavy dark brown hair that sometimes got a little long, but it wasn't now.

I reached for the eraser, invisible in his big hand, and he pulled away, a mischievous look on his face. He was goofing around with me, something that most people didn't do.

Wait—was he flirting with me?

I couldn't believe it.

I didn't know much about this stuff, but I did know you weren't supposed to seem desperate, so I turned back toward Mr. Martinez and started taking notes.

Carlos set the eraser down on top of his notebook. I reached for it, and he grabbed my wrist firmly, still grinning. "I don't think so, Nic," he mouthed.

Okay, flirting, definitely. He'd touched me on purpose. The heat in my wrist where he was holding it felt new and exciting.

Kyle was on the other side of him, watching this, clearly amused.

Carlos was strong. I could see the muscles flexing in his forearm.

Is it weird that I thought that was kind of cool? I'd never

thought about how boys were stronger than girls before, except in the they-can-beat-you-up way, but it was right there. General male strength. And I liked it.

He still had my wrist. What should I do? Tug it back? But then he might let go.

My heart sped up, because no boy had touched me in an inoffensive way since elementary school. I stopped reaching for the eraser, and he let me go with a sidelong glance, so I got back to taking notes. Not that I could concentrate.

Lately I'd been thinking if I could get a boyfriend, things might be better. Maybe people would treat me less like a freak—and more like a normal person. Carlos would be perfect because he was so normal. I loved the idea that a regular guy was flirting with me, even if I'd never thought of him that way before.

If he liked me, I wouldn't turn him away.

Although I eyed the eraser several times through the rest of class, when Mr. Martinez let us go, Carlos snagged it and tossed it in his backpack. He and Kyle grinned at me, and I followed them out, getting squeezed out by another couple of girls in the class, who gave me one of those all-too-familiar looks. The down-the-nose look, followed by the dismissive head turn away. I told myself I was numb to it.

I was pretty much used to it. I was sort of a last-picked-for-the-team kind of girl here at Emerson High School. I didn't know who they thought they were, though. Everyone knew it took forever for trends to make it to Oklahoma. We were forty-five minutes from Tulsa, and it wasn't like that was culturally cutting edge, either. All the things kids here thought were so cool were probably totally passé in places like New York or L.A. by now.

Whatever. Just three more years here, and I was gone. I couldn't wait, and wondered how I was going to weather it.

All afternoon, I obsessed over the whole Carlos thing. Could he really like me?

Admittedly, it could have simply been that I was there, and he was bored. But I didn't think so. I had a good feeling about this.

About time.

I missed having my eraser in chemistry because I decided to sketch out the periodic table while the teacher rambled on about something or other, and I messed it up counting out the transition metals. Plus, I'd need it over the weekend. Once I was on the bus, I put my headphones on and cranked up some Killers.

My asshole brother Caleb flicked me on the head when he passed me, heading for the back. He was such a douche now.

Still, the only thing in my head was Carlos, and how he maybe liked me.

My best friend Sam—short for Samantha, but she'd die if I called her that—was always getting on my case about not being brave enough socially, so I tried to think of what I could do that would be proactive and maybe even bold. We had a plan, called Operation Social Interaction for Nic—or OSIN for short—to wrangle some friends for me. She'd be proud if I did something on my own. I just had to figure out what.

It would be hard to talk to Carlos the next day with Kyle there, so it wasn't like I would be able to ask him out or anything. The idea that I'd just go up to a boy and be like, "Hey, wanna go out some time?" was sheer insanity anyway. It would be much better if he would ask me.

We rolled over a speed bump heading out of the parking

lot, and a light bulb went on in my head. I knew where Carlos lived, after all. We'd ridden the same bus since elementary school, even though he'd stopped at the beginning of this year.

I'd be avoiding the bus soon, too, because I was getting a car when I turned sixteen next month. Thank God. It would be nothing fancy. We'd already agreed on a budget of $5000.

This idea—this was an awesome idea. I could walk over there and ask for my eraser. Maybe he'd invite me in, and things would go from there. Good things.

After forty-five minutes of bus torture, because I was the second-to-last-stop on the route, I finally was able to get off into the late summer heat. My forehead beaded with sweat before I even made it to the yard.

Caleb—just ten months younger than me and a brand-new freshman—went in the front door ahead of me. I stopped to get the mail from the dented mailbox and headed up the walk to the front entrance. We had a nice covered stone porch that Mom had put a white bench and several plants on.

Of course, Caleb had shut and locked the door so I had to use my key. He was such a dick now. To me, to Izzy, our little sister, to Mom and Dad, to everybody.

I grabbed a pack of off-brand berry fruit snacks and headed up to my room.

My room was completely ridiculous. The walls were pale peach. The double bed had an antique metal frame painted white and sat centered on the wall so it seemed to take up the whole room, especially because it was tall. There were white hooks in the ceiling that drapery used to hang from because Mom had thought I needed a canopy bed.

Me, a canopy bed.

Just no.

At least she had Izzy to be her little princess of a daughter.

Not that I had a problem with Izzy. She was my favorite family member. But her princess-ness was impossible to deny.

Fortunately, my room also had a little built-in desk and shelves in an alcove. I'd been able to make it my own by claiming it for my Testors paint bottles and the little metal fantasy character figurines Sam and I painted.

I climbed onto the gray and peach bedspread because I needed to think a bit. Make a plan.

Okay, so I'd walk over there. I'd knock on the door. Carlos probably wouldn't answer—maybe his mom would. I'd just ask her if he was home, and she'd get him. No big deal. Normal people did this kind of thing all the time, I was sure.

Sam would be so impressed. I'd have engaged the en ... not the enemy. No. I'd have initiated a potentially risky social encounter on my own.

The AC kicked on with a groan and whoosh. The air was freezing because my skin was already wet from sweat—from the heat and what I was thinking about doing. But I *could* do it.

I headed out. No need to leave a note since I'd be back before either of my parents got home, unless things went really, really well. I didn't want to jinx myself by assuming the best-case scenario.

I shut the door and crossed the street. Most of the houses on this long street were two-story, in various colors. Normal, boring house colors. I'd always thought it would be interesting to paint our house bright blue, but it wasn't allowed. Not that my parents would do something so unusual, anyway.

It was a long walk down to get to a cross street. I started thinking maybe I should have left a note. What if things did go really, really well?

I replayed the scene from math class in my head. The looks Carlos had given me. He had to have been flirting. Why else would he have done all that? I mean, we'd known each other for a long time, since third grade, when he'd moved here from somewhere. Tennessee, I thought. I'd always thought he was cute. Because he was. He was a little awkward, but kind of tall, so he was still hot. He played baseball, too.

I was about halfway down toward the side street and I was drenched in sweat. I might not have thought the whole thing out all that well. My face was bound to be pink from the heat, and I'd be halfway to a sunburn.

It would have been so much better if I already had a car.

I passed the house that gave out celery sticks with peanut butter on Halloween. It was a friendly Black lady, but celery? Seriously.

I trekked further, sweated more.

There was the biggest sycamore in the neighborhood, in front of a white house with gray stonework. Finally, I reached the corner and turned, walked past the two corner lots, and turned again down Carlos's street.

Was this really a good idea? Would I look a little desperate? That was probably bad. But I had no experience with boys. I'd never been invited to those middle school spin-the-bottle parties I knew went on. I'd never sat around with a bunch of girls talking about boys and doing each other's hair or painting each other's nails. And it wasn't like I'd ever wanted to do those things, either.

I wiped the sweat off my forehead. Was it getting hotter or was it all nerves? I tugged my short sleeves back down where they'd ridden up my arms. Too fat. Which was too bad, but I didn't know what to do about it. I didn't think I had a worse diet than anyone else.

It was okay. If Carlos was interested, it would be good. I liked him.

Okay, there it was. It was a one-story on a block of mostly two-stories. But the front yard had loads of bright and warm-colored flowers—red, orange, yellow—and I guess some would say it was well-manicured. There was a set of stones that led to the mailbox, so I followed them to the door.

I stood on a small covered porch, surrounded by walls painted a dull gray that seemed in contrast to my intense emotions.

This was it, the moment of truth. I took a deep breath and knocked. Sam would be so proud of me when I told her.

After a short delay, during which I did not even ponder running, an older boy opened the door. Oh, shit—I hadn't thought of this. His eyes widened into that judgy look I was all too familiar with from school. Lip slightly curled.

Oh, God. My stomach plummeted.

"What?" he asked.

Okay, at this point I faltered. I hadn't been expecting someone else from school. "Um."

His deadpan expression didn't change.

I swallowed as a droplet of sweat trailed down my forehead. "Does Carlos live here?"

"Hold on," he grunted.

He left the door open and disappeared behind it. After a moment, Carlos appeared. He was looking off to the side when he stepped into the doorway. His brother was saying something from inside the house, though I couldn't make it out.

So for a millisecond, I got to admire his profile and be glad I'd come. He had a nice nose and full lips. I imagined what it would be like to kiss him and run my fingers through his soft-looking hair. What would that feel like?

I had never kissed anyone yet. Which was pretty embarrassing at fifteen, but maybe that was all about to change.

He turned toward me and his eyes widened in alarm, and then got wider.

Oh, God. This was worse than his brother. He was *horrified* to see me. I needed to crawl into a hole and die.

It was like I'd stubbed my toe, except it was my heart. The heat flared in my cheeks as a humiliating blush exploded onto my face.

He still stared, his hand on the door—knuckles white—and I swear the door moved like he was thinking of closing it. In my face.

I stared at him. He stared at me. Say something. Anything. "Can I have my eraser?"

"Yeah." He pushed the door almost shut and disappeared again. I stood there, dizzy with shame. His brother opened the door again, looked at me, shook his head in obvious disgust, and breezed off.

This was a fucking nightmare. I felt like puking.

Soon Carlos came back holding the stupid white eraser between two fingers like it was a stinking dead thing.

I stuck my palm out, and he dropped it in my hand, not touching me.

My tear ducts and cheeks were burning, and I knew it was a matter of time before I started crying, so I muttered, "Thanks," and turned around. The door clicked shut.

I stepped back along the stones to the street. God, I was a

fucking idiot. How could I have actually thought he liked me? I really, truly should have known better. Probably if I'd been remotely normal, I would have.

But I knew what it was. The problem was that I was an ugly freak. Everybody knew it, and I did, too, though sometimes I forgot. Apparently. I still had this traitorous well of hope deep inside me.

I clenched the eraser in my hand, wishing it could erase what had just happened.

I was not going to tell Sam about this. She'd probably pity me.

ALSO BY KELLY VINCENT

Finding Frances

New Girl

Binding Off (prequel)

Always the New Girl

The Art of Being Ugly

Ugly

ABOUT THE AUTHOR

Kelly Vincent wrangles data weekdays and spends the rest of their time with words. They grew up in Oklahoma but have moved around a bit, with Glasgow, Scotland being their favorite stop. They now live near Seattle with several cats who help them write their stories by strategically walking across the keyboard. Their first novel, *Finding Frances*, is a fine example of this technique, also winning several indie awards. Their most recent release, *Ugly*, was selected as the Honor book for SCBWI's Spark Award in the Books for Older Readers category for 2022. Kelly has a Master of Fine Arts in creative writing from Oklahoma City University's Red Earth program.